Black Roses

Staffordshire Library and Information Service

Please return or renew or by the last date shown

If not required by other readers, this item may be renewed
in person, by post or telephone, online or by email.
To renew, either the book or ticket are required

24 Hour Renewal Line
0845 33 00 740

Staffordshire
County Council

Black Roses

JANE THYNNE

SIMON &
SCHUSTER

London · New York · Sydney · Toronto · New Delhi

A CBS COMPANY

First published in Great Britain by Simon & Schuster UK Ltd, 2013
A CBS COMPANY
Copyright © Thynker Ltd 2013

1 3 5 7 9 10 8 6 4 2

Simon & Schuster UK Ltd
1st Floor
222 Gray's Inn Road
London WC1X 8HB

www.simonandschuster.co.uk

Simon & Schuster Australia, Sydney
Simon & Schuster India, New Delhi

A CIP catalogue record for this book is available from the British Library

HB ISBN: 978-1-84983-983-9
TPB ISBN: 978-1-84983-984-6
EBOOK ISBN: 978-1-84983-986-0

Typeset by Hewer Text UK Ltd, Edinburgh
Printed and bound by CPI Group (UK) Ltd, Croydon CR0 4YY

For Philip, with love

Prologue

Berlin, April 1933

The first thing Clara noticed was that it was her own shoes the girl was wearing. They were red ankle straps from Bally, with shaped heels, almond cutouts and rhinestone buckles. That is, one of them was visible, a bright splash of scarlet against the grey, rain-mottled pavement outside the apartment block in Prenzlauer Berg. It protruded from a cluster of people – two men and a hausfrau – joined by the old woman who looked after the apartment block opposite, each displaying the demeanour that was increasingly common in the city then, torn between wanting to act and an unwillingness to get involved. Clara's recognition of the shoes was followed a fraction of a second later by a feeling of dread, though she already knew what she was about to find, and a dark fear that spread in her like ink through water. For a moment she couldn't breathe, as if all the oxygen had been squeezed out of the air, and then she pushed her way past the onlookers and stared down at the girl who lay on the street below.

She had an oval face with fine features. Her eyes were wide open, as if in amazement, and her mouth, outlined in Tabu's deep crimson, was a smudged bloom on the skin's unnatural pallor. The lips were slightly parted, and dark strands of hair fell carelessly across her face. She wore a tea-dress scattered with pink and yellow flowers and the tops of her stockings could be seen where the material had ridden up. One leg was bent at an awkward angle and the arms were thrown wide. Someone had propped her up on a coat, which was rapidly blackening as blood pooled from the back of her head. She looked like a frail, exotic bird, fallen to the ground on its route to the sun.

Clara felt a violent trembling start up within her. Though she tried to control it, her entire body was shaking.

'What happened to her?'

'She fell,' said one man.

'She jumped,' said the other, gesturing towards the window of the tenement building that hung open five floors above them. Everyone followed his gaze. They had expressions of curiosity, rather than shock. Suicides, deaths, girls falling out of the sky, were not the rarity they used to be round here.

Clara took another look at the face. The skin was milky, already turning to wax as the blood contracted deep into the veins. But it was unmarked. She must have landed on her back. The smashed part of the skull was underneath, where you couldn't see, but her face was still perfect, still the same.

Clara knelt down beside her.

'She's dead,' one of the men said.

'She's breathing,' said the old woman.

With the tenderest of touches, Clara took the girl's hand in hers and whispered, 'Can you hear me?'

There was the faintest pressure against her wrist.

'You'll be all right. We're calling an ambulance.'

'We called the police,' said the second man.

A tiny flicker. The girl's eyes shifted, as though she was trying to focus. A line of blood slid from her ear.

'It'll be all right,' said Clara, stroking her hair, trying her hardest not to cry. Blood leaked onto the hem of her polka-dot dress. She brushed rain from her cheek. 'Don't worry.'

There was a movement in the eyes.

'I promise you.'

A soft squeeze.

'I promise. I'll make sure he's all right.'

A tear rolled down the side of the girl's face. Clara felt the infinitesimal pressure of the hand in hers, then nothing. The girl's eyelids fluttered. Life slid from her face as softly as a petal falling to the ground.

Standing up, Clara entered the apartment building, ran past the lift and up the dimly lit stone stairwell to the fifth floor. The door, which was sooty, with badly peeling paint, stood ajar. Breath ripping her lungs, her heart jolting with fear, she pushed it and entered.

The apartment was empty, its atmosphere brooding and heavy, as though some recent, turbulent emotion was still imprinted on the air. Otherwise it was exactly as she remembered it. The wallpaper was patterned with muddy florals. It was furnished as cheaply as possible with just a few pieces of battered wooden furniture, a desk that doubled as a dining table, with a cane-bottomed chair, an old armchair with horsehair sticking through its arms, and a raddled wool rug in front of the gas fire.

'Welcome to my penthouse! The most prestigious address in Prenzlauer Berg!'

Despite the drabness, there had been a defiant attempt to add a bright, personal touch. A pink feather boa was draped over the mantle and photo-cards of film stars were fixed with drawing pins to the walls. Through the door she could see the bedroom, with a curtained-off bathroom, and a basin into which a tap dripped. The narrow little bed was made, and a fur-collared coat laid on it, as though ready for a night out. A bottle of Scandal by Lanvin, almost empty, stood on the dressing table.

She heard a sound and turned. From the street, cars were approaching and there was the screech of braking. She guessed she had thirty seconds, a minute at most. She needed to focus. On the table there was a key and a cup of coffee. She felt it; it was still warm. Beside it was a pile of papers. The window gaped open and for a split second the girl's body floated in Clara's mind, suspended in the warm wind, caressed in its twisting currents, until a draught sent the papers crashing to the floor and on the pavement outside she was dead.

She reached down to pick up the papers and found a postcard, a black-and white portrait of Marlene Dietrich as Lola Lola in *The Blue Angel*. Everyone knew that image. Leg crooked up on a chair, deep lids like seductive shutters over the dark eyes, exuding a haughty sexuality. It was the photograph you found everywhere, in kiosks, in shops, on any street corner. Clara scrutinized it carefully, then slipped it and the key into the pocket of her navy-blue Jaeger jacket. Outside a door slammed. For a second she was paralysed, prickling with sweaty fear, then she turned quickly and left the room.

Her heels echoing like gunshots down the stairwell, she slowed to a walk as she exited the front door and headed up the street, steeling herself not to look back at the people gathering around the body, or the policemen who were climbing out of their car and marching officiously towards them. She made her way back up Rykestrasse, trying to focus on the tall apartments, their wedding-cake stucco decorated with scrolly, soot-blackened curlicues, the water tower looming above them at the end of the road like some old castle turret plucked up and dumped there, a medieval absurdity in a city that was getting a fresh taste for the medieval.

Clara's head swam and she made herself concentrate on her breathing. Her breaths were fast and shallow with shock. She tried clenching and unclenching her fists inside her pockets, a technique that had always worked before, but nothing could obliterate the picture from her mind. The dead girl, the blood like spilt ink, the frivolous scarlet shoes. Grief, anger and incomprehension struggled within her, but now was not the time to show her feelings. She walked quickly, with her head down, and if anyone saw the tears coursing down her face she would say it was the rain. It had been raining all day in Berlin, on the dour government blocks of Wilhelmstrasse, on the smoke-blackened hulk of the Reichstag, on the canals and churches, factories, breweries and graveyards. And further out, beyond the city, watering the deep forest of the Grunewald and rolling like smoke across the placid, grey waters of Krumme Lanke.

A police car passed her in a blade of sound, and instinctively she turned her face to the newspaper kiosk at the entrance to the U-Bahn. This was a city that loved newspapers, even if it didn't love the news they brought. They were bulging out of their racks, the *Morgenpost*, the *Tageblatt*, the *B.Z.am Mittag*. There were probably more titles here than any other city in the world. Next to them on the racks were postcards of devoted Germans, often alongside their devoted pets, staring doggedly up at the figure of their Leader.

She found herself staring at the title directly in front of her. On the cover was the image of an intent, swarthy man, his face dramatically half-hidden in shadow. When she could get her eyes to focus, she realized it was a horoscope paper. *The Hanussen Magazin*. Everyone in Berlin read their horoscope now. Whenever you passed a newsstand you would see them stuffed with astrology titles: *Germany's Future*; *The Seer*; *New Germany*. It was as if people couldn't get enough of them. In the back pages were classified advertisements for palm readers who could tell your fortune for a few marks. If you wanted to take it further there was no end of little rooms and offices where an old woman would take your palm in her pudgy fingers or read your cards. The theatres were full of variety acts where people allowed themselves to be hypnotized and characters in Eastern dress would profess to read your mind. It seemed everyone in Berlin wanted to know what was coming, even if they guessed it was not going to be good news.

But who could blame them? Who could have foreseen how quickly things would change? Even for Clara herself. When she arrived in Berlin she could never have imagined what would happen in such a short space of time. She could never have known how it would transform her. All that mattered now, though, was that no one else should know.

Chapter One

For a wedding, it would have made a good funeral. The bride wore black, a sweeping, lacy gown concealing, either by chance or design, the groom's deformed foot. It was probably deliberate, given that this was a groom who liked to leave very little to chance. It was a picture of National Socialist joy, if your idea of happiness was ducking through an honour guard of stiff-armed storm troopers with faces like a firing squad. Scraps of winter snow dusted the country churchyard and behind the happy couple trailed a fair-haired boy of about eleven, the bride's son by her first marriage, dressed in the uniform of the Hitler Jugend, with a look of dazed trepidation. Perhaps he was wondering what his new life would be like, under the steely wing of a stepfather with towering political ambitions, or perhaps he was dreading demotion to the second most important man in his mother's life. A little further behind, wearing a trilby and an enigmatic smile, came the honoured guest.

The wedding photograph had pride of place in the bookshop window, wrapped in a riot of ribbons, black, white and scarlet, with little twin flags bearing swastikas on each side. But no passers-by stopped to share the nuptial joy. The crowd surged on, intent on business or shopping, hats clamped on their heads and collars raised against a sharp March wind.

Their faces were as sober as the grey Prussian façades of the buildings around them. They didn't give the bookshop a second glance, any more than they did the displays of Messmer Tee and Machwitz Kaffee in the delicatessen, the cakes in the bakery, or the tall blue jars in the apothecary. Two women passed, complaining about their office manager. A woman loudly upbraided her son, 'Your father will have something to say about that!' The ground shuddered as a tram thundered past, sending a shower of blue sparks from the cables above it. Standing on the street, Clara Vine wondered if the febrile atmosphere that everyone in London had talked about really was swirling around this city. Because if so, these stolid citizens were doing their best to ignore it.

It had taken her twenty-four hours to reach Berlin. From London she had caught the boat train to the Hook of Holland, toasting her own daring with a glass of Liebfraumilch in the Pullman car as she tried to accept the enormity of what she had just done. Standing on the deck of the ferry from Harwich, staring down at the churning sea, which made her feel slightly sick, tasting the flecks of salt foam on her face, she wondered if anyone was missing her yet. She checked again the scrap of paper in her crocodile-leather purse.

Max Townsend
Film producer

From Holland Clara had changed to the Berlin Express train and watched the low, flat expanse of the Netherlands and Belgium pass through a haze of steam. Children going to school, cows waiting at a gate, villages passing like postcards. She rationed herself to one small square at a time from the bar of Cadbury's chocolate that she had bought on the platform at Liverpool Street and tried to read the copy of *Dusty Answer* she had brought, but bubbling excitement made it impossible for her to concentrate for long. She kept looking up and losing her place and staring out at the endless, corrugated fields bisected by poplars spiking the immense sky. Everything was coming into leaf, draping the landscape in luminous green. In the end she gave up and focused on an old childhood game, analysing every member of the carriage around her as surreptitiously as possible, committing each detail to memory and constructing a story for them. By dint of peering into the little rectangular mirror above the seat, she fixed on the elderly man opposite in a Loden overcoat. His clothes were quietly expensive and his face was intelligent. Surely he must be a tycoon art dealer off to snap up a Titian. The woman on the seat opposite in hairy purple tweed with a badly mended hare lip, became a governess for some exiled Russian royals. The young man with the greased slick of hair falling forward into his eyes, who kept trying to meet her glance, was clearly, from his sketchbook and metal ruler, an architecture student, off to study in Berlin.

Finally, late afternoon, with the couplings screeching and the whistle sounding up into the cavernous glass vault, they reached the Friedrichstrasse Bahnhof. In a cloud of steam and banging doors Clara passed along the platform, through the mêlée of porters in green jackets unloading the bags. Her papers were checked at the gate by a policeman in a high hat with a tight chin strap and a gleaming brass badge. Then she stepped onto the street outside.

Friedrichstrasse was busy with big cream buses and the iron clanking of braking trams. Dingy buildings crowded out the sky and the air was full of the noise of construction workers hammering at the façade of a block opposite, punctuated by the shouts of a man with a pretzel cart.

Consulting the pocket map in her *Baedeker*, Clara searched for the spot where Friedrichstrasse intersected with Unter den Linden. A jolt of anxiety assailed her as she realised she was, really, alone in a foreign city. What would her father say when he discovered her note? *"I've been offered a part in Berlin . . ."* Berlin! A city she knew absolutely nothing about. Almost her entire image of Berlin came from Greta Garbo and John Barrymore in *Grand Hotel*.

But even as she thought this, another feeling came to her. A strange exhilaration that she had travelled beyond the map of her old world, the safe confines of London squares and streets, of English houses and cups of tea, guttering gas fires and red buses, of telephone boxes and holidays on chilly Cornish beaches. Of pinched faces and pursed lips. She had stepped into a place where she was free to reinvent herself and her entire identity. Here she needn't any longer be Clara Vine, from 39 Ponsonby Terrace, London SW1, the daughter of Sir Ronald, the sister of Angela and Kenneth, connected by that intricate web of relations and background that meant people could classify you instantly, like an insect or a stamp. The world had widened before her and it was both frightening and intoxicating, like the moment swimming in the sea when the sand shelves beneath your feet and you strike out into fresh, uncharted waters.

She was running away, no doubt about it. From England, and her family, and from the path that until a few days ago she was all but certain to take. But suddenly it felt as though she was in Berlin because she was meant to be. Besides, she said to herself, what is the worst that could happen?

Checking her reflection in the bookshop window, she realized that however uncertain she was feeling, nothing about her appearance betrayed it. Her suit was uncreased, despite three days of travel, and her complexion was young and fresh enough to resist the impact of a night's interrupted sleep. She might be any young professional woman on her way to the office or out for a morning's shopping. Who could possibly guess, from the look of her, at the turmoil she had left behind? Straightening her hair, whose glossy chestnut wisps had been caught and flattened by the wind, she tucked them back beneath her blue velvet hat, tilted it to an angle and focused on finding her way to Frau Lehmann's.

Chapter Two

Frau Lehmann's finishing school for young women occupied a large villa in the leafy west end of Berlin. It was a stately, four-storey place with steps leading up to a colonnaded porch and a creamy grey frontage topped with a red mansard roof. The city was tranquil here, with substantial houses set on broad roads that spanned out towards the Grunewald. Hidden behind hedges and railings, each differed subtly from its neighbours in architectural design, from rococo to modern, from Dutch gables and mansard roofs to cool, white cubes, with large gardens thronged with oak, pine and chestnut trees, and the occasional classical statue. Perhaps it was the famous *Berliner Luft*, the clear breeze that blows across the banks of the Spree, or perhaps it was just the combination of wide streets and stately buildings, but everything about this area felt solid and unchanging.

On closer inspection, however, the houses bore signs of creeping neglect, like a mature woman whose skilful attention to make-up fails to disguise completely the attrition of age. Since the inflation, which had swept and bankrupted the nation, a seediness had overtaken the respectable elegance of this area. The lawns were mostly unmown and the hedges leant drunkenly into the street. Paint peeled discreetly from the sides of the villa Lehmann, and through the flaking railings of the first-floor balcony a climbing vine twisted, while from below poked emerald-green fronds of potted ferns, as though the unruly forces of nature were too powerful to be confined.

Frau Lehmann had in the long years of her widowhood become an institution. During the 1920s Frau Lehmann's had been a destination for well-born girls from English families who wanted their daughters schooled in German, singing, painting and music. Then it had contained a maid, who made the beds and waited at table, and a cook. Now, with things the way they were, there was only Frau Lehmann herself, offering a room with board for sixty marks a month, and an ancient parrot patched with shabby feathers like a moth-eaten fur coat. Clara had sent a letter warning of her arrival, but there had been no time for any kind of reply.

She pulled the bell and peered nervously through the glass as a shadow loomed up from the dim interior. There was a frenzied yapping, coupled with the sound of bolts rattling and being drawn back, before the door creaked open.

'You must be Clara. Come in. I have coffee waiting.'

Frau Lehmann was a huge, stocky figure, encased in a black dress that seemed somehow more solid than mere wool and silk, with a lace shawl draped like a tablecloth across the top. Her silver hair was parted with mathematical exactitude and bundled into a tight ball at the back of her head and her black eyes gleamed like currants in the doughy flesh of her face. Her make-up was applied with theatrical generosity, as if she had a stage career of her own. A small hairy dog bounced at ankle height, causing Clara to step inside cautiously. She thought of the recommendation she had been given.

"Frau Lehmann. I think that's what she's called. She's terribly reliable. Penny Dudley-Ward stayed with her. She teaches singing."

This description had a somewhat deflating effect on Clara, conjuring the picture of herself yodelling teutonic tunes with a gaggle of other English girls rather than leading a cosmopolitan existence far from drab London. But she didn't know another soul in the city, so right now she had no choice.

With an imperious wave Frau Lehmann directed Clara into a gloomy drawing room exuding a dismal smell of mothballs, dust and ancient boiled food. Clara's heart sank. All the furniture felt too big, like a giant's house into which she had mistakenly wandered. There was an enormous, shabby sofa and a couple of armchairs parked like tanks. The walls were papered brown and there was a lamp with a beaded fringe that gave off a gloomy red light.

'I keep photographs of all my young women,' said Frau Lehmann, sinking effortfully onto a horsehair armchair. 'They often come back to see me. Do you know the Cavendishes?'

'I'm afraid not.'

'Or the Ormsby-Gores?'

'Sorry, but no.'

There continued a list of families whom Clara didn't know, until Frau Lehmann relapsed with a sigh, convinced that Clara came from the lowest echelons of London society.

She handed Clara a slice of poppy-seed cake and a cup of hot, burnt coffee, which she made drinkable by adding three teaspoons of sugar. As she took it, Clara jumped at the sound of a curse, which emanated from behind her head.

'Stop it, Mitzi, you filthy creature.'

Frau Lehmann grunted and pulled a cover over a parrot's cage. Clara's eyes strayed to the mantelpiece, where a photograph of a young man with Frau Lehmann's moon faced stare was decorated by a red and black enamel *Hakenkreuz* dangling from the frame.

'Otto, that is. My son. He died at the front in 1917. Nineteen years old.' Her fingers massaged the greasy hair of the dog which was now lolling beside her on the sofa.

'I'm sorry.'

Clara felt somehow she were being held obscurely to blame.

Frau Lehmann shook her head, as though accepting Clara's complicity in her son's death, yet graciously forgiving her. 'We have lived through terrible times. But we must look to better ones ahead. Now our country is on the up again and our two nations are friends.'

'Yes, of course.'

'Your German seems rather good,' said Frau Lehmann, with a faintly resentful tone. 'Will you be wanting lessons? I know a very good gentleman who could bring you up to scratch. Or perhaps a little singing?'

'No, thank you.'

'I used to offer art appreciation, but my legs are not what they were.'

Both looked down at the dark, swaddled sausages protruding from her skirt, the stockings concertinaed in wrinkled rings.

'Though you must visit the Pergamon Museum. The head of Nefertiti is there. She is the most magnificent woman.'

'Thank you. I will.'

'And you should meet my lodgers. We have Herr Professor Hahn, who is a very distinguished gentleman. He teaches Ancient Literature at the University. And Fräulein Viktor, a very pleasant lady, secretary to someone high up in the Labour Department.'

There was a pause. Frau Lehman's jaw shifted rhythmically as she worked on the poppy-seed cake, like a tortoise eating a lettuce leaf, with about the same amount of urgency.

'So do you have plans to occupy yourself?' she enquired at last.

'I'm hoping for a part in a film. At Babelsberg.'

'How exciting.' This had plainly taken her by surprise. Her little eyes fixed on Clara with fresh interest.

'They want multilingual actresses, you see. All the best films have to have French and English versions too, so they need actresses who speak the languages. I have an appointment tomorrow.'

'I see.' Torn between the prospect of harbouring a potential film star beneath her roof, and dismay at the shortfall in tutoring income, Frau Lehman was evidently reserving judgement.

'Well, you'll want to rest before dinner. All my residents eat together, so I'll introduce you later. I'll show you to your room.'

She heaved herself to her feet and trundled ahead to the bedroom. On the way Clara glimpsed rooms stuffed with unusually hideous furniture of fretted oak, like trees in a gloomy forest. Along the end of the corridor was a bathroom, with chequered black and white tiles and clanking pipes. The bedroom on the top floor was tiny, with a brown carpet, a gigantic wardrobe into which she put her bag, and a window overlooking the conifer-lined street. There was a basin in the corner with a mirror over it, and a card attached to the inside of the door: "Dinner at eight. No hot water before bed."

Closing the door behind her, Clara sat on the green counterpane and it sank beneath her as though she were being swallowed up into the earth. She had a fleeting feeling that when she slept, she might disappear into a crevasse and never get up. She thought of all the other girls Frau Lehmann had boasted of, and wondered if they had sat here and cried with homesickness or, more likely, made sure they spent every second of their spare time at concerts and the theatre.

Then she shook herself. With any luck she wouldn't be seeing much of Frau Lehmann, or the frightful-sounding lodgers. The next morning she was to present herself at the world-famous Babelsberg Studios, find Mr Max Townsend, film producer, and audition for his new film, *Black Roses*. Gazing over at the cracked basin, down which an ochre stain snaked from the tap, Clara reflected on what had brought her here.

When Clara first stated her ambition to go on the stage, she might as well have said she wanted to enter the white slave trade and have done with it. She had ballet lessons, of course, but almost every girl of her family's acquaintance had ballet lessons as a child, and they didn't end up in rep at the Eastbourne Pavilion. To her father, the idea was at first preposterous, and then a phase. To her mother, it was simply out of the question. *'Acting is not the kind of thing I'd want a daughter of mine to do.'* Their own plan for her entry into the adult world had been via an organisation called the Queen's Secretarial College for Young Gentlewomen in South Kensington. Clara still remembered her dismay on finding the brochure on the table in the hall one day shortly before her sixteenth birthday – duck-egg blue with scrolly silver lettering. Flicking through, she read, 'Young ladies will find it congenial to learn alongside other gentlewomen in a setting where high standards of etiquette are always maintained.'

Faced with this level of opposition to her chosen career, Clara started a bit of private study. She sent off for a manual on 'charm', which she found advertised in the pages of *The Lady*, a magazine her mother took for the purpose of hiring servants, and followed its oblique wisdom as closely as she could. 'When a woman reflects her innate charm, all else of value follows as naturally as flowers turn to the sun.'

She posed before the mirror and learnt long screeds of Shakespeare by heart, for future auditions. She was Portia, Hermia, Lady Macbeth. She attended Saturday matinées in the West End and sat up in the gods. She wrote to Gerald du Maurier and Constance Cummings, and received a signed photograph from the former with a note wishing her well in her 'theatrical career', which she kept like a talisman tucked in the side of her mirror. Then her mother died, and the issue of Clara's career stopped mattering overnight. Suddenly, nobody really cared what she did.

The London School of Acting and Musical Theatre, which Clara joined the autumn after leaving school, had its rehearsal rooms in a church hall off Waterloo, where the tang of polish barely masked the smell of unwashed feet left over from dancing lessons, and leaflets for the Mothers' Coffee Circle fluttered from cork boards. The roof was crisscrossed with red painted iron rafters, and at the end of the hall was a raised platform where Monsieur LeClerc, who took Speech, Voice and Acting, went to elaborate lengths to emphasize correct pronunciation in Shakespeare and to lament the inferiority of the English stage compared to the French.

The staff were a mixed bunch. There was Miss Stuyveson, who taught deportment. *"Don't slouch, Clara. You're playing Nora, not one of the three witches. You'll have a widow's hump by the time you're thirty!"* Fran Goodbody, an athletic woman with tight red curls, taught fencing and stage technique and Miss Wisznewski, a Polish woman with a starved, ballerina's body, gave movement classes, for which they wore navy leotards and tights, and had to skip around the stage. But Clara's favourite teacher was Paul Croker, an intense young man with a patched tweed jacket and goatee beard, who had met Lee Strasberg in New York and was an avid disciple of method acting. *'You must work from the inside out, Clara. Access your emotional memory. Use everything that has happened in your life to create the character you are working on. It's not enough to look like Viola, it's not enough to sound like Viola, you must be Viola.'*

After the academy, however, work had been scarce. Clara garnered one line of praise in the *Eastbourne Courier* for her "graceful performance" as Sorel Bliss in *Hay Fever*, and she had merited a minute photograph in *The Tatler* under the caption "Sir Ronald Vine's daughter takes to the stage" when she had a few lines at the Hampstead Everyman. There had been several seasons in rep but, at the age of twenty-six, she found herself without anything resembling a career. A grown woman with no job and no husband, still living at home with her father.

Not that her father seemed to mind. He barely seemed to notice her. As often as not, after a day spent tramping around auditions and rehearsal rooms, she would return to a house full of strangers. Ronald Vine had coped with his wife's death by focusing on work, and after losing his seat in Parliament he had thrown himself into his special interest: Anglo-German friendship. He formed a society made up of politicians and businessmen, with the odd, fanatical spinster thrown in. They attended rallies and discussed plans to strengthen ties between the two countries. They held meetings at Ponsonby Terrace, a narrow street of Georgian houses in Pimlico, where they would sit and smoke in the drawing room, debating the dangers of Bolshevism. Her sister, Angela, had enthusiastically joined the cause, but Clara couldn't think of anything worse. When she came home she had got into the habit of opening the door very quietly and listening out for the sound of unfamiliar voices. If she heard them she would take off her shoes, dart silently through the hall and creep up the stairs.

Things might have stayed pretty much as they were if she had not met Dennis Beaumont.

Dennis was the kind of man who seemed to be born at the age of forty. He was a balding lawyer with a narrow moustache who had courted her assiduously, taking her out for long evening drives in his Morgan while he discussed his intention to practise at the bar until the time was right to make a bid for a seat in Parliament. Somehow, without knowing how it happened, Clara found herself part of his plan.

She didn't realize it properly until the last evening she had seen him. They were at a party in Chelsea, held by one of Dennis's friends, Gerald Mortimer, a brick-faced barrister who had just returned from a visit to the continent and was talking about the new election in Germany, and the success of the National Socialists.

'Let's hope they provide a bit of stability after the chaos that's been going on there,' said Gerald, waving a flute of champagne. 'Hitler's the only thing keeping the Germans from a tide of Communism.'

'But then,' sighed Dennis, 'the Communists will be coming here soon, won't they? All sorts will be flooding here. Jews and bankrupts. We'll have to put safeguards in place or we'll be swamped.'

'Swamped is a bit extreme, isn't it?' said Clara. She loathed Dennis's tendency to exaggerate. She supposed it was the aspirant politician in him.

'Not a bit of it. There will be thousands of them. Hundreds of thousands. I know you're half-German, my darling, but I don't think you understand the implications.'

'As it happens,' said Gerald importantly, 'an MP friend of mine, Edward Doran, asked the Home Secretary just today to take measures to prevent any alien Jews entering the country. No one wants to sound heartless, but he thinks an influx of Jewish refugees could threaten our entire civilization.'

'I think what he said was that it would be the End of British Civilization if we let them in.'

The speaker was a handsome, fair-haired man with a cigar. He paused to exhale a thin line of smoke. 'Whereas I would say it was the End of British Civilization if we didn't.'

Dennis made an irritated little gesture. 'Clara dear, do you know Rupert Allingham?'

Gerald was annoyed. 'Come on, Rupert. You have to admit Herr Hitler has a point.'

'Herr Hitler?' Allingham gave a laconic smile. 'Let's just say I'm not entirely seduced by him.'

'Rupert's a journalist,' said Dennis to Clara, as if in explanation.

Allingham gave a little bow and smiled. 'And you're the actress,' he said.

Though Clara was flattered to be recognized, it felt like false pretences. She'd been out of work for a month. That very afternoon her agent, an ancient man with a dinner-stained cravat and offices in Wardour Street, had said, 'Nothing doing, ducky,' when she telephoned about her employment prospects.

'Will you be appearing in anything soon?'

'I'm expecting an audition for the Liverpool Rep,' she lied smoothly.

'Not,' said Dennis, giving her a hard squeeze round the waist, 'that she'll have any time for acting once we're married.'

Before she had a chance to reply, they were interrupted and Clara escaped to the balcony floor. A mixture of anger and surprise cascaded through her. No time for acting! When had anyone ever said anything about that? How could Dennis presume to say such a thing when they had not even discussed it? And as for getting married! They hadn't ever discussed getting married either. Who said she was going to marry Dennis? Settle down in his home and do what exactly? Have babies and take tea with his dry stick of a mother, an intolerable woman who disliked Clara because she had German blood and had complained to her vicar because he owned a dachshund? Her heart hammering and a flush on her cheeks, Clara stared over the rail at the couples circling awkwardly round the dance floor like pairs of courting crabs.

'You shouldn't mind him.'

It was Rupert Allingham again. He leant over the banister at her side.

'I don't,' she said coolly, but the shock of Dennis's comment still burnt inside her. Looking down she saw he had started dancing with Polly Davies, a woman with a toothy face like a pony, and she could see the thinning strands of hair splayed across his scalp. She thought of all those dinners she had sat through while Dennis talked about tort and precedence and the central importance of English law in upholding the Empire, and how attentively she had listened because she thought it was important. Suddenly she felt a violent revulsion and, in an instant, her admiration turned to disgust. Dennis wasn't impressive, he was a bully and a bore, and it had taken a split second to see it. Meanwhile Allingham was studying her intently.

'Ever had a film test?'

'Afraid not.'

'You should, you know. You'd be perfect in films. I bet the camera loves you.'

'Really,' she muttered, taking a sip of her champagne and concentrating on the floor below.

'In fact, a friend of mine is working on a picture right now.'

That made her look up. 'Is he a producer?'

'Sort of,' he said languidly. 'His name's Max Townsend. He was at the BBC, until he got chucked out. But it was all for the best because he's written a script. It's called *Black Roses*. It's about a Finnish woman who's in love with a political dissident but has to sleep with the Tsarist governor, a cruel Bolshevik. It's a love story.'

Clara could barely contain her surprise. 'And you think he'd offer the role to me?'

'Well, not the heroine, my dear. He's got Lilian Harvey for that. But if you were to turn up at Ufa and ask for Max, I'm sure he could sort you out. Say I sent you.'

'What's Ufa?'

'Universum Film Aktiengesellschaft. You must have heard of it! Where Fritz Lang directs and Marlene Dietrich acts. It's in Berlin.'

'Berlin!'

'Well, just outside. At the Babelsberg studios. It's the nearest you'll get to Hollywood without being in Hollywood. And they want people who can speak both German and English. Dennis said you speak German.'

'My mother always spoke to us in German. She was born in Hamburg.'

'You'll do brilliantly then. Look, I'm going to be there myself in a few weeks' time. Why not come out and get in touch? Or, let me give you Max's number.'

He took out a piece of notepaper, scribbled on it, and pressed it into her hand.

'You should, you know. Berlin's terrifically exciting at the moment. That is,' he added pointedly, 'if Dennis doesn't object.'

★   ★   ★

From somewhere in the house, Frau Lehmann's dinner gong sounded and the unmistakable smell of cabbage wafted up the stairs. Clara swung her feet round and stood up, bracing herself to meet the other residents. Peering into the spotty mirror, she ran a trace of Vaseline over her eyebrows and patted down her hair. *If Dennis doesn't object.* Well, he hadn't had the opportunity to object. She had left the day after the party without mentioning a word of it to him.

Chapter Three

The headquarters of Ufa, secluded in the woods south-west of Berlin, looked more like a factory than a film studio. Approached through a set of imposing gates, the sprawling complex of buildings was designed in monumentalist style with its four studios projecting like the arms of a cross. It had been the centre of film making since 1911, and while the rest of the country struggled through the devastating inflation, Ufa was wildly successful, turning out the musicals and sugary love stories that Berliners loved. If it looked like a factory, that's because it was. The *Traumfabrik*, they called it – the dream factory – a production line for wholesome, rose-tinted fantasies that lightened the heart and took people's minds off what was happening all around them.

Clara crossed the car park, navigating the gleaming ranks of Mercedes and Daimlers, and paused to watch workmen erecting the set of an entire medieval street, complete with a drawbridge and wooden gargoyles on the plaster walls. Actors dressed as monks passed by, carrying bottles of beer, and a couple of ringletted actresses sat in the sunshine, reading novels. She drank it all in, taut with excitement, before entering the foyer.

The walls were plastered with posters of Ufa's triumphs. There was the dramatic advertisement for *Metropolis*, the city of the future, with its skyscrapers bisected by daggers of light, and Leni Riefenstahl clinging to a mountainside in *The Blue Light*. The famous, hooded eyes of Marlene Dietrich, her skin a severe, silvery sheen, hung next to a poster of Lilian Harvey in *The Three from the Gas Station*, sitting at the wheel of her red-leathered cabriolet, her hair bright as a flame.

A man in a small glass cubicle looked up from his copy of the *Völkischer Beobachter,* satisfied himself Clara was not important, and languidly removed his cigarette.

'Can I help?'

'I'm here to see Mr Townsend. Max Townsend?'

The man consulted a list. 'Which film?'

'*Schwarze Rosen.*'

His shrug expressed infinitesimal regret. 'He's not here.'

'Do you know when he might be back?'

He turned his mouth down and gestured at his list as though it was Holy Writ. 'All I know is, his name's not here. Perhaps he's one of those gentlemen who's smelt which way the wind's blowing. Like a lot of them who used to be here. Perhaps he's taken a vacation with a single ticket.'

'He's English.'

The man stroked a moustache which was as broad and waxed at the Kaiser's. 'English? I suppose someone has to be. I can't place him. But everything's changing here. Come back tomorrow and he may be my new best friend.'

A woman walking past in a tight pink sweater, her dark hair swept off her face, turned backwards with a smile.

'Did you say Max Townsend?'

'Yes. Do you know him?'

The woman gave a light laugh. 'All the girls here know Max. I haven't seen him lately but I can take you to his office. Leave her to me, Herr Becker, I'll take good care of her.'

Herr Becker grimaced, replaced his cigarette and returned to the newspaper reports of how Herr Hitler's aeroplane visit to Munich had been a triumph.

'Take no notice of him, he's a professional Berliner, which means his bark's worse than his bite. He sits there pretending to read his Nazi newspaper, but really he knows everything that's going on. So why are you seeing Max?'

'He might have a part for me in this film he's producing. *Black Roses*. The one with Lilian Harvey.'

'That sounds like Max. He loves Lilian Harvey. She has special appeal for him.'

'Why's that?'

'Because she's English born. It means Max can actually talk to her. He's never bothered to learn German. He says he can communicate at a deeper level. By which he means the language of love.' She pursed her lips in an exaggerated kiss and giggled. 'Oh, I hope I'm not being indiscreet. I mean Max is a dear, of course. It's just what he tells all the girls.'

'It's all right. I've never met him, actually.'

'And you say he has Lilian Harvey in his film?'

'Yes, she's playing the heroine.'

'Only,' a tiny frown formed on her face, 'Lilian Harvey's just gone to Hollywood. Didn't you know? Some of the top brass here are a little unhappy, actually. She is one of Babelberg's biggest stars.'

'I don't know much about her at all.'

'You must know her! She's just done *The Congress Dance* with Conrad Veidt. She makes about sixty thousand marks a film. Everyone expected her to marry Willy Fritsch someday soon, only now they're saying she's turned her back on Berlin. Germany isn't good enough for her. She wants to make a name in America.'

Clara felt her heart sink within her.

'But let's go and find Max anyway!' The girl thrust out her hand. 'Before we go any further, I should introduce myself. I'm Helga Schmidt.'

She had a sweet-natured face with pencil-thin eyebrows that arched above lively brown eyes, and lips outlined in cherry red. Her face was as brown and freckled as an egg. The combination of her tight skirt and sweater suggested wholesome curves, but her eyes had a knowing twinkle and her voice had a whole packet of cigarettes in it.

'Clara Vine.'

'Delighted. Oh, mind out.'

A man carrying a lighting rig nearly collided with Clara as she pressed herself against the corridor wall. He disappeared through a double door ahead of them and they found themselves staring into an enormous studio.

It was probably the biggest single hall Clara had ever seen. It was the size of a cathedral, and contained both a medieval village, with cobbled street and cosy little houses, and an Italian piazza complete with a marble fountain. A series of façades encompassed a whole host of architectural styles – Gothic windows, Renaissance palazzi, Spanish roofs. There were stained-glass windows reflecting violet and scarlet light and to one side an entire street was decked out as the American Wild West.

'Impressive, isn't it?'

Clara gazed around her. It was a sight that seemed to suggest endless transformations. Something about it reminded her of the exact reason she had wanted to act. For her, a performance was not something to appear in, but rather something to disappear into. Acting let you do that. It was a transcendent experience, even if, when you looked behind the sets, there was only plaster and struts propping them up.

'They built this studio for *Metropolis*. They used thirty-six thousand extras, can you believe, and a cool six million marks. The most expensive film ever made. It's called the Marlene Dietrich Halle.' Helga winked. 'Only since she left I don't think it's called *that* any more.'

The place seemed astonishingly busy. There was hammering and drilling from men installing a set, and others were carrying sound equipment to fix on an immense crane. Girls with scripts scurried past, dodging prop makers and electricians. Clara stared curiously at the model of an Arabian harem, right next to the background of a windswept mountain.

'Are they making more than one film at the same time?'

'More than one?' Helga burst out laughing. 'Hundreds! People never get tired of films, do they? Luckily for us actresses. The rest of the country may be going to hell but Ufa is doing wonderfully. At least, they were until recently. Now I think Max's office is somewhere along here.'

They climbed a flight of steps, turning into a long corridor, and came to a glass door, through which could be seen a man in shirtsleeves, bow-tie and red braces, gesticulating on the telephone. He was cadaverously thin, with tombstone teeth and hollow cheeks. It was hard to tell how old he might be. His face was as wrinkled as yesterday's newspaper and suggested just as much worrying news.

'Sorry to interrupt, Albert. We're looking for Max.'

'Who isn't?' he replied gloomily, raking a hand through sparse locks of hair. 'I'm thinking of putting out a police search for him. Except it's no doubt the police who've tracked him down, knowing Max. He's probably in a cell somewhere, waiting to be bailed out.'

'Clara, this is Albert Lindemann. Albert, this is Fräulein Clara Vine, and apparently she's up for a part in Max's new film.'

Albert eyed her briefly. 'If I had fifty marks for every girl who said that I could give up this filthy job and spend my life skiing.'

'Don't worry.' Helga laid a hand on Clara's arm. 'He's joking. If he tried skiing he'd have a heart attack.' To Albert she said, 'Perhaps you could ask Max to find a part for me too, darling. I'm twenty-six now and I'm getting tired of playing the chorus.'

'Tell him yourself,' said Albert, cracking open a cigarette packet, lighting up and inhaling as if his life depended on it. 'You've got far more to persuade him with. I haven't the faintest idea where he is, he's not answering his telephone and all I get is people complaining to me. What was this film he's supposed to have scripted?'

'*Black Roses*. Lilian Harvey's going to star.'

'Well, if you wait for Lilian you could be waiting a long time. She may be in love with Willy Fritsch, but I bet she'll love Hollywood more.'

'That's what I said,' added Helga. 'I'd say she's definitely there for good. Gone the way of Marlene Dietrich and all the others.'

'So that's it, is it?' said Clara, trying to keep her voice level. 'There's nothing else you can suggest?'

Noticing the dismay on her face, Albert said more kindly, 'Now I didn't say that, did I? Everyone's on the lookout for English speakers. Why not come back tomorrow? Or Max might decide to turn up for work. You never know.'

Clara thanked him and closed the glass door behind her. She took a few steps and then stopped and leant against the wall, as though her knees might actually buckle beneath her. She felt physically stunned. Her entire rationale for coming to Berlin was suddenly dashed. Max Townsend seemed to have vanished and with him her whole reason for being here.

The glamour of the studio, which just a few moments ago had seemed to offer a whole new world to her, existed now only to taunt her. How could she have been so naïve as to come all the way here on the word of a complete stranger? Everything Angela believed about her – that she was flighty, unreliable and irresponsible – was being proved true. Clara had a vision of herself returning humbly to Ponsonby Terrace just as Angela poured her evening Martini, and her sister saying, "Never mind. If you really need work I'm sure Gerald can fix you up with something at his office." Or Dennis's mother, Mrs Beaumont, with her grim stripe of a smile, declaring, "Least said, soonest mended." The thought of it ran through her like steel and she braced herself. Whatever happened, she simply couldn't go home.

Helga fell into step beside her.

'Max not being here . . . It might just be Max, but it's more likely something to do with everything that's going on.'

'You mean politically?'

At the word, Helga glanced momentarily around.

'It's a strange time at Babelsberg just now. For the last couple of weeks, since the new government, it's like everything's on hold. No one's looking at new scripts. No one wants to put a foot wrong before they know what the game's going to be. So many people have gone already. Just this morning I heard Billy Wilder and Peter Lorre took the night train to Paris.'

'Why have they gone?'

Helga rolled her eyes. 'Why d'you think?'

Close up, the elegance of Helga's appearance was diminished slightly. There was a line of grime beneath her fingernails and the kohl under her eyes was smudged, giving her the look of someone who has stayed up far too late, as she probably had. Clara wondered if she really was twenty-six as she claimed. There was a worldly wisdom in her expression that suggested she had lived longer and seen more than she was letting on.

'Catch me going anywhere though? The talkies are going to be my big break. Everyone says I have the perfect voice for them.' She reached over and touched Clara's arm generously. 'And they'll be good for you too! They're crying out for actresses who speak English. You'll have more work that you can cope with. You'll see!'

As they reached the lobby there was a commotion. A man in brown uniform bustled past, and Clara could hear the sound of doors slamming. Outside a fleet of gleaming, black Mercedes-Benz cars had drawn up, from which climbed a group of important-looking men in suits. A palpable tremor ran through the air. Heads craned out of office doors all down the corridor as the group swept in, raising their arms in swift, automatic salutes. At the front was a man in a wide-belted trench coat and a fedora with a thin black band. He was a peculiar figure. Not much over five foot and with his hair swept back in an oiled wave, he mounted the steps with a swift, dipping gait. Looking down Clara saw he had a deformed right foot that turned inwards as he walked, supported by a built-up platform sole. Quickly she dragged her eyes from foot to face.

It was obvious the man knew exactly what she was thinking. She felt his eyes travel over her, checking her colouring, the bobbed dark hair with its faint haze of chestnut, the heart-shaped face and slender physique, lingering perhaps too long on the swell of her bust. Though she was quite used to being on a stage studied by hundreds of pairs of eyes, there was something in his expression that made her squirm. He held her gaze for a second, eyes cold as a shark, then flipped a swift salute. It was only as he smiled that Clara realized she had seen him before. It was the man in the wedding photograph, the picture she had seen in the shop window as she walked up Friedrichstrasse.

'That's Dr Goebbels,' Helga whispered. 'Officially he's the new Minister of Public Enlightenment and Propaganda. Unofficially they call him the Tadpole.'

'Why?'

'Can't you see it?' she laughed. 'That big head and little body?'

'They also call him the Babelsberg Buck,' murmured Albert, who had come up behind them. 'He has a real eye for the ladies. You two had better be careful!'

'Who's he talking to?'

'Ludwig Klitzsch, the chief of the studio. And Alfred Hugenberg. Technically he's the chairman of Ufa, but he's been told to hand the whole place over to Goebbels, lock, stock and barrel.'

A glance at the assembled studio executives said it all. The men had dark, anxious eyes and smiles that looked like they were held up by piano wires. Goebbels spoke with a declamatory air, as though he was addressing a large public meeting, which meant the conversation carried clearly across the lobby.

'I assure you the government has no desire to control any films being made. Art is free and should remain so. I have always said that.'

The men around him nodded at these snippets, as though they proceeded from the mouth of Socrates. He was a devoted admirer of the power of film, Goebbels continued. There were certain films that had made an indelible impression on him. Fritz Lang's *Die Nibelungen*, for example, and *Battleship Potemkin*.

'The famously Bolshevik *Potemkin*,' muttered Albert. 'Can he be serious?'

'You wouldn't think politicians would bother much with movies,' said Clara, 'I'm sure they don't in England.' It was hard to imagine Mr Baldwin, with his pipe and his poker face, getting excited about *Love Me Tonight* or Ramsay MacDonald attending *Shanghai Express*.

'Oh, but Ufa is so important,' said Albert. 'If Ufa plays its cards right it can control film making all over Europe.'

'And I hear Dr Goebbels is planning to choose every chorus girl himself, just to ensure that they're a perfect representation of German womanhood,' sniggered Helga.

'In which case, Fräulein, you would be the ideal choice.'

Helga widened her eyes and turned round. The speaker was a short, thickset figure, his beer-barrel body encased in the brown shirt and breeches of the SA. The leer on his face had a message as plain as his swastika armband. Within a split second Helga assessed the situation, and realized she wasn't going to have to apologize.

'Well, I didn't know I was being overheard.' Her eyelids fluttered flirtatiously.

'That's because your voice is as clear as a bell, Fräulein. You're an actress, I can tell.'

Helga's whole body gave a reflexive wriggle. 'But of course.' She stuck out her hand. 'I'm Helga Schmidt.'

'Walter Bauer.' He cocked his head at the posters on the walls. 'I've probably seen your face in one of these masterworks. Only it's not usually the faces I'm looking at.' He issued a loud guffaw and turned, as if for confirmation, to his companion.

The other man was wearing a double-breasted suit, with a crest of white handkerchief protruding from the pocket, and a smile of humorous disdain. He had a dense, muscular build and his abundant dark hair was trained with brilliantine into a style of military precision. He raised his eyebrows momentarily at Bauer's remark but held out a hand to Helga, simultaneously clicking his heels. Clara had never before seen anyone click their heels.

'Klaus Müller.'

Helga allowed her hand to be kissed, and simpered. As she listed the films she had been in for the Brown Shirt's benefit, Clara was conscious of Müller's eyes appraising her.

'And what about you, Fräulein? Have we seen any of your work?'

'I very much doubt it.'

'This is Clara Vine. She's a big star in England,' cut in Helga quickly. 'And she's in line for a major part in *Schwarze Rosen*.'

'If the producer chooses to turn up,' smiled Clara, deprecatingly.

'You speak excellent German for an Englishwoman.'

'My late mother was German. She came from Hamburg.'

His eyebrows rose in polite surprise. 'So your father?'

'He's English. He's a politician.'

Clara saw a flicker of interest cross his face.

'Not Sir Ronald Vine?'

'You've heard of him?'

'But of course.'

From across the lobby, the voice of Dr Goebbels rose. 'The German film has reached the point where it must fulfil its duty to the nation. It must exercise international influence and become a spiritual world power.'

He seemed likely to go on for some time.

In a low voice Müller interrupted. 'I'm afraid, ladies, we have business to get on with. But I wonder whether you two would care to join us this evening. For a drink at the Kaiserhof. Shall we say seven o'clock?'

Clara was about to refuse politely. Everything she knew about National Socialists suggested they were not the kind of people to sip cocktails with. Besides, in England you would never accept an invitation from a man to whom you had not properly been introduced, even if he did profess to know your father. But before she could say anything Helga had spoken up.

'We'd love to!'

Chapter Four

He liked it here. Most of his colleagues had places out in the west of the city, comfortable villas in Dahlem or Wilmersdorf, where they could shield themselves behind high walls from the turbulence around them. But Leo Quinn had looked east and found a place in Oranienburger Strasse, on the top floor of an apartment block. It was only ten minutes' walk from Unter den Linden, but its proximity to the poorer districts, where the tenements housed families of Jews and immigrants from the east, made it an unusual choice for an employee of His Majesty's Foreign Office. Day and night there was the smell of frying and the sound of arguments. The back alleys were cobwebbed with clothes lines and the balconies hung with sheets like flags of surrender. Though his street might not be smart, the shabbiness suited the sombre buildings with their subdued stucco and nineteenth-century stolidity. You passed through an arched gateway into a dark, cobbled court-yard where the odd stray cat lurked, probably someone's pet in better times, and then you walked up three flights of dim stairway to find a room that was big enough only for that same cat to be swung, were it not for the piles of books that stood around the single bed and armchair. There was nowhere to cook, but Leo took his breakfast and supper in the café next door, a place of faded, high-ceilinged splendour.

Breakfast was always the same, a roll and coffee, and supper tended towards the unimaginative too: pork of some description, and dumplings, best not described. But the portions were hearty, the waitress was friendly and the café, especially in the bitter winter months, much warmer than his apartment, with its cracked gas fire.

The saving grace of his room, and the part that allowed his landlady to charge a few marks more a week, was that its tall windows looked out onto the street rather than the dank courtyard, so that in the afternoon the room was saturated with a flood of golden light that lit up every dusty corner. When he returned from work Leo would put a record on his gramophone, smoke one of his Salem Aleikum Turkish cigarettes, look out on the broad street lined with plane trees, and think it was possible to feel at peace. Almost.

He knew barely anyone here. His neighbours were mostly Jewish, due to the proximity of the grand New Synagogue along the street, a russet brick building with Moorish towers and a fretted golden dome. This gloriously exotic building was flanked on each side by leaden-faced apartment blocks like stolid German sentries in field grey. It was the largest synagogue in Berlin and seated three thousand people in a hall the size of a football pitch, exquisitely decorated with gold patterning. Leo had never set foot in it but peered into the doorway sometimes, and smelt the scent of something mysterious and ancient.

In the next apartment was a couple whose child's ragged, asthmatic cough had punctuated most nights that winter. Below him was a Fräulein Lena Goldwasser who had revealed, in their only conversation, that she worked as a nurse in a clinic out in Wannsee. Leo talked to no one in the block apart from a schoolmaster called Martin Rinkel, who would sometimes come and knock at the door with a bottle of bad schnapps and a deck of cards. Other evenings, Leo got on with a translation he was doing of Ovid's *Metamorphoses*, something he kidded himself he might have published one day. Not because he thought it would sell, but for the sheer satisfaction of seeing his name in print.

Solitude suited him fine. As an only child it had been his natural condition, and he was rarely desperate for company. From time to time he had run into a couple of men he'd known at university. They flocked here, the men who liked other men, because that was what Berlin was famous for. They discovered a homosexual freedom they could never find at home, even if that same freedom was laced with terror now as they found themselves liable to arbitrary arrest. If they were foreigners they were dealt with by the police, but their German friends risked a beating or worse from the storm troopers. The Brown Shirts took pleasure in meting out punishments of an especially perverse and sadistic nature, punishments that cast a savage light on their own benighted souls.

As for himself, there was a woman back in London, a secretary at the Foreign Office called Marjorie Simmons. Or at least she used to be Marjorie Simmons; she was married now, so not Simmons any more and not working either. She lived in Putney, but her husband was abroad, meaning that she was free to take the bus up to town pretty much whenever she felt like it, on the pretext of visiting a gallery or a day's shopping in Knightsbridge, and when he was in London she would call him and they would meet in Brown's Hotel, a place of dingy elegance, in a side street off Piccadilly.

At the thought of Marjorie's face, the freckled nose and smile revealing slightly buck teeth, Leo felt a twist either of regret or revulsion inside him. When they first met, it had been nice enough. She was girlishly enthusiastic about the plays they went to and the concerts at the Wigmore Hall, and she had listened to his travel stories with every sign of interest. Then one day, when he had returned from a vacation in Czechoslovakia, she announced blithely, as if to a gossipy girlfriend, that she was getting married, to a man whom Leo had always considered dull and unintelligent. Wrong-footed by this approach, he had congratulated her warmly.

No sooner had Majorie told him, however, than she gave a secretive little smile, and said, 'But that doesn't have to spoil our little arrangement, does it?'

And like a fool, he had shaken his head and agreed.

Since then, whenever they met, he had tried to ask about her husband, but she diverted the conversation immediately. She liked to compartmentalize him, he realized. He was part of that ribboned section of her life that was labelled pleasure. He probably had the same status to her as a trip to the theatre. Indeed there was something theatrical about the pleasure she took in lovemaking. It was like a performance in which Marjorie herself was on stage. He had noticed the way she glanced in the triptych mirror while they were in bed or as he tried to read her poetry after sex. The way she observed her magnificent body, the freckled shoulders, the curving slope of her back, the suspenders and silk knickers, as though just the experience itself was not enough. The way she stroked the reddish curls between her legs and the skin of her inner thighs, white as a boiled egg. She needed to be both spectator and performer. And she pleased him in bed, there was no doubt about it. When she undressed she possessed a seductive boldness that vanished entirely when she was clothed in twinset and pearls. She had a kind of feline sensuality that helped him forget that sex with her was at all times separated from emotion. What scared him was her assumption that they could go on like this for ever. Every time they met he rehearsed the words to tell her he was ending it, but every time, after sex, it seemed monstrously impolite. He dreaded the thought that his life could be wasted in a polite, amicable relationship of convenience. The dullness of adultery, rather than the excitement of love.

His father had been an accountant; a man whose intelligence far outshone the mundane circumstances of his life. They lived in a terraced Victorian house in Clapham, with a red tiled path and a painted porch and a scrap of front garden filled with chrysanthemums. His father would leave for work each day with a packet of sandwiches and a copy of the *Daily Herald* and when he returned in the evenings he would watch Leo completing his Latin translations on the dining table with pride and sometimes an angry flash of envy, so certain was he that education would be the route for his only son out of their impoverished lower-middle-class existence. As an Irishman he was an outsider himself, with a soft, emotional heart, and the day Leo won a scholarship to Balliol he was stiffly embarrassed to see his father cry.

Oxford had taught him several things, most notably how to mix in different social spheres with ease. He learnt how to drift on a punt downstream between banks of high yellow irises and trailing willows. He learnt the etiquette required when you were asked back for weekends to houses that possessed tennis courts and ancestral oil paintings. He understood that the English upper classes, just like his other subjects of study, had their irregular grammar and unspoken rules. The fact that they lived in the same Mayfair squares and attended Eton or Harrow or Winchester, shot on the same grouse moors and week-ended in the same country houses, meant they were far too cunning to be hoodwinked by an outsider. The tight little clan of people with money had known each other from birth. They recognized the minute variations of social status the way a birdwatcher knew a woodlark from a skylark and there were any number of subtleties to betray you. Language – not just accents or inflections, but the vocabulary itself, like the wrong word for mirror or notepaper – instantly pinpointed an imposter. Yet they liked Leo. He was good-looking, with his spare frame and high brow, from which slightly curly hair sprang. Even more importantly, he had learnt how not to obtrude.

Even while he moved among the upper classes, though, he resented them. Was it their easy assurance, or their wilful insouciance? Their carriage, the swing in their shoulders that came from hundreds of years of breeding? Their clothes, their cars, their games, their sheer damn ignorance? Their voices filled with money, their laughter that rattled with cash? Leo wasn't sure. He remembered one incident that still had the power, years on, to make him shudder.

He had been invited to a ball and it was the custom for people to be allocated to 'house parties', at which families in the nearby countryside would accommodate visiting guests. The house he had been assigned to contained a girl of especial beauty, the honourable someone, with a fine blonde bob that swung like silk, and eyes of deep violet. In the afternoon Leo was invited to take a gun out, shooting rabbits. He had never held a gun before, but when he lifted it and peered through the sites, it reminded him unmistakably of the times as a boy that he would track the elusive frisk of a bird's feathers through his binoculars. When he saw the rabbit's beady eye and delicate ears quivering with life, he found he simply couldn't pull the trigger. What if he missed? What if he merely injured the creature? He lowered it again, only to see the animal fall a second later, blasted by the blonde standing directly behind him.

'You want a clean kill,' she observed coolly, reloading her Purdey. 'And *you* couldn't do it, could you?' He said nothing, but later, as they were walking through the fields back to the house, she had made a remark that was curiously devastating.

'You know, Leo, however much you look the part, it's like you're acting. You don't actually seem like you belong.'

It stung. Because she was right.

It was dangerous, this sense of not belonging, and it was the kind of thing his own employers looked out for. He wondered how closely they kept a watch on him.

At Balliol Leo had scraped enough money to spend part of every vacation travelling, and after leaving university he worked in Geneva, Munich and Berlin, teaching English. Berlin in the high days of the Weimar Republic was paradise, sitting in cafés talking to adventurous women with short hair and monocles, having rambling discussions about art and savouring the sense that anything daring or decadent was possible.

Eventually, he ran out of money and went back to England. He thought he might go into journalism, and was poised to take a job with Reuters when he received a telephone call from a man he had known at Oxford. Hugo Chambers was an odd sort with a passion for golf, Old Masters and eclectic wildlife. He had travelled the world on natural history expeditions, seeking out creatures that were believed to be extinct. He was a respected naturalist and Fellow of the Royal Society, and also, Leo discovered, he worked for British Intelligence. He wondered if Leo might like to meet up for a chat.

Tall and thin, dressed in pepper-and-salt tweeds, and with a habit of wild gesticulation, Hugo was exactly as Leo remembered him. They spent a jovial few hours eating beef and oyster pie in Scott's, and after lengthy tales of Hugo's recent jaunt to find butterflies in the foothills of the Himalayas, they walked to 54 Broadway, a block opposite St James's Park tube station with a brass plaque announcing it as the Headquarters of the Minimax Fire Extinguisher Company. There on the fourth floor behind a padded door, was a forbidding character with a square jaw and a vigorous handshake, who turned out to be the chief of the Secret Intelligence Service. Rear-Admiral Sir Hugh Sinclair – or Quex as he was known – offered Leo a cigar from a crocodile-skin case and waved him comfortably to an armchair. He seemed already to know everything about Leo, from his school and family, to the languages he spoke and his financial circumstances. The conversation was pleasant, but there was one exchange that bewildered Leo.

'An only son, aren't you Quinn? Close to your parents?'

'Yes, sir.'

He felt Quex's gimlet eyes on him.

'They must be proud of you, getting up to Oxford and taking a first.'

'I think so, sir.'

'Yet you've spent a lot of time abroad.'

'I've travelled around quite a lot.'

'Did you take an interest in the politics when you were there?'

'Politics are not really my hobby, sir.'

'Do you keep in touch with the people you met?'

'Not at all, I'm afraid.'

'Just checking you're not a Red,' said Hugo cheerfully, as they clattered back down the stairs at the end of the interview.

'And the only child bit?'

'Some trick cyclist stuff about dependability and owing allegiance. Forget it. You're our man.'

Leo agreed to the job. He would be seconded to the Berlin Passport Control Office which was the usual cover for SIS operatives, filtering applications for British visas. He would liaise with the ambassador himself and an attaché at the embassy called Archie Dyson, and he would communicate with Head Office via communiqués carried in the diplomatic bag. He would receive a week's worth of briefing before he left. That was all, apart from the advice that he should trust no one and avoid sleeping with local women. Or men, of course.

As soon as he arrived back in Berlin it was clear that things had changed dramatically. In the wide streets men were selling matchsticks and women selling themselves. It was impossible to walk out of the Friedrichstrasse Bahnhof without being accosted by hard-faced prostitutes in high-laced boots, their faces scored by hunger and want, offering to warm your bed for the night, or even for the hour. If you strayed from the main thoroughfares in the evening, bony boys would beckon you up tenement steps where their mothers waited in rooms smelling of rotten herring, ready to sell themselves for a few marks. Old men scoured the gutters for cigarette butts and in the far stretches of the Tiergarten cities of cardboard could be found where the homeless patched together shelters of packing cases and old boxes to create semi-permanent habitations. Even the ranks of the respectable, the war widows and the families, were just getting by, holding together a threadbare gentility, existing on cabbage, turnips and bread. On Fridays Leo would pass an ever-increasing queue of people, women with fur stoles, the men neatly dressed, in suits and hats, waiting patiently outside the local office for the dole.

The current of fear that had once lurked beneath the surface, now ran through everything. In the outer suburbs there were constant battles between Communists and Brown Shirts. They killed each other daily in street brawls, two leftists to every National Socialist. Painting squads would drive in vans through the city daubing swastikas on the property of those they hated. Slogans urging '*Deutschland Erwache*' spread like black mildew on the walls of apartment blocks housing Communists or Jews. And since January, when Hitler was appointed Chancellor, a sharper edge of terror hung in the air. It drifted through the city like a poisonous gas, seeping through closed doors. There were arrests, often for no apparent reason, and men could be seen stumbling into police cars at dawn dazed with sleep. Leo observed it all with growing despair. It was like being trapped in a paralysing dream where you watched the slow disaster going on around you, but could do nothing to prevent it.

Back at home most people seemed entirely unaware of the atmosphere here, or the menace that the Nazis represented. The *Observer* had called Hitler 'definitely Christian in his ideals and keen to renew his country's moral life'. Leo had nearly choked when he saw that. Then there were the others, the pacifists, who said if Germany rearmed perhaps she should just overrun Britain and have done with it.

The Passport Office found itself besieged by streams of people wanting to leave the country. Leo spent his days drowning in paperwork. Under the League of Nations mandate, whereby Britain administered Palestine, anyone wanting to enter that region, or Britain, or anywhere in the British Empire, needed a visa from the British Passport Control Office. Since January they had been queuing in their hundreds to get one. Endless, patient queues of frightened people besieged the office, armed with paperwork, letters and offers of sponsorship, with anxiety in their voices and desperation in their eyes. Visas were what they wanted, to Palestine, Britain, or anywhere that would have them.

Now, on a dead evening in March, with the tree branches making a black scrawl against a blank sky, Leo looked over at his narrow bed and longed for some yielding female body, even if it was Marjorie's, to wrap his arms around and bury his face in and distract him from the circling savagery.

From the street below music drifted up. It was jazz, the degenerate music of the devil, according to the Nazis. The notes floated like bright balloons on the air, daring, unorthodox, unpredictable. He tried to concentrate for a moment, to isolate the song. Then he shook his head, sighed and closed the window.

Chapter Five

Until then, Clara had not unpacked her case. She was superstitious that way. She still didn't know if she was going to find any acting work, though Albert had promised to 'put her up for something', but that afternoon she began taking out the few things she had brought and stowing them away. She was used to travelling light. The years in rep had taught her the futility of carrying around a single thing more than you needed. All she had were three blouses, two spare skirts, a nightdress and underwear. The basic cosmetics, a couple of lipsticks, Helena Rubenstein face cream, Vaseline, a Max Factor powder compact, eye-liner. A blue glass bottle of Bourjois's Evening in Paris. For evenings she had her red buckled shoes, a fur wrap and a backless scarlet dress, which she had purloined at the last moment from her sister's wardrobe, just in case she needed to attend something formal. Angela would kill her when she found out. In fact, Clara reflected, she had almost certainly found out already. She pictured her sister's perfectly proportioned face grimacing in annoyance. Yet another person who would need a proper explanation once everything was sorted out.

She had a few books, a *Palgrave's Golden Treasury* and some novels, which she positioned in front of the crimson-jacketed copy of *Mein Kampf* with gold lettering which had been left on the shelf, right next to the poems of Heinrich Heine, whom Frau Lehmann had plainly not heard was now a despised author of a degenerate race. Beside them Clara propped a letter, addressed and ready for posting.

As she stowed the clothes away in a cavernous Biedermeier wardrobe that could have housed an entire family, a small silver locket fell out of her rolled-up underwear. She picked it up and held it snug in her palm, absorbing the heat of her hand. Apart from a string of pearls and a pair of earrings, this locket was the only real jewellery she possessed. It had an intricate design of entwined leaves and a filigree clasp. She opened it.

When her mother knew she was dying, she had prepared special presents for their father to give to her daughters in the years to come. The silver locket containing a minute photograph of her mother and herself had been a gift for her sixteenth birthday. Their heads were bent together, with the same dark hair, long and gently waved on her mother, cut short to the nape of the neck on Clara, with a clip holding it off her brow. They had the same slightly angular features and pointed chin which, when lifted, expressed the same look of resolute defiance. Whenever she looked at it, all Clara could remember was the day her mother died. Being brought in to say goodbye in the front bedroom, which was flooded with a mellow afternoon sun and stuffy with medicine and disinfectant. Her mother lying immobile on the bed, her hands listless on top of the faded chintz eiderdown. Clara had taken her hand gently. It was the first time she had held her mother's hand since she was small – the Vine family was not given to overtly physical demonstrations of any kind, except to dogs. She felt the heavy sapphire ring loose on the twig of her finger and looked at the papery skin of her face, creased and dusted with powder like some ancient parchment fading into insignificance. She had great brown bruises under her eyes and her black hair, no longer glossy, was wired with grey.

Clara was the only one of the children who took after their mother. Her brother and Angela were Vines to the tips of their long, sporty limbs. Clara was dark and fine-boned, whereas the others were tall, with tawny hair and the stamina of shire horses. The family of Clara's mother were bankers in Hamburg, but the Vines could trace their ancestry back to the Norman invasion. They loved the outdoors, long walks and animals, especially shooting them. Perhaps it was this resemblance to her mother that made their father more reserved with Clara than with his other children. Maybe there was something about her he didn't want to be reminded of.

Yet, Clara reflected, that distance had existed even before their mother died. Her mind went back to a summer holiday in Cornwall, where her paternal grandparents owned a handsome Queen Anne manor house a mile from the sea. They were all on the beach, Clara reading, and Angela lying prone on a picnic rug, trying to improve her tan. A golden skin had become all the rage since Coco Chanel declared it fashionable, and Angela had equipped herself with a bottle of Elizabeth Arden's Sun Oil in Honey, which caused a layer of gritty sand to stick uncomfortably to her limbs. The longer she spent in the sun, the more her skin glowed strawberry red. Kenneth was the same, though he didn't care, but Clara turned as brown as a nut after a single morning by the sea's edge. 'It's not fair, Daddy,' moaned Angela. 'Why do Clara and Mummy get a tan but never us?' Clara, looking round curiously for the answer, found her father's patrician face regarding her speculatively, as if she was entirely unrelated to him. 'It's in the blood,' he said, enigmatically. As though her veins, more than her siblings', carried some exotic mystery.

After their mother died, the family fell to bits. Outwardly they held together, but they avoided confrontations and wherever possible led separate lives. Kenneth got a job in the city and Angela tried her hand as a fashion mannequin, gathering cupboards full of expensive clothes in the process. Though their mother's photograph remained on the top of the Bösendorfer piano, they rarely spoke of her. Frequently Clara had trouble even remembering properly what she looked like. Being here now, in the country where her mother grew up, speaking her language, Clara felt closer to her than she had since the day she died. After all, her mother too had left her home for a foreign country. Hellene Vine had been twenty-two when she arrived in England, four years younger than Clara was now. She was Hellene Neumann then, a pianist with the Hamburg City Orchestra. Ronald Vine, a rising politician, had seen her playing Brahms' Piano Concerto No. 2 in B flat major and fell instantly in love. After they had married, Hellene had barely seen her German family again. Grandfather Stephan and Grandmother Hannah had visited only twice in Clara's childhood, and when they died, her mother had not even attended their funerals.

Clara guessed her grandparents disliked her father. It wouldn't be a surprise; everyone else did. Daddy's brusque and uncommunicative manner was famous for giving offence. As children the Vines had accepted the state of affairs unthinkingly, their maternal grandparents were little more than mythical figures in a distant land. But being in Berlin had brought all these questions to the forefront of Clara's mind. Perhaps that was why she had written the letter, which rested addressed and ready for posting on the bookshelf. It might be that Hans Neumann, the cousin she had never met, would be able to explain.

Chapter Six

The Kaiserhof Hotel in Wilhelmplatz, opposite the heavy grandeur of the Chancellery, was a hulking, six-storeyed building, the colour of dirty snow. The portico was decked with scarlet begonias as precisely ranked as a division of storm troopers, and from the upper floors a line of red and black banners billowed, proclaiming the Kaiserhof's status as the favourite hotel of the Nazi top brass. Inside there was a dull stolidity to the marbled staircase, the mahogany and chandeliers, that suggested the respectability of less exciting times. The air was tinged with the smell of kitchens and cleaning fluid.

They found a table in the lobby and Helga took off her coat to reveal a floaty blue silk dress with a bow at the neck and a stole of champagne fur. The dress was paper thin, and could have done with a good wash, but from a distance the impression was undeniably glamorous. She was visibly excited, glancing around her restlessly as her crimson-lacquered nails fiddled with a lighter, her head swivelling to and fro as she checked out the guests, as though she, rather than Clara, was the tourist.

'Hitler has his flat here,' she hissed in a loud whisper. 'But he doesn't eat here anymore because the Communists in the kitchen tried to poison his food.'

Clara looked sceptically at the waiters, ferrying silver trays laden with drinks and small bowls of nuts between the potted palms. The idea that potential poisoners were abroad seemed outlandish. With its red plush chairs and bowls of orchids, the Kaiserhof felt like the height of propriety.

'I still can't believe we're having a drink with Sturmhauptführer Klaus Müller!' Helga lit her cigarette and smiled broadly. 'He's the coming man. It's just a shame that he has to bring his fat friend.'

Clara was already realizing that her new friend was dangerously indiscreet. 'Shh! Remember how Sturmbannführer Bauer said your voice was clear as a bell. Well, it is. They can hear you from across the lobby.'

After the bustle of the street outside, the lobby was an oasis of calm, with National Socialists seated in comfortable seats throughout, drinking beer, or strutting around in their boots and breeches. Beyond them, up a flight of white marble steps, a cocktail party was in full swing. Clara could see a stately reception room, where light from the crystal chandeliers sparkled on the jewels of the women among the black and brown uniforms and a string quartet sawed away in the corner.

'Albert tells me both Bauer and Müller have just been appointed aides to Dr Goebbels,' said Helga in a theatrical whisper. 'They're going to help him run the Culture Department at the Ministry. Which includes film!'

'Is that good?'

'Are you crazy, Clara? It could be wonderful. A girl needs to keep on top in this business. It's all about having the right friends in the right places.'

At that moment the brown kepi of Bauer could be seen bobbing towards them, and seconds later his portly frame was visible, bustling importantly to their table. His tunic was ringed with underarm sweat and his face was gleaming. He took off his cap and wiped his brow. Without the hat his head looked too small for his body and the back of his neck bulged over his collar like soft cheese.

Müller, by contrast, was in evening dress, with a little silver swastika pinned to his lapel. He had a look of forceful energy only just contained by the stiff winged collar and white tie. Clara imagined he must be around forty. When he bent to kiss hands, his hair gleamed like patent leather. He slid into the seat next to her, and clicked his fingers.

'Herr Ober. Champagne.'

The waiter hurried off with more than usual alacrity.

Clara gestured at the party in the neighbouring room. 'What's going on there?'

'It's a political soirée.' Müller had a smile hovering on his lips. 'I assume you follow politics, Miss Vine, with a family like yours?'

Clara guessed a political discussion right then would be unwise.

'I'm afraid I'm not political. I'm just an actress.'

He laughed again. 'I think you'll find everything is political in Germany right now. Even actresses.'

They were interrupted by a shriek from Helga, a reaction to something Bauer had said in her ear.

'And I thought you were a gentleman!'

Bauer's face had deepened to shade of puce, which crept across his cheeks and extended to the bristles of his scalp. He clamped a meaty hand on Helga's shoulder and treated her to an unambiguous leer.

Müller turned to Clara with an almost imperceptible shudder, as though to provide a physical barrier from Bauer, and addressed her in English.

'It's good to have visitors from England. I hope you'll be able to give a true account of National Socialism when you return.'

'I'm not planning to go back quite yet. I've only just arrived.'

'But you have favourable impressions so far?'

What were her impressions so far? There was the mood of nervous uncertainty at Babelsberg, the graffiti she had seen spattered on walls and shops threatening death to the Jews, the brown-shirted storm troopers bullying people into parting with money for their collecting tins, and the marching band that had stamped past her as though they hoped to grind the very soil of Germany beneath their boots. Which of those would Müller consider a true account of National Socialism?

'I'm surprised to see so many men wearing uniform. I mean it's not as if anyone's at war.'

'A uniform is a mark of pride.'

'Is it? I think uniforms give people airs. It's like an actor wearing a costume. It makes people forget what they are underneath.'

For a moment Müller's eyes widened and a shadow crossed his features. No one, she realized, generally answered him back.

'I believe, Fräulein, you'll find people here like a uniform. It gives them a sense of solidarity. It gives them the opportunity to feel that they belong to the group.'

Clara took a sip of her champagne. 'I'd say it gives them the opportunity to intimidate people when they're filling up their collecting boxes.'

Suddenly Müller rose to his feet. Craning behind her, Clara was aware of a tall woman approaching them, her heels clicking on the black and white marble floor. She wore a

Schiaparelli evening gown in ivory, which flattered her
creamy skin, and pearls the size of little birds' eggs hung
round her neck. Her platinum hair was waved tightly around
her face and a gust of perfume attended her. The flesh of her
arms had the dense solidity of a Greek statue, and her eyes
had a statue's veiled, impenetrable stare.

'Herr Doktor Müller! Just who I wanted to see!'

Müller clicked his heels. 'Frau Doktor Goebbels. How are
you?'

She had a deep, fluting voice, a little clipped. 'Good, thank
you, though a little tired with the move.'

'I heard. Is the new house to your liking?'

She sighed. 'The apartment was becoming too cramped. I
liked it, but Joseph wanted something that fit better with his
official duties.'

Müller gestured towards Clara. 'This is Clara Vine. She's
the daughter of Sir Ronald Vine, the English politician.'

The woman seemed to notice Clara for the first time and
looked at her curiously.

'Is that so? I have some English friends. They have promised to come and visit us.'

'Miss Vine is acting at Babelsberg.' Müller gave a stiff little
gesture towards their companions. 'Helga Schmidt perhaps
you know.'

Frau Goebbels glanced at Helga and something in her
expression hardened momentarily.

Müller turned to Clara. 'Frau Doktor Goebbels is the wife
of the Minister of Public Enlightenment and Propaganda.'

Clara nodded politely, thinking what a dreadful mouthful
that title was to be saddled with.

'But we prefer to call her the First Lady of the Third
Reich,' he added, with a gallant bow.

The sigh was replaced with a bright smile.

'Well, it's good luck I ran into you. I'm planning a cocktail party tomorrow night at our new home. Won't you come? And bring Fräulein Vine with you?' She glanced briefly at Bauer. 'And your young lady too, Herr Bauer.'

Clara looked around her to see Helga open-mouthed.

Chapter Seven

'Filthy tea, I'm afraid. I'll ask Miss Jenkins to bring fresh, if you like. You'd think in the British Embassy tea would be the one thing we could get right.'

Sir Horace Rumbold poured a watery stream from the silver teapot, pushed a cup towards Leo, then leant on the stiff-backed sofa with a sigh. The British ambassador was a lofty man, whose benign, mild-mannered face and flaring nostrils gave him the look of a friendly camel. His neat moustache and horn-rimmed spectacles imparted a myopic expression, quite at odds with his keen wit and sharp sense of humour. He had asked Leo to see him in the library of the British Embassy, a wood-panelled room from whose walls portraits of past ambassadors stared out mistily. In pride of place above the fireplace was the King, with something of the morose bloodhound about him, looking gloomily similar to his exiled first cousin, the doddery Kaiser Wilhelm, who was now safely confined in Holland, well away from any temptations to power. Around the room burnished leather armchairs rested on slightly threadbare rugs as though a gentleman's club had been uprooted from Pall Mall and translated to the German capital.

'Tea is one of those things that can never be the same,' agreed Leo diplomatically. It sounded like a cliché but he

meant it. Tea for any Englishman evoked a cascade of associations, symbolizing consolation and continuity, a pause in
the day, a moment of reflection. He doubted very much
though that Sir Horace shared the same associations as himself.
For Leo, the thought of tea evoked his mother, with her
worn apron, reaching for the battered caddy decorated with
red-jacketed soldiers, which lived on the shelf above the
range, spooning one for each person and one for the brown
Bessie pot. The rich, musty scent of Assam brought with it
the memory of a hundred afternoons working on the dining
room table in the fading light, while his parents tried not to
disturb him, a deep russet cup of tea at his elbow. So unlike
the pallid offering here before them, in porcelain cups
stamped with the British Embassy crest.

'Sugar?' said Sir Horace, proffering the bowl.

'No, thank you.' Leo took a sip and said, 'You were going
to explain, sir.'

'Yes, I was, Quinn. All in good time.' He bit into a biscuit.
'Tell me, how is it going? You've been in Berlin what, a
couple of months?'

'Six months.'

'And you're happy? Getting around? In the evenings?'

'I'm seeing a bit of the clubs, as you do. But to be honest,
sir, most evenings now I'm dead beat.' He laughed. 'Must be
feeling my age.'

'Feeling your age!' Sir Horace guffawed, exhibiting teeth
as mottled as old piano keys. 'My goodness, man. How old
are you? Barely thirty! At your age I was good for a couple of
receptions a night and dancing till dawn. And you're a single
chap too. No lady on the horizon? We shall need to get you
sorted.'

The face of Marjorie Simmons rose in Leo's mind and he
wondered if a mention of her appeared on his file. More

curtly than intended he said, 'This is not about my social life, I take it.'

'Only tangentially.'

'Sir?'

'It's a simple brief really. Now, you were at Oxford. Not at the House, were you?'

Leo flinched inwardly at the assumption that he would not have attended the upper-crust Christ Church, popularly known as "the House".

'I was at Balliol, sir.'

'Of course. Well, you'll have seen *The Times*. This vote in the Union. "This House would not in any circumstance fight for King and Country".'

In fact, Leo had read the report that very morning. The sensation caused by the Oxford Union's vote against fighting was picked up by newspapers throughout Europe, including the *Vossische Zeitung*, the liberal-leaning paper that Leo read daily over his coffee and roll.

The university's debating chamber, the Union, liked to think of itself as a miniature House of Commons, and might as well have been, given the number of men who graduated pretty seamlessly from one to the other. The result of the debate had prompted headlines everywhere. Winston Churchill had called it "abject, squalid and shameless". But Leo had not bothered to accord it much attention. For one thing he recoiled from the kind of undergraduate posturing he remembered only too well. For another, he was too damned busy. The pressure of work was keeping him awake at night. Being called in to see Rumbold, while intriguing, only meant more piles of paperwork when he returned.

'It's in the nature of undergraduates, sir, to be provocative. This kind of thing is just an immature pose. I'm certain if war broke out tomorrow they would sign up just as fast as their fathers did.'

'I'm sure that's true. Bloody shameful nonsense all the same.'

Sir Horace put down his cup, wandered over to the window of the library and stared down at the churning traffic on Wilhelmstrasse below. Along the principal thoroughfare of the government district, housing the Reich Chancellery and the Foreign Office, a pair of gleaming Mercedes-Benz 770s containing Nazi top brass could be seen cruising.

'The thing is, Quinn, these are interesting times. We are officially still feeling our way with the new regime. We don't want to antagonize them. In some respects their hatred for the Reds is shared at home.'

Leo nodded. That much was clear from what Hugo Chambers said. For some years now the British Security Service, which monitored domestic subversion, had focused all its energies on the threats within Britain from the Left. It was only recently that anyone had taken a closer interest in the activities of the Right.

'As we all know, there's a rapidly growing body of Englishmen who favour disarmament at all costs. You know the sort of thing they say. That the last war should mark the end to all wars. Any rearming is sanctioning large-scale murder. I'm sure you've heard the kind of thing.'

'Frequently.'

'I think we both agree that a powerful England is vital to ensure peace. Yet these pacifists at home have no idea of the effect their talk has on our reputation abroad. I've already been informed that various associates of Herr Hitler believe our young people are "soft". If they think Hitler has any time for pacifists, they are much mistaken. To Hitler, man is a fighting animal and any country which does not fight back

deserves to be overtaken. I fear this new administration brings
out the worst traits in the citizens too. Jingoism, brutality, all
this business about the Jews. It leaves a very nasty taste in the
mouth.'

Rumbold turned and a brilliant, diplomatic charm suddenly
illuminated his features, as though by a switch. That was the
kind of thing you simply couldn't learn, Leo thought. It was
purely Darwinian. It had to be bred into you, as in Sir
Horace's case it had. He came from a long line of baronets,
and had travelled the globe in a distinguished career. As well
as German, he spoke fluent Arabic and Japanese.

'Now, Quinn, you're very busy at the moment, I'm sure.'

'We have Jews coming to the office daily. There's a queue
by the time I arrive, and it doesn't go away until I leave. It's
hard to turn them away.'

'I can see it getting busier. So I hope this request I have for
you doesn't take you away from your work too much. I
know you're frightfully well connected on the social side.'

Leo gave a polite laugh. 'For once I fear your intelligence
is wide of the mark.'

'None the less, this is merely an eyes-and-ears brief. It
shouldn't be too onerous. I'm leaving soon, as you know.'

'I very much regret it, sir.'

'As do I, though with the way things are, my lady wife, I
think, will be glad to spend more time in England. And what
one's wife says, as you have yet to find out, Quinn, is law.'
He smiled, removed his glasses, rubbed his watery eyes, and
replaced them.

'This is what I had in mind. I want you to keep an eye on
any visitors you may meet who pass through here from
England, especially those who are mingling with the Nazi
élite. Some of them are very young, impressionable, you
know, and they get caught up in the excitement of the

moment. They make friends with handsome Nazi officers, and they don't see the whole picture, do you get my drift?'

'I think so.'

'They see a country whose economy is on its knees, and they think Herr Hitler is the answer to everyone's prayers. It's not their fault that they are unable to see beyond the glamour, but it matters very much what they say when they return to England. Favourable reports about the new regime will only encourage elements in England who want to disarm.'

'I understand.'

'There's something else.'

Rumbold was craning towards Leo, almost as though he feared the occupants of the gleaming cars sailing down the Wilhelmstrasse might be able to overhear his words.

'If you do come across any of our compatriots who have communication with the élite, it would, of course, be useful to hear the gist of their conversations. Should they be amenable to that. I'm not talking about espionage here, merely intelligence gathering. You know Dyson, my attaché, of course?'

Archie Dyson was an unflappable Etonian who had taken Leo out for a solitary gin at the Adlon on his first night here. He was clever and not especially likeable. Manners like silk, but a mind like a steel trap.

'I've met him, yes.'

'Dyson is compiling some contacts who can give us a glimpse behind the scenes, so to speak. So if you do find anything . . .' Rumbold fingered his moustache thoughtfully, 'we might be able to put more resources into it. But you're going to have to be very careful, Quinn. You're known to be connected to the Embassy. The political police have eyes and ears everywhere. '

'I see.'

Rumbold leant back.

'I'm giving a party for Goering shortly. There'll be a host of interesting people passing through. Perhaps you could get going then. I'll get my secretary to send an invitation to your place. Where are you living, remind me?'

'Orianenburger Strasse.'

'Ah yes. How original. Well, do let Miss Jenkins have your address on the way out.'

Chapter Eight

The Goebbels' new home was in the grounds of the Ministry of Agriculture behind Wilhelmstrasse. It was a large white-washed mansion built for a former Prussian court official and looked like a small country house, surrounded as it was by a plantation of old trees. It was a princely home for one of Germany's new aristocracy, and once Goebbels decided he wanted it, a team of gardeners from the state parks authority had been brought in to restore the overgrown grounds, with their rusting skeletons of greenhouses and swampy lily ponds, and install paths and flowerbeds. In the drive stood a natty beige and brown Mercedes convertible, a recent present from the car company to Herr Doktor Goebbels, and a sparkling green cabriolet for his wife.

Clara and Klaus Müller proceeded through the door flanked by a pair of flame-shaped lanterns and into a room with ornate fluted pillars and a gigantic, sparkling chandelier. There were yellow and gold carpets on the floor and large bowls of hothouse flowers. The blond wood walls were hung with tapestries and paintings. Müller took a glass of Sekt from a tray and handed it to Clara.

'Looks like it's going to be all German wines from now on,' he murmured.

Clara gazed around her.

'Delightful place, don't you agree?' he said. There was a mocking, superior edge to his voice, which made it hard to work out what he genuinely thought.

'Very.'

He surveyed the room. 'Goering has a huge place behind Leipziger Platz, all gloomy panelling and stained glass and absolutely stuffed with Renaissance furniture. You feel like you're on the set of the Ring Cycle. Fortunately the Doktor has rather better taste.'

Clara stared around her. What on earth was she doing here? When the two men had invited them for a drink, she had agreed because that was what Helga wanted, and Helga had been good enough to take Clara under her wing. Besides, she had no other plans for anything at all. Then Magda Goebbels had extended her invitation, Helga's face had lit up, and there was no way she could have refused.

Perhaps there was no harm in it. Just this once. She would hardly have chosen to spend an evening with National Socialists, but this was a party, wasn't it, and at least she had something to wear. Angela's low-cut red satin evening dress went perfectly with her scarlet shoes, and her mother's silver locket glinting at her throat. And it was just as well she had carried out that small act of theft because she was in serious danger of appearing underdressed. All the women here were done up in the height of international fashion: Chanel, Schiaparelli, Vionnet, Mainbocher. The room was awash with shimmering lamé and pleated organza, and Frau Goebbels herself was wearing a long silver silk dress, fretted with lace on top, a diamanté belt and white evening gloves, spattered with red from the customary hand kiss of female guests.

Even so, there weren't enough women to go round. The female contingent was sprinkled among the dark male mass like a tree with too few fairy lights. Not that the men seemed to mind. Like Müller, they were mostly in uniform and stood in clusters, laughing and toasting each other. Something about them – perhaps it was the short hair and pink cheeks – reminded Clara of her brother's school rugby team, delighting in their shared masculinity, celebrating their kinship with a self-congratulatory air as if they had just won a First Fifteen match, rather than been catapulted into power on the back of a shaky electoral process. But that was where the likeness ended. There was a pent up aggression amongst these men, a sense of violence barely contained. Some of them favoured toothbrush moustaches, presumably under the impression that imitation was the sincerest form of flattery, and most of them shared a barber too, judging by the uniformly shaven haircuts, which left scalps as gleaming and knobbly as scrubbed potatoes.

Müller's heavy hand was on her elbow, steering her towards a group of men and Clara, who hated being steered, instinctively shook herself free. Instantly she felt his annoyance.

'Forgive me, Fräulein. I would like to introduce you. This is Herr Doktor Bayer.'

Bayer had the face of a gargoyle and a smile like a coffin handle.

'So this is the English actress who is to star alongside Lilian Harvey.'

Clara smiled back, disliking him on sight. 'I hope so.'

'I love her movies. So magnificently kitsch. The Germans have a sweet spot for kitsch in their soul.'

'Next to the spot of steel,' laughed Müller.

'*Ein blonder Traum*. That's my favourite. That girl really knows how to get the juices going,' said another, a piggy little man who looked as if he had been poured into his uniform with some left over. 'Did you see it?'

'Sorry, but no.' The films Clara admired were moodier and darker-edged, with dramatic, shadowy sets. The brooding Expressionist masterpieces like *M* and *Metropolis*. Monsters and murderers with haunted eyes, sinister and macabre.

'I loved *The Cabinet of Dr Caligari* though. And I thought *M* was a masterpiece. I could hardly sleep after I saw it.'

'You enjoyed that, did you?' said Müller dismissively. 'Herr Lorre, I believe, is no longer with us.'

'Anyway,' said the fat man, cranking his eyes from her breasts to her face, 'how do you find Babelsberg?'

'It's gone a little quiet at the moment.'

'While they work out who's in charge, eh?'

'So they should. It's time for change,' said another, a severe figure with eyes that were freakishly pale, and skin like white veal. 'We need to sweep out the attic of German cinema, isn't that what the Herr Doktor said? The place needs fumigating.'

'Fumigating? asked Clara, thinking how he looked like something that had been kept in an attic himself, an etiolated insect deprived of daylight.

'Herr Richter means,' smiled Müller, 'it is time we freed cinema from the hands of Jews.'

'Why does he say that?'

'Ach, they have turned the art of film into a business,' said Richter. 'That's what happens when something is Hebrewized.' He flipped his hand, as if brushing away the pioneers of the Ufa studios like dust. 'We need films that reflect the true aspirations of the German people. They're not interested in the decadent tastes of the international market.'

'But Doktor Goebbels is a great admirer of Fritz Lang. He enjoyed *Metropolis*, didn't he? And *Die Nibelungen*?' Clara tried to remember the comments she had overheard in the Babelsberg foyer.

'Oh, Fritz Lang,' Richter's voice dripped with contempt. 'Herr Lang, I think, is overrated.'

'Another one who needs his horoscope read to him,' laughed the fat man.

Clara looked around for Helga. How could she possibly have wanted to come here? Helga was on the other side of the room, her shingled hair rippling in the light of the chandelier, her ice-blue satin dress provocatively skimming her curves. Perhaps it was that which had already secured her the top spot of the party, talking to her host, Doktor Goebbels, crooking one leg so as not to tower over him. Bauer, even though he was a bull of a man, was hanging back, allowing Goebbels to pull rank. The Propaganda Minister's thin lips were stretched in a smile as wide as his face was narrow, his eyes fixed on Helga like a lizard waiting to devour an especially plump fly. Surveying his unnaturally skinny arms and strange, misshapen body, Clara wondered what on earth a woman like his wife saw in him.

Frau Goebbels was watching them too. Her face was a tense, thoughtful mask and the set of her mouth gave her an air of private pain, rigorously suppressed. As their gazes locked, she came across the room with a stiff smile that didn't reach her eyes.

'So, Fräulein Vine, how are you enjoying your work at Babelsberg? I hear you're to be in a film called . . . *Schwarze Rosen*, was it?'

'I hope so. The producer seems to have disappeared, though, so I haven't started yet. I'm at a bit of a loose end.'

'Let's hope he comes back soon. We simply couldn't live without the cinema! We're having a cinema installed here, so we can see all the latest films.'

'The Führer is a great fan of the movies too, is he not?' enquired one of the men, deferentially.

'Of course. We watch together. The Führer watches one every evening, sometimes two.'

'And what kind of films does he like?' asked Clara politely.

'Oh, nothing dreary or tragic. Happy films. *Grand Hotel* is his favourite, and we hear good things of *King Kong*.'

'Let's hope that under the Doktor's new Film Chamber the industry can at last begin to fulfil its true purpose,' intervened Richter, pompously.

Clara was about to ask what the true purpose of the industry was, if it wasn't simple things like entertaining people and giving them a good time, but before she could speak a frisson ran through the air. It was a kind of electric ripple that travelled through the room with no apparent cause. Black uniforms were moving through the throng, taking up positions in the crowd, and eyes were turning towards the central doors. Conversation dropped to a hush. Next to Clara a woman clutched at the arm of her companion, trembling visibly. Frau Goebbels sped away.

The next minute the doors were flung open and a bodyguard, with a distinct resemblance to Al Capone, entered, followed by a small man in a dinner suit. Everyone raised their right arm in salute. Clara didn't know what she had been expecting, but it wasn't this. His face was pale and indeterminate, strangely unplaceable, like a ghost's face or one you might see in a dream. There was something opaque in his countenance. Dark hair flopped over his forehead, which he swiped away with a nervous hand. Only his eyes were startling, slightly protuberant and hypnotic, like blue ice cubes, as they swivelled around the room seeking out people and familiar faces. Instinctively Clara looked away. She didn't know why, but she didn't want that blue gaze to fall on her. She saw him go towards Magda, heard the kissing of her hand and the "*Gnädige Frau*".

The room felt stifled and airless. Clara had expected to be fascinated by her first sighting of Herr Hitler, but instead she had an intense compulsion to escape. Perhaps she could slip away without anyone noticing. She could take a tram home and explain to Helga the next day. She would be perfectly inconspicuous. Klaus Müller's eyes, like everyone else's, were trained on the group at the centre of the room. No one wanted to chat to some unknown actress any more. Moving to the door, she turned to look back at the corner of the room where Helga was, to signal her intent, and found her gaze snagged in the direct stare of Goebbels himself. His eyes were curious, calculating.

She slipped along the corridor to the front hall. Out on the drive a number of Brown Shirts lounged, keeping guard over the entrance and an eye on the cars, taking the opportunity for a quick cigarette. But no sooner had she wandered through the door than a black Mercedes limousine, with long curving fenders, tubular exhausts and polished chrome head-lights, glided towards her and the driver leapt out to open the door. Behind her she heard the crunch of gravel and Müller appeared at her shoulder.

'Fräulein Vine, you're not leaving already, surely? Were you not enjoying yourself?' His voice was heavy with irony. 'Let my driver take you home.' He gestured to the car. 'Please.' It was not a question, but a command.

She had no choice. Embarrassed that she had so obviously been leaving without telling him, she nodded, and climbed into the car as he held the door open, and then her heart sank as he climbed in alongside her.

The car smelt of tobacco and expensive new leather, and the mottled walnut dashboard gleamed. As they swept west through the dark streets, the shadowy mass of the Tiergarten to each side, she saw the driver's eyes flick towards her in the mirror. His neck was pink and raw, a thick, shaven sausage. She could feel Müller regarding her with jocularity, as though he saw something ridiculous in her clumsy attempt to escape.

'The Herr Doktor certainly knows how to throw a party, don't you think?'

'The house is very impressive,' she said noncommittally.

'Ach, the man is a genius. He has such an eye for colour. It was he who chose the red for our banners, when everyone else wanted a dull black. He understands aesthetics, you see. That's why he's so interested in film. Unfortunately,' his eyes slid towards her knowingly, 'he is also very interested in film actresses.'

'I hope Helga's all right.'

'To me it looked like she was getting on just fine.'

'His wife seemed a little unhappy.'

'I doubt it. The Frau Doktor adores cultural conversation.'

'Was tonight what passes for cultural conversation? Discussing how there are too many Jews in the cinema?'

He smiled tightly. 'You are rather hasty in your judgements, Fräulein. This is politics, you understand.'

'Are you a politician, Doktor Müller?'

He exhaled thoughtfully, as though she had posed an interesting philosophical question.

'I suppose I am really. I qualified in law originally. But I didn't practise for long. My uncle wanted me to take over his business.'

'What was his business?'

'He produced magazines and newspapers. It was very profitable, though he published nothing you'd have heard of. Trade papers, mostly. Hardly the *Deutsche Allgemeine Zeitung*.' He leant towards her, mock confidentially, 'though not *Der Stürmer* either.'

'Yet you're in uniform tonight,' she said, looking at his buttoned brown jacket and tie, and his cap, on which a silver eagle spread its wings.

'I'm proud to be.' He ran a hand down his breeches. 'Until recently this uniform was banned, if you can believe it.'

'But if you're not a soldier, why would you want to look like one?'

He folded his arms and looked at her quizzically. 'You dislike the military, don't you, Fräulein Vine? Let me tell you, if Hitler had not come to power there would be half a million lying dead in the streets.'

'I'm not sure I understand . . .'

'You can't understand because you haven't lived here.' His voice hardened. 'You haven't seen what the Communist rabble can do. I have. When it was at its worst, after the war, you couldn't drive down the Ku'damm without some mob attacking the car. The Reds were everywhere. They shot my father.'

'I'm sorry.'

'It was 1921. He was in the Freikorps. So now I'd give my life's blood to exterminate Bolshevism. In fact, if every Communist in Germany was lying dead in the streets, I couldn't be happier. But what? You seem surprised? Why?'

'It's not the way people talk in England.'

'Oh, England.' His contempt was withering. 'I'm sure it's different in England. England is rich, she has her empire, she has the luxury of moralizing. But don't fool yourself. That British Empire of yours was built on war too. War, oppression and blood.'

The combination of his words, uttered so scathingly, and his uniform with its hard ridged leather and glossy knee boots lazily extended, was chilling. Clara watched him out of the corner of her eye as the bars of sodium from the streetlights slid across his face. He took out a cigar and lit it, letting the thick, noxious smoke envelop the car.

'Perhaps my words seem harsh. But you're much younger than I am, Fräulein, so it's harder for you to see. How can I forget hauling a suitcase of notes to the baker's shop to buy bread? Or my mother arguing with swindling Jews when she tried to pawn her rings?'

He was looking out of the window pensively. 'Since the war our country has been bleeding to death and the Communists have tried to throttle what life remains. We've been weak, but now we're going to be strong again.'

'You seem very certain.'

'I am. It's our time now. The Führer has a description. He says he is building up our country again like a stonemason builds a cathedral. The people are his stone. A mason needs to cut sometimes, to shape his art. But the result will be beautiful.'

'People lying dead in the street doesn't sound especially beautiful to me.'

She saw his jaw tense and a muscle ripple in his cheek.

'Perhaps, Fräulein, you need to see a bit more of Germany before you jump to your conclusions.'

'And perhaps you should see a bit more of England before you jump to yours.'

There was a silence, like a sharp intake of breath, and then he laughed delightedly. 'Maybe you will be my teacher. In fact, to tell the truth, I have a great admiration for England. As do all of us in the Party.'

He leant forward and tapped the chauffeur on the shoulder.

'Fräulein Vine will be joining me for a nightcap before she goes home.'

His words sent a prickle of anxiety through her. It was one thing to attend a party with a man like this, but to visit his home? Already the car was drawing up in a square of tall apartment buildings, and the driver was jumping out to open her door. She followed Müller out warily. No one, she need not remind herself, knew she was here. A shiver of sexual apprehension stirred beneath her skin. She looked around, but the square was dark and there were few passers-by. The chauffeur smirked, as though smirking was part of the uniform.

Müller opened the door of his apartment and ushered her inside. He lit a lamp to reveal a gloomy, high-ceilinged drawing room papered in green stripes, with a piano at one end and dusty velvet curtains drawn. A spiky pot plant withered silently in a corner. While he went over to a drinks trolley and poured from a decanter, Clara looked at the photographs on the piano. There was a picture of a small, plain woman wearing a dirndl, with plaits like ear muffs and an alpine scene in the background. In the foreground a giant Alsatian drooled at the camera.

'My wife, Elsa,' he said shortly. 'And our dog, Rolf.'

'Where is your wife now?'

'I am a widower. She died in '26, in a tram collision. She was on her way to see a doctor because we could not have children.' He gave a harsh bark of laughter. 'Hence I have no children.' He handed her a cut-glass tumbler, glinting amber.

Clara sipped it, feeling the brandy burn her throat. His mention of his wife had exposed a crack of vulnerability in his grandiloquent demeanour. He gestured to a capacious leather chesterfield, but she chose an armchair, so he plumped himself down on the sofa instead, crossed his legs and spread his arms expansively along the back.

'You seem wary of me, Fräulein. There's no need. I'm nothing like my acquaintance Herr Bauer, whatever your friend may have told you.'

'She told me nothing.'

He gestured to the photograph of his wife. 'Perhaps it's just as well we had no children. The Party takes up all my time now. Tell me, is there a fiancé back in England for you? Or a boyfriend?'

'Not any more.'

'I'm surprised.' He lit two cigarettes and gave her one. Then he flung off his cap, took off his jacket and tie and unbuttoned the collar of his shirt. She glimpsed a curl of dark hair below his throat and caught the scent of lime cologne, mingled with cigars. There was something intensely masculine about this apartment, with its well-used drinks trolley, its drab furniture and musty undertow of loneliness. She hoped he wasn't going to start confiding in her. She didn't want to relax in his company for a second.

'So tell me about this *Schwarze Rosen*. What kind of film is it? Not another one of those gloomy murder stories you were saying you liked?'

'No, actually. It's a historical costume drama. About a young woman who falls in love with a soldier.'

'Now that sounds much more my sort of thing! Call me bourgeois, and I don't pretend to know anything about art, but I'd say Germany is well rid of all those creepy dramas about insane murderers and such like. Give me a love story any day, and a pretty actress with a figure, not one of those mannish skeletons who've become so fashionable.' He winked at her and drained his glass. 'There, I've said it. You'll probably think me uncultured, but I'm only telling you what a man really likes.'

Clara shifted uneasily. The last thing she wanted to start discussing was Müller's taste in women. She needed to change the subject.

'About Frau Goebbels . . .' The minister's wife had been puzzling her all evening. There had been such a contrast between the glittering evening and her air of private misery. 'Does she not enjoy parties?'

'She should do. She gives them all the time. The Goebbels are famous for their receptions. In fact, the Führer spends most of his evenings with them, listening to the piano or watching movies.'

'She looked unhappy.'

'Unhappy? Really?'

'She was rather cold.'

He laughed. 'Ah, well, that's true. No one needs ice in their schnapps when the Frau Doktor is around.'

'Perhaps she just doesn't like actresses.'

'She sees enough of them. She always gets some actresses along for the Führer to provide feminine distraction from his work.'

'She didn't seem too friendly towards Helga.'

'Well since you ask, I think your friend should watch herself. She seems the chatty sort. She should be careful. Especially with a man like Walter Bauer. Bauer is not known for his tenderness towards the fair sex.'

'I'm sure Helga can take care of herself.'

'That's an admirable opinion. I hope it's justified.' Müller got to his feet and made for the drinks trolley. 'But as for you, Fräulein Vine, don't worry. I don't think Frau Doktor Goebbels saw you as a mere actress. You are the daughter of Sir Ronald Vine and a welcome guest.'

'A *mere* actress?'

He poured another schnapps for himself and smiled. 'Well here in Germany acting is not a job one would wish one's wife or daughter to undertake.'

'Are you serious?'

'But of course.' He waved his glass expansively. 'Only because we believe in better things for women. There is no objection to a young woman having a career, of course, but the proper place for a German woman is in the home.'

Clara was about to argue, but what was the point? It would only prolong their encounter. And it was no different from what Dennis believed. Briskly, she said, 'As it happens, the producer I was expecting to meet hasn't arrived yet. So I don't have a part at the moment.'

'Perhaps I might have a word with someone.'

'But I don't see how you . . .'

'Don't worry about that.'

His eyes lingered on her thoughtfully. 'You know, despite what I said, you have a face that should be on screen. There's a freshness about you.'

'Thank you.' Now was most certainly the time to leave. Clara reached for her fur wrap, but Müller placed a restraining hand on her arm. Up close, his breath had the sour, yeasty odour of cigars.

'What I meant was, you have a purity that appeals to me.'

'I'm sorry, I really do have to go. Frau Lehmann is expecting me.'

He smiled and offered her an ironic bow. 'Of course. My driver will see you home.'

He walked to the door, but instead of allowing her through he stood in front of it. Her skin prickled. Despite the fur, she was shivering. Up close his acne-scarred neck looked like sand pitted with rain. He seemed huge and muscular in the semi-darkness. She knew he was using his physical bulk to intimidate her. Standing over her he suddenly reached out and tilted her chin towards him. She wondered what she would have to do if he tried to kiss her.

He caught the look in her eyes, and held up his hands in mock surrender.

'You look frightened, my dear Fräulein. Now tell me, what could you possibly have to be frightened of?'

Chapter Nine

The waitress had the body of a goddess and the eyes of a devil. Wearing a nude costume with silk fig-leaves sewn on strategic places, she pressed her chest against Leo's as she passed, giving him a sly wink.

The Katakombe was Leo's favourite club. It wasn't anything to look at: a cramped underground den, crowded with wooden tables and a stage on which a variety of musical acts and sketches were performed. Crimson Chinese lanterns swung from the ceiling and the air was heady with the clash of cheap perfumes. The smoke was as thick as a London smog and the beer was indifferent. Your waitress might be a pretty girl, but was just as likely to be a six-foot male with a dress like Cinderella's ugly sister and knuckles like a beer-house thug. Still, Leo liked it here.

There were any number of clubs like the Katakombe, most of them with lashings of straight or unconventional sex. There was the Blue Angel and the Tingel-Tangel, and most famous of all the Weisse Maus, where Anita Berber would perform her naked, drug-induced dances to an audience of spectators wearing black masks to conceal their identity. Excitement ran high, and if the spirit took you, for a few extra pfennigs a back room could always be secured for a sweaty, furtive consummation.

Seedy as they were, the clubs were a magnet for intellectuals and dissidents, artists and writers. The menu of satire,
sketches and songs had enough of an edge to help people
laugh at the reality outside them. Years before, back in the
high days of Weimar, patrons would sip champagne as they
laughed at the innuendo. But since then the luxury had worn
thin, like the plush on the gilded chairs.

The audiences had worn thin too. The Nazis considered
the clubs nests of degeneracy, and leftists and writers of all
kinds were skipping town as fast as they could. That month
the *Berliner Tageblatt* had run a list of the venues closed by the
city chief of police: the Dorian Gray, the Monokle, the
Mikado. The Silhouette in Geisbergstrasse, where Conrad
Veidt and Marlene Dietrich mixed with lesbians in smoking
jackets, had disappeared the previous year. The famous
Eldorado, the fashionable ballroom where cross-dressing
women mixed with Berlin high society, had even been
requisitioned as a Nazi Party HQ, complete with Nazi posters on the windows and a pair of storm troopers on the door
whose uniforms were certainly not part of the fun.

The jazz band on stage began to pack up and Leo's
companion turned to him.

'There won't be much of this any more. They hate jazz,
don't they? It's nigger music they say. Or was it Bolshevik? I
can't remember.'

'Whatever it was, it's going to be all Strauss waltzes and
Bavarian folk music from now on.' Leo grimaced. 'Get used
to it.'

'You might enjoy the odd waltz, Leo, if you tried it.
There's something to be said for a dance that requires you to
clasp a beautiful woman in your arms.'

Leo looked at Rupert's broad, good-natured face with
affection. He had met Rupert Allingham in their first term at

Oxford. They'd discussed politics, women, and even God. Rupert described himself as "Church of England by race, rather than religion", Leo was a more conflicted agnostic. They had talked as honestly as possible about their backgrounds. Rupert's mother was a landed aristocrat, who indulged her only son's every whim, and tried hard not to mind when he dropped out of Oxford after the second year and opted for journalism rather than managing their thousands of Northumbrian acres. Leo tried to explain life in Clapham, and had even taken Rupert home to meet his parents. They had sat together at the same kitchen table where Leo had had his tonsils removed as a small child, and Leo's parents had asked Rupert respectful questions about Lord and Lady Allingham, while Rupert had responded with unfeigned interest in Mr Quinn's accountancy work. Yet although his friend had a boundless curiosity for other people's lives, and it was that which made him a good journalist, Leo knew Rupert would never properly understand the life of the lower middle class, with all its inhibitions and dull propriety. Rupert's was a different England from his own. It was that "precious stone set in the silver sea" England that Shakespeare wrote about, whose identity was distilled in architecture and ancient places. While they were at Oxford, treading the same cobbles and honey stone quads, they had shared a country. A decade later, Leo wasn't sure they did any more.

After university, they drifted apart. Throughout the second half of the twenties Leo would see Rupert's name above a story from Paris, or Cairo or the Lebanon. Colour pieces, he thought they were called, about local life, a row about antiquities in the Valley of the Kings, the last interview with Gertrude Bell in Iraq. But even though he knew Rupert was a foreign correspondent, it had still been a pleasurable surprise when he turned up one morning last month, announcing that he was to run the *Chronicle*'s Berlin bureau and asking where the best restaurants could be found.

The audience chatter died down as a handsome man in a suit peered round the curtain and edged shyly onto the stage. He had a strong face, round, horn-rimmed glasses and an expression like an accountant about to break bad news. His appearance drew cheers from the customers. This was what they had come to see.

'Oh!' he said in mock surprise. 'Are we still here?'

Another laugh. Everyone knew Werner Finck. He was renowned for sailing close to the edge in poking fun at the Nazis. He had a technique of allowing the end of his sentence to fall away, so his jibe was implied rather than directly stated, but still everyone knew how it ended. They liked to finish his jokes for him, and all too often they shouted the punch lines out. Rupert looked bemused.

'It's a skit about Hitler,' Leo explained. 'It's a favourite. He's done it before.'

'That's one joke where I'd like to know the punchline.'

Finck moved onto the next part of his story. "Goering, who as you know is to be made Reich game warden, likes to take his animals for a walk now and again. He is walking past the Reich Chancellery, and Hitler looks down and says "Hermann, I see you are taking a tortoise for a walk." And he says, "No, this is just Goebbels in a steel helmet".'

The audience erupted, banging their tables in appreciation. Suddenly Finck leant towards a man in the audience, a small man with a fedora and a face as bony as a bag of spanners, whom Leo had not seen before.

'Am I going too fast for you? Do you want me to slow down so you can take notes?'

The audience laughed, but more quietly this time. Finck had identified a police informer. The man shifted uncomfortably, turning scarlet with embarrassment and anger. As faces turned towards him, the man rose and shouldered his way roughly out of the room, to the accompaniment of clapping. As he ducked out of the door he shouted a parting shot.

'Filthy Jew!'

'I'm afraid not, good sir,' Finck called after him. 'I'm not a Jew. I just look intelligent.'

'Gestapo nark,' said Leo tersely.

'It won't be just jazz they're getting rid of, if he keeps taunting Nazis like that,' said Rupert.

'I don't know. Finck is careful. It's all puns and innuendo. He doesn't say anything directly critical of them. Besides, the manager here is a Party member.'

A gust of laughter greeted Finck's next gibe. He was telling a joke about Erik Jan Hanussen, Hitler's personal astrologer. The intense, dark-featured Viennese psychic, with his persuasive voice and mesmeric eyes, had come to public notice the previous year when he began casting prescient horoscopes and astounding audiences with his feats of mind reading. Then, more audaciously, his own weekly newspaper, the *Bunte Wochenschau*, printed the startling prophecy that within one year Hitler would become Reich Chancellor. It was a long shot then. The Nazis were short of money. The results of the November Reichstag elections were disappointing for them. Even his avid supporters were doubting that Hitler really had it to become their country's leader. Berliners in particular scoffed. But they weren't laughing now.

'Hanussen should watch out himself,' said Leo quietly. 'He's lent a lot of money to the SA. That doesn't go down well. Nobody likes to be in debt.'

The waitress arrived with Leo's Weisse, the traditional Berlin light beer with a dash of raspberry juice. It was sweet enough for a child, but he liked it. As she leant across Leo, the waitress gave him a look that needed no translation. If he was prepared to wait until the end of her shift, it said, there would be something worth waiting for. She batted her black spider eyelashes at him and wiggled away. Rupert laughed.

'At least she's a woman,' said Leo, dryly.

'So how are things on that front? Anyone special?'

He shrugged. 'There's a girl at work. But you have to be careful.'

Irene was a receptionist. She was an English girl born in Berlin and she had the kind of blonde, Aryan prettiness that would have melted the heart of any storm trooper. He couldn't ignore the looks she gave him as he dashed past her desk in the morning, or handed her a sheaf of paperwork to type up. Or the way she lingered when she handed him a letter she had prepared, as if there was something he needed to ask. He knew what that meant. He had thought about asking her out somewhere, but dismissed it instantly. You had to be careful, they had stressed in London. You were being watched and you knew it.

'You're a lone wolf Leo. You always have been. You probably always will be.'

'Well, I'd like to see the woman who could get you to settle down.'

Rupert grinned. 'I'm far too young for that. You won't find me on my knees in front of a priest till I'm at least forty. If ever. Enough of that. What's this onerous task you were talking about?'

'It's complicated.' Leo took a draught of his beer and wondered how far Rupert could be trusted. Then he gave a mental shrug. If he couldn't trust his oldest friend, what had things come to?

'It's about certain English visitors to Germany. I've been asked to keep an eye on them. Anyone who fraternizes with the Nazi élite. Young men who come to learn the language. Girls who've been packed off to finishing school or music classes. They might take all sorts of ideas back home, and the worry is that favourable reports about the new regime will only encourage elements in England who want to disarm.'

Rupert's habitual warm laugh rolled out of his mouth. 'And they pay you for that?'

'It's not frivolous, Rupert. These people, our compatriots, they're coming over here to look at the Nazi regime as though it were the Chelsea Flower Show or the Lord Mayor's Show. It's a spectacle to them. They see all the marching and speeches as the sign of some tough, hard-line discipline, rather than a militaristic display designed to rehabilitate Germany in the eyes of the world.'

'We're not all taken in, you know.'

'Of course not. It's just . . . at first glance it looks so normal here. Everyone going about their business, visiting the cinema, the cabarets, the parks, the dance halls. They're like sleepwalkers. People under anaesthetic!'

'And what kind of operation do you think the doctor has in store for them?'

'War. Within ten years. Perhaps even five or six.'

'What a doom-monger you are!' Rupert laughed. He possessed the kind of optimism, whether of birth or disposition, that no amount of experience could entirely erase. It provoked in Leo a little wave of bitterness, a ripple of class consciousness, that made him momentarily angry at his friend and he said more sharply than necessary, 'Hitler's bound to re-introduce conscription. Haven't you read *Mein Kampf*? You'll need to if you want to do this job properly. It's a blueprint.'

'I'll do my homework.'

'Good. Or listen to Goebbels on the subject. Goebbels is intelligent. He proves even intelligent people can fall under Hitler's spell.'

'I've yet to meet the cripple. What happened with his foot, by the way?'

'He had a botched operation as a child. Though he prefers people to think he got it in the war.'

'The surgeon who did that has a lot to answer for.'

'He likes the limp apparently. He thinks it makes him look distinctive.'

A ripple of laughter at Werner Finck caused them to look round. Leo studied the patrons, their faces relaxed in laughter. How long could all this go on for? Surely it was only a matter of time before Hitler and his crew shut these places down. Laughing at themselves was not on the prescribed list of National Socialist pastimes.

'Anyhow, Rupert, about this other thing. All I'm asking is, keep in touch. Let me know if you see anyone coming through that I might like to know about.'

'Well-born young English girls, you mean? I can't promise that, but there's a rather sweet American girl just turned up in the press corps. Perhaps she'll fall for your strong and silent routine. I'm meeting up with her tomorrow night. At the Romanisches Café. Why not come along?'

Chapter Ten

Ten long-stemmed roses stood in a cut-glass vase. Pearls of dew clung to the deep cleavage of the petals and the colour seemed to throb through the air around them. They looked so expensive, they might as well have had a price tag attached, instead of a note. Frau Lehmann was eyeing them with approval, evidently relieved that her lodger had turned out to have the right connections after all.

'A gentleman delivered them.'

Clara's heart sank. One look at the note that accompanied them confirmed it. Sturmhauptführer Müller would not, it seemed, be easily shaken off.

At that moment the telephone rang. Frau Lehmann answered it, then turned to Clara, proffering the receiver as cautiously as an unexploded bomb.

'Fräulein Vine?'

She recognized his commanding, jocular tone immediately.

'I'm so glad to reach you.'

'How did you get this number?' Even as she said it, she realized it was a foolish question.

He gave a brief laugh. 'I had my driver ask.'

'Of course. Thank you for the roses.'

'That is my pleasure. And I have a request for you.'

Clara braced herself. She was going to have to tell the aide to the Minister of Propaganda she had no intention of seeing him again.

'It has been passed to me by the wife of the Minister. She wonders if you might call on her.'

'Frau Goebbels wants me to call on her?' Surprise made her raise her voice so that Frau Lehmann who was hovering at the end of the hall, pretending to adjust the clock, had no trouble catching every word.

'She has something to ask you. It seems you made quite an impression the other evening. She asks if you could visit her at two o'clock, if you are free. I've arranged to send my car.'

Clara rang the bell and heard the quick clip of heels on the marble floor before a maid dressed in black and white uniform opened the door.

'Please come in.'

As the maid led her down the corridor and into the drawing room there were the distant sounds of an animated discussion in progress, but when a few moments later her hostess entered, wearing a soft cream jacket and pearls, she appeared entirely controlled, apart from a spot of high colour on her cheeks. It was the only hint of warmth in an otherwise glacial demeanour.

'Forgive me, Fräulein Vine. We are having the whole house remodelled, but my decorator's taste in wallpaper does not always accord with my own.'

She pressed a small buzzer and a second maid appeared instantly with a tea trolley. A silver pot suspended over a small flame sat in the centre, surrounded by cups of delicate bone china, and a platter of sandwiches. On a separate plate was butter cake, speckled with cinnamon, and slices of fruit cake with a yellow marzipan rind.

Clara looked around her. In daylight the Goebbels' home appeared no less impressive. Everything about it was sumptuous. One might have been in a small art gallery, rather than a private home. The parquet was covered with rich Turkish rugs, the furniture was antique and gleaming. Fat armchairs were clustered round a low marquetry table and French Louis XIV chairs stood by. The walls were hung with oils, all in exquisite taste – gorgeous Italian hunting scenes and pink-fleshed cherubs fluttering round a Madonna. Pride of place above the fireplace however, was given to a photograph of Hitler. His face was bathed in light as if from some divine revelation and his eyes were fixed mystically on the middle distance, yet no amount of soft focus could disguise the undistinguished profile and jutting, stumpy nose. Clara wondered how an Old Master would have tackled Herr Hitler. But even Michelangelo had to paint the odd Borgia, she supposed.

'You have a lovely home, Frau Goebbels.'

She gave a tight, formal laugh. 'Thank you.' She poked at the open fire, which felt like the only warm thing in the room. 'We've only just moved in but Joseph already dislikes it, I'm afraid. It's not the house, it's the city really. He's never liked Berlin. He calls it "asphalt culture". He thinks it will be much healthier if we move further out. He has an eye on a place up by Wannsee.'

'And would you like to move?'

Magda Goebbels shrugged. 'I lived in the country for years. My former husband had an estate in Mecklenburg. If I'm honest, the country bores me to tears. I love the city, don't you? Berlin is the loveliest city on earth. The Führer always says Paris is the most beautiful city and I suppose I know nothing about architecture, but I was born here, in Bülowstrasse, and I'd die here too, given the choice.'

Just then the maid returned with a pile of post, which Magda waved impatiently away, then turning to Clara, she sighed, 'We receive so many letters. Of course it is lovely that ordinary people write to Joseph and myself all the time, but to answer them . . . you have no idea of the work. Please, eat something.'

She had a way of issuing invitations so that they emerged as commands. Clara, who was always hungry, decided it would be polite to obey. As she selected a liverwurst sand-wich, Magda leant forward in her chair, crossed tan stocking-ed legs and fixed on her an unnervingly intense gaze.

'Tell me, do you know much about fashion?'

'Fashion?' Clara was mystified.

'Yes, I noticed you were wearing a lovely gown the other night – by Jean Patou, wasn't it?'

'I think so. Yes. But I can't pretend to know much about clothes and so on. It was my sister's dress, actually. Angela's terribly interested in all that.'

'No matter. I still think you'd be perfect.'

'Perfect for what?'

Magda got up and went over to the mirror. Absently she adjusted her hair, then walked to the window and sighed, crossing her arms in front of her and cupping her elbows. It was almost as if she had forgotten Clara was there. Clara remembered what had struck her at the party: the sense that some private misery preoccupied this woman, some secret unhappiness hovered just beneath her steely surface. Outside, gardeners were raking the gravel and tending to flowerbeds packed with tulips that were, by accident or design, National Socialist red. But Clara felt sure that gardening was not uppermost on Magda Goebbels' mind. She turned.

'This is a rather confidential thing I have to say. I hope I can trust you to keep it to yourself for a while. Until it's made public.'

Clara nodded.

'I have had a rather special request from the Führer. He wants me to establish the Deutsches Modeamt. A Reich fashion bureau.'

'A fashion bureau?'

'Yes. I am to be honorary president.' Magda came over and clasped her hands, her vivid grey-blue eyes taking on a look of intense urgency.

'You see, he has very strong feelings on this. You might not expect a man to take such an interest in women's things, but the Führer is exceptional. He doesn't think like an ordinary man. He understands how all parts of our culture affect the German people. Even something that a lot of other people might think trivial, he has opinions about, and ideas for change.'

'And what sort of opinion does he have about fashion?'

'For a start, he believes French couture is absolute poison. It has been wreaking havoc on German women.'

'Poison?' Clara said, mystified.

'Yes, and it's not just clothes. The Führer has strong feelings about cosmetics too.'

'He doesn't like them?' hazarded Clara. She couldn't help recognizing Frau Goebbels' perfume – Elizabeth Arden's Night and Day. Angela wore it all the time.

'He hates artificial hair colours and cosmetics. He says they're all about feigning health and youth.'

Clara wondered if the Führer's dislike of adornment stretched to jewellery. A row of chunky pearls nestled on the Frau Doktor's neck, a diamond and emerald clasp was fixed in her hair and twin diamond teardrops dangled from her ears.

'Then there's this cult of unnatural slimness. It makes it so much harder for women to . . . procreate. Did you know that?'

'I had no idea.'

'It's true.'

It had to be said, Frau Goebbels was not herself an obvious advertisement for German fashion. She was wearing a black lacquer Chanel bracelet and her jacket was by Vionnet. Her own make-up had been freshly and immaculately applied. But on hair dye at least she was in line. Her wheat-blonde locks clearly owed nothing to the bottle.

'So you see, Fräulein Vine, I have been given the task – well, the honour I suppose – of calling together designers and creating an entire new look for the German woman using German materials, German workers and German designers.'

'That's quite an undertaking,' said Clara, thinking how exhausting it sounded.

'It is. And the Führer knows that my health is delicate and that such a task might be too much for me alone. That's why he has asked me to involve many of the wives of our top people. Together we will plan a showcase for the new German fashion. And that is when I thought of you!'

'Me?' Clara gave a little choke of surprise and put down her tea.

'Let me explain.' She came over and sat on the sofa next to Clara. 'Look at this article. I had it placed in the *National Socialist Women's Yearbook*.'

Clara looked. The article was titled: '*How Do I Dress Myself as a German, Tastefully and Appropriately?*' Beneath were a section of pictures of tight-laced bodices, full gathered skirts, embroidered blouses and aprons, as well as a photograph of a smiling woman wearing a green checked dirndl dress. None of them, Clara knew for certain, would she ever be seen dead in.

'Frau Goebbels, this is very interesting, but I can't imagine what it has to do with me.'

'You mentioned that your acting career was on hold for a short while.'

'Just until the producer returns, yes.'

'So I thought, how would you like to model some of our new designs? In my first fashion show? We have a planning meeting next Wednesday. Five o'clock tea at the Adlon.'

'Modelling! I'm afraid I've never done any modelling.'

Magda shook her head as though this objection was incidental. 'You have the looks, and you are an actress, after all. An international actress. I plan to get many of our leading ladies involved, Kristina Söderbaum, Olga Chekhova, Zarah Leander. It's quite an honour to be the first.'

'But Frau Goebbels, the problem is . . .' Clara thought of Angela's stint as a mannequin at Harvey Nichols. A photograph of her, in a gold lamé evening gown, looking more elegant than Clara could ever hope to be, had even appeared in *The Times*. 'I don't really want to do it.'

A slight frown creased Magda's brow. Clara's refusal seemed to have introduced a note of vulgarity into their encounter. 'If it's difficult, I'm sure we could also manage a fee of some sort.'

'Oh it's not that.'

'No, I insist.' She snapped the magazine shut. 'You will be paid a proper rate.'

'What I meant was, modelling is quite a different talent. And if you wanted well-known actresses, I can't imagine why you would start with me. Nobody here would know me from Adam.'

'To be honest,' Magda regarded her coolly, 'I would have to agree. It was my husband who suggested you.'

With a shock Clara remembered the look Goebbels had given her as she slipped out of the party. She had guessed his thoughts, but the involvement of his wife added a calculating edge to his interest.

'I'm flattered, and thank your husband for me, but I still don't think I can help.'

Frau Goebbels' eyes, which a moment ago had been fixed on her with such intensity, had turned implacable. Clara's equivocation seemed to go nowhere. 'Nonsense. You will be wonderful. Remember this is an honour, as much as an invitation. To refuse it might be taken as an insult by Herr Hitler.'

Clara reflected a second. She had just two hundred marks to her name. She was going to need to make some money somehow if she were to stay in Berlin. And exactly how onerous could modelling actually be? Only until some more acting work came along.

'What would you like me to do?'

Magda rose and extended her hand. 'We shall expect you at five o'clock on Wednesday. Now, if you don't mind, I must get going. The Führer is coming to tea.'

At the mention of it, a glimmer of girlish boastfulness escaped her controlled exterior. In a softer, more confidential tone, she added, 'He loves a gossip you see. He doesn't always want to talk about affairs of state or ideas. He needs somewhere he can feel safe and comfortable, and a woman who knows what he likes. He has a very special diet, and we make a particular little caramel pudding he appreciates so much. And my cook does the finest cream horns you can imagine. The Führer adores them. He has such a sweet tooth.'

Chapter Eleven

The glow from the yellow lamps on Unter den Linden had dimmed since the bulbs were changed to a lower wattage, but the wind was still as sharp as a knife. It came from the east, straight from the steppes of Russia across the Prussian plain and right into the marrow of the bones. Like everything Berliners feared from those frozen Soviet wastes, it was harsh and relentless and utterly without mercy.

Leo was making his way back to the apartment after a draining afternoon's work. The lines outside the British Consulate had been growing longer by the day. They were well-kempt queues of men in soft hats with brims pulled down, carrying briefcases and newspapers, trying their hardest to appear inconspicuous. Intelligent faces with round glasses and strained expressions. They were professional men mostly, accountants, lawyers and doctors, respectfully waiting to argue their case for a British visa. And they would argue as if their lives depended on it.

The phone would ring non-stop from nine o'clock in the morning. There were calls from Palestine or Trinidad or Rhodesia from people vouching for visa applicants and calls from Berliners who had got all the way to the aerodrome and booked their seats on the plane, and needed only the visa to leave. There were desperate enquiries from wives and girlfriends whose loved ones had disappeared. The girls on the telephones were brisk, but they never lost their temper and just occasionally you could see the glint of a tear in their eyes.

Each day Irene brought piles of letters to open and visa requests to file. The applicants varied. The richer, smarter people had often opened foreign bank accounts already and planned ahead. Others had nothing but their desperation to propel them.

Leo's boss, Foley, the chief of the Passport Office, was a short, thickset man in a Harris tweed suit, who looked out on this mayhem phlegmatically through a pair of horn-rimmed glasses. He was a gentle man who spoke little but had immense patience. Under his guidance, staff on the visa desk knew they had an unwritten authority to bend the rules. They would issue holiday visas that could be transferred once the refugee arrived, or organize sponsors, or create visas that helped people out of prison. Foley remained available day and night with rarely a dent in his good nature. 'Remember,' he would say, if anyone pressed him to go home, or take a rest, 'these people are depending on us.' Very often Leo ended up staying late too.

Tonight, however, he had left at six. He had been thinking that he might be able to get in an hour's translation of Ovid. He was working on 'The Transformation Of Daphne' and had reached the moment when the infatuated Apollo first sees the nymph and pursues her, before she prays to her father, the river god Peneus, for a disguise to save her. The lines ran through his head. 'He saw her eyes like stars of spar-kling fire, her sweet lips made for kissing, her hands and fingers and her arms; her shoulders white as ivory, and he knew, whatever was not seen must be even more beautiful.' He had been looking forward to it. There was something about translating that appealed to him at a profound level. It was both an act of impersonation and self-effacement. To think himself into the mind of another man and enact his thoughts, leaving only the lightest touch of himself, gave him a particular pleasure. It was also, undeniably, a superior form of escapism to the kind to be found in the Katakombe or any of the other nightclubs he regularly visited in search of oblivion.

Yet the more Leo thought about it, the more he was thinking that he might prefer to sit in his chair and allow the schnapps to burn in his throat before heading out to eat his regular supper in the shabby café downstairs – sausage in gravy with a paving stone of bread to mop it up and a tankard of blonde beer by the side.

Turning off Unter den Linden and passing down the street, he sidestepped to avoid a man up a ladder defacing a perfectly innocent office block with a gigantic loudspeaker. Loudspeakers like this were sprouting all over the city, in cafés, bars, factories and offices, mushrooming on walls and lamp posts, at the zoo, in the parks and anywhere you might go to get away from the Führer's shriek or the sarcastic hectoring of Doktor Goebbels. Radio was the new weapon of the revolution, evidently. Apparently the little doctor believed Hitler could never have crowbarred his way into the Reich Chancellery without it. There were speeches every day now, in amongst the sport and the light music and the cultural discussion programmes. Great rambling diatribes, bloated with all those long words the Germans preferred to simple short ones, calling for swastika flags to be raised at every house "behind which Germans live". These addresses were interspersed with frequent pauses, too, to remember fallen soldiers in the Nazi struggle, which meant everyone was obliged to stop what they were doing and stand in awkward silence or risk the wrath of a passing Brown Shirt. As to what the Berliners thought about it, that was harder to fathom. The Führer's voice wasn't Leo's idea of background music when you were drinking your beer, but he hadn't yet seen anyone complain. Last time it happened, a woman in the bar beside him clapped.

This time, though, the voice that proceeded from the radio was not the hectoring bark of Doktor Goebbels, but a lighter, female voice. It took him a few moments to realize it was Frau Doktor Goebbels, the Propaganda Minister's wife. He paused and stood for a moment in the doorway of an electrical goods shop, and lit a cigarette.

"We are on the threshold of an era of strong men. Women must not struggle for the place of men, but fulfil their own important destiny. That is why the professions of the law, government and the military have been closed to women. No one is saying that a German woman may not work, but when it is a case of choosing between marriage and a career, the German woman will always choose marriage."

Leo looked at the toasters and electric food mixers in the shop window beside him. It was bad news to be female right now. Alfred Rosenberg, the mad head of the Foreign Affairs Bureau, whom the Nazis held up as some kind of philosopher guru, had even suggested women should go back to the spinning wheel and the loom. Leo thought of the girls you would see in the Tiergarten. Those groups of Bund Deutscher Mädel marching past with their rosy cheeks and shining faces. Drawing admiring glances for all the wrong reasons in their gym vests and navy shorts. The government said these girls were happy to be serving the state, absorbed in one great endeavour. But what did they really think? How would you ever find out? It was not as though women were writing in the newspapers, or performing sketches in cabarets. Only the female élite, the Frau Goebbels of this world, were allowed to broadcast. And perhaps even she held very different views in private, if you could ever get to hear them.

He thrust his cigarette away and carried on in the sooty darkness. It would be useful to know what those Nazi women thought. It could tell you a lot about the cohesiveness of the top brass. Behind every powerful man was a wife, after all, who heard things he would tell no other living soul. They may be Lady Macbeths, or Caesar's wives. They may urge caution, or goad their men on. But how would you ever get to the wives? There, Leo had to admit, he was stumped. It was not as though he knew much about women at the best of times.

Chapter Twelve

The girls' faces were painted in livid white, and elaborate silver wigs were piled in looping curls on their heads. Their bosoms swelled like fresh dough from their tightly stitched bodices and they wore pale yellow crinolines frothing with lace. They had tangles of pearl necklaces, dainty eighteenth-century satin slippers on their feet, and cigarettes hanging from their mouths. Either they couldn't read, Clara thought, which was just about possible given the silliness of their laughs, or they were so far in character they assumed that the notice behind them on the Babelsberg lot which said *Rauchen Verboten* simply couldn't apply to them.

There were numerous historical films being made just then. Light hearted films about Italian heiresses, aristocrats in danger, Bohemian kings who had been denied their crowns or, as in this case, candyfloss comedies about the lives of Louis XIV. Sweet, syrupy confections that rotted your brain instead of your teeth. They were popular, upbeat and instantly forgettable.

Perhaps people preferred to focus on the past rather than the realities of the present, Clara reflected, as she passed through the lobby and made her way to Albert Lindemann's office. Perhaps those French costumes were the truest kind of

Nazi fashion, because they were expressly designed to take your mind off what was really going on.

Still, she didn't need to think about that now. Not after the good news.

Albert had called the previous evening, as she was sitting in Frau Lehmann's front room after another dreary dinner with the other lodgers. Her fellow guests were Professor Hahn, who taught at the university and sported a bow tie and a monocle, and Fräulein Viktor, who had wide, rabbity teeth and staring eyes, and spent her evenings knitting. Professor Hahn in particular had welcomed the arrival of another lodger, and used the opportunity to practise the English he had learnt on a visit to Bournemouth in his youth. He had fallen into the habit of bringing home English newspapers from the university, in the mistaken belief that Clara might be homesick. Nonetheless she took one eagerly that evening, because flipping through reports about the financial crisis in America or a review of *42nd Street*, was a foolproof way to forestall further conversation.

She had told no one about Frau Goebbels' extraordinary suggestion. There was no one to tell, really, except Frau Lehmann, who was already regarding her with more circum-spection than before. Modelling! Let alone modelling for the National Socialists. Yet, without any other work, how else was she going to pay the bills? And she was astute enough to see that refusing would be awkward. The invitation was at the behest of Goebbels himself, who was now in control of Babelsberg. Turning down his request might mean giving up any chance to act in the studio's films. And she couldn't go back to London. Not yet. She simply couldn't face it.

Just then, as she worried away at the problem while the professor tried and failed to engage her in conversation, had come Albert's call with the promise of a part.

Clara took the call in the hall, well aware that Frau Lehmann would listen in as much as she could. As soon as she realized that she might have some work, she raced up to her room with a light heart. At last! With the prospect of a part and a salary there would be no need to go slinking back to London. Even better, she would be too busy to model dirndls for Frau Goebbels.

From Albert's office, high above the great hall, it was possible to look right down into the set of the eighteenth century French film as it was shot. Cameras slid backwards as they followed a couple strolling through a painstakingly realized interior, complete with lovingly crafted Louis XIV furniture. A director in shirtsleeves kept bounding onto the set and asking them to repeat the scene. Clara couldn't tear her eyes away. What must it be like to stand before those painted flats, with the clapper board in front of your face, and walk convincingly through a make-believe world of cardboard walls and forests with fake branches? To appear entirely unaware of the great glass eye that tracked your every gesture?

Albert had his feet up on the desk with one thumb hooked into his braces and in the other hand a cigar, like the movie tycoon he obviously hoped to be.

'I think we might just have found a part for you,' he announced, airily. 'A new film directed by Gerhard Lamprecht. He recently made *Emil and the Detectives*, which, as you know, was a fabulous success. He's very highly regarded.'

'He does know I haven't been screen-tested yet?' she asked anxiously.

Albert waved his hand. 'He'll arrange that. He's editing at the studio on Cicerostrasse right now, but he's due back at Babelsberg next week. He'll give you an audition.'

'And he realizes I've never been on a film set before?'

'My dear, don't worry. A lot of people aren't going to survive with the talkies. It's no good having the face of an angel if you have the accent of a barmaid. Your voice, I'm sure, will melt hearts.'

'So what's the film?'

'It's a spy story. *Ein gewisser Herr Gran – A Certain Mr Gran*, in the English version. He's got Hans Albers and Olga Chekhova. It's set in Venice. Hans plays a special agent who needs to save some military secrets from the enemy.'

'A spy story! So what would my part be?'

'You would play Alicia, the daughter of the hotel owner. In the German version they have Karin Hardt, so you'd double up for her. Herr Lamprecht would like you to come for a read-through. If you come here on Monday I can introduce you. How does that sound?'

She could have kissed him.

'Albert, it sounds wonderful. I'd love to! How clever of you to arrange it for me.'

'It was nothing.'

He stood up and together they gazed down at the monumental great hall spread out beneath them.

'It certainly looks busy.'

'It is. Things were quiet for a while, until people worked out what this government wants, and now it's picking up again.'

'So they know what the government wants?'

'Let's just say the Doktor has not been slow to acquaint us with his thoughts.'

He clapped a clumsy hand on her shoulder.

'Still, I'm glad we've got you fixed up. It's a small part to start with but you could go far.'

'And how about Helga? Do you think Herr Lamprecht could offer something to her?'

'Don't worry about Helga. There will be plenty of parts for her.'

There was something in his expression, a wariness perhaps, that Clara couldn't read.

Either that, or she chose not to see it.

Chapter Thirteen

With a curse, Mary Harker, special correspondent to the *New York Evening Post*, slammed the phone down on her editor with a furious clatter. Or in her dreams she did. In reality, she replaced the receiver and stared crossly out of the newspaper office's fifth floor window, which looked directly onto Unter den Linden. Way below there was a military march – another one – drilling its way down the street, giving the players foot-ache and the listeners earache. She scowled as she replayed the editor's infuriating instructions in her mind.

'It's about that Hitler interview, Mary. I'm taking you off it and putting Tom onto it. I've got other plans for you. I'd like you to focus on how life is for ordinary people. Women and kids, you know. We'd like to see what the Third Reich means for them right now.'

'Ordinary people?' She strove hard to keep her tone level. 'With respect Frank, anyone could do that. I'm not some rookie reporter. I should be interviewing Hitler and Goering at a time like this, not filing fluffy colour pieces on what the Berlin hausfraus are baking in the new Reich.'

'I don't want fluffy colour, as you call it, Mary. And believe me I know you're not a rookie. I want the best you can give me. We already decided Tom should cover the interview with the Chancellor, and I can see you're feeling sore, but

given that Herr Hitler says the Reich's going to last a thousand years, I'm sure there'll be plenty more chances.'

'Damn it, Frank, Dorothy Thompson interviewed him last
year!' said Mary, hating the whine that had entered her voice,
but too annoyed to do anything about it.

'Mary, I'm not doubting your prowess. I'm just saying
that Tom is the man for this. Besides, from what I hear,
things are going to get tougher for women under our pal
Hitler. There's a rumour he's about to ban married women
from holding jobs. Restrict female university students to ten
per cent of the total. Hell, from what he's said, he doesn't
even believe in the vote. That's a pretty important area,
wouldn't you say?'

Mary sighed. Even from a thousand miles away, she could
picture him in his eyeshade and braces and scarlet spotted
bow-tie, giving her that quizzical look that said he knew best.
Frank Nussbaum was a great guy. Mary had met him back in
New York and he had been personally responsible for getting
her hired when she came out here and applied for work as a
stringer in the bureau. After six months he had ensured she
was taken on full time. She owed Frank more than she could
say, but sometimes he was so obdurate she could scream.

It had not been easy negotiating the break from her New
Jersey home to come out here. She was the only daughter of
elderly parents, who regarded a visit to New York as foreign
travel and whose lives revolved around their country club
and their bridge nights. Her mother had taken to demanding
grandchildren like a kid demanding a puppy. But that wasn't
going to happen in a hurry, or ever, as far as Mary was
concerned. She felt about as enthusiastic about staying in
New Jersey as a medieval nun would feel about being bricked
up in the walls of an abbey. She had experienced a twinge of

guilt as the liner sailed from New York harbour, but by the time they passed the Statue of Liberty she was over it.

Europe was glorious. Everything was dirt cheap and you could travel around third class for nothing. Everywhere was swarming with Americans, painting and writing and editing literary magazines. A lot of them headed for Paris, where the franc was depressed and life was great, but Mary preferred Berlin. Here people seemed to like Americans, perhaps because they weren't tangled up in any of these European affairs, or perhaps because the dollar was strong. Everywhere there were flags flying, brass bands playing, flowers tumbling from the window-boxes, smiles on faces and food in the shops.

There was plenty of work too. Newspapers and magazines and wire services like AP and the United Press were all offering work to freelancers or people who were prepared to take short-term contracts. Then Frank had taken her on full time for a hundred dollars a month and she found a lovely apartment near Nollendorfplatz in Schöneberg, which was one of the liveliest areas in town, full of bars and late night jazz joints. She got by in German with the help of a tutor and a dogged determination to practise on everyone she met. It was a further relief when her mother back in New Jersey began to concentrate all her attention on her daughter-in-law, who had furnished her with a grandchild in a way that her own daughter seemed incapable of.

The first cracks had come last month, soon after the Nazis had secured power. It was a little thing. Mary was locking up one night when Lotte Klein, the woman who kept supplies of typewriter ribbons and carbon paper, typed letters and generally managed the office, took her aside. Lotte Klein was a mousy young woman in her twenties, whose sober navy suit and spectacles put a good couple of decades on her.

'I noticed, Fräulein Harker, when the delivery man came the other day you made a joke to him about the German newspapers.'

It was true. Rudi Koch, who brought up a stack of papers to the bureau each morning, was a friendly old guy, whose eyes always lit up when he saw Mary. They frequently joked about the contents of the press. There were two hundred newspapers in Germany and nowadays they divided into two camps – those that supported the Nazis and those that opposed them. You made your choice there, but there was no choice when it came to journalistic standards. Party newspapers like the *Völkischer Beobachter* thought nothing of printing news that was weeks old, or running the same piece twice. The efforts of the *Angriff*, Goebbels' paper, left even more to be desired.

That morning Mary had jokingly complained, 'How come the *Beobachter* says Germany is being swamped with Jews coming into the country when all the other papers say they're trying to leave?'

Rudi took off his cap, screwed up his eyes and pretended to contemplate the question.

'Here's an idea, Fräulein. Take everything in the *Beobachter*, and work out what would be the complete opposite. And that's what you want to go with.'

At the memory of it Lotte grimaced.

'Fräulein Harker, Berlin is not like your own country. You can't say everything you think. Don't give your opinion to anyone you don't know.'

'I'm a journalist, Lotte! It's my job to give my opinion.'

'I know that. But in the new Germany – how can I say this? – individual opinions are not so important.' She cast around for inspiration. 'This is difficult to explain but . . . people here are happy to be part of something larger and stronger than themselves. They feel they have struggled for long enough.'

Mary recognized that. The crowds she saw who flocked beneath Hitler's balcony at the Chancellery, or who attended the rallies at the Sportpalast, obviously loved to be part of something bigger than themselves. The air was charged with emotion. She could see people thrill to it, and it made her realize there was something in the human soul that longed for drums and flags as much as ordinary things like warm beds and home cooking. Those parades had a way of making Mary, who as a reporter was already apart from it all, feel even more alone. Yet she had never properly considered that other Germans might feel the same way. People like Lotte, who took off her glasses and moved closer, though there was no possibility of being overheard.

'You may not be afraid to say what you feel, Fräulein Harker, but it's not the same for us. You don't know what it's like. We don't dare say anything bad, in case we might be denounced or reported to the authorities. My friend went to the post office the other day to complain that the post service had been unreliable and she had to wait two weeks for a parcel. The clerk behind the counter threatened to report her. And then just last week I was queuing in the grocer's and a woman moaned to me about the price of milk. Right in front of other people! I pretended not to hear and had to go away without buying anything.'

'It wasn't you complaining!'

'I can't risk it. Every night before I go to bed I think through what's happened in the day and ask myself if I've done or said anything that could put us in danger.'

Mary reached out a hand to her arm. 'But surely, Lotte, you don't need to be afraid? You're not Jewish. You're not a Communist and, as far as I can see, you're not an enemy of the state. Why should you?'

Lotte shook her head and drew her coat tighter like a flimsy shield against the dangers she saw around her.

'It doesn't matter about me. What I meant to say was, for you, perhaps, there could be risks.'

Lotte was probably right. Perhaps Mary did have a tendency to shoot her mouth off when she felt strongly about something. Was that why Frank Nussbaum felt she couldn't be trusted to interview the Nazi top brass? In case some comment affected the delicate balancing act between America and the National Socialist regime?

She sighed. It was quiet in the office now, apart from the faint chuntering of the ticker tape machine. She stretched, gathered up her jacket, switched off the lights and locked the office door. As a result of her talk with Frank she had made plans to visit one of the new *Arbeitsdiensts*, the labour camps for young men and women, which were springing up all over the country. It had been Lotte's idea actually. Her younger sister Gretl had just signed on for a six month stint at a place on the outskirts of Berlin. It was a good idea too. It would make the kind of simple colour piece about 'ordinary' German girls that would be sure to please the editor. And no danger of insulting anyone of any consequence. Meanwhile a handsome Brit reporter had asked her out. Perhaps that would be enough to take her mind off it.

Chapter Fourteen

Judging by the map, Helga's apartment was in the east of the city, the other side of Mitte, with all the galleries and state buildings that Frau Lehmann had instructed her to see. Clara took a tram to Alexanderplatz and then walked. This part of the city was a world away from the prosperous, leafy streets of the western outskirts, or the affluence of the Ku'damm. No shiny Mercedes were parked in these streets and no one was painting and primping their houses the way they were in the smarter parts of town. Clara passed pale old men with wizened faces and eyes full of shadow. Children paused in their play to stare at her as she went by. There had been money here once, and gentility, yet now within the flag-stoned inner courtyards the buildings were in a state of severe dilapidation, with paint peeling from rusting balconies, sooty windows and water dripping from broken pipes. Turning a corner, she came to a street of five-storey tenements, dominated at one end by the tall cylinder of a brick water tower, and found the number of the building where Helga lived.

She opened the door and pushed the light, but nothing happened. A notice on the wrought-iron doors of the cage lift said the elevator was out of order so she climbed the staircase to the fifth floor in darkness. Helga flung open the door.

'Welcome to my penthouse! The most prestigious address in Prenzlauer Berg! *Klein aber mein.*'

It was a joke, obviously. The apartment consisted of two rooms, one with a stove and sink in the corner, and a narrow bedroom, with an iron bedstead. Marlene Dietrich and Conrad Veight shared space on the patterned wallpaper. In front of a flickering gas fire a pair of stockings hung. There was no bath, and the pile of damp clothes beside the chipped, enamel basin suggested that Helga did all her washing there. It reminded Clara of the digs she had had in Eastbourne, except, with Berlin's chill evening air whistling through the cracks at the window edges, it was infinitely colder.

Helga herself was a splendid contrast to her dingy surroundings. She was wearing a leopard-skin coat with only underwear beneath it and crouched in front of a tiny mirror, plucking her eyebrows.

'Just giving Nature a helping hand. Pluck them all away then shade them in. And never use mascara on the lower lashes. It makes you look tired. Marlene Dietrich told me that.'

Clara plumped herself down.

'Have you always lived round here?'

'Not far away. I was born in Wedding actually. Not such a swish area as your Frau Lehmann's, in fact Kosliner Strasse where we lived was the poorest of the poor. But my darling mother did everything she could for us. She's a nurse, and the kindest woman alive. I'll never forget her coming home each evening and scrubbing her apron which was red with blood, then hanging it to dry before checking that we children had finished our lessons and there was bread and milk for the morning. I never met my father, but as my mother used to say, that's his loss.'

She paused to apply lipstick, rub her lips together and kiss the air.

'Then a kind uncle – well, not really an uncle but one of my mother's friends, if you get my meaning – offered to pay for some dance lessons so I went to the Grimm-Reiter school – where I met Leni Riefenstahl, you know? Who made *The Blue Light* last year? Don't say you haven't seen it? It was wonderful! Though, my dear, she's *much* older than me. Anyway, after that I found work as a dancer.'

'How exciting! What kind of parts?'

'This and that.' Helga smiled brightly. 'You can't be too choosy. Work's work, you know? You'll have to wait. I won't be ready for ages. Make some coffee. There, on the stove.'

Clara went over to the stove. She held her hands over the gas ring, warming herself, and spooned coffee out of its paper box into green china cups. Through the bedroom door she could see Helga hooking her stockings to the suspenders, and dabbing a touch of scent behind each ear. Clara looked around the room and as she did an oil painting caught her eye.

It looked like a headache in the form of art. The canvas was filled with manic swirls, like an explosion in a firework factory. In the foreground a woman lay, rendered in a harsh, angular light, legs sprawled across a purple sofa, intersecting planes of pallid flesh grotesquely convoluted, her face lascivi-ously contorted. Around her were men with hideous expres-sions, a beggar, a priest and a solider missing one leg, waving his crutch. The background was blood red and desolate, and a church with a broken steeple stood on the skyline. Clara had never seen anything like it. It took a few moments to realize that the woman was Helga herself.

'If that's your reaction, you can imagine what I thought,' Helga smiled, emerging from the bedroom. 'I only put it there to cover the damp. And because the artist is a good friend of mine.'

'What's it supposed to be?'

'It's a portrait. I did say: Darling, couldn't it be a little more flattering, couldn't it at least look like me? But he said something about needing to transcend the tyranny of external forms. I forget now. It seemed to make sense at the time. Anyway, enough of that. What matters is, how do I look right now?'

She was wearing a satin maroon dress which was too tight for her, with cleavage spilling over the low neck line.

'Beautiful. So where are we going?'

'Just to a bar. My old friend Frieda works there. I'm going to introduce you.'

'Is Bauer coming?'

'Not tonight.' She fingered her necklace and gave a coy laugh. 'But next week, you'll never guess, they're organising a meeting of film stars at the Lustgarten and he's invited me! I need to look sensational.'

'I'm sure you will.'

'Can you imagine? Just a year ago I was dancing naked in the Tingel Tangel, and now I'm mingling with the new film stars of the Reich!'

She came over, caught Clara's face and kissed her impulsively. 'You've brought me luck, I'm sure of it.'

Helga ran her fingers down her dress with pleasure. There was something flighty and exotic about her, Clara thought, like some tropical bird which has fluttered down into a cold grey clime and decided to stay for the winter.

'In fact, I have a teeny favour to ask.' Helga pursed her lips. 'For next week. I'm wearing a cocktail dress – a girl at the studios is going to lend it to me – and I wondered if those shoes you wore the other night, the ones with the rhinestone buckle . . .'

'You can borrow them if you like.' Clara looked at Helga's own shoes which were scuffed and worn, the leather beginning to fray at the edges. 'We're obviously the same size.'

'Could I? Really?' Clara smiled. Helga's excitement was rejuvenating. The tiredness in her eyes had vanished and she looked like a little girl who has been promised a treat.

'Of course.'

'I'll take great care of them. I promise. It's for a special occasion.'

'I'll bring them when I next see you. Keep them as long as you like.'

'But,' Helga paused, struck with a sudden thought, 'what about you? Won't you need your best clothes for evenings with Doktor Müller?'

'I doubt it. I'm not planning on seeing him again.'

Helga stared at her, flabbergasted. 'Why not?'

'I realized he's not my type.'

'Whatever gave you that idea? You've only just met!'

'The idea occurred to me when he started talking about wanting to see Communists lying dead in the street.'

Helga raised her eyebrows at this absurdity. 'They all say that. That's just men.'

'Not the men I know.'

'But can't you simply, you know, pretend?'

'Why should I?'

'You're an actress. You need to stay in work, don't you?'

'Not if Doktor Müller's the price. Besides, I've already been offered an audition. For a Gerhard Lamprecht film.'

'Oh, that's wonderful!' Clara noted the flash of envy in her eyes. 'You should have told me. All the more reason for us to celebrate tonight.'

'What's more,' Clara added quickly, 'Albert says there will be plenty of roles for you too.'

'Don't worry. I know.' Helga relaxed. 'Bauer will see to that. But still,' she added coaxingly, 'there's no need to be nasty to Müller. He's awfully handsome. Not even married, from what I hear. And Bauer was telling me they're all interested in you.'

'Me? I can't imagine why.'

'You fascinate them. They're used to putting women in two camps – wives and actresses. They sleep with the wives but they make love to the actresses. Actresses are for sex, but they get no respect. You're a respectable girl, and an actress, so they can't make you out. They don't know what kind of bird you are.'

'I don't care. I'm not interested.'

'Please, Clara.' She came over to Clara, knelt theatrically and took her hands. 'I need this. Bauer is useful to me. He could be the best thing that's ever happened to my career. But if you offend Müller, then Bauer might be obliged to drop me too.'

'Don't worry, I won't offend him. I'll just keep away.'

'That's the same thing.'

'I'll be otherwise engaged.'

'Please,' she wheedled, 'just think about it.'

She went across to collect her cigarettes and as she did Clara picked up a photograph from the mantelpiece. It was a little boy, perhaps six years old judging by the gap in his cheeky smile, holding a banner. Helga came over and snatched it away from her.

'That's private.'

Startled at her tone, Clara apologized. 'I'm sorry. I was only looking. Who is it?'

For a moment, as she replaced the picture and straightened it, Helga looked as though she was not going to answer. Her previously pert expression had clouded, her features drooped.

'It's Erich.'

'Who's Erich?'

'My son.'

'You have a son?'

'He lives with my mother.'

'You never mentioned him.'

'You never asked. Besides, what business is it of yours?' She hesitated. 'I was very young. Only sixteen. I was so innocent I hardly knew what I was doing and this big bruiser came on to me. I was too young to know any better and too scared to get myself out of the fix. So I had my son. I've made a couple of mistakes since then but I've dealt with them.'

'You mean . . .?'

Helga smiled briskly. 'There's a woman in the west end who works in a maternity hospital and does a little private business on the side. Lots of the actresses have used her. It hurts like hell and it costs a hundred marks a time, but it's better than the alternative. Only now it's been outlawed she doesn't dare perform operations any more so God knows what I'll do if another mistake comes along.'

'So where's Erich's father now?'

'Long gone, thank God.'

'How old is he?'

'He's ten now. He's just joined the Pimpf – that's the junior part of the Hitler Jugend. I didn't want him to, but the school . . .' She grimaced. 'They say it's an important part of a boy's development. There's hiking, sports, den evenings. They say they're developing the whole boy – you know, his spirit.'

'We have something like that at home. It's called the Scouts.'

'I don't like it. When you join the HJ they give you this pamphlet with a quote from Hitler. "The Hitler Jugend are as agile as greyhounds, as hard as Krupp steel and as tough as leather." And that's about the last way you'd describe my Erich. He's such a sweet thing. Small for his age, but so intelligent.'

'Where is he now?'

'They live out in Havelberg, about two hours from here. He visits, whenever she can afford to send him. I'm hoping he can come soon. You could meet him! We could go to Luna Park, there's a funfair there. Once I get my big break, he's going to live with me all the time. Until then, he's best off with Mutti. Besides, I don't want him meeting savages like Bauer.'

'If you think that about Bauer, why do you see him?'

Helga crossed her arms and took a deep drag of her cigarette. The eyes she fixed on Clara were swimming slightly.

'Here's the thing, Clara. I'm not like you. I'm not a foreigner with a family back home and a big-shot politician for a father. I'm Helga Schmidt with a lousy apartment in the worst part of town and about two Reichsmarks to rub together. I have nothing to my name except this body and a little bit of talent. I need to take every opportunity that comes my way.'

Chapter Fifteen

The five o'clock *Tee und Tanz* sessions at the Adlon Hotel were the height of social sophistication. All the top hotels held them – the Esplanade, the Bristol, the Eden and the Kaiserhof – but the Adlon was where the cream of Berlin society took their tea. With its palm court and its fountain and its magnificent view of the Brandenburg Tor, the Adlon's dances were so well attended that two orchestras played alternately, to ensure the music didn't stop.

They were especially popular with elderly matrons who would order an *Eintänzer*, a professional dance partner, the way other people might order *Apfeltorte* or *Spritzkuchen*. The *Eintänzer*, a breed of fetching young man, would approach the old ladies and ask politely for a dance, before steering them like ancient tugboats round the dance floor. Some were said to provide services that went beyond professional dancing, but there was very little erotic frisson detectable among the potted plants that afternoon as Clara threaded between the marble-topped tables, determined to tell Frau Goebbels that she was sorry, but she would not be available for modelling, after all.

Magda Goebbels was wearing a black Persian lamb jacket with a matching hat. She was seated next to a statuesque blonde of about forty, with a broad face and a disconsolate

expression, eating a slice of chocolate cake. At her feet a
schnauzer sat, its oily eyes switching alternately from cake to
mouth, like a spectator at a tennis match.

'Fräulein Vine. I'm so glad you could come.'

Magda indicted her plump companion with a gold-tipped
cigarette. 'This is Frau Emmy Sonnemann.'

Clara had heard of her. She was Minister Goering's girlfriend, a provincial actress who had, through her relationship
with Goering, been catapulted into starring roles in Berlin
theatres. She looked like a Wagner heroine might look, if
Wagner heroines ate chocolate cake. She wore a Vionnet
bias-cut dress, whose sinuous folds were designed to drape
flatteringly over the wearer's curves but were failing hope-
lessly in their task. She seemed engrossed in a newspaper.

'Emmy is celebrating. She's been given the lead at the
Schauspielhaus. The play is *Schlageter*. About that brave man
who was executed by the French in the Ruhr. Do you know
it?'

'I'm afraid not.'

'Don't worry,' said Emmy, scarcely looking up. 'You're
forgiven.' She was poring over a report of the Aviators' Club
ball. She pointed to a picture of Goering. 'He'll loathe this
picture. He hates looking fat.'

Clara looked. Fat was an understatement. In his tight
airforce uniform Goering was a sweating hippo, whose spindly gilded chair was bending dangerously under his weight.

'It's Hess who's to blame. He asks to see every photograph
of Hermann and then he only allows the most unflattering
ones to be published.'

Magda motioned to a ravishingly attractive blonde, perched
across from her. She had marcelle-waved hair and matching
wine-red velvet cape and muff. It was impossible not to
notice how her slender figure and shapely legs contrasted

with Emmy's thick waist and stolid calves. She offered Clara
a white-gloved hand.

'Pleased to meet you.'

'Frau Ley's husband is the new head of the Labour Front,'
said Magda. 'He's going to get our people working again.'
Then, gesturing to the third person, a tank of a woman in a
flowery dress with puffed sleeves, she added, 'Do you know
Frau von Ribbentrop?'

The girlish prettiness of Frau von Ribbentrop's outfit was
in unfortunate contrast to her square-jawed, pudding face
with a mole above one lip. She was a formidable figure. Her
necklace looked like bunting on a battleship. Her neck was
swathed in a mink stole on the end of which the head of its
previous owner stared out glassily, teeth bared. She looked at
Clara as though she were a housemaid who had just broken
the Dresden china.

'Annelies is extremely interested in fashion, so we are rely-
ing on her to have some great ideas.'

All Clara knew of Annelies von Ribbentrop was that she
was an heiress to the Henkell sparkling wine firm. The von
Ribbentrops were rich, and they lived in some style at a
handsome villa in Dahlem.

'It is my Führer himself who has the best ideas,' she said
ingratiatingly. 'He even helped design the uniform of the
BDM.'

From what Clara had seen of the uniform of the Bund
Deutscher Mädel – the German Girls' League – it was not the
kind of costume many people would put their name to. It was
guaranteed to transform the most elegant girl into a frump.

'He has an artist's soul,' agreed Magda. 'He tells me he sees
fashion as another form of artistic creation.'

It was clear that the two women were engaged in some
kind of competition for the favours of Hitler. Which was

doomed, Clara knew, given that Frau Goebbels' access to the Führer was second to none.

'Now to update you. Doktor Hans Horst has been appointed acting director of the Deutsches Modeamt and I am the honorary president. We don't want our designers to be unduly influenced by what other races might choose to do so we plan to hold our first show before the Paris collections, at the Grunewald Horse Race Track. I shall be sending invitations to Zarah Leander, Olga Chekhova and Kristina Söderbaum, but Fräulein Vine has already graciously agreed to model. I thought we should donate the profits of the first show to the Winterhilfswerk. Is that agreed?'

'What is it the Führer wants exactly?' enquired Emmy, looking up from her paper.

'As I was explaining,' said Madga, a trifle tersely, 'he has been thinking of the importance of fashion, not just as an industry but as an indispensable part of German culture. Fashion is a way by which women too can play their part in strengthening the nation.'

'How would that be?'

'Well, for a start, the Führer wants French fashion replaced with German fashions. I have had some preliminary sketches made.'

Out of a leather portfolio she pulled a sheaf of sketches. Clara saw women in flat heels and black skirts down to the ground. Tyrolean hats. Tight-fitted bodices with puffed tartan sleeves. Gretchen braids and little brown jackets. Emmy looked over and made a face.

'The Leader dislikes fur, too, doesn't he?' she said regretfully, patting her mink.

'He hates killing animals, as you know. Short or long hair?'

'Oh, short, please, we're none of us getting any younger,' sighed Emmy. 'And you won't find many film stars willing to wear their hair in braids. *Butterkuchen*, Frau von Ribbentrop?'

Annelies von Ribbentrop winced as though someone had offered her cyanide and shook her head. She leant forward to look at the sketches with a wrinkle of disdain then said, 'What does Joseph think?'

'Joseph is very supportive of our plan. He says too much of German culture has been hijacked by cosmopolitan intellectuals.'

Frau von Ribbentrop nodded. 'The Führer told me that fashion is interwined with the racial problem.'

'Exactly so. He feels the international silhouette encourages women to remain too thin to have children.'

'He has my vote there,' said Emmy, crossing her legs to reveal a plump stockinged knee.

'So no haute couture then?' ventured Frau von Ribbentrop.

'Absolutely not. We need to compete with Paris. Here. I placed a piece about it in *Die Schöne Frau.*'

'Ach, I can never bother with that,' said Emmy. 'It's one long nag.'

Frau von Ribbentrop produced some spectacles and read the magazine aloud.

"Finally the possibility is given for the fashion makers of Germany to unite in a great work to rid themselves of foreign influences and to create proper standing and status for German products in fashion, industry and in the field of arts and crafts."

'Actually,' said Emmy. 'I don't mind a dirndl. It's very supportive. When you get to a certain point, you need all the support you can get. And Hermann adores a low-cut dress. How about you, Frau von Ribbentrop? I know how you love all those French fashions you find abroad.'

'I don't think anyone has ever questioned my commitment to German culture,' she said stiffly.

Emmy laughed and popped another piece of cake in her mouth, then turning her back entirely on the others, addressed herself to Magda. 'So are you enjoying your new home?'

'It is beautiful, thank you. The Speers came to our film evening last night. Albert is remodelling the house, and adding a reception hall. I was hoping that Margaret Speer could become involved in our fashion enterprise, but sadly she felt it was beyond her.'

'Hermann is having the palace at Leipziger Platz remodelled too. He's planning a cinema room with a Wurlitzer organ. I don't know if our taste in movies will ever agree, though! He asked me to watch a stag movie the other night and I thought it was something naughty but it turned out to be a film about stags! Lots of footage of Hermann walking around in his leather suit.'

'Anyway,' Magda said quickly, 'it was a good idea of Joseph's to involve figures from the film world and it's lovely to have Fräulein Vine as our first model.'

Emmy shot Clara a glance. 'Did the Herr Doktor specifically recommend Fräulein Vine?' she enquired sweetly.

'Fräulein Vine is the daughter of a prominent English politician,' replied Magda, with a touch of acid. 'She wants to help us in any way she can.'

'Is that so?' Emmy looked at Clara with renewed interest.

'My father was formerly a Conservative MP. Sir Ronald Vine.'

'Fascinating,' said Annelies von Ribbentrop. 'My husband is a great admirer of England. We have visited many times.'

Magda tilted her head towards the ceiling and exhaled a plume of smoke. 'So can we count on you, Emmy? To participate in the Deutsches Modeamt?'

Emmy sighed. 'Of course. I'm at the Führer's disposal.' As she stood up, the schnauzer truffled for the crumbs that fell from the folds of her dress. 'Time for me to go. The curtain's up in two hours.' She allowed her hand to rest briefly in Clara's.

'So pleased to meet you, Fräulein Vine.'

As she bustled off, flanked by a grovelling hotel manager and eyed by a sprinkling of drinkers at the bar, Magda leant back with a sigh.

'I feel sorry for her really. Hermann adored his wife, Carin. He keeps a room in his home devoted to her. Pictures of Carin, her furniture, her harmonium, everything. Emmy's not allowed to set foot in it. He's even ordered a sarcophagus so they can both be buried together. How is poor Emmy to compete?'

'She can't. And he shows no signs of making an honest woman of her,' added Frau von Ribbentrop, snapping her snakeskin cigarette case shut. 'He's issued instructions that she is to be known only as his "private secretary".'

'The theatre loves her though,' said Magda. 'The box office takings have shot up because people think Goering will come to see her. They keep a box reserved for him at all times.'

These confidences were interrupted by a commotion taking place across the lobby. A large, bearlike man with floppy hair and a clownish face had commandeered the piano and the bandleader had given way. The couples who had been circling the dance floor hesitated uncertainly as the music changed, then quietly departed. Magda looked pained.

'That's Putzi. The fool.'

The piano player was hammering out a number of his own devising choreographed with strange jerky movements of his head.

'Who's Putzi?' asked Clara.

'Putzi Hanfstaengl is our Foreign Press Chief. He considers himself very musical.'

'And he has to be the centre of attention,' added Frau von Ribbentrop. 'Still, as long as the Führer enjoys his playing, I suppose his jokes will be tolerated.'

Catching sight of them, the man abandoned the tune midway, rose and came across the dance floor. He was very tall with a lantern jaw and limbs that looked too big for his body, like a puppet whose strings are not quite tight. He was wearing a brown uniform with little gold epaulettes.

'Oh dear, I had hoped he wouldn't notice us,' murmured Magda, then standing she extended a hand and said,

'Fräulein Vine, can I introduce Putzi Hanfstaengl? Foreign Press chief. Fräulein Vine has come from England to join us. Putzi's half American, aren't you?'

'Indeed.' As he kissed Clara's hand his eyes lingered on her thoughtfully. In perfect, American-accented English, he said, 'Wonderful to have you with us. Can I ask you ladies what the occasion is?'

'We're discussing a fashion initiative,' said Magda brusquely.

'How marvellous. I'm a great admirer of the fashionable woman.'

'German fashion,' clarified Frau von Ribbentrop.

'Ah well, there you have me. I'm a sinner, I'm afraid. This uniform, you see . . .'

'I was just thinking I haven't seen you in uniform before,' said Frau von Ribbentrop, sounding bored.

'I decided I would join the club. But that SA uniform is so dreadful. Such a ghastly dun colour. So I sent for a length of chocolate brown gabardine from Savile Row and had my tailor make it up. It makes all the difference, don't you think?'

'Considering we're launching a bureau to promote the use of German materials, Putzi, I would say that your decision was especially ill-timed. I advise you not to mention it to the Führer.'

As Putzi stood open-mouthed, Magda rose and addressed herself to Clara and Frau von Ribbentrop.

'Now I have to leave you. I have a piece to record for the radio. I shall be in touch with you shortly, Fräulein Vine.'

With that she was clipping across the Adlon's marble floor before Clara had had a chance to explain.

Chapter Sixteen

Ever since Helga told her about the Romanisches Café, Clara had been wanting to see it. It was an enormous space the size of a barn, opposite the Kaiser Wilhelm Memorial church and famously packed with artists, film directors, writers and intellectuals. Or as Helga more simply put it, everyone went there. Outside, awnings and trellises of greenery sheltered tables for those who wanted to watch the world go by; inside, the marble topped tables were crowded with people wrangling and disputing. In the old days customers could spend twelve hours nursing a single cup of coffee before a discreet card would be placed on the table top, asking them to order more or leave. But since January, the atmosphere had changed. As the regular clientele realized it was only a matter of time before they were arrested or went into exile, an uneasy lull had fallen on the long, disputatious discussions. Who wanted to talk politics, when politics were all around them, threatening to report them to the police or haul them off to the cells in the middle of the night?

Eyes flickered upwards as Clara walked through the café. She had been planning to find a quiet corner where she could enjoy a cup of coffee and a cigarette before going home to Frau Lehmann's for the evening. Beneath her coat she was wearing a yellow cardigan over a new china blue polka-dot dress which she had bought that afternoon, a purchase she had justified as a vote of confidence that work was on the way. And it teamed well with her blue hat, as the glances she got confirmed.

As she made her way to a table, a man sprang to his feet and blocked her way.

'Good heavens! It's Clara Vine!'

For a fraction of a second, Clara was bewildered to be accosted by the handsome Englishman with a loop of fair hair, until she recognized him as the man she had met at Gerald Mortimer's party. The man who had given her Max Townsend's number. Rupert something.

'Rupert?'

'So you came after all.' He held out a hand. 'I wondered if you would. I should have mentioned I'd just been made head of the *Chronicle*'s Berlin bureau. Fancy joining us? This is Mary Harker.'

He gestured at a fair woman in spectacles and a heavy tweed suit which looked a little warm for the occasion. 'And that's Leo Quinn.' The other man was lean and broad-shouldered, with a suit that hung off him, and striking green eyes that could pierce a sheet of steel. 'Leo has the dubious distinction of being one of my oldest friends.'

Clara took his hand. Beneath a thatch of thick brown hair he had a fine, sensitive nose and a serious face, which was transformed when he smiled. In his jacket and flannels he struck an almost donnish figure.

'Leo is working at the British Consulate.'

'Sit down, won't you, Clara?' said Mary, throwing her jacket off. 'We're all drinking Pilseners. Rupert told me the froth is supposed to be so firm you can lay a coin on it and thanks to him I've lost three pfennigs already.'

Rupert laughed and pulled out a crumpled packet of cigarettes from his pocket, offering Clara one. He tilted his head to survey her.

'I never thought you'd actually come.'

'Well, I'm here,' she said, taking off her gloves.

'What did Angela say?'

'I don't know. I didn't tell anyone I was going. I just left a note saying I'd been offered an acting job in Berlin and I'd explain in good time.'

He raised his eyebrows. 'They must be worried.'

'I doubt it,' she said briefly.

'Clara's an actress,' he explained to the others. 'And she has me to blame for her appearance here. I advised her to contact an old friend of mine, a film producer. So how's it going? Are you having any luck in Naziwood?'

'Yes, actually. Though no thanks to your friend. Max Townsend seems to have disappeared off the face of the earth.'

'Oh dear. That sounds like Max.'

'*Schwarze Rosen* has been delayed, but luckily I've been offered a part in a spy film instead.'

'I'm glad it's worked out.'

'It has. What about you?'

'Oh, I'm in disgrace.'

'What happened?' asked Leo.

Rupert shot him a look. 'I just got in a bit of trouble with Putzi Hanfstaengl for something I wrote.'

'What now?' asked Mary.

'I said despite everything Herr Hitler is saying about peace, Germany is determined to recover everything she's lost. And if it can't be done through peace, it'll be done through war.'

'War?' said Clara. 'Surely not.' The thought of it sent a cold shudder through her. She thought back to childhood, of the lines of men she had seen tramping the street. A troop train at Waterloo station. Two teachers at her school who had come to lessons red-eyed as the news went round that their fiancés had been killed.

'I'd bet on it,' said Leo sombrely. 'Only I'm not a betting man. And it's not a betting topic.'

'I've come round to your analysis, Leo. At the very least I said Hitler wants to carve up Europe the way he likes it, preferably with some colonies thrown in.'

'And they didn't agree?'

'Apparently not. They told the office back in London that they'd prefer someone more concerned with facts than trivialities.'

'So you know you're doing something right,' said Mary. 'We could do with a few more sceptical correspondents.'

'Perhaps. But sceptical correspondents are like giant pandas in Berlin. There aren't very many of us and we're disappearing fast.'

'*I'm* certainly not going anywhere,' said Mary. 'It's the most extraordinary time. Every journalist in Europe should want to be here. Things are changing day to day, it's almost too hard to keep up.'

'All the same,' said Rupert gloomily, 'the Nazis are making it harder for people like us. They have dossiers on every foreign journalist in Berlin.'

He turned to Leo. 'It's got worse since Putzi fixed up Hitler for an interview with Dorothy Thompson from the *Chicago Daily News*. She called Hitler an insignificant little man and said he was so dull you needed smelling salts to keep awake. That went down like a bucket of cold sauerkraut, as you can imagine.'

Mary Harker burst out laughing, but Clara noticed that Leo looked quickly over his shoulders.

'Are you still safe then, Rupert?' asked Clara.

'For a while, I reckon. They're still very sensitive about international opinion. They know if they chuck us out we can write just as effectively from elsewhere. They take their feelings out on the domestic press instead. Bully those in a position of weakness, that's their motto.'

'It's true,' added Mary. 'Last year *Vorwärts* ran a jokey piece about Goebbels, saying he had always ranted against high society yet now he was mingling with aristocrats and his wife was curtseying to princesses. The next day an SA man with a riding whip turned up at the offices and beat the editor to a pulp. None of the journalists dared intervene.'

Rupert turned to Clara. 'Tell us about this film then. It's a spy movie, you say?'

'Just a caper called *A Certain Mr Gran*. The hero is played by Hans Albers.'

'How exciting,' breathed Mary. 'He's damn good-looking, Hans Albers.'

'You'd better watch out,' said Rupert. 'It's a dangerous occupation, being the girl in an Ufa movie. The heroines tend to die. They commit suicide usually. They're careless with women, these Nazis.'

'Stop trying to scare the girl, Rupert!' Mary turned to Clara. 'At least you can count on good reviews.'

'How would you know that?'

'They've issued an edict. All film criticism is to be positive, no negative reviews. The Doktor is going to great lengths to ensure that only the films he likes become popular.'

'How on earth can he determine that?'

'Any way he can. Didn't you hear what happened at the launch of *All Quiet on the Western Front*? It was premiering at the Mozart cinema near my place on Nollendorfplatz. The Doktor hated it. He said it was an unpatriotic insult to the brave men who fell. So he arranged for sackfuls of live mice to be released into the cinema at the start of the movie, which prompted all the females to run screaming from the stalls.'

'And that's a guy who really knows how to make women run screaming,' laughed Rupert.

'Hitler and Goebbels are obsessed with the cinema, though, aren't they?' said Mary. 'You're always seeing them at premieres, surrounded by stars, or having all those glamorous women at their receptions. You'd think their wives would be jealous.'

'Have you seen most of the wives?' Rupert rolled his eyes. 'The Nazis don't believe wives should be glamorous. You know the phrase "Kinder, Küche, Kirche". The first calling of a woman is as a wife and mother.'

'Why don't those double standards surprise me?' said Mary.

Rupert picked up his hat.

'We have to be off, I'm afraid. Mahatma Propagandi is holding a press conference in the morning at his new ministry. Apparently we're to be treated to a daily newsreel before the event.'

'I met his wife the other day.'

Rupert stopped in his tracks.

'Did you? How?'

'I went to a cocktail party at her house.'

'A cocktail party with Magda Goebbels? What did you make of her?'

It was the first time anyone had asked Clara that, but she had been asking herself the same question for days. Given that the Nazis had at long last achieved the power they craved, Magda Goebbels, First Lady of the Reich and Hitler's favourite hostess, should be having the time of her life. Instead, she seemed tense and preoccupied, as though behind the dazzle of diamonds and pearls, a darkness lingered.

'I think she's miserable.'

'Married to the Doktor she has a lot to be miserable about,' said Mary. 'I wonder if she shares his views.'

'I don't doubt it,' said Leo. 'She's a fully paid-up Nazi. There was a big row last year when six National Socialists murdered a Communist down in Silesia. They woke him up in the night and beat him to death in front of his mother. They were all sentenced to death but the Frau Doktor told the wives and mothers of Germany it was a duty of humanity that they should be released. It worked.'

'So how was the cocktail party?' persisted Rupert.

'I didn't stay long,' Clara said noncommittally, taking a deep draw of her cigarette. She regretted mentioning it now.

'Well, well,' said Rupert, standing up and removing his hat in farewell. 'You really must tell me more next time. And remember, watch out for those movie heroines!'

There was an awkward silence after he and Mary left. Leo Quinn was fiddling with his glass and staring at the tabletop. Clara hesitated for a moment, wondering if she should stay or leave. She didn't want to go back to Frau Lehmann's now, especially since she had missed the evening meal, and the thought of hours in the cramped front parlour listening to the wireless, chatting to Herr Professor Hahn and watching Fräulein Viktor do her knitting was more that she could bear. Either that, or shivering in her bedroom, which was icy cold and smelt of mothballs. But nor was she bold enough to invite a comparative stranger out to supper. Eventually, she was about to say goodbye, when he looked up and said, 'Do you fancy a walk? It's still quite early.'

'All right.'

They walked out of the café and turned eastwards, towards Budapester Strasse. Rain had fallen. The black asphalt was striped with vivid bands of sodium, and the neon shop fronts turned the rain into blue and ruby puddles. In the far distance the pale beam of the Funkturm radio transmitter flooded the sky.

'You should have seen this place on the night of the torch-light procession,' said Leo. 'You could hardly take in how many people there were. Four hours it went on. People were hanging out of the windows of the Adlon. You could even see Hitler craning out of a window in the Reich Chancellery with the crowd below all chanting.'

'It must have been an amazing spectacle.'

'Spectacle is the right word for it. It's hard to explain how it felt. You sensed that you were there, and yet not there at the same time. As if you were watching something staged.'

It was, he had thought at the time, like the light and dark of a silent movie, with the torches and flames against the night sky and the spotlights passing through the Nazi banners, causing a stream of light to pour onto the upturned faces. Watching it provoked the curious sensation of seeing fantasy and reality collide.

'They burned the flag of the Weimar Republic and when the bands passed the French embassy on the Pariser Platz they actually stopped and played a new tune, "*Siegreich wollen wir Frankreich schlagen*"

'We will defeat France?'

'Yes, and they mean it.' He remembered the excitement of the mob in their brown shirts, surrounding the embassy with their arms outstretched and shouting. It was almost a religious ecstasy on those faces, as though salvation was at hand, along with a lot of less pleasant things like vengeance, and petty power.

'Do you really think there could be another war?' Clara asked. 'Surely it would never come to that.'

'I wouldn't be so sure.'

It felt strangely intimate, walking beside this man she had only just met, in the fresh evening air that smelt of mingled petrol and rain. There was something closed and impenetrable about him. In his dark suit and soft brimmed hat, with his hands in his pockets and his mackintosh flapping behind him, he reminded her somewhat of a medieval monk. She knew nothing about him, yet she felt close to him. Why should that be? Probably because it was the first time she had spoken English for days.

'There are so many things I love about Germany,' he said. 'Rilke, his wonderful poems. Do you know them?'

'Of course. *The Duino Elegies*. Or that lovely one, "Exposed on the Mountains of the Heart".' Clara laughed. 'I used to learn great long chunks of poetry as a child. Heaps of Tennyson and Shelley and Browning.'

'I like Browning. He's underrated.'

'You know "My Last Duchess"? The one about the evil Duke who murders his wife because he suspects her of having an affair? I adored that one. And I won the school prize reciting "Ozymandius".

"My name is Ozymandius, king of kings:
Look on my works ye Mighty, and despair!"

I still say it to myself when I'm about to go on stage. I know it's supposed to mean the opposite, but it's awfully good for stirring you up.'

They walked on for a while discussing poetry until they came to the Tiergarten, and followed one of the winding paths lit only by the occasional iron lamp. It was cold for the time of year, and their breath made spindly clouds in the icy air. Between the pools of light it was properly dark, and it was possible to imagine the deer and wild boar that were said to still roam out there in the trees. She thought for a second she could see their eyes glinting, but it was only the glow of cigarettes studding the distant spaces like fireflies against the inky grass.

'I wonder, Clara.' Leo bent to light a cigarette and snapped the lighter closed with a deft movement of his wrist. 'You mentioned that you had met Frau Goebbels. Without wanting to intrude, could I ask how you come to be attending Nazi cocktail parties?'

'I was invited by a man at the Ufa studio. Klaus Müller.'

He raised his eyebrows at this. 'Sturmhauptführer Müller? Goebbels' new aide?'

'That's him. He invited me to the cocktail party and then we had a drink at his apartment.' She felt suddenly defensive, as though she were being asked to account for herself. She shrugged. 'That's about it, though.'

'And did you like her? Frau Goebbels?'

'Not exactly. She's not the kind of person you'd warm to. Or ever really feel you'd know.'

'Might you see her again?'

'That's the funny thing. She's been asked to set up a bureau for German fashion and she wants me to get involved.'

'Why you? Do you know a lot about fashion?'

'Absolutely nothing. She said she wants actresses to do the modelling and she thought she'd start with me.'

She decided to omit Magda's comment about her husband. Leo didn't need to know that.

'She invited me to a tea party at the Adlon, to meet some of the other women involved. Goering's girlfriend was there. And Frau von Ribbentrop.'

Leo was silent for so long she guessed he must be horrified. Well, let him be, she thought. It was not as though she had any intention of spending any more time with Frau Goebbels.

Or Sturmhauptführer Müller. Leo obviously disapproved, or considered her frivolous or ignorant, but he didn't say anything so she added sharply, 'Not that I've any intention of getting involved.'

'Why not?'

'For a start, fashion modelling isn't my thing.'

He remained silent.

'More importantly, I dislike everything they stand for. I'm not one of those English girls who are fascinated by fascism. I don't get carried away at the sight of a man in uniform, especially not if it's a Nazi uniform.'

Leo seemed to be looking at her intently. Then he said, 'I wonder if you might do something for me. I would be very grateful if you would get involved. See Frau Goebbels every time you can. Listen to what she says, then come back and tell me.'

'What a strange request. Why?'

'I'd be very interested.'

'So you want me to keep seeing them for the sake of your curiosity?'

'Not just my curiosity.'

'It sounds like you're asking me to spy.'

'For Christ's sake!' Leo looked around swiftly, but there was no one nearby. A group of young men – students, they looked like – were up ahead laughing, and showing no sign of eavesdropping on a pair of visitors speaking English.

'Sorry. Just . . . speak more carefully, please, Clara. What I'm asking, what I mean is, the information could be useful.'

Something about the way he said it, made her burst out laughing. How melodramatic he was. 'Useful! What information? I haven't got any information. It was only very trivial chat.'

'What did you chat about?'

'First we talked about films, and then we talked about clothes.'

'I don't mind what it is. Anything. It doesn't matter if you think it's important. Just tell me.'

'Why should I?'

'As I said, I'd be grateful.'

'And who could Frau Goebbels' views on fashion possibly be useful to? Apart from her dressmaker?'

'To people at the embassy. And I give you my word it would go no further. '

Her face grew grave. 'At the embassy. Why? Why do they want to know?'

'It's politics really. We're trying to build up a picture of these people. The way they think, what they're like in private.'

'I can't imagine I'd be any help.'

'You'd be surprised. They harbour great hopes for increased friendship with the English. Last year, Winston Churchill and his wife were over here, hoping for a meeting with Hitler, only at the last moment Hitler ducked out of it. But it's certain to come up again and when it does, they'll need briefing.'

'You're telling me Mr Churchill would need to know the Nazis' views on fashion?' Clara said incredulously.

'Not only that. Anything could be important.'

'But why me?'

'They plainly don't suspect you. And . . .'

'And what?'

'And it helps that this Müller is friendly towards you.'

His green eyes held hers unblinkingly. Although it was dark, a flush crept up her neck as she began to divine what he was suggesting. He thought she was having a relationship with Klaus Müller. Images of herself making love with a Nazi official were playing through his mind.

'He has taken me for a drink. Once.'

'And back to his apartment.'

'Once.' Her voice was tight with indignation. 'Look, I'd better be going now. I'm in the opposite direction, I'm afraid. I'm going to look for a cab.' She pulled her coat more tightly around her, as the rain flicked into her face.

'I'm sorry, Leo. But the fact is, I'd already decided. I don't want to see these people again so whatever it is you want me to do, I can't do it.'

He looked down at her, frustration and annoyance warring in his eyes. For a second his expression made her shiver.

'Let me give you my address. Just in case.'

He threw away his cigarette and bent his head in the darkness to write an address in a notebook. As he did so there was the faintest rustle and scurry in the darkness.

He froze and laid a warning hand on her arm. 'Quiet!'

As they peered into the gloom they saw a figure had dashed out and taken the still glowing cigarette butt from where it fell. Leo laughed, a short, joyless laugh.

'Sorry. Sharp ears everywhere these days.'

He tore off the paper from his notebook, gave it to her, and held her hand briefly.

'Here. Take this. And think about it. Seriously, please.'

Chapter Seventeen

The rain had come on again but Leo decided to walk all the way home to punish himself. He pulled up his collar yet the stinging rain still drenched him and the cold air flayed his face. However warmly he dressed, the freezing Berlin wind still took him by surprise. The English expected their weather to be soft. In weather, as in other things, they disliked extremes. He plunged his hands in his pockets and carried on.

At the end of the Tiergarten he crossed the Platz der Republik and passed the blackened hulk of the Reichstag. It had been more than a fortnight since the fire and the embers were cold now, piles of rubble and masonry shifted into the street. For days passers-by had had to navigate charred planks of wood and sooty bricks, with many of them stopping to stare at the crumbling parts of the stately old building and reflect on everything its destruction stood for. Which was the devastating fires of Marxism, if you thought along National Socialist lines, but for most people, the home of democratic parliament standing in ruins meant something far more ominous.

Leo had been in a bar that night, not far away, eating a pile of noodles with the first of several beers at his side. Alerted by the clanging of the fire engines, he had run out into the street with the rest of the clientele to see the red glow in the west and plumes of smoke coil into the night sky.

The fire had started around a quarter to ten that evening, in five different corners of the assembly hall, where cloths soaked in petrol had been placed at the oak panelling. The glass cupola glowed scarlet and the flames funnelled up it until it burst and crashed to the ground. It was only minutes before two black Mercedes screeched into view, passed through the police cordon and Hitler could be seen running up the steps, two at a time, closely followed by Goebbels and his bodyguard.

Once Hitler had entered the smoking hulk, he stood at a little balcony in the hall, laid his arms on the stone balustrade and peered down into the flames. His voice rising to an uncontrollable screech, he announced, 'There will be no mercy now. Anyone who stands in our way will be cut down. The German people will not tolerate leniency. Every Communist official will be shot where he is found.' If it was proved to be the work of Communists, he would round up the murderous pests with an iron fist. The bit about being "proved" was plainly superfluous, because the same night hundreds of Communists were dragged from their beds, given a beating in the local SA cellars, followed by interrogation, imprisonment, and in many cases a bullet in the back of the head.

In the days that followed, even though a young Dutch Communist was quickly apprehended and charged with setting the fire, the reprisals carried on regardless. Squads of Brown Shirts in trucks raged through the Communist districts enacting mass arrests, smashing windows and raiding businesses. Swingeing new measures against personal liberty followed. The German Communist party, the KPD, was banned, and hundreds of people crossed the Swiss border into exile. The result of this fresh fear of Bolshevist terror meant a surge in the Nazi vote in the March 5 elections, since when the euphoria of the Nazis had known no bounds.

Tonight, though, the rubble heaps were being shifted. Labourers had been brought in with spades and shovels, and neither the late hour nor the rain was going to stop them. Hitler had acted swiftly. First thing tomorrow he was to re-open the Reichstag in Potsdam. The old President had been dragged along in his dotage to provide a fig-leaf of respectability for the dismantling of democracy. Deputies would no doubt have to pass through a cordon of SA men and the mandatory cheering crowd. The Day of Potsdam would symbolise the continuity between the Third Reich, Prussia and the German empire. In the evening Hitler and his friends would return to Berlin for a performance of *Die Meistersinger von Nurnberg* at the State Opera. It made sense that the National Socialists loved opera. Presumably it was the only art form loud enough to drown out the shouts of protest on the streets outside.

Leo waited as a lorry bristling with SA men and banners passed, and it was only when he had crossed Pariser Platz and headed up Unter den Linden that he at last let his mind turn to the matter that was troubling him. Not so much troubling him as clanging through his head like a klaxon in a frenzy of alarm and recrimination. Clara.

A young British woman in social contact with the new regime. It was exactly the thing Horace Rumbold had asked him to look out for. Her story of the meeting with Frau Goebbels had amazed him and at the same time seized his imagination. What astonishing access she had. Listening to their conversations, their complaints and their confidences. Entry to social circles that would be closed to almost every foreigner. And a woman on her own, out of contact with her family back in England. After what Rumbold had asked him, he would have been irresponsible if he'd passed up an opportunity like that.

And yet . . . he had fumbled it. He had been crazily, disastrously, unprofessionally reckless. On the slightest acquaintance he had been guilty of the most extraordinary clumsiness and broken the first rule of intelligence work. Not to trust anyone. And the second rule, not to give away too much information. And all sorts of rules down to about the tenth, which had to be not to alienate a potential source. The memory of Clara's pretty, dark-eyed face staring at him with shock and a certain amount of disdain, rose lividly in his mind.

His first instinct had been simply to befriend her. When he asked her for a walk, he had been thinking that a stroll might allow the gossip to flow more naturally. A young Englishwoman alone in a foreign city would probably be glad of some company. If he was honest with himself, he had found her attractive. She had fine, delicate features, and a petulant fullness to her lips that hinted at sensuousness. Her enquiring, intelligent eyes, coupled with a sense of reserve, brought to mind the perennial lover's question, 'What are you thinking?' All these impressions had passed through his mind as she sat before him in the café wondering whether to stay or go.

And then he had to come right out with it and ask her! Something about the intimacy of the evening, the soft, enclosing trees of the Tiergarten, the tenebrous darkness speckled with the pinprick of cigarettes, had provoked his rash confidence. Or perhaps it was the girl herself, all that talk of poetry, or a sudden, unexpected shaft of homesickness. Since he arrived in Germany Leo hadn't spoken about England much, except in a professional capacity, with people at the consulate. And despite the reserve, she seemed the kind of girl who was easy to confide in. He could have kept on walking with her all night. He still held the memory of her handclasp in his, cold and surprisingly soft.

And now he risked compromising the entire operation. He had behaved like a madman. Heaven knew who she would run and tell. Perhaps even Sturmhauptführer Müller, God forbid. He should never have alluded to her acquaintance with Müller. She was outraged and annoyed, as she had every right to be.

There was another, more agonizing, concern. He had placed the girl herself at risk. If she talked to anyone about his proposal, there was no telling what dangers she was getting herself into. Would she understand how vital it was to say nothing?

He cursed himself and lit another cigarette. It wasn't as if he hadn't enough work to get on with at the consulate.

He had reached the end of Orianenburger Strasse when he heard the shouts and a sparkling shower of glass spilled across the pavement in front of him. It was Zimmerman's, the place he bought his morning paper and tobacco. He liked going into that shop. It was stacked like a tightly packed suitcase, with every surface filled, shelves piled high with tins and the whole place smelling of sugar and newsprint and a deep musty scent of polished wood. Its owner, Herr Zimmerman, was a dapper little man in his sixties with a moustache and a pipe, who liked to ask Leo about English football. He had relatives in north London and he claimed to support Arsenal.

As Leo approached, a pair of Brown Shirts crashed out. They had been drinking – he could smell the beer on their breath from where he stood – and they were cursing the shopkeeper for being a filthy Jew. Herr Zimmerman, though he was half the size of the men, had taken one by the arm and hustled him to the door. His friend had picked a stone from the gutter and broken his window for his pains. Now jagged teeth of glass surrounded a gaping hole.

'Count yourself lucky that's all we broke!'

They sprinted off up the street, and Leo fought a powerful urge to give chase. The second man was fat and ran slowly with splayed feet. His lumbering backside reminded Leo of a boy at school who was routinely and universally bullied, and in turn bullied those smaller than himself. Leo could easily overtake him, probably call the cops on him, yet he resisted the idea. For one, he had already caused enough problems for himself tonight. A punch-up with a Brown Shirt and a night in the cells at the Alex were more than he needed. And the sense of inertia that was seeping through the entire population of Berlin was starting to have a paralysing effect on him.

In normal times, when people witnessed a crime, they called the police. Now people knew better. They would avoid the huddled body in the gutter. They slept through shrieks in the night, and the sounds of car engines and door slamming that meant their neighbour was being arrested. It was as though the Nazis were conducting an experiment on the entire populace, hoping with small and regular acts of violence to inoculate them, and as a result, they were all becoming immune.

Herr Zimmerman had already armed himself with a broom and was sweeping the scattered glass. The window was not so bad. He could patch it with cardboard, no trouble. Leo noticed spots of blood on his white shirt, but there was no sign that he was hurt. Herr Zimmerman looked up from the pavement and gave Leo a quiet, despairing smile with a hint of a shrug. As though he was aware of the catastrophe that was coming towards them all in slow motion.

Chapter Eighteen

As it turned out, there was a whole week to kill before the read-through for the new film. Lamprecht needed to edit rushes of his last movie, so Clara passed the time like a tourist, walking through the Englischer Garten in the Tiergarten, gazing at the Brandenburger Tor with the Goddess of Victory lashing her stone horses to war, visiting churches and galleries and roaming round the city, going to cafes and eating sugary cakes swathed in cream.

Sitting in Kranzler's in the early morning sunlight, sipping her coffee, she took out a postcard for Angela, and wrote in the blandest possible tone, saying she was having a glorious time at Babelsberg and would be in contact soon. What she had told Rupert about her family's independence was true. Without their mother, she, Kenneth and Angela led quite separate lives and their father, who had never been very communicative at the best of times, found it almost impossible to stray beyond formalities.

Poor Daddy. At a distance his intemperate curtness became possible to explain. He was a widower, robbed far too early of the wife he had loved and he was cursed with more than the usual allocation of an Englishman's emotional reserve. Thinking about it like that, Clara was almost able to feel sorry for him.

She also forced herself to write to Dennis, telling him she had been offered work in Germany and was not expecting to be back for some time. It had been cowardly of her to leave without explaining, she knew, but she also knew the biggest blow would have been to his pride, rather than his heart. How could she tell him that he was the reason she came to Berlin or that she had wanted to feel closer to her mother, who had died almost a decade ago? Dennis wouldn't understand and it wouldn't be kind.

Thinking about Dennis brought into her mind again the question she generally tried to suppress. Why had she never met a man she wanted to marry? At twenty-six most of her school friends were married or engaged. Only Dennis, who had not so much proposed as announced his intentions to a general audience, had ever seriously suggested marriage to Clara. Normally she didn't let it bother her. She had no shortage of male admirers after all. But yet again she wondered if it was something in herself, some deep inhibition, that deterred true intimacy. Was she too choosy, or was it simply that she had never yet met a man she could imagine spending years talking to?

She left no address and dropped both cards in a postbox before she could change her mind.

Strolling round the city, she found it impossible not to notice how Berlin was changing, even in the short time she had been here. Leaflets and pamphlets fluttered from every railing. Political posters framed harsh warnings in the dense German Gothic script that looked like a thicket of thorns. It was not just Nazi propaganda either. On the sun-warmed seat beside her at the Café Kranzler Clara had noticed the fluttering pages of a pamphlet and, picking it up curiously, found inside a cartoon of a goose-stepping Nazi and the legend "Fight Hitler for our Future". Underneath was the strapline of the KPD, the German Communist Party. She looked at it for a moment, before quickly putting it down again and pushing the seat under the table.

She remembered what Rupert Allingham had said about war, and how Hitler wanted to carve up Europe. She thought of the map they had at home, the countries beautifully marked out, the shape of England like Britannia, the upright old dame, France, vast and sprawling, Italy poking into the sea like a lady's boot, Poland, Germany, Czechoslovakia. Other places in Middle Europe you hadn't even heard of, towns jagged with consonants, villages with names like anagrams. Then she imagined a great pair of scissors cutting the whole thing up and reassembling it like a giant jigsaw. Except war wasn't neat like that. War was about deaths, hundreds and thousands of deaths.

Her encounter with Leo Quinn troubled her. What he had asked, though it had surprised her, was not such a great request. It wouldn't be hard for her to comply. She knew she had acted rudely, rushing off into the night like that. She regretted it almost immediately. It was his mention of Müller, and the implication that she might be having an affair with him, that had caused her to react so angrily. If it hadn't been for that, she might very well have agreed with his proposal. But then she wouldn't be seeing much of Frau Goebbels any more, so there wouldn't be any need for it, would there?

That morning she was planning to visit the Kaufhaus des Westens. When she had first passed the KaDeWe store a few weeks ago, she had pushed through the brass doors and marvelled at the racks of hats and gloves and handbags on display, the gleaming escalators that rose to the upper floors. Exotic perfumes hung and mingled in the air and beautiful assistants stood behind the counters, their countenances as creamy and impassive as Japanese geishas while grim-faced housewives with fur-collared coats and cloche hats rammed on their heads fingered the lingerie and picked over the fashions. Clara had been longing to return for a leisurely morning's shopping. But when she approached that day, a quite unexpected sight awaited her.

A clatter of trucks and shouting from further along the street heralded a series of lorries containing a detachment of Brown Shirts who jumped out brandishing paint pots, intent on despoiling the windows and doors of the store. A large caricature of a Jew with a gigantic nose had been painted on one window and thick streaks of paint were dripping down others as the men laboriously spelt out slogans saying "Drop Dead Jew", "Danger to Life", "Jews to Palestine". Mostly it was spelled correctly. Some passers-by stopped and smiled, others gawped, but most continued with their heads down, mentally abandoning any plans for Saturday morning shopping. They seemed to melt into each other, a vista of turned backs and cold shoulders, undulating away from the trouble.

The storm troop commander, a tall, blond man with a leather crop that he kept swatting on his own calves, was supervising the hanging of a banner between two lampposts reading "The Jew Is Our Enemy". Clara stopped to watch as he strutted along, the whip switching impatiently against his polished boots, with a smile as thin and vicious as barbed wire. He must be in his twenties, no older than her own brother, with rosy cheeks and flaxen hair that conformed precisely to the Aryan archetype and eyes as narrow as shards of ice. Until recently he might have been a country boy, with only farm animals on which to exercise his whip, but now, in his smart uniform with the silver shoulder cord glinting in the sun, he looked like a man who had found his vocation. A poster boy for the Sturmabteilung.

At that moment a shop manager emerged from the department store and began to remonstrate with him. He was a fat little man in a three-piece suit and a scarlet spotted handkerchief blooming flamboyantly from his breast pocket. He spread his small hands in a pleading, conciliatory gesture and cocked his head to one side, like the maître d' of a restaurant explaining why the fish would not after all be available that evening, but perhaps sir would enjoy the chicken instead. He kept gesturing to the storm troopers who were desecrating his shop, as if suggesting they be directed to paint their messages a little more tidily, or perhaps confine their efforts to a single door, rather than slapping the paint all over his windows which would be such an effort to remove once their perfectly justified demonstration was finished. The commander towered over him, head cocked and smile still fluttering on his lips as though politely considering his petition, until in a sudden movement he lifted his crop and lashed it down the side of the manager's head.

'I do not take lessons from Jewish vermin!'

The man staggered to one side. Blood was already beginning to seep from a savage stripe on his cheek. His eyes widened, as if more in astonishment than pain at the commander's swiftly executed stroke. Clara, rooted to the spot, felt an involuntary gasp of shock escape her, at which the commander looked round.

His pale blue eyes passed over her Jaeger coat, the chestnut hair tucked beneath her navy felt hat and the shopping bag hanging from her arm, as if he was assessing whether she, too, should be subjected to his whip. She returned his stare and a shudder of something she had never felt before, sheer hatred, went through her like a knife. The emotion rose up in her so that her head was pounding, and the blood rushed in her ears. It took all her effort not to reach forward and snatch the whip from him and bring it down on his own head. What must it feel like to depend on this man's tender mercies? To be beaten like a dog? She really couldn't imagine.

Without taking her eyes off him, she stepped forward past the manager, who had propped himself up against the window and was holding his handkerchief against the side of his face in a stupor, and made for the great brass door.

By now the entrance was obstructed by five storm troopers with huge placards hung round their necks. The one nearest her, a bear of a man with a dull, angry look in his eye, had a sign saying, "Germans defend yourselves, don't buy from Jews". As she tried to pass him he moved to block her way. He was so close she could smell the stink of sweat on his shirt and the buckle of his belt dug into her side. She dodged and he moved again, leaning against her so that she was pressed against the shop door.

'*Ausländerin!*'

She had not used the "foreigner" explanation before, but it worked. He did a double take and shifted slightly, just enough for her to slip past and enter the shop.

The store was thinly populated, and the assistants seemed more formal, and distant than usual, as if embarrassed. Clara's heart was pounding against her ribs and she had lost any appetite for shopping, but almost at random she chose a beret in cherry red and smiled at the salesman who stood behind the till. He served her with the barest of courtesies, without meeting her eye. His face was rigid with a kind of extreme self-restraint, as though every fibre of his being was straining to step outside and order the hooligans away. She noticed that he was wearing a row of medals, and when she looked around she saw that several other staff had medals pinned to their clothes.

'Can I ask what medal that is?'

'This is the Iron Cross.' Her question seemed to have animated him and he met her eye. 'First Class. Herr Hitler holds the second class, I think. And Frau Mann here,' he gestured to a stout woman behind the till with terror in her eyes, 'wears the Emperor's Service Cross and the Cross of Honour for being a soldier's widow. She received it from Hindenburg himself.'

Clara was still shaking when she left the shop and boarded a tram. As it proceeded onto the Ku'damm she stared out at the smart stores and the Saturday morning shoppers without seeing them. She felt a sudden sharp longing for Swan & Edgar in Piccadilly, where she would be taken by her mother as a child to buy school uniform, followed by tea and Fuller's walnut cake in Lyons on the Strand. It was the first time since she had been in Berlin that she felt any kind of nostalgia for London. She thought of the Thames moving slowly beneath the morning light, wet leaves gleaming beneath the lamp-posts on the embankment, and the comforting smell of oil and damp clothing on a red bus. And how unthinkable it would be to find a banner saying "The Jew Is Our Enemy" draped across Oxford Street.

When she got back to Frau Lehmann's there was a letter waiting for her propped up on the hall table. For a wild moment she imagined that her father had managed to track her down, but on closer inspection she saw the envelope bore a Hamburg postmark.

"Dear cousin Clara, what a surprise to hear from you after all this time!"

It was Hans Neumann, the son of her uncle Ernst and the cousin she had never met. She took the letter up to her room and read it on the bed, with her legs curled up on the green eiderdown beneath her. Hans, it emerged, was working as a teacher at a *Gymnasium* in Hamburg. He enclosed a photograph of himself surrounded by three grinning children and a pudgy wife, and went into a schoolmasterly amount of detail about the achievements of his gifted offspring, who seemed to play enough instruments to staff an orchestra on their own. There were pages and pages of it, in his meticulous, spidery scrawl. "My wife Lieselotte was the daughter of the mathematics master in my first teaching post! . . . Ute, Franz and Jacob have been selected to perform in the city's foremost string quartet. Ute has also competed for the school in athletics." If Clara cared to come to Hamburg he would be delighted to put her up and give her a guided tour of the city. She made a mental note to postpone that visit indefinitely. It wasn't until the end of the letter that he came to the part she had asked about.

"Our grandparents, you must know, longed to see more of you. They were a lovely couple and it must have been very sad for you not to see them as you grew up. It was your father, I understand, who was reluctant. They always suspected he disliked the fact that our grandmother was a Jew . . ."

Clara almost dropped the letter right there. She tried reading on but it was hard to focus on the rest of Hans's news with that short, spiky little word banging through her mind. A Jew. She read it back, incredulously. Grandmother Hannah! Why had she never known? She thought of the Jewish girls she had known at school, who held mysterious Friday evening dinners with their family and were excused hymn-singing and Religious Studies; their mothers, who wore sable stoles and too much jewellery. She pictured the men she had seen in the east of Berlin with their flapping black coats and yellowed faces, and the shopkeeper that morning wearing his iron cross. Then she thought of her tiny, smiley grandmother with her high-collared blouse, black hair polished to a shine, the slow accented voice rich and dark as bitter chocolate. How she had carried a little box of sweets in her bag, to be smuggled to the children, confidentially. A Jew.

A Jew in a country that hated Jews. Those banners in the street, that Brown Shirt with his riding crop, the filthy slogans daubed on the walls. Klaus Müller's disdainful laugh. Until now, all that had nothing to do with her. Only now, she saw, it did.

"It's in the blood."

That was what her father had said when he saw her honeyed complexion turn brown on the beach. Jewish blood must be what he had meant. Yet Hellene Neumann had carried her inheritance in silence. She had loved to tell the children about her German childhood, but that part of her story had stayed unspoken. Clara did not need to wonder what power her father had to enforce that silence. Her mother had always been subservient to his whims, always anxious to keep the peace. Smoothing over arguments, quieting the children's squabbles. It was a tendency Clara had detested, resolving that it would be different for her.

She stood up and looked at herself in the mirror, and felt a new identity emerge from its silvered surface, gradually sharpening like a grainy photograph in a developing tray, gathering nuance and perspective. She was no different from the person she had been that morning, and at the same time she was entirely changed. She had come to Germany to feel closer to her mother; in the process she was learning more about herself than she could ever have imagined. It was from

Grandmother Hannah that she inherited her cheekbones, her watchful eyes and her sharp, defiant chin. Perhaps, too, her inclination to perform. Yet no one had mentioned that Clara's inheritance did not stop there. She thought again of her mother's adamant objection when she first mentioned wanting to go on the stage.

"Acting is not the kind of thing I'd want a daughter of mine to do."

She should know. She had been acting for half her life.

Chapter Nineteen

When she walked up from the station at Neu-Babelsberg the following Monday Clara noticed immediately that changes were taking place. The squat red-brick building opposite the main entrance was being renovated. Granite door posts and pseudo-medieval porch lights had been fixed to the frontage. Outside, a van was parked and chairs, tables and filing cabinets were being carried in. A white BMW sports convertible was parked next to it.

'What's happening?' Clara asked Becker.

'The minister is setting up an office here. He wants to keep a close eye on everything.' He checked her pass, even though he knew her by sight now, and nodded her through with a wink. 'There are a few things the Doktor likes to keep an especially close eye on.'

Normally, the studio complex was a mass of people, passing busily through the corridors into studios and dressing rooms. Today, the place seemed unnaturally quiet. People were moving tight-faced down the corridors, with briefcases and arms full of scripts. A couple of well-known actors who would normally take the gaze of others' as their due, hurried past, heads down, as if loath to draw attention to themselves.

Albert had a new office up on the fifth floor, with a sofa and a bigger picture window giving on to the great hall. Clara found Helga lounging there, riffling through *Filmwoche*. She looked up and smiled broadly, waving a whisky tumbler. Something about the flush on her cheeks suggested it was not her first drink of the day.

'Good news! We're celebrating. I've got a part! There's a new movie called *Barcarole*, using that Czech girl Lida Baarová. Oh, come on,' she said as Clara looked blank, 'you must have heard of her?'

'Is she the one whose photograph has just gone up in the foyer?' The girl looked very young, with serene, classical features.

'That's her. Anyway, she's to play next to Gustav Fröhlich. I've got a massive crush on him. And I'm to play a beautiful temptress.'

Throughout this Clara noticed that Albert was sitting at his desk, with his head in his hands.

'Albert, is something happening?'

'Oh, that,' said Helga. 'Yes, there is some other news.'

'He's finally done it.' Albert picked up a memo and read aloud. ' "As a result of the national revolution now taking place, it is now Ufa policy to terminate contracts with Jewish employees".'

He looked up. 'They're going through the place right now. They're going from set to set and announcing that those who don't have pure Aryan blood must leave the studio immediately.'

'Everyone's saluting like crazy,' said Helga, flapping her arm upwards in mimicry of a Nazi salute. 'Don't they just remind you of seals at the zoo?'

'Most people with any sense have left already. Erik Charell is going. Erich Pommer is already gone.'

'Erich Pommer?' Clara thought of the formidable producer of *The Blue Angel*, *Metropolis* and most of Ufa's greatest hits. 'Surely not?'

'He's had his contract rescinded and he's headed for England, apparently. He'll survive. He can work anywhere. But that's only the beginning. There's to be a new Reichsfilmkammer headed by You Know Who which will control everything to do with the film industry. There's a lot of people today tidying their desks.'

'And leaving their offices,' said Helga. 'Which is how Albert came by this one.'

Albert gave a tiny shudder.

'The good news is,' said Helga, tossing her head, 'Ufa's going to be producing more patriotic films. Featuring healthy Aryan actresses.'

'They like good hips and blonde hair. Perhaps you should think of having yours dyed, Helga,' said Albert acidly.

'Nonsense.' She ran a hand through her hair. 'I'm not a Jew, thank God. And, besides, they love brunettes too.'

Clara felt a creeping horror. 'Isn't anyone going to protest? Are you all going to stand by and watch everyone get fired?'

'Protest! Are you mad? You think we want to end up in Prinz Albrecht Strasse too?' Prinz Albrecht Strasse 8, a formidable barracks of a building on the border of Mitte and Kreuzberg, was being taken over by Goering for the headquarters of the Gestapo. 'Besides,' she added testily. 'if you're a baker and you don't like the government, you don't stop baking bread. Why should actresses stop acting? You're not Jewish, are you? You don't need to worry.'

Despite the alarm coursing through her, Clara remained impassive. Not a flicker of fear, she knew, appeared on her face. For once she was glad of her deep-rooted instinct to repress her emotions, to bury her secrets deep within her and affect a composure she didn't feel.

'Bauer told me a joke,' continued Helga. 'He said that before the Nazis, an actress's career depended on her favours to Jewish playwrights. The good thing is, that's no longer the case. The bad thing is, it's the Nazis' turn now.'

'And you laughed, I suppose,' said Albert glumly.

'Of course I did. I laugh at all his jokes. Walter might be a monster but at least he's an ordinary monster with ordinary tastes. If you know what I mean. Some of the others are far worse. Someone was telling me Geli Raubel said you wouldn't believe what Hitler made her do. That kind of thing is too obscene for the filthiest nightclub in Berlin, let alone with your niece! No wonder she did herself in.'

'Geli Raubel,' Albert explained to Clara shortly, 'shot herself in Hitler's apartment two years ago. Apparently he keeps a portrait of her beside his bed.'

'And they say he once beat his dog to impress a girl.'

'This is hearsay,' Albert mumbled.

'But he rather likes being beaten himself.'

'Helga!'

'As for that Emmy Sonnemann. I feel sorry for her with Goering on top of her. He must weigh a hundred and twenty kilos. He does love his Currywurst.'

'For God's sake, Helga!' Albert sprang to his feet. The colour had bled from his face and his starved figure seemed to be trembling. 'What's wrong with you today? You're a terrible one for gossip. You should be careful what you say.'

'Oh, who cares?' Helga's delight at the prospect of work had caused her to throw caution to the winds. 'The Nazis are no better than anyone else. What about Herr Ley? Didn't he make all his money selling contraceptives? He must know a thing or two about decadent desires.'

Albert advanced, as if physically to silence her.

'Oh stop it Albert. I'm only having a joke! Perhaps you should concentrate on getting yourself a girlfriend before people start to talk.'

Albert threw her a shocked look but didn't answer. Clara stepped forward.

'Albert's right. You could be overheard.'

'So what? Who's going to inform on the girlfriend of one of Doktor Geobbels' most important aides?'

She kicked up her leg, expensively clad in new stockings. '*Bleyle Strumpfhose!* The special ones that never run!'

'A present, were they?' said Albert sourly.

'Don't ask me questions, I won't tell lies,' she said, happily.

The white of Clara's knuckles gripping the handle of her bag was the only outward evidence of her apprehension. She turned to Albert.

'There is just one thing. You said all foreigners were to be banned. That has to include me.'

'I think, said Albert, 'you'll find you are exempt from this particular ban.'

'Why? I'm half-English, after all.'

'How do you think you got the job?' laughed Helga.

'What do you mean?' Clara looked over at Albert, who glanced away defensively, but not before she had caught his eye.

He sighed. 'Herr Lamprecht had a call, from Klaus Müller. He was left in no doubt that a part for you would be a good idea.'

'Klaus Müller?' she said, but Albert's face was rigid and he jumped to his feet. He was staring behind her at the door.

'Did I hear my name?'

'Herr Doktor,' stammered Albert.

Clara turned to see the figure of Müller, wearing a dove grey herringbone suit, navy tie and the habitual slight smirk on his face. He was carrying an armload of files and a couple of aides hovered behind him. Müller, she realized in a flash, was here to dismiss people.

'What good luck, Fräulein. I was hoping I might run into you. Perhaps you'd like a lift back to town later?'

Gerhard Lamprecht had been a matinée idol once, and his good looks, well-cut three-piece suits and status as Ufa's star director meant his face featured in the film magazines as much as any leading man. But the events of the past few days had aged him ten years. Ashen, chain-smoking and raking his hands constantly through lanky hair, he ushered Clara to a corner of his cluttered office, cracked open a fresh packet of cigarettes and proceeded to interview her as though the idea of his next movie was about as pressing as a trip to darkest Africa. Every time someone passed he jumped, and didn't relax until he had escorted Clara down to the Great Hall and they were standing in the deep shadow of the set.

He confirmed what Albert had told her. The part he had in mind for Clara was the English version of Alicia, the role played by Karin Hardt, an exquisite blonde.

'Won't there be a problem? I mean, we look nothing like each other. I'm much darker than Karin.'

Lamprecht waved his hand. 'This is cinema, my dear. Illusion is our business. In fact illusion, you might say, is all we have to offer right now. Given that we are able to persuade people that black is white, we ought to have no difficulty persuading people that blonde is brunette.' He gave a phlegmy laugh, which turned into a cough, then recovered himself.

'All the same, we should be able to furnish you with a wig.'

Clara was given a script and asked to learn the first few pages, which she would rehearse with Hans Albers, the actor scheduled to play the lead. She had seen Albers' face beaming out of a hundred posters, and knew he was one of the studio's biggest stars, but it wasn't that which proved the problem.

The film was set in Italy, so an entire reproduction of Venice had been built with lavishly painted flats depicting canals and gondolas and the gilded interior of the Danieli Hotel. Standing on set, surrounded by the rigs and cranes and cameras, Clara swiftly discovered that acting for the camera was an entirely different art from that she had learned in the theatre. When she projected her voice, Lamprecht assumed a pained expression as though she was hurting his ears.

'You're declaiming, my dear. Try talking.'

She started again, but he interrupted almost immediately.

'Less is more, remember.'

After her third attempt, he took her by the arm.

'Don't talk too loudly. Remember, no one needs to hear you at the back of the circle. There is no circle. On film, everyone's in the front row of the stalls.'

The scene required Clara to walk across the marble floor towards Hans Albers, and confront him. She was supposed to sway seductively but each time she attempted it, Lamprecht would spring out from behind the camera and ask her to repeat it. She found it impossible to ignore the black-hooded eye of the camera inches from her face. Nerves made her moves heavy and deliberate. Her gait became more exaggerated, her limbs turned to lead, and although Hans Albers squeezed as much encouragement as he could into his few lines, she was not so much swaying seductively as stumbling across the stage like a pantomime horse.

Eventually the director drew her aside.

'I'm sorry, Herr Lamprecht. I've never acted in front of a camera, you see.'

'Take your time. It's a question of adaptation. When you do your first film you have to learn a whole new way of acting. I've seen hundreds of theatre actresses who have this problem. They all learn to overcome it.'

'But how exactly?' Her voice trembled with frustration.

Lamprecht leaned against the rig, and looked down at her. 'Well, now. Do you want to know what I tell them?' His face melted into a slow film star smile, a legacy of his heart throb days. 'I tell them, think of the camera as your lover.' He sucked at his cigarette held between finger and thumb and regarded her thoughtfully. 'You understand? The camera studies your face very closely. It sees your slightest expression. It understands each tiny nuance. Every little frown. You can break a heart with the bat of an eyelid. You can destroy a man with the merest flicker of your lovely face. When you act in the theatre, you need to be seen as well as heard at the back of the circle, but film is not like that. Film is intimate. When a thought crosses your face, it should be like the wind on the water. Just a ripple and pouf . . .' he waved the cigarette lightly, 'That is enough.'

'I'll try.'

His face creased kindly. 'And don't apologize, my dear. I can see you have talent, and besides, on a day like today, we're all learning new ways to play things.'

So in the dazzling limelight of the set Clara tried to keep her expressions precise and controlled, to subdue her responses until she had complete mastery of them. She managed to ignore the huge cameras that slid in and out of the shadows around her and the microphones that hung above her head. The effort of it was so absorbing, it was simply impossible to think of anything else. After an hour, Lamprecht declared the audition a success. She was issued with a script and told she would be called for fittings and rehearsals the following week.

Müller was waiting for her in the lobby. His cheeks were shadowed with stubble, suggesting that he had been working flat out, but he seemed energised by it, and exuded an air of suppressed excitement. He was in high good humour as he ushered her into the front passenger seat of the car.

'Is it true that you organized the part for me?'

He pulled the BMW out of the main gate and fell behind a large convoy of trucks carrying construction workers off to build the autobahn. Bands of men armed with picks on the sides of the road were an increasingly frequent sight these days. Müller gestured to them with a grin.

'We National Socialists are committed to reducing unemployment. Unemployed construction workers first, then unemployed actresses.'

'Then I suppose I should thank you.'

He raised an eyebrow. 'I'm sure you'll think of a way.'

He pulled her towards him on the seat and reached his arm round her shoulder, lightly brushing her breast. There was no longer any ambiguity in Müller's intentions towards her, Clara realized. It seemed clear that he thought it was only a matter of time before she succumbed to his advances. She pulled away.

'So you're in charge of making sure that Jews leave the studios?'

'That's not the summit of my responsibilities, I hope. But if you want to put it like that.'

'Don't you realize what impression of National Socialism this will make? Don't you think this will make enemies abroad? In England, for example?'

'But we have many friends in England.'

'Like who?'

He looked across to her, and she saw a flicker of bafflement in his face.

'I would have thought it was obvious.'

'Well, it's not.'

'Your father, most particularly, has been a great help to us. Surely you knew?'

'My father?' Her voice faltered.

'Your father, *meine Fräulein*, has been instrumental in advancing the fascist cause in England. Our relationship could not be warmer.'

'But my father doesn't know . . .'

'What doesn't he know? He has known von Ribbentrop for many years. As I understand it, von Ribbentrop visited your family home. You probably met him.'

'I . . . I don't think so.'

Yet even as he spoke, it became as clear as day. An individual moment, entirely disconnected yet resonant, like music. Frozen in her mind, but at the same time floating free of all context.

It was the smell she remembered first, of leaves and her own hot skin. Herself lying, slightly awkwardly, in the boughs of an apple tree, braced in the crook of its branches, with the reddening fruit all around her. Her plimsolls were frayed and grubby and a bee lurched drunkenly towards her, as though the air was too thick with heat to fly. There was a smell of mown grass and distantly, the scent of damp vaporizing from the recently watered rosebeds. Across the lawn Angela was sitting in the shade of the huge ilex tree. Her brother was on the swing and she could hear the bark of her sister's laugh, falsely grown-up, like the high, imperious cry of a peacock.

Above the lawn was their house, wide and low-set in warm brick with yellow, mullioned windows. Her parents were making their way down the steps of the terrace and towards them. Her mother was wearing a white dress printed with roses, and Clara thought that her lipsticked mouth looked like a rose too, blooming in her powdered face. It was her mother's last proper summer but no one knew it then; the shadow inside her had not yet darkened their lives.

With them was a tall man with a weak chin and a jolly face. He was wearing a white linen suit, but he still looked hot. As he came nearer Clara discerned little beads of sweat forming on his forehead. She began, as was her habit, to imagine life for him. He was a toymaker with a shop full of wooden puppets. He was a baker, who crafted fat chocolate éclairs. Reluctantly, she swung her feet around and dropped out of the tree vertically, silent as an arrow, like the savage she was half-imagining herself to be. She waded through the long grass and approached her father.

'And this is my younger daughter, Clara.'

It turned out that the man was German. One of her father's political friends. He was visiting England, and he admired it very much. He spoke to her in German, as though he expected her to be fluent.

'And you have never seen your mother's homeland?'

'Not yet.'

'Don't leave it too long. What do you want to do when you grow up?'

That was what all adults asked children. And that was the first moment it had ever come into her mind.

'I want to be an actress.'

Now, she looked across at Müller and saw that he was smiling confidentially, as though about to let her into a secret.

'In fact, your father will be pleased to know the Doktor has argued for supporting his most recent request. When he last visited, your father mentioned that his organisation was in need of funding. It looks like your father is going to get what he asked for. Only please Fräulein, keep that news to yourself for the moment.'

He paused at the traffic lights, and rested his elbow on the rolled-down window, drumming his fingers happily on the car door.

'Oh, and I almost forgot. I have a message from the Frau Doktor. Could you please accompany her to Minister Goering's home tomorrow morning?'

Automatically Clara said, 'I'm working, I'm afraid,'

Müller laughed. 'My dear Fräulein, you must understand, a visit to Herr Goering's home is more important than any other work. Certainly more than acting. I'm sure Herr Lamprecht will understand.'

She lapsed into silence.

It made sense, of course. The travelling, the meetings, the time when she had come home from Eastbourne to find the house shut up and deserted. Daddy travelled, she knew he did, it was part of his job. His group was active in promoting international friendship, she knew that too. But forming links with the National Socialists was another thing altogether. Asking them for funding. Surely her father could not possibly understand what they were like?

And yet . . . if he had met them, then he must know. In Germany he must have seen, just as she had, the casual violence, the brutal justice handed out on the streets. Most of all the persecution of the Jews.

Her own father. Whose wife was half-Jewish.

At the same time she realized she must not betray a jot of what she was feeling. Everything Müller assumed about her was wrong, but it was essential that she did not enlighten him. Clara had told Müller she was not political, so that was how she would stay. She would maintain absolute composure. She would stick to the teasing, bantering nature of conversation that he seemed to prefer.

'So when am I going to take you to dinner?'

He glanced across at her and she returned a coy smile.

'You must be busy. With all those sackings to carry out, I'm surprised you can spare the time.'

'There's a lot to do, but it's good to get away. Being with the Herr Doktor can be like being an audience of one at the Sportpalast.'

He gave a conspiratorial wink and from a compartment on the dashboard produced a tin of fruitdrops and offered her one. *'Lutschbonbons'*, it said on the lid. Each sweet, to her amazement, had the hard sugary imprint of the swastika etched on it. She held one up.

'I can't believe it.'

'You mean the attention to detail? But we're famous for it! The company makes them specially for the Führer.' He smiled. 'They know what he likes and they know what's good for them.'

Müller took a hand off the steering wheel and placed it on her knee. He let it linger there and gave it a slight squeeze. She smiled flirtatiously at him, then gazed out of the window at a passing store, as if there was nothing else on her mind but where she might find her next evening dress. As she sucked her cherry bonbon, her tongue found the ridge of the swastika on the fruitdrop's sugar coat, the sourness beneath the sweet, and the image of grandmother came to her, with her gentle eyes and her bagful of Gummi bears and marzipan pigs.

What would her grandmother have said?

Leo Quinn believed war was coming. What if he was right? And was there something, anything she could do to help stop it? What if she could play even the tiniest part in bedevilling this new regime? To become even the smallest of stones in the shoe that was stamping all over Germany. She would do it, wouldn't she? Not because of Leo or the British government or Mr Churchill, or any of those things. But for her grandmother.

Chapter Twenty

The Passport Office of the British Embassy was based in a stucco-fronted hunting lodge at number 17 Tiergartenstrasse. At the beginning of the century, this road, which bordered the old hunting grounds of the Dukes of Brandenburg, had been a plush, residential area of handsome villas, but when the price of property crashed, the British Government had been able to buy up the house cheaply, to be used as a base for consular services, and other, more confidential activities. A flight of wide stone steps led from the courtyard to the first floor, and the windows looked out onto the lush greenery of the Tiergarten, giving it an almost rural aspect.

It was five o'clock in the afternoon by the time Clara arrived, but there was still a queue from the courtyard, through the door and down the corridor. They were professional men, smartly dressed, waiting patiently. She guessed they had been waiting all day. Along the queue, a woman pushed a steel urn on a trolley, dispensing cups of steaming tea.

As she passed up the steps, one man stopped her and said in perfect English, 'Forgive me, miss, but I have an urgent message for my cousins in England. Mr and Mrs Daniel Cohen. They live in Chatham, Kent. I wonder if you could . . .'

'Hey, wait your turn.'

The next man in the line began to berate him for his inter-ruption and others joined in.

'I'm sorry.' Clara fled through the door and asked a resent-ful-looking blonde with plaits to show her the way to Mr Quinn's office, where they waited outside a room until an elderly man with a briefcase emerged. He looked like a doctor who had just diagnosed a terminal illness. An illness that afflicted himself.

The blonde girl nodded and Clara went in. It was a grand room painted in pistachio green, with a fireplace and glass-fronted bookcases. It might have been a ballroom in its earlier, fin de siècle existence, a place where young couples waltzed to a string quartet on the polished parquet floor. But now it was cluttered with tables stacked with pile upon pile of paper files. Leo sat at an enormous desk in the centre with his head bowed over a sheaf of papers. For a split second before he looked up, Clara almost didn't recognize him. She took in the intensity of his concentration, and the utter weariness in his frame. The look in his eyes when he glanced up her sent a shiver through her.

'Miss Vine?'

'I wondered if you might be free for a talk. I thought we might go and walk somewhere.'

'As you can see, I'm busy right now. There's rather a lot of people here and they've been waiting some time. But . . .' He replaced the cap on his fountain pen and nodded at the secretary, who left reluctantly, shutting the door behind her. Standing up, he came round to the front of his desk and stuck his hands in his pockets.

'Can I ask what this is about?'

She shivered at the chill in his voice. He might just have been tired, but he sounded unfriendly. As though she was wasting his time.

'What do all these people want?'

'They want to leave, of course. They're Jews.'

'Do they all want to go to England?'

'Not at all, no matter what your friends in London may tell you. Most Jews are going to France and Holland. They think things will improve, you see, and they can return when this lot are kicked out. The realists are going to Palestine. Because that's our mandate, they need visas from British Passport Control.'

'And do they queue like this every day?'

'Right now we're overwhelmed with applications. They're pleading with us to get anywhere in the British Empire. They're mostly professional people – teachers, doctors, war heroes. We think there'll be more than fifty thousand leaving the country this year.'

'And have you been told to give them all passports?'

He smiled slightly. 'We haven't been told anything. We have no special instructions at all. But as my boss sees it, our job is to make sure as many of them get passports as need it. Anyhow,' he glanced at the clock. 'If this is just a social visit . . .'

'It's not a social visit. Leo, I've just been at Babelsberg. All non-Aryans have been fired today. Under the orders of Doktor Goebbels. In the interests of making Ufa more patriotic.'

'Yes, I heard it on the wireless.' He had been called late the previous evening to provide a document enabling one of the country's best-known actors to pass into Britain. 'I can't say it came as much of a surprise.'

'Klaus Müller told me the Jews would be given every encouragement to leave.'

'That sounds like the sort of thing he would say.'

'And I just want to tell you, the thing we were talking about before, the other night?'

Leo came nearer, so close that she felt uncomfortable, though she didn't show it. Could he possibly think they would be overheard? Instinctively she reduced her voice to a murmur.

'I'll do it.'

He was surprised, she could tell that from the way his eyes widened.

'Can I ask why?'

'Do you need to ask?'

He went back to his seat, took out his pen and bent his head over his work again, so she added, 'I've been invited to call at Goering's house tomorrow.'

'That's good,' he said tersely.

'Should I go?'

'Yes. And meet me on Thursday. At the front entrance of Wertheim's department store in Potsdamer Platz. The one nearest the U-Bahn. Let's say one o'clock.'

Clara was startled at the speed with which he accepted her proposition. She had acted on impulse, stunned by the revelation of her father's dealings with the Nazis and the discovery of her own Jewish heritage. Yet having asked for her help, Leo's manner was now distinctly cool and businesslike. Dismissive, almost. It wasn't as though she was expecting gratitude, but did he realize how hard this would be for her? She had thought there would be some discussion, or acknowledgement of the risks she would be taking. Instead there was just this curt acceptance. Dismayed and bewildered, she turned towards the door.

'And, Clara . . .'

'Yes?'

'Don't go straight home from here, will you? Pop into a department store and spend a good long time in the ladies' fashions.'

Chapter Twenty-one

The former official residence of the Prussian Minister of Commerce was a grand, balconied block off Leipziger Strasse, which Hermann Goering had recently picked out for his new townhouse. It was a bright morning and as Clara and Magda waited, a shout of laughter could be heard from behind the massive door. It was opened by a butler wearing white cotton gloves and Emmy Sonneman bustled through to welcome her visitors into the gloomy interior.

'Come in!'

She led them through a warren of rooms crammed with Renaissance furniture, Gobelin tapestries and Old Masters so exquisite they looked like they belonged in a museum. As indeed they did.

'I have my own apartment, of course, in Bendlerstrasse, but Hermann likes me to be here,' said Emmy airily. 'Now if you come through, Frau von Ribbentrop is waiting in the study.'

Annelies von Ribbentrop was perched on the edge of a huge, over-upholstered sofa as though wary it might eat her. It wasn't the only thing that was larger than life. Everything about the place was enormous. The sunlight that poured through the French windows fell on a giant swastika embedded in blue and gold mosaic floor tiles. In the corner a stuffed bear reared on hind legs with its mouth open, as if it shared its owner's gargantuan appetite. An antique rifle, possibly the very one that had dispatched it, was displayed on the wall. An elephant's foot, mounted in silver, served as a side table, and to one side of the room stood a mahogany desk, with what looked like a throne behind it. It was like being in a cross between a museum and a hunting lodge, where every exhibit had something ominous to say about its owner.

Beside a pair of silver candelabras the size of antlers was a large photograph of Hitler. Magda picked it up.

'How curious! This is similar to mine, but so much bigger. And yet the Führer always presents the same size photograph in the same size frame. I know because he has them especially designed by Frau Troost, the architect's wife.'

Emmy looked momentarily abashed. 'Oh, Hermann had it enlarged. He likes everything big.'

'Including his women,' murmured Frau von Ribbentrop in English, just loud enough for Clara to hear.

'Hermann likes décor to reflect his personality,' said Emmy, fondly. 'It's the actor in him. I often wish he'd gone into the theatre instead of politics. He has such a good eye for display.'

There was a sudden scuffle and from the corner of her eye Clara saw something large and golden bound into the room. For a fraction of a second she thought it was a Labrador, until she realized it was a lion cub. It approached Annelies von Ribbentrop, who sprang away with a shriek.

'Get down, Caesar!' shouted Emmy merrily, as the cub raked its claws down her skirt. 'If you ruin another pair of my stockings, I'll have you sent right back.' Then, to the others, she said, 'Don't worry, he's a darling. They roam completely free, they wouldn't hurt a fly.'

'Lion cubs?' said Frau von Ribbentrop, incredulously.

'Hermann had them sent from the zoo. They're perfectly adorable little things, completely safe, though they shred the stockings with their claws if you get too close. I've been through so many pairs but when I complain Hermann just laughs.'

'Why can't they keep cats, like everyone else?' murmured Magda.

'Hermann is devoted to them.' Emmy crouched to fondle the animal around its glossy neck. It relaxed, blinked its dark gold eyes and a rasping purr filled the room. 'He fed Caesar himself from a baby bottle.'

'So charming,' said Frau von Ribbentrop, a smile frozen on the pallid expanse of her face.

'He washes them every week and puts them under the drier,' said Emmy, cupping the animal's face to hers and kissing its nose. 'Can you imagine! When he's finished with them they're all round and delicious like furry little plums.' The lion rose to its hind legs and narrowly avoided ripping the pearls from her neck. She disentangled the huge paws and lowered him to the ground. 'The only thing is, we have to send them back when they're a year old. It's so sad. They get too big. They frighten the guards.'

The animal scampered off and she came and plumped herself down.

'Ooph. You must forgive me. We're so busy with the play I hardly know what time of day it is. There's to be a special performance for the Führer's birthday and you can't imagine how nervous that's making us.'

'But you have wonderful reviews,' said Frau von Ribbentrop sweetly. 'All except for the *Angriff.*'

'Oh,' Emmy flicked her hand as though swatting a particularly irrelevant fly. 'Who reads the *Angriff?*'

Clara noticed Magda stiffen. The *Angriff* was Goebbels' personal newspaper, dedicated to the most extreme kind of

Nazi propagandizing. Could it be that Emmy didn't know? She seemed entirely insouciant, passing round cake and pouring a stream of fragrant, creamy chocolate for her guests.

'I adore chocolate! My father owned a chocolate factory, so I had all I wanted as a child. Now I can't do without it. I'm addicted for life!'

'None for me,' said Magda briskly, opening her files. 'I find too much sugar so bad for the figure, don't you? Now let's get on with deciding which designs to make up for our first photographic session.'

Clara sipped her chocolate and tried to focus. She had been awake for most of the night and her face was washed out with fatigue. She had brushed a bit of life into her cheeks with rouge, but her eyes were red-rimmed and the contents of several cups of coffee were already buzzing through her veins. She felt acutely alert, her every nerve standing on end, yet full of trepidation. How was she going to do this? It was essential to behave as normal, but what was normal? She was an imposter now, and for that reason, normality was a façade. Yet it was a façade that felt impossible to achieve.

Leo's parting advice to her the day before had startled her. *'Don't go straight home'*. She had no idea why she could not go straight home, but she had obediently visited KaDeWe and tried on some dresses, though she would not be able to afford another thing until her first pay packet, whenever that might be. The idea that someone might be watching her was new. It had taken her an hour and a half to make her way back to Frau Lehmann's and even there she found it hard to relax. For most of the night she had lain awake, turning the arguments over in her head. Am I a spy now, if I do what Leo wants? What is a spy anyway? Is it someone who watches at windows, listens at doors? Someone who discovers things that other people might want to keep hidden? Or just a sceptical observer? Surely, if I do it, it can't cause any harm, and might do some good.

Eventually, these thoughts swirling round her head, she fell into a fractured sleep in which her father and sister were talking, facing away from her, and she could not make out a word they said.

Magda had taken out the sketches that had been made up for her by Hans Horst, the design executive assigned to the Bureau, and circulated them. The women stared at them quizzically.

'As I mentioned, we felt that the international silhouette was too restrictive for the German woman. All those tight waistlines and hips are going to discourage women from having children. And we want to reflect the German national character.'

'I suppose Hermann would like this one,' said Emmy, holding out a teal green suit with leather inserts and a Bavarian hunting hat with a feather in the side. 'All it needs is a gun and a brace of pheasant to set it off. Perhaps we should go the whole way and add a pair of lederhosen?'

'The Führer detests trousers on women, as you know.'

'Frau Goebbels, I was joking. Though it's true that Hermann would like it. He adores hunting. His latest plan is to recreate a primeval German forest. He's bought some land on the Schorfheide. He's going to have real herds of bison roaming, just like they did in the Ice Age. Only German bison, of course.'

Magda pressed her lips together as though her patience was being sorely tried.

'I do wonder if the folk influence is a little strong,' commented Frau von Ribbentrop dubiously. Her own navy suit, with puffed shoulders and a row of buttons down the front, was by the Jewish tailor Fritz Grünfeld, as was Magda's sleek black jacket with its mink cuffs. 'The young woman in the city might find this a little . . . rural.'

'There's a different feel for the urban woman. No one is saying that our women need to look primitive. The Führer himself says it makes him happy when a woman looks pretty.'

'I suppose so,' said Emmy, mournfully. 'But this one has an apron. Can you imagine me wearing an apron? Someone might mistake me for the cook!'

With her heavy hips and weighty forearms, the image was far too accurate for anyone to risk a comment.

'So we're decided then,' said Magda briskly. 'When we stage our presentation it will involve all German designers and all German materials, like cotton, wool and worsted.'

'Such a shame about the fur,' said Emmy. 'Personally I couldn't live without my ermine cape.'

'It would be wrong,' said Magda, impatience cracking through the ice. 'Hitler hates killing animals for fashion. You know that. And he's specially asked that our models do not paint their nails or pluck their eyebrows.'

At the mention of models, Clara was aware of all faces turning towards her. Frau von Ribbentrop in particular had a hint of suspicion in her eyes. 'On that subject, surely,' she said, 'it might be more appropriate to have a full German as our first model. After all, Fräulein Vine is half-English.'

Clara bent down to stroke the lion cub, which had come up to her and was now purring round her legs. Its fur smelt hot and sweet, and she tried to picture Reich Minister Goering shampooing the struggling animal in his bathtub.

'Fräulein Vine is only one of a number of actresses who will be modelling. Olga Chekhova is Russian and Lida Baarová, as I'm sure you're aware, is Czech, but they still reflect the German ideal.'

'And the Doktor wanted Fräulein Vine to be involved,' added Emmy, her voice laden with heavy semaphore. 'It was his *specific* wish.'

Frau von Ribbentrop tightened her lips in disdain. The message was clear. The Herr Doktor's inclinations were well known. However humiliating that might be for his wife.

'Well then of course.'

'How about Leni Riefenstahl?' said Emmy. 'I hear she's been appointed the party's Film Expert. And she has a figure to die for.'

'Entirely unsuitable,' said Magda sharply. Her neck coloured, the way it did, Clara had noticed, whenever her emotions were charged. 'So let's concentrate on more important matters. There is another thing. The Führer has suggested that we compile a special book to be given to all newly married couples. So they understand how to live in a truly German culture.'

'Yes, I heard him mention that,' Frau von Ribbentrop cut in. 'He has a dream that all German brides should be able to consult a book with instructions for marriage. A kind of marriage manual.'

'Why on earth would you need instructions for marriage?' asked Clara.

'Oh, there are many things.' Magda consulted her notes. 'He suggests brides should be taught how to hem curtains, how to plan a budget and keep a house clean.' She ticked off a list. 'How to create an attractive table decoration. Correct behaviour before a husband. Fashion guidance obviously, and advice on children and cooking and so on.'

It astonished Clara that Herr Hitler should have time to be troubled by the question of whether the Reich's new brides were capable of hemming curtains, but Frau von Ribbentrop leant forward.

'The Führer told me that he would like to create a school for brides, where they might learn this kind of thing before they are married.'

Magda nodded. 'You know, we're fortunate to have a Führer who gives so much thought to marriage. He has such interesting plans. Because he wants to encourage more babies he's thinking of giving a medal to prolific mothers. And he says if a man has not established a family by the age of twenty-six, then he should not be eligible for promotion.'

Clara thought of Müller's face when he described his wife's battle to have children. The expression had seemed more grim frustration than tight-lipped grief. Had the death of his wife held him back? Or did the Nazis' views on large families not apply to the senior ranks?

'Must all married men have families?'

'Of course. It matters that we set a good example. Joseph wants at least five! It doesn't apply to the Führer, though. He tells us he will never have children, because they would never be able to live up to him.'

Emmy flicked her fingers through her hair, with the slightest trace of impatience. She must be in her late thirties, Clara guessed. Her first marriage was over, so presumably she wouldn't be collecting a medal for prolific mothers any time soon.

'What else do we need in this manual?' she asked.

Magda consulted her notes. 'Every girl should know how to make simple meals, with ordinary ingredients like herrings, chicken or veal. I'll ask my cook to suggest some recipes.'

'Mine too,' added Frau von Ribbentrop quickly.

'And we'll include some of the Führer's favourites,' said Magda. 'He has entrusted me with the details.'

'Speaking of cooking . . .' Emmy smiled.

A housekeeper had emerged and hovered by the door. Emmy waved her across.

'Don't worry, Cilly, you're not disturbing us. Bring it here.'

The little housekeeper presented a sheet of paper.

'It's the menu,' Emmy explained. 'Actually, we have Herr Hitler dining tonight and Hermann has drummed it into me that I must get the menu right. Last time he came I ordered cold dishes from Kempinski's, and to make sure they were special, I said they were for the Führer. The salmon arrived decorated with his initials in mayonnaise. I thought it was so pretty, but you should have heard the fuss! Silly me. Hermann told me he hates anyone to know where he eats.'

Magda looked aghast. 'You should be more careful, Frau Sonnemann. The Führer is aware that there are enemies out there who could poison him. He needs to take great care with his eating arrangements. Besides, he prefers a home cooked meal anyway. He has a delicate constitution.'

'Well, I'm sorry. I find it enough of a trial with all those raw vegetables he eats. He sits there nibbling a lettuce leaf and taking sips of orange juice and everyone else feels bad about having a good hearty dinner. Last time we dined, I said to him sorry, but I'm going to order a juicy steak. And do you know, he laughed and said go ahead!'

Magda began collecting up her designs. 'Obviously if you have the Führer to entertain you must be very busy, so we should be getting on. I shall assume we pick these two for our first outfits. I'll have them made up and modelled by Fräulein Vine. I hope very soon we will have our own headquarters and staff but until then . . .'

'Perhaps we could meet at my place?' cut in Frau von Ribbentrop swiftly.

'Of course. How kind of you.'

They were making their way to the door when Emmy stopped them.

'Wait! Before you go you have to see this.'

She flung open a door and led them into a room entirely devoted to a model train set. The vast table was covered in mountains and fields, intricately crafted from baize and wood and papier mâché, over which ran intersecting tracks connected by tunnels. The entire vista was like an idealized representation of Germany, with its beer houses, stations and town halls. Little villages with gabled roofs and timbering were separated by pine forests, a posse of hunters chased a deer and milkmaids laboured in the farmyard. A group of children on their way to school waved at the train track and a dog ran alongside.

'Hermann keeps this for his nephews, or so he says,' laughed Emmy. 'There's three hundred feet of track. Incredible, isn't it? Now gather round, everyone. You have to watch carefully!'

She selected one train and set it running round the track. On its side it bore the beautifully painted livery of the French flag, and inside portly French gentlemen in evening jackets could be seen dining in the restaurant car, raising miniature glasses in a toast as they passed through the tiny countryside. After the train had performed one lap, Emmy flicked a switch on the side of the table and from one side of the room a Junkers aeroplane attached to a wire puttered through the air.

'It's a four-engine bomber. Hermann had it specially made when he was given the Ministry of Aviation. He loves his toys.'

When it reached the French train, the model plane released a tiny parcel which fell with precision, knocking the back half of train from the tracks. The parcel gave off a crack and a puff of white smoke. Inside the derailed train, its wheels whirring uselessly, the little Frenchmen could be seen, glasses still raised in futile celebration.

'He did that for the French ambassador. It was so funny. You should have seen his face!'

For a moment they gazed as if dumbfounded at the train set, until there was a sudden cry from Annelies von Ribbentrop.

'*Mein Gott!*'

One of the lion cubs, which had followed them in and had been scampering round the room, had urinated on her handbag.

Magda had plainly had enough.

'If you come now, Fräulein Vine, my driver can give you a lift as far as you want.'

Chapter Twenty-two

The labour camp in Spandau was an old poorhouse that had been taken over by the Party, disinfected, cleaned and furnished. There were forty-eight girls, twelve to each dormitory, squashed in on narrow wooden bunks with blue gingham bedspreads, and sheets which looked like they had been straightened with a set square. They probably had, for all Mary knew. This place was a long way from the summer camp her parents had once forced her to attend, in the mistaken belief that a dose of countryside and communal living was all their daughter needed to cure her quirky, solitary addiction to books. She'd bet there were no toasted marshmallows and apple-pied beds round here.

'It's very tidy.'

'But of course. There is an inspection check every morning.'

Frau Hegel, the supervisor, a flat-faced ideologue in braids, who could have done with a lick of make-up, explained how the girls made their beds every day at five a.m. The occupants of this hut had also saved their daily allowance of thirty pfennigs to buy a portrait of Hitler, which now glowered above them on the dormitory wall.

Mary jotted down details on a notepad as she followed the supervisor round. Labour camps were a relatively new institution in Germany. They had been established on a voluntary basis to provide work for young people, in the belief that menial labour, moving away from home for six months and mixing with other classes was an emancipating experience. The boys made bridges and roads, worked on wasteland and shovelled coal, while the girls laboured on farms and in private houses. A six-month spell at an *Arbeitsdienst* was soon to be compulsory for all German youth. And from what Mary could see, it looked as though singing songs and being insanely cheerful already were.

She gazed through the window at the field outside where someone had marked out a track and the girls were staging running races. Large and small, fat or thin, they all wore the uniform of the BDM and it was not a good look: white blouse, tied at the neck with a black scarf and leather knot, belted navy-blue skirt, short white socks and clumping leather shoes with flat heels.

'Every girl must run sixty metres in fourteen seconds, throw a ball twelve metres and complete a two-hour march,' boasted Frau Hegel.

Just watching them reminded Mary with a shudder of school sports days and herself flailing along at the back of the hundred metres while her mother, in her best dress and too much lipstick, cheered weakly on the sidelines. Not putting a child through all that was yet another advantage to having no kids, she thought grimly.

She had suggested the trip to the labour camp with bad grace after Frank Nussbaum told her he wanted to know about ordinary women's lives, and he had been predictably excited.

'Great idea, Mary! It'll make a change from writing about storm troopers roughing people up and depressing everyone.'

And it had to be said, no one looked especially depressed here. Even the girls on kitchen duty who got up at four a.m.

to chop carrots and peel potatoes for the army camp nearby. Everyone else got to lie in until five a.m., Frau Hegel explained, after which there was roll call, then an hour's run through the woods, before a day hoeing or ploughing in the fields.

'Hard work,' said Mary, who felt exhausted just hearing about it. It had been tough enough getting up at six to drive here. She was simply aching for a cup of coffee, but nothing had been proffered so far. She reached in her handbag for a cigarette and lit up, ignoring the supervisor's steely glare.

'But it needs to be hard. The idea of the *Arbeitsdienst* is to teach girls the value of work, to harden them up.'

'Harden them up for what, exactly?'

'For marriage, of course,' said the woman, as though to an idiot. 'At the end of the course they will get a certificate, which marks them out as fit for marriage. The idea is that they should make good wives.'

'Very romantic.'

Frau Hegel's face crinkled in disdain. 'Come and see our little farm.'

They walked out to the outhouse where along one wall stood a long row of cages, like a military barracks, with hundreds of pink, twitching noses protruding through the wire.

'This is our special experiment.' She gestured at the cages with pride. 'It could be a very profitable enterprise for us. They are angora rabbits, so we can use the meat and sell the fur. It's very luxurious. The Luftwaffe use their skins for lining flying jackets. Here, take a look.'

She opened a cage and hauling a rabbit out by its scruff, plumped it in Mary's arms, where it sat, its tiny heart juddering, as she stroked its velvet ears uneasily. What was it about the rows of docile creatures, palely fattening in their cages,

that made her think of flaxen girls obediently breeding for
the Fatherland?

Mary replaced the quivering animal carefully in its cage. A
couple of girls were washing down the yard, and, as she
passed, the supervisor scanned their scrubbed faces as if checking for evidence of ideological disobedience.

'There should be no shame about manual labour,' she told
Mary. 'Nor should the daughter of factory owners shirk the
company of children of factory workers. Now you wanted to
find Gretl. There she is.'

Mary looked across to where a red-faced girl in glasses, her
cheek squashed against the flank of a cow, was tugging squirts
of milk unevenly into a tin pail. She was recognizably Lotte
Klein's sister, though younger and fatter.

'Gretl had never been near a cow. Now she is an *Arbeitsmaid*
she loves them. She can milk as though she was born to it.'

Mary thought the plump and sweating Gretl resembled no
more a natural milkmaid than she did Greta Garbo.

'What if she doesn't want to work on the land? Is there any
point learning how to milk a cow if she's going to spend her
life in a city?'

'But of course. Besides, our girls learn the kind of domestic
skills that will set them up for life.'

'Such as?'

'Cooking, sewing and knitting. Baby care.'

Frau Hegel left her side to reprove a group of giggling
girls, who were bungling the herding of goats. Mary took the
opportunity to crouch down beside Gretl.

'Hi Gretl. I work with your sister Lotte and she suggested
I visit. My name's Mary Harker. I'm a journalist.'

'Oh, Fräulein Harker! I've heard of you.'

With a broad smile, Gretl let go of the cow's teat and offered
a damp hand, which Mary tried to take without flinching.

'Lotte has told me all about you. She loves working in the office. And meeting your friends. It sounds so stimulating!'

'It is, I suppose. So, do you like it here? Do you really enjoy learning how to cook and milk cows?'

Gretl removed her glasses and blinked. 'If it helps to make me a better woman, then of course!'

Mary wanted to take her by the arm, shake her and say, "Milking cows never helped anyone be a better woman! Finding your vocation makes you a better woman!" Instead she waited while Gretl finished the bucket, emptied the milk into a giant churn, wiped her hands on her apron and accompanied her across the yard to the poorhouse block.

From the cows, it seemed a natural progression to the baby lesson, where Mary stood and watched while a howling infant was prised from its crib and passed between a group of girls, having its nappy inexpertly removed and replaced several times. The poor creature rolled and kicked to no avail, thrashing its fat legs, its little face scrunched in scarlet protest, its wails resounding round the concrete walls. Mary gritted her teeth. She tried to switch off but the cry went through her like a knife. She wondered who the baby belonged to.

The previous night she had told Rupert Allingham she was coming to visit the labour camp and he had laughed.

'Baldur von Schirach told me all about those camps for Hitler maidens. From what I've heard, most of them aren't maidens by the time they return.'

The pass-the-parcel continued around the circle of girls until the baby came to a stop next to Mary, where it was seized by a tough-looking girl with a peasant's face and muscles like tennis balls on her upper arms.

Mary recalled what she'd read. "A minimum of intellect and a maximum of physical aptitude are required to make woman what she is intended to be: the womb of the Third Reich."

'Your turn.' The peasant girl passed the kicking infant to Mary.

'I think I'll pass.'

Gretl came up beside her and took the baby, gently placing it in Mary's arms. By now the infant had exhausted itself. It stopped resisting and stared up passively, its little face wet with tears, exuding a mingled smell of urine and soap. A tiny belch of milk leaked out of the side of its mouth. As she looked into its navy gaze and felt the damp weight of it, nudging and stretching in her arms, Mary had the most unexpected feeling. A deep, almost physical tug somewhere inside her, a hot, protective urge, which was different from anything she had felt for the legion of dogs and horses she had owned throughout her life. She had loved all her animals fiercely, especially her dog Walt, and her favourite horse, a gorgeous Appalachian called Dora, who jumped like a dream. But this was different. This was visceral and frightening.

She guessed that must be how it felt to want children. Luckily, almost as soon as the feeling had come, it passed.

'Don't you adore babies?' asked Gretl.

'I think they're an acquired taste,' Mary said, passing it on.

'But surely you want to be married yourself, Fräulein?'

'I'm not sure I do.'

'I suppose you would have to give up your job then,' said Gretl, thoughtfully.

Mary declined the invitation to stay for an evening of folk singing. She had another date that night with Rupert. No doubt it would involve visiting his favourite bar, drinking too much and talking about the way things were going. But at least a girl didn't need a certificate for that.

Chapter Twenty-three

If you wanted to find the busiest place in Berlin, you would probably choose Potsdamer Platz. With its five-way streetlight and spaghetti of tram lines, the intersection was a torrent of cars and people. Leo was weaving, quite fast, through the crowds past the Josty Café and along the western side. Clara was trying to keep up with him without obvious exertion but with his long stride he far outpaced her, forcing her to patter inelegantly at his side as she ducked through the shoppers, and making her very slightly breathless.

He kept up a rapid, clipped commentary as he walked.

'First thing is, you will need to know if you're being watched.'

'I thought I was being asked to watch them.'

She dodged as they crossed the road and a number 15 tram seemed certain to run them down.

'Befriend them, is your task. That's all.'

'Surely they wouldn't watch me.'

'They have no particular reason to suspect anything about you, but even so, the Gestapo will be wary of an unknown British female. They will be curious about you. But they won't necessarily be heavy-handed. Bear in mind that anyone who is following you will look unremarkable, absolutely mundane. The type of chap or girl you wouldn't give a second glance. Anyone who sticks out, who does anything unusual, is absolutely bound to be innocent. If you notice a chap hanging round a shop, looking in the windows, coming back time and again to look in the windows, he's not following you, he's wondering if he should buy that suit. Don't spend your time looking over your shoulder because he's as likely to be ahead of you than behind you. He might be the other side of the street. He or she might change their appearance to suit, they might sport a very bright jacket, or scarf, which they can easily remove. Look at the shoes. They're the giveaway. It's very hard to change shoes in a hurry.'

Whatever else she thought Clara was certain she would never be able to tell anything from looking at people's shoes.

'So what do I do if I am followed?'

'If you think you are being followed, it helps to engage someone in conversation. That way, they will have to follow the person you spoke to as well, which reduces their effectiveness. And if they're still following you, lead them a dance. Give them some exercise. And meanwhile work out how you can lose them. It might be more than one, of course.'

'But wouldn't that make them more noticeable?'

'One behind and one in front. Then they swap positions. It's called a box. It could be a man and a woman. Expect the unexpected. It could be a woman with a pram. If you find there's someone on your tail, you'll need to find a way of disguising yourself. That's what this game is about. Concealment.'

'I don't know if I'm really suited to this game, as you call it.'

'Oh, I'm sure you are. Concealment comes easily to the English upper classes. I bet you were taught never to speak in front of servants.'

'Well, yes, but . . .'

'Besides, you're an actress. It's what you do.'

'But . . .' How could she explain that this wasn't anything like the acting she knew, where you were on a stage, and repeating lines in front of a delighted audience, who would clap at the end and, if you were lucky, write a complimentary review of your performance in a newspaper.

'It's not just about acting,' Leo continued, slowing a little, 'it's about observation too. You can tell an awful lot about people from the slightest glance. For example, that woman over there.' He pointed to a woman of about thirty, in a headscarf, walking calmly along the pavement. 'You can tell she's not a mother.'

'How can you tell that?'

'Because when that little boy fell over, just beside her, she didn't stop. She didn't even turn to look.'

'He has his nurse with him.'

'That's not the point. A mother would stop. Mothers always think they know best.'

Clara was beginning to suspect that Leo Quinn, too, always thought he knew best.

'You seem to know a lot about mothers,' she said testily. 'All mothers aren't the same.'

He shot a look at her. 'The main thing, Clara, is that if you want to help us, you'll need to be on your guard. Observe everything. Get into the habit of noting everything around you, even if it seems inconsequential. And sounds, too. They can be important. You need to look in a new way. To notice the kind of details that would pass everyone else by.'

'How do you mean?'

'Absorb everything about a person. Be acquainted with their actions and their habits, and think what they say about them. Haven't you ever done that?'

Clara couldn't help thinking of her childhood game for long train journeys: observing her fellow passengers unawares and making up stories for them.

'I suppose I have.'

'Good. Follow me.'

A tram had drawn to a halt beside them and Leo jumped into the rear carriage as if on a last-minute impulse, so swiftly that she had to scramble to follow suit. The tram was packed and she guessed, from the way he stood hanging onto the rail and gazing into the distance, that he didn't want to continue their conversation just there. It was fascinating, she thought, watching him in the window's reflection, swaying with the tram's motion, how easily he managed to fold in on himself, to appear practically anonymous, despite his height. He might have been just another clock-watching commuter in a mackintosh dreaming of five o'clock after another dreary day in the office.

When the road passed under an elevation where a train thundered above them, making the metal pillars shake, he gave an almost imperceptible nod, which she took as a signal to dismount. They had arrived at the Zoologischer Garten.

The zoo was thronged with people enjoying the sunshine. A blanket of begonias bloomed tidily in rectangular beds. A couple of fat old men, with no sense of absurdity, were pulled along by minuscule dachshunds in tartan coats. Leo and Clara walked along the winding paths between the animal enclosures, beneath palm trees and over a little wrought-iron bridge. Leo bought a zoo guide in Italian, which he consulted gravely as if he was really trying to choose between the tigers and the reptiles.

They passed the Ostrich House, done out in ancient Egyptian style, complete with pillars, and an Antelope House with stone centaurs standing guard, along a quiet path that led to the great cats. In one cage a panther padded restlessly, the muscles rippling beneath its sleek pelt, an agonised intelligence in the depths of its liquid black eyes. It paced and paced, measuring out its confinement the way a blind man gets to know the precise dimensions of his home without touching them.

'Rilke wrote a poem about a panther, didn't he?' said Clara. 'Do you know it?'

Leo leant on the rail beside her.

"To him there seem to be
A thousand bars, and out beyond these bars exists no
    world."

Perhaps, he thought, there was some strange satisfaction to be derived from confining savage animals here, given that the savagery outside this place was the kind that couldn't be confined. He turned his back on the panther and said, 'Tell me about Magda.'

'What do you want to know?'

'What would you tell a friend?'

'A girlfriend?'

'Sure.'

'Well, I suppose a girlfriend would want to know what she thinks about Hitler. I'd say she's very devoted to him.'

'In a romantic way? Or like a mother.'

'Both.'

'How does she show it?'

'She cooks him special meals, or has her cook do it, and she sends them over to the Kaiserhof in travel Thermoses.'

'What sort of food?'

'Sweetcorn, he loves, and some kind of caramel pudding. And baked potatoes with curd cheese and unrefined linseed oil. He's a vegetarian. Though I can't see how this is any use to you. Unless you're planning to poison him.'

'Details. What does Goebbels think of the Fashion Bureau?'

'He's not too keen on it, apparently. Though he does think Hollywood vamps with all their glamorous clothes are having a bad effect on German women.'

'That's rich, coming from him. Given that he's all too well known for his love of film stars.'

'And considering how fashion-conscious he is himself. Would you believe he has more than a hundred suits?'

Leo gave a silent whistle.

'All the wives are terrifically well dressed too. Frau von Ribbentrop has gloves sent over from Italy, and Magda has her shoes handmade in Florence.'

'Do the wives like each other?'

'Not a bit. Magda told me in the car yesterday that Joseph hates her having anything to do with Emmy Sonneman. He considers her a silly woman and disapproves of her affair with Goering.'

'There's no love lost there. Goering dislikes Goebbels. He thinks he's of a lower rank, not really aristocratic enough to associate with. Whereas Goebbels feels superior because he's a Prussian, from the north, and a purer kind of German than the Bavarians. How about Frau von Ribbentrop?'

'She's rather forbidding. Magda says she's the power behind the throne. Her family, the Henkells, are hugely rich. Magda says von Ribbentrop bought his name and married his money. But the Henkells are quite liberal too, and she likes to shock them apparently.'

'So flirting with National Socialism is the best way she can think of.'

'It is pretty shocking, isn't it?'

They came to the children's corner. Piglets, llamas, goats and even a bear cub were frolicking around, being grappled by tiny children.

'What is it about these women, Leo? What do they see in Hitler?'

Leo shrugged. 'You see it everywhere. Women hurl themselves at him when his motorcade passes. The SA has banned them from throwing flowers because he was getting hit too often by flying roses. It would be funny, if it wasn't true. He has an uncanny knack of making women cry in his presence.' He paused. 'I dare say he's made a lot of women cry *out* of his presence too.'

'I suppose it's because he's powerful.'

'It was like that before he came to power. Back in the twenties there was a Bavarian newspaper, the *Munich Post*, which ran a piece about various women who were infatuated with Hitler and pawned their jewellery to help his cause. They did everything – sent in their pearls and their diamond rings and their watches. And Hitler took the money, of course, for the Party. But he had the newspaper's editorial offices demolished.'

'When I saw him he seemed much smaller than I had expected. His face was kind of pouchy and boneless. Almost inconsequential.'

'That's what everyone says. Until they realize how consequential he is.'

They had come to the Aquarium. Inside, the echoey damp of the floors and the eerie blue light lent it a feeling of hushed privacy. Standing side by side and watching the fish drift in their secret oblivion, both of them relaxed a little. There was a tank of deep-sea creatures, pale and hideous, with eyes that seemed strangely misplaced and wide gasping mouths. According to the information label, they needed a specially pressurised tank because they could only live at high pressure. Watching the faces loom up and veer away into the murky depths, Clara was transfixed by their languid slithering. To think that such perversions and ugliness should be produced simply by the pressure bearing down on them.

She turned away, feeling a little sick.

'The thing is, Leo, I keep worrying why they should trust me.'

'Because they trust your father, of course. Also, Goebbels is reckless when it comes to women. I wouldn't be at all surprised if he was behind your recruitment.'

Startled by the accuracy of his assessment, she said nothing.

Then, more gently he said, 'Tell me about your acting. When did you first want to act?'

She hadn't been expecting such a personal question. But even as he asked her, she remembered something else. That childhood day when the German man had come to visit the house. She had told him she wanted to be an actress, and everyone had laughed, and then the whole party turned and went back to the house, where a loaded tea tray was being brought onto the terrace. There was the distant clink of cups as Mrs McKee divided the Victoria sponge and handed round isosceles triangles of cucumber sandwiches.

But Angela had come back across the lawn to her. She came so close that Clara noticed she had been experimenting with make-up, a slick of lipstick riding up over her cupid's bow and a line of kohl – their mother's no doubt – emphasizing the violet eyes. Her teeth were as perfectly enamelled as a Fabergé jewel.

She hissed an urgent whisper, *"Don't talk about being an actress, Clara. You won't ever be an actress. I can tell everything you're thinking. Every single thing you think is written all over your face. You couldn't act to save your life."*

Why had Angela said that? What did she mean?

Turning to Leo she said, 'A German man came to visit our house in Surrey. He was a friend of my parents and he asked me what I wanted to be when I grew up. It was then I decided to be an actress. I hadn't ever thought about it before. I only said it for effect, to annoy my sister. She was always telling me what to do. She thought she knew best. It made me terribly cross.'

She looked up and found him smiling at her.

'Why are you smiling?'

'I can imagine you as a cross little girl.' For a moment his eyes gleamed with humour and something flashed between them. 'And I can just imagine you hating being told what to do.'

'And I can just imagine you thinking you knew best.'

'Guilty as charged.'

'Do you know,' she said slowly. 'I think that man, the man who came to visit us, must have been von Ribbentrop.'

'He was.'

She stared at him, as comprehension dawned.

'You knew?'

His answer confirmed everything she had feared. It gave her the impetus to broach the question she had been avoiding all along.

'That my father had been meeting the Nazis?'

'Yes.'

'Before you met me?'

'Yes. But I didn't connect him with you until later.'

She felt a sinking dismay. 'So what else do you know that you're not telling me?'

'That he has been working hard to advance the fascist cause in England. Clara, tell me, have you heard of Maxwell Knight?'

She shook her head.

'He runs a unit called B5b. It's part of the British Security Service, investigating political subversion. They observe the activities of various groups and their political tendencies. It was he who alerted us to your father.'

'Are you saying that the British secret services are watching my father?'

'He's being watched, yes. Though it's a pretty recent thing. Back in London they're really more interested in sympathizers of the Left, but since last month there has been a little more interest in those who are keen to develop relationships with the Right.'

'But my father was a Conservative MP until the last election!'

'I know. And now he's keen to forge alliances with fascist organizations across Europe. He's part of an enclave of the British ruling class who are determined to avoid war at any cost. They will deal with Hitler, or anybody, if it avoids war.'

'Surely there's nothing wrong with wanting to avoid war?' she said, but even to her own ears her voice sounded hollow and uncertain.

'It depends on what terms.'

Clara looked away, so that he should not see the tears pricking the corner of her eyes.

'How long have they been watching him?'

'I don't know that. But there was something particularly that alerted our attention. Earlier this year your father visited Germany and met Hans Frank, who has just been made Minister of Justice for Bavaria. He had a friend with him. A lady called Anna Wolkoff.'

'Anna? Whose family owns the Russian Tea Room?'

Anna was a White Russian, an intense, dark-haired woman whose family had once been in the service of the last Tzar,

and whose life in exile, running a little café on Harrington
Road near the South Kensington tube, struck everyone as a
bit of a come down. In fact, Anna Wolkoff preferred to
describe herself as a couturier rather than a café owner. She
had, after all, designed dresses for the Prince of Wales's friend,
Mrs Simpson.

'Anna's a dress maker. She made an evening gown for my
sister. Emerald-green silk with sequins.'

'She's also made several trips to Germany in the past few
years and held meetings with senior Nazis, including Rudolf
Hess.'

'With Hess? What were the meetings about?'

Leo raised his eyebrows. 'I don't imagine she was measuring him for an evening gown.'

They came out of the Aquarium, blinking in the bright
sunlight and drifted over to the elephants. A line of sharp
nails set into the ground prevented the animals from over-
stepping their enclosure. A new baby elephant was being
offered pretzels by some children. It kept trying to reach their
outstretched hands with its trunk, before teetering on the
edge of the nails and having to step back.

'I've decided I hate zoos. Let's have a drink.'

Clara headed towards a little café and sat, as she knew Leo
would want, in the quietest corner facing the room. The
other occupants of the café were an elderly man reading a
copy of the *B.Z. am Mittag*, a couple holding hands and stealing kisses across the table, and a pair of women, enjoying
creamy wedges of cake and what looked like equally delicious gossip.

Leo waited until a waitress in a black uniform and lacy cap
had taken their order, then said softly, 'You know, of course,
you mustn't mention any of this to your family. Or indeed
anyone. That's imperative. You do understand?'

'I do.' She bit her lip and focused on a child nearby who was eating *Bratwurst* and onions from a paper container.

'And you are absolutely committed to helping us?'

'Yes.' His green eyes were on her intently. Without knowing why she added, 'I've never been so sure of anything.'

'Good. Well, the first rule is, keep yourself safe. Otherwise you endanger others.'

'What's the second rule?'

He laughed. 'I suppose the second rule is, sometimes you have to abandon the rules.'

She was playing with her coffee spoon, twisting it round in her fingers so that it made her two-faced, at first narrow and concave, then round and moonlike. She hesitated while the waitress served them and then said slowly, 'Just because I'm an actress, Leo, doesn't mean I'm good at deception. They're not precisely the same thing. The people you act for actually want to be deceived.'

'A willing suspension of disbelief.'

'That was Coleridge. And he was talking about literature. This is something different. These people don't want to be deceived. You might say, "Just act natural" but how do I do that? How do I act natural?'

'Well, let's see.' He paused. 'How would you do it on stage?'

She looked at him suddenly with a flicker of understanding. 'You'd do it by degrees.'

'Tell me.'

'All right,' she said slowly. 'The first thing you do is study the character, so you absolutely know the way she talks, the way she carries her shoulders, say, or swings her hips as she walks, whether she would hold her cigarette like this.' She took the cigarette from his hand and held it between her second and third fingers and curved her palm round her mouth, 'Or like this . . .' she flicked her hand carelessly outwards, away from her, in a pose he always thought of as intensely feminine.

'You have to know the way she stands, and the way she relaxes. For example, does she cross her legs, does she hold her head to one side?'

She tilted her head at him coquettishly and pursed her mouth in a way that reminded him suddenly of Marjorie Simmons. 'Is she one of those women who just loves being centre stage all the time, or does she like to fade into the furniture? Does she have any little habits, like twirling her fringe, or biting her lip, or, I don't know, blowing smoke rings?' She inhaled and blew a perfect ring of smoke which hung trembling in a shaft of sunlight. He couldn't help but laugh. It was a trick he had tried many times and never managed to achieve.

'Then, when you've worked all of that out, you have to forget it. Say you're playing a bold, careless, flighty girl, like Sorel Bliss in *Hay Fever*, who doesn't think too deeply about anything, and just wants to have a good time. Well, you have to become that person, so it's natural for you, so you do all that without thinking about it. Because usually onstage you have so much else to think about.'

She looked about her brightly, smoothed a curl of hair behind her ear and for that second she seemed totally transformed. It was true, Leo thought. It was as though, through the tiniest of gestures, she actually had become that flighty girl she had mentioned, who just wanted to have a good time. He felt a prickle of envy. How liberating it must be to have that release, to be able to escape from yourself and inhabit a different personality entirely.

They left the café and walked to the oriental elephant gate that led out onto Budapester Strasse. Its gilded arch and green

Chinese turrets couldn't have looked more out of place in the modern Berlin, with its clean lines and sombre, monumental architecture. The arch looked gloriously defiant, a crazy, extravagant gesture of an architect who'd let his fantasies go mad. Though nothing like as mad, of course, as the minds behind the buildings now being planned for the streets of the new Reich.

Gazing upwards, Clara said lightly, as if commenting on the sunshine spilling through a rent in the clouds, 'So what do I do now?'

'Just what we've been discussing.'

'And what if I don't have anything to tell you?'

He turned his head away from her, looking down the street, as if searching for a taxi.

'Tell me what they talk about, that's all. No matter how trivial. And go along with anything Magda asks of you. The main thing is, they mustn't suspect. Don't ask questions. Don't talk about England. Don't ever write or type anything. No addresses or names.'

'How am I supposed to remember, then?'

'How do you remember lines? You must have a method. And Clara . . .' He paused and for a moment looked at her directly. 'Don't trust anyone.'

'You sound so suspicious.'

'Why should the Nazis have a monopoly on suspicion?' He glanced around him. 'Berlin is full of sharp ears and eyes. Everyone's watching. Everyone's on the alert. The number of informers is increasing constantly now. The police encourage people to report anything they might think odd. Someone away from home, someone printing pamphlets, someone entertaining a lot of men. A woman like you, frequenting the Herr Reich Minister's home, is bound to attract attention. Despite everything I said about blending into your surroundings, that might not be easy for you.'

There was something in the way he looked at her. A flicker of attraction in his eyes. He hesitated for a second, but didn't elaborate.

'And if you go straight from the Goebbels' to the British Consulate, well, even they can make elementary calculations.'

He pointed to the red-jacketed *Baedeker Guide to Berlin* that was poking out of her bag. 'Wait a minute. Pass that to me.' He flipped through. 'They know where I live and they may well know where you live, but tourist spots are always difficult. Crowded and busy and full of people speaking other languages. That's where we should meet.'

'How will I get in touch with you?'

'You won't. From now on you mustn't. I'll contact you. In fact, I'll send you tickets. They'll have the time and the date on. All you have to do is turn up.'

He leafed through the book and found a sketch of a nine-teenth-century red sandstone building in the style of a Corinthian temple.

'Everyone should visit the National Gallery. Have you seen it?'

'Not yet.'

'It's easily found. On Museum Island. Mostly edifying German art but a lovely collection of French Impressionists, and I think there's still some of what the Führer describes as degenerate art.'

'So when will I see you?'

'Look out for the tickets.'

He tipped his hat and she felt a slight pang of disappoint-ment as he turned without saying goodbye and walked quickly away.

Chapter Twenty-four

It was fortunate that the sunny weather continued because on Saturday Helga's son, Erich, arrived and she invited Clara to spend the day with them at Luna Park.

Luna Park was a vast amusement park at the end of the Ku'damn, the largest one in Europe, Helga said, as if that was proof that Germans really were having a bigger, better time than anyone else. From some way off the thunder of the roll-ercoaster could be heard and the tinny music carried in the wind. Inside there were attractions like the Swivel House, where an entire house tilted precariously to one side, and a spinning machine called the Devil's Wheel, which whisked people round and left them feeling sick. There was a Tin Lake, where little boats sailed on a metallic expanse while artificial waves beneath billowed and coiled. At night, Helga said, there were cabarets and boxing matches and firework displays that spattered a glowing graffiti on the sky.

That Saturday was as loud as ever with the screeches of the rides and the calls of the men behind the stalls. A rime of petrol hung in the air, mingling with the hot oil from the sausage stalls and the yeasty baking scents of the pretzel carts. But up close everything, from the fairy tale palace, with towers and a staircase leading down to the lake, to the stalls and the rides, was going very obviously to seed. There was a sad, down-at-heel feeling to it, not made any better by rumours that the Nazis planned to bulldoze the place shortly, on account of the decadent fun it represented. Their own favourite hobby was building new roads and as it happened there was one planned right through the centre of Luna Park.

'So what do you think of my boy, then?'

The two of them had met Erich that morning off the train from Havelberg. Short for his age, with a crew cut and carefully pressed clothes, Erich was far more polite than the children Clara knew in England. Compared to her brother Kenneth, who at the age of ten had spoken to adults only under sufferance and had scarred knees and pockets stuck together with melted chocolate, Erich was a model of maturity and decorum. He had shaken hands solemnly with Clara and risen to his feet without prompting on the tram to give a seat to an elderly man. Clara couldn't help thinking Erich's grandmother had made a rather better job of raising him than his own mother would have. Yet the affection between the two of them was plain to see.

Helga was transformed by his presence. She couldn't take her eyes off him. She repeatedly touched his arm and stroked his hair. She fluttered around Erich, insisting that they drop into a café for tea and a roll because he might be tired after the journey, peppering him with questions about his friends. Another boy might have hated it, but Erich himself seemed equally proud of his mother, who, in her tortoiseshell sunglasses and floaty pink and yellow tea-dress did exude an eye-catching glamour.

'Mutti is a film star,' he informed Clara solemnly. 'She is almost as famous as Marlene Dietrich but much more beautiful. Soon she will have earned so much money she will bring me to live with her in Berlin. And Oma too?' he added, anxious eyes on Helga.

'And Oma too,' said Helga, winking at Clara.

'And Bruno?'

'Who's Bruno?' said Clara.

'Hush,' said Helga. 'An old friend of mine. An artist. Erich took a liking to him.

'He made a lovely poster of Mutti. I have it on my wall.'

'Do you, sweetheart?' Helga beamed. 'Well then. Why don't you tell Clara everything you've been doing? Are you doing well at school?'

'Of course. I always do well. And I'm excited about the Führertag.'

'Hitler's birthday is coming up,' explained Helga. 'They have a special day at school.'

'We all put flowers on his picture and sing songs, then the teachers bring cakes and we play special games. We are going to have a tug of war. Only,' his face drooped, 'no one picks me on the team.'

'Of course they'll pick you!' said Helga brightly.

'No. Because I'm small.'

'If anyone leaves you out you must tell the leader.'

'That would be stupid, Mutti! The leader says it is good for the bigger boys to bully. It stops us being weak.'

'What nonsense!'

'No. He's right. It's better to be strong. We have to learn to fight.' Erich brightened. 'But soon we'll be going hiking, and that will be fun. We'll cook at a camp fire and sing and sail in canoes down the lake. And when I'm fourteen in the Hitler Jugend I'll get an HJ knife with "Blood and Honour" written on it. I can buy one, can't I, Mutti? They're only four marks.'

'Of course you can, darling. Now take this and go and fetch us some food. I'm ravenous.'

They watched him run off and join the queue at the frankfurter stall. The stallholder had a little monkey on a chain, which all the children were allowed to pet. Once Erich was out of earshot, Helga frowned.

'You don't know how I worry about him, Clara. It's probably why I drink when he's not here. It helps me not to think about him. He'll have a dreadful time in the HJ. They do boxing and they have terrible tests like being marched into ice-cold lakes up to their waists. How will Erich cope with that? He's always been delicate. He has a bad chest.'

'Does Bauer know about Erich?'

'Yes, of course.'

'What does he say?'

'What can he say? The Party is all in favour of children. The more little Nazis the better. Bauer says it's better for a woman to have a child even if she's single, than to stay barren.'

'Nice of him.'

'Don't worry, Clara. That doesn't extend to having his kid. I'm being very careful in that respect, I assure you.'

Erich returned, balancing three steaming cartons of wurst and fried onions and little wooden spears to eat them with. They sat contently on the bench opposite a newly erected poster of a roadworker with rippling muscles and the slogan, "Hitler is building. Help him. Buy German goods."

Clara noticed Erich was screwing up his face in unconscious parody of the heroic worker.

'I would like to meet the Führer one day.'

'I'm sure you will, darling,' said Helga, running an indulgent hand over his closely cropped skull.

Through a mouthful of sausage he said, 'Perhaps if I am accepted to the Napola school.'

Seeing Clara's raised eyebrow, Helga clarified. 'National Political Academy school. It's a new boarding school being created for special children. They want to raise the boys to be part of the Nazi élite or something. Erich has set his heart on going there. It's in Potsdam, but they're only taking the brightest.'

'I will pass the exams, Mutti. You'll see. My teachers say I can. And the lessons will be so much more interesting than what I get now. They study Germanic heroes and Luther and Frederick the Great and proper German history.'

Clara wanted to ask what proper German history might be, but she guessed she already knew. It would be like the films, a special take on the past, seen through Joseph Goebbels' eyes.

'But, aren't these places all about sport? I've heard they're planning athletics and boxing and shooting morning and evening. They don't allow boys who wear spectacles, do they?' Helga sounded fretful.

'Why should I care, Mutti? I don't need spectacles.'

'What would they say about your chest?'

'They'll never know about my chest if you don't tell them,' said Erich glaring at his mother from dark-lashed eyes that were identical to her own. Then he tugged at her hand. 'Look, it's the china stall! I want to go on it! Please?'

A short way off was a ramshackle stall in which customers paid to throw hard rubber balls at old plates and crockery. A large crowd had gathered, egging on the players, who had six balls a time. If they failed to smash anything, they complained loudly that the crockery was glued to the shelf, but generally they managed to smash at least one item each turn, resulting in cheers and congratulations. Something about the violence of the players, their evident pleasure in seeing the plates and dishes fall to the ground in a shower of multi-coloured fragments, made Clara flinch. Even though the crockery was chipped and shoddy, and came in job lots from second-rate hotels, she couldn't enjoy seeing people take such pleasure in wanton destruction.

Erich disappeared and Helga sat back on the bench, face upturned, basking in the sunshine.

'He makes you very happy, doesn't he? You look quite different today.'

Helga grinned, without opening her eyes. 'Perhaps it's not just Erich. Perhaps it's someone else too.'

'Bauer?'

Helga sat up indignantly. 'Of course not Bauer! That bonehead. It's Bruno.'

'The artist?'

'He designs posters for Ufa. That's how we met. He did the poster of a film I was in and said he'd used the picture of me because I was the prettiest.' She sniffed. 'Though he's a proper artist too. '

Even before she said it, Clara realized. 'He did that portrait of you, didn't he? The one in your room.'

'Yes. I know what you're thinking. It took me a while to see there was anything good about his style. He's quite famous, actually, but when he first took me back to his studio all he was painting were prostitutes or dreadful violent scenes. Skeletons and men being hanged. His latest one had a dead woman mangled with a river of blood flowing round her. I can't imagine what it's like inside Bruno's head.'

'But you posed all the same.'

She bit her lip. 'When he first asked to paint me I said no, straight away. But then he started talking to me about art, about why he paints things the way he does, and it made sense. He said his art was a church where people could scream out their rage and despair. He said you need to look horror in the face if you're ever going to overcome it.'

'It's not how I'd imagine having my portrait painted.'

Helga sniffed. 'Me neither. But I thought frankly, who's going to recognize me? Anyway, now it turns out he's been commissioned to make the poster for that new film I'm doing, *Barcarole,* and he came into the studio. It was so lovely to see him. I could tell he'd missed me.'

'So he took you home?'

'Why not? It's such a relief to be with a decent sensitive man. One who doesn't boast about how drunk he got last night like he deserves the Iron Cross for it.'

'Is he married?'

'He was, but it didn't work out. His parents made him marry young, but his wife was completely wrong for him. She got the house and everything and he has to live in a squalid little apartment in Pankow. But who cares?'

'Well, you, I'd have thought.'

'I know. But it's different this time. So he can't take me to restaurants or plays, but then I've got Bauer for that.'

'And what happens when Bauer finds out?'

'He'll never find out. How could he?'

Erich kept up an animated chatter all the way back to the station, but when the moment came to get on the train he reverted to the child he was and clung to his mother's neck so that she had to prise off his fingers one by one.

'I don't want to go, Mutti. I want to live in Berlin, I don't care about the Napola school, I just want to live with you.'

'Now don't be silly. And besides, I only have one bed.'

'I'll sleep on the floor then. I don't care. I'll be good, you'll hardly notice me. Please.'

'And how would Oma like that? You'll come again soon, my darling, I promise,' said Helga, bundling him into the carriage and shutting the door. 'Don't cry.'

He sat obediently in the third-class carriage, and placed his palm briefly against the window, as Helga touched the glass with her own. Then there was a clamour of doors and whistles, and the blur of his small face behind the glass gradually receded as the train disappeared down the track. He didn't cry. It was Helga who had tears sloping down from behind her sunglasses half the way home.

Chapter Twenty-five

Clara could tell from the maid's face that there was a row going on. From behind the drawing-room door there was shouting, accompanied by the thin wail of a baby elsewhere in the house.

'The Frau Doktor asks you to wait up here.'

The card in an envelope marked with the crest of the Hotel Adlon had asked her to call at ten a.m. the next day. Surprised as Clara was to receive another summons to the Goebbels' home so soon, she was even more startled to find herself being shown up the stairs into Magda's dressing room.

It was a light, sunny room, papered in yellow, with oil paintings of still lives with flowers, and a pair of French armchairs in apricot watered silk. The mirrored dressing table was clustered with bottles of perfume, amber and pale green liquids stoppered, and a cut-glass spritzer with a trailing scarlet cord. The warm, sweet fragrance of the mixed perfumes mingled with the scent of fresh laundry on the bed.

"Observe everything".

On the chest of drawers were two photographs. The first was an autographed picture of the Führer in a silver frame bearing the letters 'AH', his standard gift to loyal friends. The other, Clara registered with a jolt, was a wedding photograph of the couple emerging from an honour guard of storm troopers in shirtsleeves and caps. The one she had seen that first day in the bookshop. She picked it up. There were Magda and Goebbels with Hitler trailing diffidently behind, looking like someone's affable uncle. How happy the bride looked, how proud the groom.

In the distance there was a shout, which made her jump, then the bang of a door. A few seconds later Magda entered.

Her face was flushed and her eyes glazed. For a second she stared at Clara as if perplexed to see her there, then put up a hand to her neck. As she did, Clara saw a row of fading fingerprints on the skin, and wondered at the ferocity of the argument. Magda's necklace was broken. She stood motionless but too late to prevent its unravelling as it rolled and scattered, spilling a pearly diaspora across the carpet. Clara bent down but Magda waved a hand.

'Don't worry. The maid will collect them.'

She went across to her dressing table and sat down, bending her head, to apply a dusting of powder to her face. Her shoulders could not have been tighter if she had been wearing a steel brace. Given Magda's normal rigid self-control, Clara was shocked by her loss of composure.

'Thank you for coming, Fräulein Vine. I asked you here because the first designs we have had made for the Bureau have arrived and I thought perhaps you could try them out. We have been given some splendid headquarters in the Columbushaus, did I mention?'

'No. How lovely.'

'Very appropriate and so kind of Joseph to arrange it. We move in next month . . .'

She stumbled to a halt. In the mirror Clara could see her mouth working, trying to maintain control.

'I'm sorry. Perhaps you could come back another time.'

'If you like.' Clara made for the door, but something stopped her. Tentatively she went over and hovered a hand above Magda's shoulder.

'Frau Goebbels, is something wrong?'

She had no idea how Magda would take this gesture and for a moment guessed it would be considered an unforgiveable breach. At first Magda shrugged off her hand and summoned her accustomed formality. 'I must apologize, Fräulein Vine, for this emotion. I was only discharged from the clinic last month and my constitution is delicate . . .' then she broke off, and buried her face in her hands.

'Do you know, Fräulein Vine, I sometimes ask myself why I ever married again?' She stared defiantly at Clara in the mirror. 'I had everything I could want – a car, a seven-room apartment in Reichskanzler Platz, maids, all the clothes I needed, a generous allowance from Gunther, my first husband. I was only eighteen when I married him, and he was twenty years older than me.' She dabbed at her reddened nose and looked up at Clara meaningfully. 'Klaus is an older man too, I know.'

With a shock Clara realized that Magda must assume she was sleeping with Müller. She blushed, but Magda was staring at her own reflection in the mirror.

'Twenty years is a lot.' She fumbled for her gold-tipped cigarettes with trembling fingers. 'Yet Gunther Quandt was a decent man. When we divorced he took me to dinner at Horchers. Roast partridge we had, if I remember rightly.' In a quieter voice, almost as if she was talking to herself, she continued. 'Four thousand marks monthly allowance, plus fifty thousand marks to purchase a house.'

Clara couldn't help thinking of Leo Quinn's face.

"Ask them questions. And just tell me what they talk about. That's all."

She sat on the apricot silk chair, and said, 'So how did you meet the Herr Doktor?'

'I had had an accident. A car smash, and though I was not badly hurt, I spent several weeks in hospital. While I was there, lying in bed day after day, I did some serious thinking. I became convinced that I should find a purpose, and that was when I began to get interested in politics. There was a NASDAP meeting one evening, and I went along. At first, I felt so embarrassed, so out of place – the people, and the smell, the sweaty bodies in that hall, all the Brown Shirts, you can't imagine. But when I heard Joseph talk, something in me answered that. In the midst of all that excitement, the shouting, the roaring, he was so calm. And his suit was shabby. He needed mothering. That's what I thought.'

She looked down at the wedding photograph on the dressing table beside her.

'I taught him so much too. Do you know he had no idea how to eat lobster before he met me? And when he tried to use French, he would mispronounce the words. Can you imagine? I taught him table manners. I smoothed his rough edges. That easy charm he has in society, it was all down to me.'

She blew her nose. 'Perhaps I shouldn't have bothered. We married just over two years ago. Just two years ago, and now he looks at me like he wishes me dead.'

'Everyone has tiffs,' said Clara, aware how lame her advice sounded. But if Magda considered her reassurance inadequate, she didn't show it.

'This is not what you would call a tiff.' She stabbed her cigarette in the cut-glass ashtray. 'He's completely irrational.'

Clara kept silent. It was almost as if Magda thought she didn't matter. As if she were a servant. Was it because she was half-English, and may not be in the country for long, that she could be confided in without risk? Or was it that way Magda had, of disregarding most of humanity, as if they had no private thoughts or feelings? She realized Magda rarely asked anything about herself, where she lived, for example, or her acting. Magda was simply consumed by the drama of her own existence.

'Do you know I have people sending anonymous letters telling me my husband is seeing actresses?'

'People are always ready to say spiteful things. Especially anonymously.'

'Oh, but what they say is true. He betrays me at every turn. The other day I made him swear by the life of our daughter that he hadn't betrayed me when I knew that very night he planned to meet a woman. It's so ironic. My husband has very firm views on the role of women, as I'm sure you know. He's very keen to restore their dignity to them.'

'I heard him talking about that on the wireless.'

The Doktor's latest pronouncement had come on Frau Lehmann's set just the previous evening, while Clara was tackling an overcooked chop with kale and dumplings, one of Frau Lehmann's spécialités de la maison.

"The first, best, and most suitable place for the woman is in the family," came Goebbels' sharp bark, "and her most glorious duty is to give children to her people and nation. This is her highest mission."

'Today he's going to open an exhibition on the German Frau. Such firm views on the German Frau, but when it comes to the Fräuleins,' Magda almost spat. 'Skinny little foreigners.'

She slammed the wedding photograph face down and reached for the other, the silver-framed one from which Hitler stared off enigmatically into the distance.

'You know, when this happens I tell myself, "Love is meant for husbands but my love for Hitler is stronger." It might be hard for you to understand, but it's true. I would give my life for the Führer. He is a wonderful man. Sometimes, when he has left, you feel a kind of vacuum.'

'But if that was the case then why . . .?'

'Why did I marry Joseph? Hitler told me he can love no woman, only Germany. Perhaps that was why I consented. So I could be close to the Führer.'

This thought seemed to console her and she blew her nose and looked earnestly at Clara.

'Forgive me for being so emotional, but I feel I can talk to you. It's hard to talk to people here. Joseph hates me to gossip and everyone here tittle-tattles. They just want political advantage, but that doesn't really apply to you, does it?'

'Not at all.'

'You know, my first husband was jealous. He wanted to know exactly what I was doing every moment of the day, but I thought Joseph might be different.' She sniffed bitterly. 'It seems not.'

'But your husband has nothing to be jealous about.'

Clara noticed the hand holding the photograph was trembling. Magda raised her face in the mirror and there was a flicker of truth in her eyes.

'I wonder, Fräulein . . . there's something you might help me with. A matter of some delicacy. You see . . .'

Just then, there was a sharp little cry outside and a bash against the door.

'*Gott im Himmel!*'

The maid peered round, holding the baby in her arms. She had a feathery shock of dark hair and chubby limbs encased in an exquisitely stitched, smocked-front white dress.

'I'm sorry, Frau Doktor,' she stammered, 'but you said eleven o'clock.'

When she saw her mother the baby held out her little arms and at the sight of her daughter Magda brightened somewhat, stubbed out her cigarette and took her on her lap.

'Isn't she lovely? Joseph was so disappointed not to have a boy but now he adores her. He gets her up no matter what time he gets home. It's not good for her routine, but what can I do? She loves her daddy.'

She held up her silver hand mirror and the baby reached for it, staring round-eyed at her own face.

'The Führer finds her enchanting. All the senior men play with her.'

'She's very pretty.' Clara reached out and stroked the fine downy hair of the child as she sat on her mother's lap.

'I've always loved children. I adore being surrounded by them. I only married my first husband because he had two motherless sons, and then after I had Harald we took in three others, whose mother had died. But now the others are gone, Harald's with his father and this little one is all I have.'

She hugged the child to her and said, 'Forgive me, Fräulein, forget what I said. Perhaps we should try the clothes out another time. On Thursday perhaps? Would that suit you?'

'Of course.'

As she bent over the child, Clara's silver locket dangled irresistibly and the baby clutched at it.

'What a pretty necklace!' said Magda.

'My mother gave it to me. At least she bought it for me before she died.'

'When did she die?'

'Just before my sixteenth birthday.'

A new expression entered Magda's eyes. 'I'm so sorry. I always think it must be the hardest thing in the world for a child to be without its mother.'

Chapter Twenty-six

On the days when Clara was required on set, Herr Lamprecht sent a car to ferry her to Babelsberg. She was glad of it. Not only did the sight of a gleaming Mercedes pulling up at the house visibly impress Frau Lehmann, but it gave Clara an hour each day when she was spared the anxiety of wondering if she was being spied on or followed.

Since agreeing to Leo's request, her behaviour had changed at some profound level. She had become as sensitive as if she had shed an entire layer of skin. She didn't use the telephone because Leo had told her it could be tapped. You could generally tell, he said, because the police were still pretty inept at it and audibility was always affected, but it was better not to risk it. Not that she had anyone to telephone anyway. Yet the very notion of surveillance, that telephones might be tapped or mail intercepted, had opened up a whole new way of seeing the world.

In turn, she learnt how to notice and recall far more than she had before. She looked at things, not in the clinical, indiscriminate way that a camera might, but scanning for incongruity. Already, as an actress, she was used to observing human tics and behaviours, but now she was being asked to remember aspects that might otherwise have escaped her entirely. She decided to practise. When she walked around the city she searched out other people and tried to memorize the colour of a man's tie, or the rings on a woman's hand. She had always had a good memory. As children they had played a game involving ordinary objects on a tray – a box of matches, a corkscrew, a pencil – which increased each time in number until only one person recalled them all, and it was usually her. Now she dug out those old skills and polished them up again. She read car number plates and tried to retain the first three digits. She noted the number of windows in a house, or the number of flags on a shop. She counted railings and associated them with an image in her head, a trick her mother had taught her with a shopping list. She was constantly on alert. It was like looking at a picture where everything was significant, each detail mattered and nothing could be discounted.

She would wait a second at street corners to see if the people who came after her were the same who had been behind her at the corner before. She would stop just before a road crossing to light a cigarette, obliging anyone coming after her to pass and cross in front of her. She watched out for discrepancies. Why did the old woman who walked into the shop with a stick come out again and appear to manage perfectly well without one? Why were there two men sitting in a parked car? Once, passing a man on a bench in the Tiergarten, she noticed that his newspaper was turned to the same page ten minutes later.

It was impossible when she did this to forget that her father back in England was being followed too. Perhaps there were shabby men in macs outside Ponsonby Terrace who would trail him every time he left for the Carlton Club, or note down the visitors who came to the door. Maybe they even opened his mail, or employed bright young men to chat to Angela at parties. She wondered what Daddy would say if he knew and it was telling to realize that she had simply no idea. She may have learned to observe the world in detail, but when it came to her own father she had no insight whatsoever. She supposed he would regard her own behaviour as treacherous. Acting against his interests while trading on his reputation with the Nazis. He would probably cut her off entirely for such a betrayal. But finding out about Grandmother Hannah had convinced her more than ever that she was right. She may have nothing of significance to give Leo, but that didn't mean she wouldn't try. Gradually the nervous tension dissipated and she felt instead very calm.

On set between takes, Clara spent most of the time chatting to Karin Hardt, the young blonde actress whose role she had to reproduce in English. The script, with its story of a secret agent on the trail of stolen military secrets in Venice, was shambolic, and her character, a flighty love interest whose actions unwittingly helped military intelligence to perpetrate a daring coup, was paper thin, but the actors were friendly and even the grand Olga Chekhova smiled and offered cigarettes. Karin was obsessed with beauty tips and spent her time chewing gum, in the belief that it firmed the jaw. She looked with dismay at the tan that was forming on Clara's skin as a result of the spring sunshine and advised her to splash her face with ice water and massage sugar and lemon juice into her skin before going to bed.

'She's a girl, not a pancake!' said Herr Lampecht who had overheard.

'Besides,' added Hans Albers gallantly, 'Clara doesn't need any help in that department. She's an English rose.'

So Clara guessed the face she presented to the world must be convincing enough.

Privately in the dressing room, amid the pots of scented cream and jars of thick beige make-up, she perfected her new persona in the mirror, emulating the kind of flirtatiousness that Helga practised, with a girlish flippancy and a touch of the scatter-brained actress. She put on the blonde wig she had been given and saw how it transformed her face, spilling light on the skin, evening out the subtleties of expression. Every natural instinct, such as her unfortunate tendency to flush at times of emotion, or to talk too much when nervous, must be suppressed or disguised. Yet the process of erasing her natural self and cultivating a different one had little to do with costumes or wigs. It needed to start from within. She thought back to Paul Croker, her old acting coach. "*It is not enough to look like Viola, it is not enough to sound like Viola, you must be Viola.*" She must learn her role as though it was written on her skin in invisible ink, until she carried it around with her, like her own shadow.

She saw Magda only once, when she called in to help send invitations for the celebration of the National Socialist People's Welfare. Frau Ley was on her way out, her skin as polished as Sèvres china, her fair hair rolled at the nape of her neck.

Clara found Magda in the drawing room, mournful and depressed. Between signing invitations personally and stuffing envelopes, she told Clara all about the Leys' luxurious home in Grunewald, with its swimming pool and marble hall, and the gossip that the squat, thick-lipped Ley regularly attacked his wife in an alcoholic rage.

'To think a woman like that is made to suffer by a brute of a husband.'

Somehow, though, it felt like Magda was not thinking of Frau Ley at all.

Once she met Clara's eyes directly and she felt sure that Magda was about to raise the 'matter of some delicacy' she had mentioned before. But Goebbels arrived home at that moment and the sight of him passing in the corridor made the hair rise on Clara's neck, even though he marched straight to his study without a greeting.

Back at the villa, Frau Lehmann hung a portrait of the Führer in her bedroom. It was colour tinted in an amateurish way, giving his lips and cheeks an odd, rosy glow that suggested he had defied his own strictures on lipstick and rouge. At night Clara turned it to the wall.

Then one evening about a week later she found an envelope in an unfamiliar hand waiting for her on the hall table.

Chapter Twenty-seven

Leo stood before the landscape, absorbed. A Brueghel, it must be, with peasants battling through a wintry landscape quite unlike the bright spring morning outside. The scurrying figures in the foreground, bent beneath their burdens of logs and herding their geese, seemed entirely unaware that in the far distance, a crucifixion was taking place on a patch of waste ground outside the city walls. How brilliantly, Leo thought, the painter had depicted the ordinary objects: a straw basket, a leather hat, a little dog on a chain. A fashionable woman, in a rich orange gown. Her husband, in a leather hat and cream cotton scarf. All had been rendered with loving faithfulness. The horror of the crucifixion, an event of dreadful cruelty, was taking place to the far right of the frame. A phalanx of soldiers followed the condemned to the gallows. Some watched curiously, mothers sat excited children down to enjoy the procession. Others went about their business entirely unmoved. This spectacle of misery was nothing special. The death that awaited the felons came to everyone sooner or later. In the distance, an exquisite city, like a new Jerusalem, rose with gleaming towers.

He saw her reflection on the glass of the picture, but did not turn.

'The *Crucifixion*,' she said. 'Brueghel the Younger.' She fingered the ticket that had arrived the previous evening in a plain envelope with no accompanying note.

Wednesday 5 April, Alte Nationalgalerie. Admit one.

'At least it's still here,' Leo said conversationally, as if engaging in art appreciation with a fellow visitor. 'I've heard Goering has begun helping himself to whatever catches his eye. All the gallery owners are terrified when he comes to visit. He's already had Rubens' *Diana at the Stag Hunt* taken out of the Kaiser Friedrich Museum and put up in his own place.'

'Goebbels disapproves of robbing the galleries.'

'As does Hitler, apparently. Mind you, given his taste, it would be a favour to everyone if he did spirit his favourites away.'

They walked around the gallery like tourists. Part of Leo wished they were. They peered into glass cabinets jumbled with watercolours and gouaches. On the second floor they entered a side room of foreign artists, and found Millet and Corbet, and Constable's house on Hampstead Heath. They stopped in front of a Degas, flush with the pink and apricot flesh tones of a woman dressing. It reminded Leo a little of Marjorie Simmons, in the deft way she refastened her brassiere after lovemaking, putting herself firmly out of reach. Repackaging herself. That way women had with their bodies, of controlling them after an ecstasy of release. He wondered about Clara too, whether she loved to watch herself during sex, the way Marjorie did. But then he reproached himself. Today she was wearing a navy suit and a blue hat tipped to one side. From the shadows under her eyes, it seemed she was a little tired.

'How is your acquaintance?'

'Not good. She looks exhausted and she's constantly on edge . . .' Clara hesitated.

'What?'

'It may be nothing, but I think there's something wrong.'

'Go on.'

'I can't work out what it is. I thought she was going to tell me the other day. She said she wanted to talk to me about "a matter of some delicacy." She started crying.'

'Crying? Why?'

'They'd had a row.'

'What about?'

'That's just it. I'm not certain. Though I'm sure it was serious.'

'Politics perhaps?'

She gave a short laugh. 'I shouldn't think so. She did complain that Joseph is betraying her.'

'He's a famous womanizer.'

His eyes were surveying the room while they talked. There was only one other visitor, American it looked like, by the Kodak Brownie he was carrying.

'Yes, and it's hard for her. Apparently the girls just swarm over him. She has to take such care over her appearance. She obviously feels she needs to keep up.'

'Without the help of cosmetics, one assumes.'

'Not at all. And forget no drinking or smoking either. She changes outfits several times a day. He's just the same. He takes manicures and he sits under a sun lamp. He thinks it makes him more attractive.'

'I shouldn't think it's the suntan the women are falling for.'

'It's strange though, isn't it?' she mused. 'All this talk of making women more simple and natural, when Magda and the other women are doing their level best to be as glamorous as possible.'

'It matters, glamour. People believe that an élite should be glamorous. The Nazis don't want to actually *look* like a gang of murderous roughnecks now, do they?'

A gaggle of schoolchildren, satchels on their backs, entered the room, accompanied by a teacher with a booming voice. The girls, in short white socks and gymslips, stared obediently up at the Brueghel, but the boys at the back glanced at Clara. Leo drifted away into a room of Post Impressionists and she followed him.

'I suppose he'll end up leaving her,' she said.

'I doubt it. She reflects well on him. It's more a case of whether she will stay with him, I'd have thought. I wonder why she stands it.'

'I asked her that. She says he's a brilliant man. He lives three times as intensively as other men. He can't be judged by a middle-class moral code. She's very proud of him. She remembers the days when he would give talks in Communist neighbourhoods and they would throw beer mugs at him, and now he's the youngest ever minister in Germany.'

'So she does share his politics?'

'I didn't say that. They argue a lot about women. He thinks that women should concentrate on being mothers. He says he respects them too much to allow them involvement in politics.'

'That's rich. Without the votes of women, the Nazis wouldn't be where they are.'

He stopped to admire a nude, looking closely at the thick, stippled paint of the thighs, marvelling at how a painter could conjure such a convincing illusion of living flesh from oil and greasy pigment.

'She seems to talk quite readily to you.'

'I think she's lonely. They don't have many friends in high command. I suppose she just likes having someone to chat to. Someone who's not going to spread gossip.'

'So this latest row then. It's just about the womanizing?'

The American had entered the room and begun photographing the paintings. Leo wondered briefly why. There were plenty of postcards weren't there, in the kiosk downstairs? Then again, Americans tended to photograph everything. It was a habit of theirs. Perhaps they thought looking through the lens of a camera was the only authentic way of seeing the world.

'I don't think so. She was talking about him being jealous.'

'Who would he be jealous of?'

'That's just it. She's there at home most of the time, unless she's out with him. They seem to spend every night watching films.'

He drifted away as if transfixed by a Seurat of three women at the seaside in varying stages of undress. Clara caught up with him.

'I still can't understand why you want to know all these trivial things. What use is it to you?'

He gestured to the painting in front of them. 'Pointillism.' She frowned, so he continued. 'The amassing of tiny specks of colour, which when seen close appear meaningless but from a distance create an effect. They got the idea from tapestries originally. When French restorers worked on them, they noticed that the only way to replace missing sections was to look at the colours surrounding them. You need to look at the interplay of colours, the role of every little bit, to find out what's missing. It all counts. When you're trying to see the big picture, you need details.'

Clara stared at the women and the seascape behind them, letting the focus of her eye relax until the turquoises and the azures of the water blurred into one brilliant blue. She spoke softly, without moving her head.

'Goebbels distrusts me, I know. You should have seen his face when I visited the other day.'

She remembered the shining, intent dark eyes that flickered over her as he passed down the corridor.

'Don't worry. You're doing well.'

Leo loved being here, surrounded by scenes from the past, reminders that beauty and sensitivity and civilization had flourished and would flourish again outside this brutal regime. He wished they really were a pair of ordinary sightseers, drifting around discussing art, with nothing more pressing to decide than where to go for lunch and whether to visit the Brandenburger Tor or Sanssouci. He'd like to know if Clara felt as passionate about painting as she did about poetry. He longed to debate the pictures in front of them. Instead of which, he had a pile of work waiting for him back at the office, no chance of lunch and his conversation with Clara must be confined to the business in hand. He stared over at a small Manet pastel of a woman naked in a tin bath. It was a graceful, understated study, the light glancing off her ordinary, imperfect curves. The model's back was turned to the painter, and she was looking up at him, bold and unashamed, as the water ran in sparkling rivulets down her thighs. She seemed utterly unconcerned at being observed. Not proud and theatrical like Marjorie, but spontaneous and fresh.

'You haven't mentioned Müller.'

Clara was looking at the nude too, and immediately detected his train of thought.

'I haven't seen much of him,' she said shortly.

'That's a shame.'

'Not for me.'

'But this isn't for you,' he said, with an edge of impatience, as though he were talking to a subordinate, or a child.

'I know it's not. But I don't see how this . . . whatever you call it . . . can profit from my seeing Sturmhauptführer Müller.'

'It will help. Just the appearance of it would help.'

'Why?'

'You need to be someone they would never suspect. Anyone liaising with a Nazi official would have to be above suspicion.'

'I don't see . . .'

'You may not see, but that doesn't matter, Clara. Just keep meeting him.'

He was riffling through a French guide to the museum's pictures, consulting the notes on the Manet.

'It's perfect from every point of view,' he continued as if he was explaining the style of the work in front of them. 'It suits them, because they're keen to build up connections with people from England, and it suits us because Müller is valuable cover.'

Clara looked down at the page too. 'But if I keep meeting him he'll assume I return his interest. What can I do about that?' He didn't answer, so in a low tone she added, 'It's difficult to go on meeting a man who . . . who expects something.'

Leo turned a leisurely page. 'No one said doing this was going to be easy. It's for your own safety. You'll think of something.'

This remark had a curious effect on her. She looked him full in the face, with a high spot of colour in her cheeks and a kind of frustration in her expression, and then in a tight voice she said, 'I'm starting to wonder why I'm doing this at all.'

After which she turned abruptly, and made her way down the wide marble hall and out of the gallery.

Leo stared at her retreating back in astonishment. If he had been taking notes, he would have had to include the impression that there were tears in her eyes.

Chapter Twenty-eight

Goering's pale grey airforce jacket was studded with strips of medals, marching across the broad expanse of his chest.

'If he gets any more he'll have to start going round the back,' murmured Leo's boss Foley, in a voice drier than the sherry he was sipping.

Dyson, the embassy attaché, grunted. 'Goebbels has a new nickname for him apparently. He calls him the Christmas Tree.'

'They say he's had a rubber set made to wear in the bath,' added Leo.

The new Prime Minister of Prussia was attending a party at the British Embassy for which a collection of dignitaries, socialites and assorted journalists had been assembled. No matter how grandiose Goering might be, he was never likely to outshine Number 70, Wilhelmstrasse. The grand colonnaded Palais Strousberg was a magnificent and stately building, designed originally for a railway pioneer and bought by the British Government when the previous owner, a banker, went bankrupt. The visitor passed through a two-storey marble hall, where fountains splashed gently, to a spectacular ballroom, which that evening contained a large gathering of National Socialist officials, fortified by liberal quantities of His Majesty's champagne. They had all been there quite a while. In the new regime everyone who was not a Nazi, even if they were foreign ambassadors, expected to be kept waiting. And Nazis themselves were kept waiting by officials of a senior rank. This etiquette of unpunctuality broke down a little, however, towards the top. Although Goering had arrived promptly, Goebbels was late, which could either have been unavoidable, or a calculated snub, and going by everything they knew, the British assumed the latter.

Leo moved to talk to a group of aides. It was incredible to him how easily the National Socialists had eased themselves into high society. Industrialists and aristocrats fought to host their evenings. These men who just months ago were staging fist fights on street corners, now spent their evenings being courted by ambassadors and princes. Though Herr Hitler was not attending tonight, there was a big turn-out of all the top brass. The rising young architect Albert Speer was there and von Ribbentrop had just arrived with his hard-faced wife, her gaze raking the room like a searchlight for the most prestigious guests. Across the room the bushy-browed Rudolf Hess glowered at Goering with a look of invincible hatred. Goering himself was kissing hands as he circulated, his pudgy fingers glittering with rings like some ancient potentate.

'The Minister is celebrating his success on today's hunting trip,' said one of the lackeys, stiff as a ramrod with an expression to match. 'He has managed to shoot more than three hundred in a single afternoon.'

'Animals, I trust,' murmured Leo.

The Nazi gave him a contemptuous look. So much got lost in translation with these British. He was a desiccated fellow with a face of parched solemnity and all the conversational skills of a Ministry press release. He tried again.

'Let us hope that tonight will be evidence of the friendship between our two nations. Germany has a great love of

England, whereas France plans to squeeze her like an orange. It is France that England should beware of.'

'Is that so?'

'Of course. Although it is important that England recognizes she has responsibilities too.'

'What might they be?'

'England must be the breakwater to stop the Communist flood. You saw how the Communists set fire to our Reichstag? They would like to set fire to the whole of Europe.'

Leo noticed Hitchcock, Archie Dyson's deputy, coming towards him, signalling that he lose his companion. He carried two glasses of champagne and nodded towards a side door that led into a corridor. A few feet further on was an empty office, the typing pool, which Hitchcock entered, kicking the door closed behind them. He didn't turn on the light.

'Thanks, Quinn.' He handed over a glass. 'Just to say. We're rather pleased with your progress.'

He perched on the edge of a table and leant back. Hitchcock liked to cultivate the air of effortless establishment superiority he thought was essential for someone working for the British Government's secret service. In that, as in so many things, he was mistaken, Leo thought. From what he had seen of it, the secret service was full of oddballs and misfits. Lone wolves like himself who knew how to assimilate, but never properly belonged. Besides, he never really saw the point of Hitchcock, who seemed to spend most of his time playing golf and being dined by businessmen in the Ku'damm's classier bars.

With difficulty Leo wrenched his thoughts back onto the subject of this conversation. Hitchcock was referring to the communication Leo had sent a week ago to London and was now regretting.

"Fluent German speaker. In regular contract with Frau Docktor Geobbels and Goering's girlfriend. Privy to an enormous amount of inconsequential chatter, but possibly information."

The message had come back that Leo was to "maintain contact". His next report must be written the day before Bag Day, the day the diplomatic bag went to London, which was tomorrow. He should be aware there was increasing Gestapo surveillance of foreigners. Telephones would be tapped and there would be routine shadowing of people with embassy or journalistic links. It went on to say his source should be made fully aware of the operational difficulties and take all the "requisite precautions".

'That's good.'

Hitchcock was lighting another Corona. He would never have bought his own cigars. He was probably making the most of the Embassy's supplies.

'Yes, and it's a stroke of luck for us to find a source so close to the high command. That kind of high-grade intelligence is going to get increasingly valuable, I'd say. Head Office are beginning to wake up to the realities of this regime. There's talk of budgets being increased.'

Leo was only too aware that Clara was a valuable prize. The opportunity she had to peer below the surface of Nazi society, and glimpse the fault lines and the fractures that lay beneath, made her an extraordinary asset. Unique probably. But hearing Hitchcock talk about her put Leo's teeth on edge.

'Pleased to hear it.'

'In fact, while you're at it, there's something else I'd like you to take a look at.'

'What's that?'

'Probably nothing. But they're quite interested in London. He's a walk-in. He says he represents the Red Front Fighters Union. He wants paying for identifying Communist contacts in Britain.'

'And would he be in a position to know?'

'Yes, but they want us to check him out first. I wondered if you'd see him. You might need Xantener Strasse.'

The apartment in Xantener Strasse was in an anonymous beige building situated a block south of the Ku'damm. It was a tall, nineteenth-century block, with frosted glass in the front door, and a long, dark hallway lined with pocked tiles. The owner of the bakery next door lived on the ground floor and the rest of the block housed the kind of transient population that passes through any large city, travelling salesmen, the proprietor of a ceramics factory in Munich, a visiting academic from the University of Hanover. Neighbourliness was in short supply, which made it pretty much ideal. The British apartment was on the third floor and contained a bedroom, a bathroom, money and a small amount of tinned food. As far as the owner of the block was concerned it belonged to a Herr Edvard Zink, who ran a small company supplying cigarettes and spent most of his time away, leaving the apartment deserted, apart from the occasions when Herr Zink's employees spent the odd night in Berlin. The company's brass plaque was by the bell. It was generally used as a safe house by whoever needed it.

'There's a lot of interest in that direction just now,' said Hitchcock. 'It's down to the Nazis' haul after the Reichstag affair.'

He was referring to the day after the fire, when vans of storm troopers had descended on the headquarters of Social Democrat organisations and the KPD, the German Communist Party, seizing the members and carrying off lorryloads of documents.

'There was a cache of papers seized by the SA from the KPD. Goering claims there were plans for attacks on public buildings and assassinations of public figures. London takes the Comintern threat seriously, as you know. Guy Liddell from B division has been invited over to discuss the haul with Rudolf Diels. I take it you know who I mean?'

Leo nodded. It was hard to miss the man Goering had appointed head of the political police, if only because his hatchet face was badly marked by duelling injuries inflicted when he was a student. Diels was a lawyer by training, an expert on building up information to incriminate political radicals and, if that didn't frighten them, the three long curving scars that puckered and bisected his visage never failed to induce a shiver. The challenge was to tear your gaze from those scars and fix instead on his narrow, calculating eyes.

'The Prince of Darkness? Friendly chap. I think I saw him talking to the Ambassador earlier.' Leo stood, hands in pockets, studiedly neutral.

'Yes, well. From what they say, apparently there's records of Soviet funding for organizations in Britain and details of individuals who pose a threat.'

'You'd think if we're talking about threatening individuals, there's no shortage of them right under our noses.'

'Price of liberty is eternal vigilance and all that,' said Hitchcock, tapping the side of his nose in a way that irritated Leo intensely. 'Names have come up that need checking out.'

'Right.'

'So you can take care of the walk-in then? You'll set up a meeting?'

'Sure. Ask him if he likes Rilke.'

'Rilke?' Hitchock's face expressed a mixture of suspicion and incomprehension that made Leo think of the line in that

Schlageter play: "When I hear the word culture I reach for my gun." Already several senior Nazis had been heard parroting the line for their own amusement, but it could have been coined for Hitchcock too.

'He's the Germans' favourite poet. Tell him there's a bookshop on Leonhardstrasse which has a great selection.'

'Right you are.' Hitchcock cast him a quizzical glance, then patted him on the back. 'Good man.'

They went back into the ballroom, and Hitchcock said, 'Ah, I see old Mickey Mouse has arrived.'

It was fascinating to see Goebbels close up: the huge ears, which had earned him the nickname, the tight, clever-looking face, the alert brown eyes. But it was his companion whom Leo was looking out for. Sturmhauptführer Müller, a dark, good-looking brute in his forties, was whispering into the little minister's ear. He was a burly, muscular man with a tan that suggested a life outdoors and a physical energy only just confined by his perfectly pressed uniform. At once Leo's senses were on the alert. Every instinct in his body united and he felt a stab of emotion, which he identified as professional attention. He signalled to the waiter for another glass of champagne.

So this was the man who had taken an interest in Clara. What had she said? "It's difficult to go on meeting a man who expects something."

He knew exactly what she meant, but he had ignored her perfectly normal female delicacy. It was hardly a surprise that Müller should take an interest in her. There was something about those dark brows, not the plucked, pencilled lines German women went in for, and the violet eyes beneath them. Something that suggested turbulence barely contained, along with the petulant lips and the curly hair that constantly escaped from its style. That scent she wore, with its spice and vanilla, that you caught a snatch of when close. He pictured again the flush on her cheeks and the filmy eyes as she left the art gallery and yet again regretted being so curt with her. God knows what she thought of him. But there was no choice. It was the only way. The sooner she understood what she had signed up for, the better really.

Leo accepted another glass from the waiter and took a large gulp. An agreeable numbness was starting to take the edge off things. It was time to concentrate on his duties as a host. Yet it was impossible to stop thoughts of Clara running through his mind. He heartily wished he had never mentioned her existence to Head Office, only at the time it had just seemed too promising an opening to ignore. With the result that he had raised expectations and placed her under a threat she couldn't properly understand.

The nature of that threat had in a matter of months become only too plain to him. Since their seizure of power, the brutality the Nazis had employed on the streets had become legitimized, and violent interrogation, torture and arbitrary imprisonment were now the norm. The mere fact of being female did not guarantee decent treatment. The first reports from women who had been arrested in the recent crackdown suggested they suffered the same beatings and savagery as their male counterparts. The fate of a woman found spying didn't bear thinking about.

A sick feeling of disgust arose in him. He felt contagious. As though merely by meeting Clara he had infected her with some kind of disease that also ran through him. He looked across at the circle of National Socialists laughing and drinking and standing slightly apart from them he saw Bella Fromm, the upmarket gossip columnist from the *Vossische Zeitung*, spikily aquiline with her raven hair, and the hooded eyes that implied, before she had written a word, the profound scepticism she felt towards the new regime. Then he thought back to the problem of the message from Head Office.

"The source should be made fully aware of all operational difficulties and take the requisite precautions."

What did those "requisite precautions" include? There were so many skills Clara would need to learn. To listen out for the click on the telephone line that suggested the police were present. To cultivate that sixth sense that recognized a pattern and when it was changed. To vary her route, think before speaking, never relax and as much as she could, with the figure and face she had, avoid attracting attention. Most of all she must never underestimate the savagery of these thugs masquerading as statesmen with their medals and armbands, sipping His Majesty's champagne. In truth, the best precaution for a woman like Clara was to be as far away from here as possible, in England preferably, performing in *Hay Fever* or whatever that play was she had talked about. He thought again of the moment she had come to him at the office, eyes shining with some defiant emotion, and he wondered what had provoked her desire to help.

'You're miles away.'

A woman touched him on the elbow. It was Rupert's friend. Mary Harker. She had what Americans called 'the girl-next-door look'. Not exactly attractive, with her glasses and stubborn straw coloured hair which stuck out awkwardly and looked like she brushed it once in the morning, and then not again all day. She had sallow skin and a beaky nose, but they were more than compensated for by a sweet, downturned, deprecatory smile. From what he knew of Rupert's romantic tastes Leo didn't rate her chances of a long-lasting relationship with his friend, but he couldn't help warming to her.

'I enjoyed the other evening. Rupert pretended he needed an early night, but that lasted about two minutes before he gave in and took us off to a nightclub. We were there until three a.m. and totally bleary when we rolled into the press conference the next day. We could hardly keep awake, which wasn't helped by the fact that we had to spend hours taking notes on the precise division of the Propaganda Department into ministries for the press and film and broadcasting and paperclips and so on. Infernally boring! How about you two? I bet you went dancing.'

'I went straight home.'

'Did you? And I was sure you two were going to sneak off somewhere!' She gave him a knowing look, which Leo blanked.

'How is she anyway? Clara?'

She was persistent. Leo had to give her that.

'I really wouldn't know, I'm afraid.'

'Ah well.' She gave up. 'It's quite a turnout tonight, isn't it, considering the low opinion they seem to have of you Brits. That chap over there told me that there's a gigantic conspiracy of international Jewry being organized from London.'

'So I hear.'

He lit a cigarette for her and they stood companionably, looking out at the assembled throng. The senior Nazis progressed around the room in a complicated gavotte, designed to avoid encountering each other.

'They don't look like they're enjoying themselves much, do they?' he observed.

'I guess a British Embassy cocktail party is a long way from a Bavarian beer cellar.'

'I hear there was another wave of arrests last night.'

'I heard that too,' she said. 'It came up in the morning press conference. But when my colleague from the *New*

Republic asked Goering about it, he said there has been no violence, the violence is over and anyone suggesting that there is still violence will face reprisals.'

'Violent reprisals, I take it.'

Leo noticed that Goebbels and Müller, in order to avoid crossing paths with Goering, were heading straight for them. Müller, immaculate in his SA breeches and knee boots, was already smiling speculatively in their direction. Seized by a violent aversion, whose cause he could not precisely define, Leo took Mary's elbow and hastily turned away.

Chapter Twenty-nine

The photographer from the *B.Z. am Mittag* was a fussy little man with a pernickety expression and a relentlessly worried manner. He had good reason too, considering that he had taken the best part of twenty minutes to set up his equipment in the drawing room of the Goebbels' home, where Clara was to be photographed wearing the designs of the first collection. There were a couple of large cameras on rickety tripods and both had to be fitted with the correct lenses, and then the lights placed in precise locations around the room. The curtains had to be drawn too, to get the light exactly right, and he was issuing his harried assistant with increasingly sharp orders as the lady of the house waited impatiently upstairs. Clara had compounded the problem herself by arriving late and Magda was at her most imperious, brimming with irritation. She was sitting at her dressing table, primping her hair with aggressive little jabs.

'I'm sorry I'm late. I overslept a little, I'm afraid.'

In reality Clara had sat in a coffee house by the tram stop, collecting her thoughts and bracing herself for the morning ahead. She regretted her bad temper with Leo the day before. At first she had put it down to tiredness or a lack of breakfast. But the truth was, she knew it wasn't that. It was Leo's assumption that she would be willing to do anything that was necessary with Müller. Did he realize what he was asking?

She was also engaged in what Paul Croker had called "getting in character". There was always the chance that Magda might regret her indiscretions and resolve to place a distance between them, so it was essential to preserve the breezy informality that she had created, if she was to gain any useful information. To be the young actress, thrilled to find herself at close quarters with the Nazi High Command, but so far out of politics that she was easy to talk to. She ran though her character in her head, the way she had in the past before going on stage. She straightened her shoulders, tidied her hair and tilted her hat so it sat at a slight angle. She caught a glimpse of herself in the coffee house window and tipped her head coyly. Up by the counter a man winked at her and she gave a broad smile. It was working all right.

It was hard to preserve the breezy informality, however, when the maid showed Clara into the dressing room. Magda's face was like thunder.

'Late? You need discipline Fräulein! I am never late. Routine is vital. No matter what time I go to bed, I always follow the same routine. In the morning, forty-two strokes of the hair-brush, two minutes exactly on the teeth. I always change for lunch and dinner and never go out without fixing my make-up. It's half the battle. That's what they taught me at the convent school in Brussels and it has stayed with me for life.'

'I didn't know you were in a convent,' said Clara, perching casually on a chair. 'Did you like it?'

'It was a regime,' she said coolly, spritzing her perfume. 'Like any regime it had good and bad points. The secret is to learn to live with it.'

With a shaking hand she reached for her pillbox and extracted a small blue pill. She was always taking pills, but

then, Clara had noticed, pill-taking was a great hobby among
women in Berlin. Helga too had her own little box of some
non-specific medication, which she said was herbal and
calmed her nerves. It was all of a piece, Clara thought, with
the astrology and the superstition and the fortune-telling. All
ways of alleviating a sickness no doctor could define.

Magda ran a lipstick round her mouth and flicked a final
nimbus of powder on her immaculate face, perfecting the
mask Clara had seen so often in newspapers and magazines.

'These photographs are such an ordeal,' Magda sighed.
'Still, it's important to appear as beautiful as I can. You may
think this is foolish but I see it as my duty to Germany.'

'I don't think it's foolish, but I can't see why it's your
duty.'

'Why do you think?' She directed a reproving look
through the mirror. 'It's wonderful of the Führer to create
this opportunity for me to serve. After all, we all want to help
in the great endeavour of transforming Germany.'

'By looking beautiful?'

'Do you think that sounds frivolous? In fact, it's something
I learnt from abroad. It wasn't until I went to America and
saw what hostesses those women are, that I decided how I
should live. They were so well-dressed and beautifully
groomed, I realized then just how influential a hostess can be.'

'I never knew you'd been to America.' Clara gave a girlish
sigh. 'I'd love to visit.'

'It's an amazing place.' Magda gave a little laugh, fixing a
pair of pearl studs in her ears. 'I had such a time there. It was
before I met Joseph, of course. President Hoover's nephew
wanted to marry me. I went to Fifth Avenue! And Broadway!
But in the end it bored me. I wanted to come home.'

She braced her shoulders and gave herself a little shake.
'Now, if you wait here, I'll have my photograph taken, while

you change. Then it will be your turn. The outfits have been delivered in your size and I've chosen two contrasting styles to begin with. One for the rural woman, another for the girl-about-town type. Shoes too. They're over there.'

Magda disappeared and Clara picked up the clothes that had been made for her. They weren't quite as bad as the preliminary sketches had suggested, but not far off it. The first had the feel of a folk costume. It was made of heavy green woollen fabric, with a close-fitting top, bell shaped skirt and a sweetheart neckline. There was embroidery round the hems and cuffs. Presumably it was to be worn with Gretchen braids and no make-up. The girl-about-town costume could not be more different. It had a military look to it, made of brown worsted, with padded shoulders and a sleek pencil skirt. It was marginally less hideous than the first, so Clara took off the skirt and blouse she had arrived in, stripped to her slip and stockings and pulled it on.

She stood in front of the mirror and sighed. There was something about these outfits that drained all femininity and defied any kind of flirtatiousness. If she had wanted to play second tuba in a marching band, then the clumpy, low heels and military shoulders looked just right. But if she wanted to turn heads as a sophisticated girl about town, forget it.

It occurred to her that while she was on her own she should look around. Swiftly she ran through the cupboards in Magda's dressing room. The contents could not be further from those designed for the Reich Fashion Bureau. The wardrobe was fitted with special compartments for her shoes, dozens of them in satin and velvet, some bearing the label 'Hand Made in Florence by Ferragamo'. There were shelves of linen, and fur coats in a line. On one shelf stood her alligator handbag, and a clutch bag in black crocodile with a diamanté clasp. Above were evening gowns in diaphanous

chiffon with low-cut bodices and beaded straps, some backless and others with short capes floating from the shoulders.
Below were nightdresses in ivory crêpe de Chine, and a lace
bedjacket. As she rummaged, Clara kept her eye on the door
in the mirror. She even ran her hand beneath the frothy silk
slips and underwear folded with precision in the drawers, but
there was nothing here that could be of any interest at all.

After ten minutes she ventured down the corridor past the
bathroom, a magisterial affair with black marble bath and
gold taps, then downstairs and along to the drawing room.
Through the crack in the door she could see Magda being
photographed. The little man's nerves were in shreds, causing him to make numerous mistakes. First he dropped the
light, then he clipped the tripod with his foot, requiring him
to reposition the camera at length. Then he bustled across the
room to reposition Magda physically, a proposition that he
almost dared until he saw the expression on her face and
backed swiftly away. It was too painful to watch. Clara
wandered back down the corridor, passing the door to
Goebbels' study which had been left open, and on impulse
she slipped inside.

The study was obsessively tidy. Three sides of the room
were devoted to bookshelves, which extended floor to ceiling. A pair of leather armchairs stood before a tall window,
which looked out onto the gardens at the back of the house.
From a hook on the wall, she noticed, a suit hung and beneath
it a pair of patent leather shoes, one of them with a built-up
platform to accommodate the crippled foot, giving the
unnerving impression that Goebbels was present in ghostly
form. Positioned precisely on the desk was a row of sharp-
ened pencils, and beside them a cut-glass ashtray, a typewriter
and a framed photograph of Magda and the baby. Everything
was immaculate and nothing out of place. It spoke of

someone to whom control was all important. Not even a pencil would be allowed to step out of line.

Clara made her way over and pulled out the drawers. In the top one was a nail file, a hairbrush, a jar of pomade and a small atomizer of Scherk's Tarr cologne. In the second was a manila file of papers. They were subdivided into smaller files. Leafing through them she found one headed 'Employees of Ufa'. There followed a list of names. Quickly, and efficiently, she ran through them until she came to 'V', but hers was not there. She replaced the file and pulled out the drawer below. It contained a thick, leather-jacketed notebook, a diary by the look of it. The handwriting was small and densely packed. The first entries had been made in January that year and from what she could see Goebbels completed it several times a week. She looked at the entry datelined 1 April.

The boycott against the international atrocity propaganda has burst forth in full force in Berlin and the whole Reich. All Jewish businesses are closed. The public has everywhere proclaimed its solidarity. There is indescribable excitement in the air. The boycott is a great moral victory for Germany. We have shown the world abroad that we can call up the entire nation without thereby causing the least turbulence or excesses.

There were several more entries, pondering administrative changes in his office and his anxiety over the dated décor of the Palais Prinz Friedrich Leopold, which had been allocated to the new Propaganda Ministry. The most recent entry had a large X beside it. What did the X signify, Clara wondered. It couldn't be, surely it wasn't, the most obvious code of all, the one teenage girls put in their diaries, the mark that signified a secret liaison?

'You should be more careful, Fräulein.'

She jumped, and the acid taste of alarm sprang into her mouth. Heart racing, she found herself looking directly into the eyes of Klaus Müller. How was he able to approach so soundlessly? She hadn't heard a thing. It must be the thickness of the carpet. He was frowning, the fleshy mouth compressed into a harsh line.

'The Herr Doktor might want to know that there's a curious young English lady creeping around his house.' He closed the door behind them and came over. 'Exactly what do you think you are doing?'

She had never heard his voice without its jovial edge. At the sound of it her hands had dropped and the book fell back to its place in the drawer.

'The Frau Doktor asked me to wait while she was photographed.'

'In her husband's study?'

'Oh!' she laughed and placed her hand to her hammering chest. 'Is that what it is! I wondered why you were so angry. I thought it was the library!' She gestured to the shelves. 'All these books.'

She leant her body against the draw that held the diary, pushing it shut.

'It's the private office of the Reich Minister of Public Enlightenment and Propaganda and anyone snooping in here gets to explain themselves to the political police.'

'But,' she looked around the desk and picked up the silver-framed photograph, 'I was just admiring the picture of the Frau Doktor. There's nothing wrong with that, is there? And the baby is so adorable.'

Flustered, she talked on, protesting too much. 'Frau Goebbels said I should make myself at home. How should I have known this was his study? I was just killing time because that man from the newspaper is taking so long with these wretched photographs. He must think we have all day. And she has a headache. I don't like to think what kind of mood she's going to be in when she comes out.'

He continued glaring at her for a moment, then broke into a laugh. 'Oh, don't look so worried. I can keep your secret. Come here.'

She came out from behind the desk and stood in front of him. She noticed that he was growing a moustache. He placed his hands on her shoulders and looked down.

'Though I preferred you in what you were wearing before.'

He reached out a hand to her hip and she felt it travel across the ridge of her suspender belt. Her heart was racing but she tossed her head and struck a pose.

'Frau Goebbels chose the design, actually.'

'So this is the famous fashion enterprise, eh?' His fingers passed the curve of her hip and strayed lightly towards her groin. 'And I thought you hated uniforms.'

She forced herself to adopt a light, bantering tone. 'By wearing a uniform, the German woman subjugates her individual desires to the communal destiny of the German race. Surely you heard your boss on the radio the other night?'

'But of course. I would never miss it. Though I can think of more enjoyable ways to spend my evenings.' He extended one arm to prevent her stepping backwards and reached his hand up to twirl a lock of hair at her brow.

'On the subject of which, perhaps you'd like to come for a drive with me?'

'Now?'

'Not now. I have work to do with the Doktor. But tomorrow perhaps. We could drive out to the Grunewald. There's a villa I want to look at. It's just become available and I need

a country place.' His brown eyes were studying her meaningfully. 'We could stop on the way.'

'Perhaps some other time. I'm afraid I'll be at Babelsberg.'

'Well then.' He pulled her more tightly towards him and
she felt a surprising hardness against her belly. 'It's a long time
to wait, but on Thursday night there's a gala performance of
Madame Butterfly at the Staatsoper. Perhaps you would like to
accompany me?'

Clara braced herself. It was no good trying to avoid him.
She could think up endless excuses but the fact was, she was
supposed to be seeing him more. She freed herself from his
grasp with a little wriggle and smiled.

'I'd love to,' she heard her own voice, brightly flirtatious.
'I can think of no more enjoyable way to spend my evening.'

He adjusted his collar and checked his watch. 'Excellent. I
shall send my driver at six. And by the way, how is the film
going?'

'Very well, thank you.'

'Don't thank me.' He turned to go and stopped at the door
and winked. 'Or not entirely.'

Chapter Thirty

The next day, leaving work slightly early, Leo jumped on a tram, got off at the next stop, crossed a crowded street and took another up to Tiergarten. Slipping off the tram he changed to the S-Bahn and waited at the platform for the S5 to arrive. As it approached, he crossed swiftly to the opposite platform and grinned at the elderly lady who held the door for him just as the train was pulling out. Once he had settled down it was satisfying to see, above the top of his *Vossische Zeitung*, that a young man, slightly out of breath, was standing alone on the platform, watching distractedly as the train trundled westwards. When Leo reached Charlottenburg he left the train, paused momentarily at the S-Bahn entrance to light a cigarette and glanced behind him. There was no one there.

He had known he had a tail for some time. A skinny youth in a shabby overcoat could often be seen outside the café where he took his breakfast, pretending to interest himself in the morning news. It was to be expected. Everyone at the embassy here knew they would be followed sooner or later. There was a certain look, they called it *der deutsche Blick* – the German glance – which described the casual over-the-shoulder check everyone made now before talking to a friend in the street. Leo had caught a glimpse of this particular tail earlier. Sallow and pinched, with a spidery moustache, he was the kind of lad who had been throwing bricks at Communists in Moabit just a few months ago. Now he had now found a new career opening up to him, one that offered exercise and plenty of travel. Leo might have shaken him off for now, but he'd be back again tomorrow, no doubt. It shouldn't be a problem.

When he first accepted this job, before he came to Berlin, Leo had spent a couple of days in a shabby country house in Suffolk being taught the basics of the espionage agent's craft. A genial colonel with a gun dog trailing at his heels, who might well have been the house's owner, taught him all about communicating with Head Office and how to send messages in the diplomatic bag. A fey young man in a Fair Isle sweater, who looked more like an art historian than an intelligence agent, chatted about the political situation in Germany and quizzed him on how to assess the value of any information he might receive. The third part of the training, taught by a brusque character called Ralph Sidebottom, who had worked in Russia during the war, was what they called the Practical. Put that way it sounded more like a chemistry lesson than the grimly serious business it was, to do with disabling a man in a fist fight, executing a choke hold and handling a Beretta 418 pocket pistol, so small it could easily be concealed in the palm of a hand. But the main part of the Practical was about avoiding surveillance and general evasion, which was where the observation skills came in. Though in truth Leo's preparation had begun much further back than that.

When he was a boy he had loved bird-watching. For several years he had even entertained thoughts of being a naturalist. It had started with *The Observer's Book of Birds*, and progressed with a pair of binoculars and regular trips to the Essex marshes with his father, who would patiently lie alongside his son for hours in a hide, probably with no interest at all in lapwings or plovers, fortified only with a Thermos of tea and a bar of chocolate, until Leo would call it a day and the pair of them could cycle back to the station.

In time, academic work took over and Leo's enthusiasm had waned, and it was only when he began this business that he discovered how many others in the job shared his early predilection. Not just Hugo Chambers, with his passion for exotic creatures like the Indonesian vole, but Maxwell Knight, the eccentric head of B5b, who kept parrots and snakes in his Sloane Street flat.

There was a reason, of course. Spies and naturalists had a lot in common. Love of travel, the ability to familiarize oneself with a different habitat, an obsessive attention to detail. Secrecy and camouflage became second nature. Anyone interested in wildlife knew the necessity of becoming invisible, or at least innocuous, to the creatures they studied, in order to observe them at close range. There were other things, harder to explain, concerning a sixth sense for the environment around you. Sometimes it was only by observing the small nuances of change, that you could tell when a bigger change was coming.

One of those signs was apparent at the café he passed in Leonhardstrasse. He had been in there once out of curiosity and found it an unglamorous place, specializing in towering steins of beer, wooden benches and the kind of food that restaurant guides liked to call unpretentious. But recently the place was gaining a popularity out of all proportion to its gastronomic merits. Every evening the tables were full of burly Brown Shirts showing off their women. A newly completed portrait of the Führer hung on the back wall. Perhaps it had something to do with the fact that the fat, cigar-smoking, moustachioed proprietor was called Alois

Hitler, and was lucky enough to be half-brother to the fellow in the picture. Leo chuckled to himself. He probably shouldn't have chosen this street, but really, it helped to have a sense of humour in this job.

The bookshop two doors down from the café was empty and a bored salesgirl looked as though she was summoning extra sensory powers to speed the clock on its way to closing time. The poetry section was badly lit and right at the back of the shop, like one of those distant, windswept outposts of the Reich where no one important lived and no one else wanted to visit. But for Leo it was an old hunting ground. He leafed through a couple of books until he found it, a volume of Rilke with a slightly battered blue dust-jacket, pages beginning to fox at the edges. No one had bought it for the best part of a year and it seemed unlikely anyone would be buying it in the next ten years either. He leafed through until he came to what he was looking for.

> Exposed on the mountains of the heart, see how small there
> A last hamlet of words, and higher and still so small
> A last homestead of feeling.

Holding his place, he inserted a used envelope, addressed to Herr Zink, Xantener Strasse, 9, which was postmarked most unusually with a time and date two days from hence, replaced it carefully on the shelf and left the shop.

The man from the Red Front would want money, of course. And much of his information about Communist activity in Britain might be lies. But they couldn't afford to pass up opportunities like this. All over Berlin, an invisible web was being formed of people who might be of help to British interests. A delicate, unseen network linking those from the very top of society, the aristocrats and industrialists who instinctively disliked Hitler, to others on lower rungs, men with grievances, drivers, publicans, policemen even. It wasn't just information that Head Office was after. There were the men who might own garages or warehouses, where something could be quietly stored, or people who had access to documents, rubber stamps or printing materials. Nor would they stop at the willing ones. Sometimes there might be other ways to convince individuals to part with information. Homosexuals, petty criminals, and anyone who walked in fear of the State might be persuaded that helping out the British was in their interests. There were a variety of methods to employ. Bribery, threats, or promises for those in financial or moral trouble. As they said at Head Office, this wasn't cricket.

Leo thought of Clara, and hoped she was safe at Babelsberg that day, acting out her light-hearted spy movie. He lamented the end of all those shadowy expressionist masterpieces Ufa was famous for, but the atmosphere that ran through Berlin now, of suppressed frenzy and suspense, more than made up for them. No wonder they didn't need movies about murderers any more.

Chapter Thirty-one

The Rio Rita Bar on Tauentzienstrasse had dazzlingly elegant panels of cream and gold on the walls and marble-topped tables surrounding an intimate dance floor where, in happier times, girls would circulate with champagne, fruit and fresh gossip. But now, despite the upmarket fittings, it had a melancholy air. A perfumed fug of luxury-brand cigarettes hung beneath the ceiling like a low cloud, and the tables were lit by red-shaded lamps, expressly designed to disguise the age of the businessmen and the weariness of the bar girls. The girls wore basque tops made of grubby feathers, like pigeons with tired plumage. A couple of them were at that moment sprawled at the back, legs akimbo, exuding a force-field of apathy that deterred anyone from approaching them before their shift began.

Helga looked around at the band, where a saxophonist in shirtsleeves was playing a melody as if it were the Last Post.

'I used to work here for a while, but it's changed.' She wrinkled her nose. 'Not so much fun.'

Despite the lighting, she had on a pair of Zeiss sunglasses, and although she never normally wore one coat of make-up where two would do, it was impossible not to notice that her foundation could have been laid on with a trowel.

'Thank you for coming to Luna Park the other day. Erich loved meeting you. He told Oma you're almost as big a film star as his Mutti.'

'What's the matter, Helga? You don't look yourself.'

'Nothing. At least, well . . . we had a row.' She lit a cigarette and Clara noticed that her hands were shaking. 'Remember the picture Bruno did of me?'

'The one that no one was going to recognize?'

'That's the one.'

'So Bauer did.'

'Not at first. I'm not that dim!' she retorted with sulky indignation. 'I hid the picture under the bed because I knew that even if he didn't recognize me, Bauer wouldn't like it. But he found it. And straightaway he recognized the signature and started taunting me, saying I was sleeping with Jews. The picture was *Judenkunst*. I had sold my body to a degenerate artist. He was really jealous. I was scared.'

'What did you say?'

'I said Bruno was just a friend. I had to. Though even being friends with a Jew could be disastrous for my career.'

'How could it be?'

'Don't you see? They don't like actresses who befriend Jews. Even if they can't prove anything against you, at the very least they can starve you of publicity. Keep you out of all the film newspapers and magazines. Your picture doesn't get taken. Your name never gets mentioned. You stop getting work.'

'Surely not.'

'Look at Henny Porten, a huge star, but married to a Jew, so she can't work at all. She spends all her time now shut up at home. She's thinking of leaving for America, but the rumour is they won't give her an exit visa because it would be bad for business.'

'But Bruno's just a casual friend. You don't have to go on seeing him.'

'Makes no difference,' she said, taking a mournful drag from her cigarette. 'Bauer's started calling me one of those sluts in furs.'

'Sluts in furs?'

'It's what they call actresses who don't fit the picture.'

She sniffed fastidiously at her glass of cognac, downed it, and signalled to the barman for another.

'Bauer told me that women who sleep with Jews have their heads shaved and signs put round their necks and get dragged in carts through the streets.'

'That's just talk,' said Clara, with a confidence she didn't feel. 'How many girls in carts do you see on the Ku'damm?'

'He suggested I find myself a new career as a Telephone Girl, one of those whores who dress up as famous actresses on the orders of their customers. Because that was the nearest I was ever going to get to being a movie star.'

Suddenly Clara understood the reason for Helga's pan-stick.

'You're not saying Bauer hit you?'

'No.' She shrugged. 'Well, not because of that. It was something else.'

Suddenly all the feelings Clara had about her own mother, and the way she had always done what her father wanted, welled up. Their parents' arguments were bitter and frequent, and on numerous nights the children had listened behind doors or from the banisters on the stairs. Her father had never stooped to physical violence, but his icy silence was a weapon every bit as brutal. Her mother would retreat, cowed by her husband's fury, acquiescing to his overbearing demands. Clara had vowed she would never be like that. She would never let a man even think he could dominate her.

'How dare he!'

'How dare he?' Helga gave a tired laugh. 'What are you talking about? He can do anything he wants, can't he? Who's going to stop him?'

'So if it wasn't the painting, what provoked it?'

'It was the night we went to the Sportpalast. It was a lovely evening, and there was tons to drink. You can't imagine how glamorous it was. Zarah Leander was there and everyone was in a jolly mood. I was joking and I probably went too far.'

'What kind of joke?' asked Clara, though she had already guessed.

'Lots of jokes. Everyone jokes, don't they? But when we got home, Bauer asked me to repeat the last joke I told, so I did. "There's two girls. One girl says, 'At last I've met the perfect German man." The other girl asks, "So what's he like?" And the first girl says, "He's gorgeous. He's as blond as Hitler, as slim as Goering and as tall as Goebbels!".' She spread her hands in petition to Clara. 'Tell me that's not funny! But when I told Bauer, he knocked me down.'

'He knocked you down?'

'He couldn't stop himself. He said if I keep making jokes I'm going to find myself in a cell at Prinz Albrecht Strasse. He said people have got four months in a concentration camp for less. But he didn't mean it. He can't have. I mean, that would reflect badly on him, wouldn't it?'

'It's not worth finding out.'

'He said people will think he's associating with a subversive. So I said if he felt like that, then why did he sleep with me?'

Clara could just imagine it. Helga's eyes, flashing defiantly, the hint of mockery in her laugh. What effect that had on a man like Walter Bauer didn't bear thinking of.

'You have to stop seeing him!'

'I can't.' Her shoulders sank. 'Didn't you hear the latest

announcement? It went out two days ago. They pinned up the notices in the foyer at the studio this morning. As part of the Aryanization process you now need proof of descent to work in the film industry.'

Clara's heart buckled. No one had asked for her papers, and they weren't likely to as long as Klaus Müller was in charge of the studios. But that only served to remind her that she had agreed to keep seeing Müller. And the prospect of what he would want in return.

'You have to take a form and give all the details of your grandparents,' Helga was saying. 'But I never even knew my father. Bauer takes great pleasure in that. The fact is he protects me. If I couldn't get film work, I'd have to go back to taking my clothes off for fat businessmen in dives like this.' She shot a contemptuous glance at the girls at the back, decked out in their feathery two-pieces. 'And I need the work for Erich's sake. I . . . oh, you wouldn't understand.'

'Try me.'

'There's no point,' she said briefly, lighting up. 'You have no children. You couldn't possibly.'

'All right, I don't have children, but give me credit for trying to imagine what it means. I'm an actress, after all.'

'What's that got to do with it?' Helga said scornfully. 'Acting can't tell you how something really feels. It can't tell you what it means to have someone totally dependent on you, really needing you. The fact is, having Erich means I have to keep in work, and to keep in work I need Bauer.'

Clara laid a hand on her friend's arm. 'Then please, Helga dear, at least be more careful. I can't bear to think of that man being violent to you.'

'You'll be glad to know we're going to be filming in Prague. It will mean I can get out of town and away from that bastard for a while.'

'Thank God for that.'

'Yes. I know.' Her face softened. 'But, Clara, that's not why I wanted to see you. The thing is, there's something else. Something worse.'

She beckoned to the barman for another cognac, slapped a note on the table, and waited until he had gone.

'It's about Bruno. The other night he told me that someone had come to his room and thrown ink. They also trashed some of his canvases. He was out at the time, but he was worried. He hoped it was just a jealous rival – those artists are always having tiffs with each other – you know, one is Expressionist and the other is a Non-Realist or something. I can't remember the labels, but you wouldn't believe the rows they have. Anyway, Bruno hoped it was that but he guessed it was more likely political. And when I called him earlier today, he wasn't there. I went straight round but he'd disappeared.'

'Perhaps he's gone away.'

'Clara, you don't see! He wouldn't go away without telling me. We talk every day. I know everything he does. He's been taken, I'm sure of it. He must have been arrested. I went up and down all the doors and tried talking to the neighbours, but most of them didn't want to get involved. They must know something, the cowards. I only found one who would speak to me, an old guy who keeps rabbits on his balcony. Bruno painted him once. Anyway, he said Bruno had been there yesterday evening. So they must have come for him in the night.'

'Surely they wouldn't arrest people in the night.'

'That's exactly what they do! You know that water tower at the top of my road? The one that looks like some kind of crazy castle? Every night you see police vans turning up, stuffed full of people, and men in uniform going in and out all the time. I bet that's where they've taken him.'

'Did you call the police?'

'Of course I did. I ran outside and found a policeman in the street and begged him to help. I explained about the canvases being attacked and he just laughed. He said, "Now the Jews will see that we mean what we say".'

Clara reached over to her.

'Helga, you're overreacting. It's probably nothing. A family emergency, perhaps, or a customer of his who wanted to see him. He'll be in touch, I'm sure of it. I don't see why you're imagining the worst.'

Helga snatched off her sunglasses, revealing the full purplish yellow of Bauer's handiwork, and wiped her eyes.

'You don't see why? Can't you see anything, Clara? I love Bruno, that's why! He loves me too, though he would never admit it. He doesn't like talking about that kind of thing, but I can tell.' She replaced her sunglasses and drew herself up. 'Anyway, that's why I need your help.'

'My help? How can I help?'

'The Frau Doktor. Just a word from her would help.'

Clara's heart sank, but she took Helga's hand and smiled brightly.

'Of course. I can try.'

Chapter Thirty-two

Leo laid down his Latin edition of *Metamorphoses* and rubbed his eyes. His attachment to the classics was a psychological prop, he knew. The ancient world had a huge pull for him, though whether he was nostalgic for the world of the Greeks and Romans, or for the sunny schoolroom where F. J. Earnshaw had first introduced his thirteen-year-old self to the works of Homer, Herodotus, Ovid and Pliny, he wasn't sure. Either way, it had sparked something in him that refused to die down.

One vacation he had taken a villa that looked out over the cobalt-blue Ionian sea. As he watched the purple mountains rise unchanging across the bay it was almost possible to believe that two millennia had simply not passed and the four rivers of antiquity, Styx, Acheron, Phlegethon and Cocytus, still moved beneath his feet. Standing in the little courtyard with its ancient cypress tree he had thought himself back to fifth-century BC Athens, the birthplace of democracy, when Solon and his followers first established the rules by which people could determine their own lives. Now, sitting in his apartment bent over his Ovid, he thought how perverse it was to immerse himself in the classical world at a time and in a place where democracy was being systematically dismantled.

The walk-in had found his way to Xantener Strasse that afternoon. He was around forty, a weasely type with a face that had more lines than the Berlin U-Bahn. A sour smell of herrings and unwashed clothes rose off him, there was an angry boil on his neck and the edges of his collar were frayed. He introduced himself only as Heinz and before he uttered a word he had insisted on going round the apartment, poking underneath the radiator, around the ceiling lamp, in the open fireplace, looking for recording devices. Leo had watched him amazed. If he thought they were inefficient enough to allow their safe house to be bugged, why was he even thinking of entrusting them with his information and, in all reality, his life?

Then again, Heinz was illegal, of course. Most of his friends were probably in prison. The Red Front Fighters League was the paramilitary wing of the Communist Party in Germany, the red equivalent of the SA. For years they could be found engaging in street fights in the outskirts of the city, or wielding table legs, truncheons and bottles in the beer halls, giving as good as they got and matching the storm troopers in savagery and violence. Then last year the League was outlawed, and its members had been hauled off to moulder in cells or face firing squads. Since when the existence of people like Heinz had become fraught, and any neurosis on their part could probably be justified.

Leo drew the shutters, sat him down at the table, which was situated on the opposite side of the room from the window, and made coffee. Heinz was smoking heavily, glancing around him at the dull little room with its striped wallpaper and single sofa covered with faded chintz. He had a malnourished look and charmless air, which would suit him well, Leo thought, if he chose the Soviet Union for his adopted home. Were he to opt for England, however, he might need to learn a few courtesies if he didn't want to frighten the horses.

Heinz didn't bother with preliminaries. As Leo had accurately guessed, he did indeed want money in return for a list of names who he said were active Communist agents in England. The names would be passed back to Maxwell Knight and checked out. Leo took the list and scrutinized it, then put it in his pocket.

'So why are you doing this?'

Heinz shrugged. 'What do you mean?'

'Why would you want to turn your back on the people you worked alongside?'

Heinz regarded him, as though calculating whether he could be trusted, then realized that he had already made that choice.

'I joined the Party ten years ago. I was a young teenager, and everywhere here things looked bad. What with one thing and another I decided to go and study in Moscow. When I was there I was recruited by the GRU. The idea was that I would come back to Berlin and set up an intelligence network, training members of the Comintern to prepare for world revolution. I would work under the cover of the Red Front.'

He cast an anxious glance at the window.

'It worked well. A few years ago I was to be sent to England to meet members of the Comintern leadership there and assess the readiness for increasing party activity. But the trip never happened. The reports were that the English didn't seem ready for it.' He waved a disparaging hand. 'The British are a lethargic people. All that unemployment and hunger, but still they're suspicious of a political solution.'

'That doesn't answer my question,' said Leo. 'If you feel the British are beneath contempt, why would you be wanting to help them?'

'I'm not sure I do want to help them.'

'Then injure the interests of the Comintern?'

Heinz looked evasive. He stubbed out his cigarette in the saucer and wiped his nose on a sleeve. Leo wondered idly what would happen if he were ever to repeat either of those actions in one of the elegant houses deep in the English countryside that MI5 kept for debriefing agents.

'A woman . . .'

It was always a woman.

'A woman I met. Katya Stein. She was my girlfriend for two years and an agent too. We were going to get married. She worked in a bar, one of those smart places up in the West End where rich businessmen go and she would talk to the men there, the foreigners, and report back on what they were doing, what deals they were making. The Party was very pleased with her, it was said. She was so quick, so clever. I was amazed, actually, that she ever looked at me. Anyway, one day last month she was supposed to come back to my place but she didn't appear. I couldn't find her anywhere. I searched everywhere she knew.' He pinched his watering eyes between two fingers. 'Then she turned up in a back street with a hole in her head. Murdered by the Reds.'

'How do you know they killed her?'

'I know the way they work. They had some suspicion she betrayed them. The fact was, you never met a better girl.'

'I'm sorry.'

Heinz shook his head. 'Sure. So I had nothing to lose.' He took another of Leo's cigarettes. 'That reminds me. There's something else.' His face twisted into a dentist's nightmare of a smile. 'A big fish.'

'Oh, yes?'

'Who is coming to swim into your net.'

Metaphor had its place, Leo recognized, in this world of evasions and codes, but sometimes, frankly, one yearned for plain speaking.

'What exactly are you getting at, Heinz?'

It seemed there was another agent, a Ukrainian Jew, who was known to be active in seeking a link between the Nazis and the Soviets. An alliance there, however unlikely it seemed, would not bode well. London was alert for signs of increasing friendliness between Germany and Russia. Heinz said this man had just arrived in Berlin from Holland. And he was a danger.

'How is that?'

'He has a lot of contacts among the Comintern agents in Britain. And he is disgusted by what he regards as the betrayal of Jewish interests in Palestine by the British. He believes they side with Arabs every time. The British don't fear him because as far as they know, they have high-level contacts with him. He is here only briefly before going to attend a Zionist conference in Warsaw.'

'Can you give me a name?

Heinz passed a piece of paper. It was not a name Leo recognized.

'Thank you, Heinz. Your help is appreciated.'

'And you will help me, too?'

'Of course.'

'My life is very difficult already. I think they're onto me. I'm staying in a different place every night.'

'We'll keep in touch.'

Heinz rose and embraced him unexpectedly. Up close he smelt worse, clutching Leo as though starved of human contact. Leo fought the urge to back away and patted him on the back, like a parent comforting a child. There was an unexpected shade of vulnerability in his eyes.

'If I come to England? Will I like it? Is it very different?'

Leo frowned. How could he explain in any way that Heinz would understand? What kind of life could Heinz look forward to if he came? He would be debriefed first, of course, probably in some secluded rural manor house that smelt like a boy's prep school, staffed by military types with tweed jackets and poker faces. Then he would be run as an agent domestically, living in some anonymous south London basement flat, holding regular meetings with his controller and continuing to inform on every new friend he made. That was a spy's life in a foreign country. In a bigger way, Leo supposed, a spy's entire existence was a foreign country, where they must think before speaking, and attempt to fit in, without ever going native themselves. Still, no need to depress the man.

'England's very different.'

'How?'

Leo racked his brains and attempted a cheery smile. 'Well, I suppose one difference is, if someone knocks on your door at some unearthly hour in England, you can be pretty sure it's only the milkman.'

On his way home he dropped into Hoffmann's, his barbers, as if the act of being washed and clipped and shaved would somehow purge him of the contact with Heinz. He had been using the same place since he arrived in Berlin and always found it relaxing to sit amid the glinting chrome, the clouds of steam and the scents of hair oil and eau de Cologne, listening to the polite conversation of Herr Hoffmann as he went about his shaving like an artist, a snowy napkin draped over one arm. Herr Hoffmann was a cultivated man, who was proud of the fact that his son played the clarinet in a chamber orchestra and had pressed Leo with tickets on a couple of occasions. But this time he was flanked by two National Socialists talking loudly across him about a meeting hall in Wedding that had burned to the ground the night before. It appeared the hall had been a meeting place for Communists.

'They said Marxism is a fire, so it stands to reason when you stamp out a fire then sparks are bound to fly!' laughed one.

In the mirror Leo's eyes snagged on Herr Hoffmann's for a fraction of a second, before he looked away. They forewent their usual pleasantries.

Chapter Thirty-three

Even though they were built for the ample German backside, the seats at the Staatsoper were still too narrow for Clara's liking. They forced her to sit tight up against Klaus Müller, feeling the muscled warmth of his thigh through the dark serge of his trousers. She was wearing the scarlet dress again, and the silkiness of the pearlized satin caressed her bare skin. Before them, ranks of officials sat in a magnificent VIP box, which was hung with tassled crimson drapes and surmounted by a golden eagle. Everywhere was red, from the plush of the seats, to the damask walls of the boxes, to the shades of the gilt lights on the wall. It was like being in a lurid crimson cavern. Inside the dark, beating heart of the Nazi regime.

Before her, rows of men stared with grim determination at the stage. The lyricism of the diva's love song seemed to leave them unmoved. They looked more like people observing a public execution than an opera. It was a miracle Madame Butterfly managed to keep singing. Hitler, of course, was in the middle, flanked by Goering, and Rudolf Hess. Hess, with his undertaker's face and clenched jaw, was separating Goering from Goebbels, evidently by design. She spotted Walter Bauer wedged a few rows back, rigid with boredom. The men were in full uniform, decked with ribbons and medals and swastika armbands, the women in their own uniform of evening gowns and competitive jewellery. Frau von Ribbentrop was in a green sheath wearing emeralds the size of walnuts, and to her left was Magda in a crimson gown, her hair like a pale flame lighting up her face, a tight necklace of rubies round her neck, making it appear from a distance as if someone had slit her throat. Even from where she was sitting, Clara could see Magda's eyes were red and her mouth was tense with misery. Following her gaze she caught sight of the reason. The film maker Leni Riefenstahl sat in the opposite box, languidly beautiful in the soft light, her skin golden and her dress a silky, caramel drape. Clara studied her curiously. It was the first time she had seen her closely. She was exceptionally pretty, with a strong nose, a high clear brow and tumbling curly hair. No wonder Magda suffered.

The opera was wonderful, even without the Staatsoper's star conductor, Otto Klemperer, who had left Germany that week. Puccini's music rose and soothed Clara so that for a while she almost forgot where she was until Müller's hand descended and began massaging her thigh, gently stroking his fingers upwards. She repressed the urge to shift in her seat and tried to imagine herself relaxed, enjoying the evening. She was an ordinary girl, spending a night at the opera with a man to whom she owed a debt of gratitude. It was a part like any other, which required a little extemporizing perhaps, a touch of improvization, but nothing beyond her talents. It required her only to separate the sensation from the emotion, to shut out all thoughts of place and circumstance, and focus only on the rhythmic touch of his hand, the mingled masculine aroma of cologne and cigars. If she did that, it almost worked. She pictured herself as a young actress excited by the splendour of the opera house, dazzled to be at the heart of society and oblivious to its dark undercurrents. Indeed, when she felt the warm pressure of his thigh against hers and laid her hand lightly on his arm, a brief, treacherous flicker of arousal ran through her flesh, before the sly, lascivious glances directed at her by other Nazi officials shocked her back into cold reason. Through her mind ran Leo's comment, "You're not doing this for you, are you?" But what exactly was she doing? And how far could she remain in control?

By the time Butterfly had killed herself and the opera ended, Müller's normally suave manner had been replaced by a heightened excitement and she sensed an expectation in him that filled her with dread. There was to be a champagne reception in a private room, at which Hitler would be introduced to the performers, but before that they were obliged to wait for a number of standing ovations and *Heil Hitlers*, and then for an enormous bouquet of roses to be brought on stage and presented to the diva, tied with a scarlet sash which spelt out 'Adolf Hitler' in gold lettering. Then, in a new convention, everyone had to salute and sing *Deutschland Über Alles* followed by the Horst Wessel Song. After that the etiquette was to allow the Führer's party to leave first, but the process was slow, given that Hitler was besieged by well-wishers, beaming and wanting to salute in his face so, seizing her hand, Müller ducked through a door marked 'Private', and into a concrete-walled corridor. A little way off two SA men were sneaking a cigarette. No one wanted to risk smoking in Hitler's presence.

Müller lit up himself with greedy desperation and passed one to her.

'I can't stand all these women wailing and killing themselves, but that's opera for you. The Führer loves it, of course.'

He looked down at her with his habitually sardonic edge. 'Speaking of wailing women, how's our First Lady?'

'She's fine. The Fashion Bureau is going well. We have a new headquarters now.'

The new HQ had been organized by Goebbels. It was in the sumptuous Columbushaus in Potsdamer Platz, an ultra-modern office building with a Woolworths at the bottom and a restaurant at the top. The building was considered an architectural triumph, but that was rarely mentioned now since its architect, Erich Mendelsohn, had bought a one-way ticket across the border.

'Someone told me she was throwing another fit this morning.'

'Really?' Yet again Müller seemed to be looking to her for information. She was valuable to him too, she realized. A spy behind the scenes of his boss's private life.

'Yes. One of the men was saying she'd consulted a fortune-teller who has prophesied that she will meet a violent death between the ages of forty and forty-five.'

'How terrible!' Perhaps that had been the reason for the red eyes. 'They're so irresponsible, these people. They can't imagine the hurt they cause.'

Müller's face was contemptuous. 'Exactly. No wonder the Herr Doktor find this superstition stuff repulsive, if it makes women hysterical. He calls it witchcraft. He's planning to ban all this astrology and fortune-telling; those charlatans who claim to see the future through the bumps on your head. What would they make of mine, eh?'

He took her hand and ran it playfully over his hair. He had just had a cut, so it was shaved even shorter at the sides, but the top was lustrous and springy. Clara had learned to control her instinct against physical contact, but it was hard. She kept her touch light and clinical, like a nurse's.

'I can't feel any bumps.'

'Perhaps I have no future then. Is that what you think?' She didn't answer so he shrugged. 'Anyhow, what do we need hypnotists for? You've seen the Doktor talk. He mesmerizes millions. He has them eating out of the palm of his hand. What hypnotist could beat that?'

Clara frowned. 'But doesn't the Führer have an astrologer of his own? Herr Hanussen?'

'Ah, Herr Hanussen, he's different. He always gets it right.'

'Why's that?'

'Because he has the good sense to know what the Führer wants to hear.' He shrugged. 'The Doktor hates him. He's convinced he's a Jew. But, you know, Hanussen's quite an act. One of the sights of Berlin. In fact, you should see him. I'll take you to his place next week. The House of the Occult, he calls it. It's extraordinary.'

He leant one arm against the wall, and looked down at her. 'On the subject of acting, how is Frau Sonnemann?'

'She's invited us all to her latest performance.'

'I feel sorry for you. Emmy can't act her way out of her own sweater. But still,' he touched her cheek. 'I like to hear what these women are up to. What they fill their little minds with. It helps me know what kind of mood the boss is going to be in tomorrow.'

'So that's why you like to see me!'

'It's not the only reason, my dear, as you know.'

He leant closer and put a hand on her shoulder. His grip was weighty and rough. He eased a finger through the strap of her dress, as though he was about to undress her.

'I think you've enjoyed making me wait.' His voice was thick with desire. 'But it's not good for a man in my position to be without a woman. People make assumptions.'

'Of course they don't. No one could think you were that kind of man.'

'They think I may be going to parties with Ernst Röhm.'

'But you've been married. You had a lovely wife.'

'Perhaps. But it's been years.' Her mention of Elsa had the desired effect. He recoiled slightly. 'However, I'd better watch out. The boss has his eye on you, I think.'

'What makes you think that?'

'I've seen the way he looks at you. He's been asking a lot of questions about you.'

'Questions?'

'About your opinions. He's desperate to know if you have boyfriends. He wants to know if you are spoken for.'

'And what do you tell him?'

'What would you like me to say?'

'Tell him I live for my art.'

He laughed. 'All right then. I will. But I warn you, the Doktor doesn't trust you.'

'Why should he not trust me?'

'I don't know. He said the other day that he dislikes the company you keep.'

A cold current of fear went through her. Could it be that she was being watched, just as Leo had said? She forced herself to keep smiling.

'And what would the Doktor know about the company I keep?'

He shrugged. 'I assume he's talking about your friend Helga.'

'Helga?'

'Yes.' He lowered his voice, though there was no one listening. 'In fact, I should give her a little advice if I were you. Tell her to be more careful. Tell her that her sense of humour is not shared by everyone.'

'What do you mean?'

'It's just what I've been hearing. At the Sportpalast the other night. She has a loose mouth.'

'Why? You're scaring me now.' She gave his arm a little push. 'What has she done?'

'Do you want to know?'

'Obviously.'

'Then I'll explain in more detail.' He ran a hand down the curve of her body and she smelt his sweat beneath the clean starch of his shirt. 'Tonight, in fact. I've reserved a room at the Adlon for later.'

At that moment he broke off and straightened up. From the end of the corridor a slight figure had emerged. Even from a distance his hobbling gait was unmistakable. He had donned a camelhair coat over his uniform and was accompanied by a woman whose dark head was bent close to his, a black velvet cape round her shoulders. It was Leni Riefenstahl.

'Damn,' Müller's face darkened and he threw the cigarette away. 'The brass neck of the man. He can't stop himself.'

'What are they doing?'

'Officially? Officially they're discussing a film he wants her to make about Hitler. Unofficially, they're going to spend some private time at the Adlon. He sneaks her in the Wilhemstrasse entrance. He imagines his wife is unaware.'

Clara sensed her escape.

'Poor Frau Goebbels. She'll be upset. I must go to her.'

'Wait.'

Müller barred her way with his arm and leant down to kiss her. At the last moment she turned, so that his kiss landed on her cheek. He scowled, frustration rising from him like the scent of the lime cologne he wore. For a second, his face twisted in annoyance, but he swiftly repressed it and summoned a smile.

'Very well, gnädige Fräulein. We are still getting to know each other. But don't make me wait too long. Unlike our dear Leader I do not intend to be married to Germany. I'm too young for that.'

Chapter Thirty-four

'So Goebbels' home is burgled, and he comes home and says to Magda, "What did they steal?" And she says, "Only the results of next year's election!" '

Rupert Allingham threw back his head and roared. The others clustered around the table followed suit. Die Taverne restaurant was an Italian place of low ceilings and long wooden tables, fogged with cigar smoke and the deeply ingrained scent of beer. The proprietor was not Italian at all, but a big, bluff German called Willy Lehman, who ran the place with his amiable Belgian wife and provided for British and American correspondents not just a hearty meal but a sanctuary. Here they gathered most nights, trading jokes and news and information, notwithstanding the fact that young storm troopers liked to meet there too, plus a sprinkling of government spies who eavesdropped despite the best efforts of an American jazz band.

Most evenings, until the small hours, their regular table was occupied by journalists swapping stories. Mary had discovered that the burning instinct all journalists felt to safeguard a scoop was actually less pressing than their desire to relay the facts behind the new Nazi Germany. If Americans were ever to know just what it was like here, everyone involved in reporting it would need to overcome their competitive instincts and help each other out.

In here, crowded around the table, with a huddle of journalists making jokes and telling stories, it was intensely warm and relaxed. There were five of them that evening. Next to Rupert was a British friend of his, a handsome man with a shock of blond hair, called Stephen Spender, who wrote poetry, Rupert said. Alongside him sat Quentin Reynolds, the Hearst correspondent, a huge man with curly hair and a big smile who had just arrived in town. Mary had squeezed in next to Sigrid Schultz, of whom she was slightly in awe. Sigrid was the bureau chief of the *Chicago Tribune*, a feisty American who had grown up in Paris, attended university in Berlin and was known for speaking her mind to the Nazi leaders. She had the porcelain complexion of a china doll, which was entirely at odds with her penchant for smoking a pipe. It was either the pipe smoke or the personality that inspired Goering's nickname for her as "the dragon from Chicago".

Mary had almost given the meal a miss that night, but she was glad she came. For one thing she was famished. They were eating a knuckle of pork with sauerkraut, and it was delicious. The heavily marbled meat had been braised for hours and was covered with a thick layer of crispy fat, perfectly complemented by a plate of pickles. It was a chance, too, to see Rupert and try to work out exactly where she stood with him. He always beamed when he saw her and flung his arm round her shoulders, throwing out compliments about 'the cleverest correspondent in town', but then Rupert was always ebullient and good-mannered to a fault. That was the problem with these damned Brits. It was so hard to know what was going on underneath.

They had spent several evenings in each other's company now, and she had gathered that he was very close to his mother, whom he called the Countess, although that was not her actual title, just an expression of affection. Confusingly, she did have a title, her name was Lady Isidora Allingham, not plain Lady Allingham as you would imagine (though Mary wouldn't) because she had the right to use her Christian name as the daughter of a duke. Mary said in America everyone had the right to use their own goddam Christian names, but when she asked Rupert to explain all the ranks and titles and so on, he had just laughed and said if you thought you understood the English aristocracy, it meant you hadn't understood it.

It wasn't that he was self-obsessed. Like any good journalist he asked her a ton of questions about herself, her home and family, he'd even got the name of her dog out of her. Walt. Whitman or Disney? he asked, then got it right first time, and even quoted Whitman, to boot. He knew her dream was to settle in Europe, going wherever the story led her, and said for his part he was simply longing to visit New York, and perhaps she could show him some day. It was just that she felt she existed for him as a specimen of curiosity. Something you might observe in order to write about, a character who might pop up in a sketch one day, when the veteran correspondent finally published his memoirs. Yet however baffled and frustrated that made her feel, she wasn't going to let it spoil the evening.

She flicked through the pile of newspapers they always brought along with them while Rupert dominated the table with an incessant stream of tales and jokes.

'Have you noticed how these Nazis boast of their prowess in the war? I was talking to one the other night who insisted that Hitler won his Iron Cross second class for capturing fourteen Englishmen singled-handedly.'

'Quite an achievement,' said Sigrid drily. 'No doubt he surrounded them.'

Reynolds guffawed. 'I heard a good one the other day. There's a German steelworker whose wife wants a new pram. He can't afford it, so he steals the parts one by one and attempts to assemble the pram. But he's puzzled because every time he does, it turns out to make a machine gun!'

'Does anyone really doubt that rearmament is underway?' asked Spender.

'No one I know,' said Rupert, attacking his pig's knuckle with gusto. 'It's proving it that's difficult. And even if you did, it's a problem getting anyone interested. You can practically hear my editor yawning down the phone. They're getting tired of atrocity stories too. It's come to something when your own newspaper agrees with Doktor Goebbels.'

'Of course, you know why Goebbels detests us all,' said Sigrid languidly. 'He wanted to be a journalist himself. He sent fifty articles to the *Berliner Tageblatt* and they rejected them all. That was after all his novels and plays and poetry got rejected too. He decided it was because all the publishing houses were owned by Jews. The Ullsteins and the Mosses. I suppose we should recognize that rejection does dangerous things to a man.'

'It's not all bad.' Rupert grinned. 'He's opening a fancy new press club on Leipziger Strasse for all the foreign journalists. So we can learn to love the new regime.'

'Hey, Rupert.' Mary passed him a copy of the *B.Z. am Mittag* that she had been reading. 'Here's a picture of your friend.'

In the middle pages was a story about how Magda Goebbels was choosing actresses to spearhead a new push for German fashion. There was a half-page photograph of the minister's wife sharing space with a potted palm in the drawing room of her new home and on the opposite page a smaller photograph of Clara Vine posing in a brown, military style outfit that did nothing for her.

Rupert frowned. 'What the hell is she up to?' He took the paper and pored over it. Then he thrust it away again. 'And to think it's my fault she's here.'

Observing the change in him, Mary wondered for a second if Rupert might be in love with the girl. The thought made her heart drop in the pit of her chest.

'How did you meet her?'

'What?' he looked distracted. 'Oh I had a friend back in London. A slightly raffish chap called Max Townsend, who's been producing films out here. Clara was looking for work and I thought he'd be able to give her a part. To be honest, I never actually thought she'd take me up on it.' He shrugged. 'I suppose she's just another one of those well-born English girls who are all too happy to see the sights, without seeing what's underneath them.'

'She didn't strike me like that.'

'What's this girl doing anyway?' said Sigrid Schultz, removing her pipe and leaning across.

'She's modelling that natural German look being promoted by Magda Goebbels.'

'What natural German look?'

'You know, no make-up, no trousers, no jewellery.'

'No jewellery?' queried Quentin Reynolds. 'Frau Goebbels wears so many diamonds it's like she had a fight with a chandelier.'

'As for cosmetics,' added Sigrid sourly, 'those women look like they've won a free day on the beauty counter at KaDeWe.'

Their conversation was interrupted by a commotion from the opposite corner of the room. Two men in the brown shirts of the SA had entered the restaurant and walked towards

the back. One was a huge meaty man with a face like a side
of ham, the other an old–fashioned German, with tawny
moustache sprouting from his face like the whiskers of a wild
boar. Their target, a pallid man in his thirties, was sitting
alone, sipping tea and doing his best to disappear into the
newspaper he read. The fatter Nazi barged into the table,
knocking the tea cup to the floor.

'You're taking up too much room!'

'Forgive me.' The pale-faced man apologized and ducked
down to retrieve the broken cup.

'His people always take up too much room,' said the other.
'They're taking up too much room in Germany.'

'Not for long!'

Before the others knew what was happening, Rupert had
sprung up, approached the men and engaged in an energetic
row. Mary saw them cast a glance across to their table, assessing how many men could be ranked against them if it came
to a fight. They obviously decided they were outnumbered
because after a large amount of shouting but no actual blows,
the Brown Shirts left, overturning chairs and a further table
as they went, sending tea glasses and plates flying and leaving
the sound of smashed crockery lingering in the air. Rupert
came back and inserted himself into his seat with unruffled
ease as the waiter hurried across to clear the mess.

'So you actually want to get yourself arrested then?' said
Quentin Reynolds with amusement.

'The benefits of playing for the first fifteen.'

Rupert looked over at Mary, his good humour entirely
restored. 'I've got something I wanted to ask you.'

Chapter Thirty-five

The cinema was a cheap, unremarkable place in Neukölln, where people huddled to while away a dull, weekday evening. It smelt of old beer and bodies, damp tweed coats and the smoke of a thousand cigarettes, ingrained forever in the velour seats. Clara's ticket had arrived that morning.

Reifende Jugend, 7 p.m., admit one.

Reifende Jugend was one of those films of "purely German character" that the authorities had decided everyone wanted to see. That probably explained the fact that the cinema was almost empty. It had been raining all afternoon, the dark clouds marching like storm troopers against a leaden sky, so Clara wore the old Burberry trench coat she had brought from home, with a hat pulled down over her eyes. Inside the cinema she stumbled in the dark for a second before making out the figure of Leo already sitting at the back of the stalls, his face ghostly in the flickering light of the screen. She felt a rush of relief to see him.

The newsreel was on, the *Ufa-Tonwochen*, which always came on before the main feature. A field full of young men wearing only shorts were performing press-ups. They were being addressed by an Obersturmbannführer about their commitment to a Fatherland of healthy comrades.

'Hi.'

Clara took her coat off and slid into her seat. In the silver darkness Leo looked alien, the planes and angles of his cheek-bones accentuated, making him appear more severe and mysterious. He smiled briefly but stared straight ahead, so Clara too, focused on the screen. The newsreel had moved on to a story about villagers in an Alpine setting gathering in last season's harvest with their scythes. It could have been a scene straight out of the nineteenth century, with the corn making its way to vast barns where it glowed in golden heaps. The message of abundance and plenty throughout the Reich was unmistakable.

'Have you seen our friend?' he murmured.

'Once or twice.'

'How is she?'

'Changeable. She can go from warmth to ice in an instant. She calls and asks me to see her, then she cancels.'

'Why? Does she suspect something?'

'I think she's tired. She has a lot of entertainments to organize. Her husband has arranged for her to give a talk on the radio for Mothering Sunday. Then there are collections to arrange for the Winterhilfswerk – you know, raising money for coal and food for the poor. There's the baby too. And I think she has something on her mind.'

'His womanizing?'

'Not that. Though there's a new woman now. Leni Riefenstahl, the actress? He's crazy about her, Madga says. He's asked her to be his permanent mistress, but she rejected him.'

'Surely Goebbels wouldn't be that blatant? Isn't Riefenstahl a big favourite of his boss?'

'Yes, but someone told Magda he'd been seen looking at an apartment in Rankestrasse, near the Zoo Bahnhof. She suspects he's looking for a safe place to take her. And I think . . .' Clara hesitated, uncertain of whether this information was sufficiently sound to pass on, 'she might be considering a divorce.'

Leo gave a little disbelieving snort. 'I'd like to see the lawyer prepared to handle that.'

The newsreel had moved on to a story about Goering taking the salute at a Nazi march. Even by the rose-tinted standards of the *Tonwoche*, the crowd around him were ecstatic. It was noticeable, Clara realized, how people liked Goering. Whenever Goebbels appeared, the crowd fell silent.

'Goebbels hates Goering. He calls him Fatso.'

Leo suppressed a grunt of amusement. 'She said that did she?'

'I read it in his diary.'

Leo sat up and gripped the arms of the chair. 'A diary? My God, Clara. Where did you see that?'

'I found it in his desk.'

It gave Clara a little glow to say this. She knew how it sounded, but she didn't want to give Leo the idea she would be able to leaf through the Minister's private thoughts on a regular basis.

'I had the chance to look in his study.'

'Does he complete it every day? Is it political, or just chit chat? Anything about the leader?'

'I only saw a couple of pages. It looks like he writes it every few days but the entries are pretty long.'

'And what does it say?'

'There was stuff about the boycott on Jewish shops. How successful it was. I didn't get a chance to see much, I'm afraid. But there was also an entry about how he and Goering have been fighting over the budget for propaganda. He wants more, but they're spending so much money on planes.'

'On planes? He actually wrote that?'

'Yes. Also Goering wants to spend more on the construction of concentration camps. They're sort of detention places for Communist enemies of the state.'

'I know what they are.'

'For re-educating people.'

'That's what he says, is it?'

The film had begun. It concerned three young girls who wanted to go to an all-boys high school, and only managed because the boys stole the exam questions on their behalf. Clara watched with interest. This, after all, was the type of film she could expect to be acting in, if her career at Ufa continued.

'So when's the next meeting?'

'We're going to have lunch at the von Ribbentrops' house next week.'

'Are they close friends?'

'Hardly. Frau von Ribbentrop gives herself tremendous airs, but the others still feel superior to her. Apparently von Ribbentrop has ambitions to be Foreign Minister, but Magda says he hasn't a hope. She says von Ribbentrop knows nothing about England except whisky and nothing about France except champagne.'

'How are things otherwise? Do you have any sense that you might have been followed? Have you noticed anyone looking at you?'

'Not more than usual.'

Leo's face creased in a transitory smile. 'I suppose a girl like you gets used to being looked at.'

Was that supposed to be a compliment? If so, it was the first time he had ever made any kind of reference to her being attractive.

She continued to stare at the screen, then said, 'Actually, there is another thing, Leo, I wanted to ask you. A friend of mine, Helga Schmidt, needs to trace someone who's gone missing. He's called Bruno Weiss.'

'The artist?'

'You've heard of him?'

'He's rather well known.'

'He produces posters for Ufa on the side. That's how she met him. But she thinks he's been arrested because he's Jewish.'

'More likely he's a pamphleteer. He's known for his Communist sympathies.'

Clara recalled the pamphlet she had found on the seat beside her at the Café Kranzler.

'Is there anything you could do for him? Anyone you could ask?'

'I suppose I could try.'

There was a man in the stalls below them. He was wearing a dark suit and an overcoat and had been shooting them curious glances for some time. Suddenly he got up out of his seat and walked up the aisle towards them. As he approached, without any warning Leo turned towards Clara, seized her face in his hands and kissed her full on the mouth. Seconds later, when the man had passed he released her and muttered, 'Sorry about that.'

Clara stared at the screen. She tried to focus on the scenes of young girls arriving at school, but her mind was in tumult and her heart was hammering in her chest. She was in shock. Not because he had kissed her but because she had enjoyed it so much.

Chapter Thirty-six

For the past five months passers-by had been peering curiously at the dilapidated mansion in Lietzenburgstrasse. Construction workers had gutted it, and now, rewired and utterly renovated, it had been transformed into the Palace of the Occult, a pagan temple decked with Carrara marble and decorated with Egyptian and Babylonian words, astrological signs and religious statues. The walls were painted in gold leaf, gessoed and inlaid. Great caryatids held up a roof that was spangled with silvery symbols and painted with airy clouds. It was a magical place, a theatrical confection of hidden doors and sliding panels and concealed spaces. And if anyone wondered who was responsible for it all, a huge bronze statue of Erik Jan Hanussen, arm uplifted in a Nazi salute, could be seen in the entrance.

There was a thin glitter of rain on the street outside but it hadn't deterred a small huddle from lingering to watch the parade of visitors emerging from their gleaming cars to the dazzle of camera flashes. This was a reliable patch for a bit of celebrity-spotting. Since the launch a few weeks ago, politicians, celebrities, newspaper owners, princelings and aristocrats had already passed through these doors. Rupert and Mary looked around them in wonderment. In the main vestibule stood priestesses in white silk gowns which left nothing to the imagination, their nipples protruding pinkly beneath the voile. Nazi officers were stuffing themselves with canapés and helping themselves to trays of champagne as though French wine was about to go the way of Paris fashions. As they processed through the hall Rupert passed a pillar and tapped it. It gave a hollow sound.

'Should suit the Gestapo. They say there are recording devices hidden in every one.'

'Why?'

'So they'll be able to read your mind later on, of course.'

The two progressed through a series of rooms to the centre of the complex, a gloomy arena called the Hall of Silence lit by the flicker of crimson candles. A crowd waited expectantly while searchlights played on an empty stage. In the front row could be seen the uniformed figures of Hanussen's private SA bodyguards.

'There's a lift hidden in the centre of that stage,' murmured Rupert. 'Just wait. Hanussen will rise into the rafters and commune with the gods. It can give you quite a turn if you're not expecting it.'

They stood at the back and waited as a green fog swirled into the hall, a distant band struck up some Wagner and the lights dimmed, leaving nothing but a single spotlight. Sure enough, slowly and majestically, a black throne bearing the seated figure of Hanussen wearing a flowing scarlet cape rose thirty feet into the air.

'Smoke and mirrors,' hissed Rupert. 'Just what we've come to expect from our National Socialist friends.'

'So you've been here before?' murmured Mary.

'On the opening night. He got Maria Paudler, that blonde Czech actress, to sit on the throne and he massaged her brow. He asked what she saw, and she said "red". He said, "Could it be red flames?" And she said 'Yes, and they seem to be coming from a great house'.'

'I heard about this.'

'Then Hanussen says he sees a bloodcurdling crime committed by the Communists, a wilderness of blazing flames that lights up the world. A couple of hours later, the Reichstag burnt down. Don't tell me someone didn't know what was going to happen.'

They stood for a while longer, as Hanussen continued to speak. He had a sultry, brooding expression and his gaze was fixed on the middle distance. Mary tried to make out what he was saying but it was rambling and indistinct. It seemed to centre around a blood feud between Britain, Germany and Russia.

'I can't hear.'

'You don't need to. Come on.'

They threaded their way out of the hall and ducked into a smaller chamber which had a sign over the lintel saying 'The Room of Glass'. Cages of snakes and other reptiles were set into the walls and in the centre was a circular table. In the dim candle-light all they could make out were a number of Nazi officers seated, with their hands placed on the table. A séance was under-way. A woman with dramatic black eyeliner and a costume embroidered with Egyptian motifs turned crossly towards them.

'This is a private hearing.'

'Sorry.'

Rupert led the way back to the vestibule.

'I can't take much more of this. At least, not without a drink.'

'They love all this mystic stuff, don't they?' Mary observed. 'It's like they want to think the Nazis' power is written in the stars or something.'

'Makes up for electoral legitimacy, I suppose. And you can't deny it's worked for Hanussen. He has seven apart-ments and a yacht the size of Rockefeller's. There's all kinds

of stories about what goes on there. He holds the most decadent parties. He gives his guests drugs and gets the girls to . . .
well, you can imagine.'

'No Rupert, I'm not sure I can!' Mary laughed, delighted
to notice that he was actually blushing. 'This is all a long way
from New Jersey, you know.'

'Hitler is the jewel in his crown, of course. He gives him
mandrake root apparently, as well as voice lessons. They say
the Führer is going to return the favour by setting up an Aryan
College of the Occult Arts. But Hanussen has made one
mistake. Last year he published a horoscope for Hitler that
prophesised a violent end. His tenth house presaged disaster,
apparently, Jupiter and Saturn not getting on or some such
nonsense. No one else repeated it and all the other astrologers
decided to move the time of Hitler's birth by two hours.'

'Rupert, I'm dying to write about this! The horoscopes,
the séances. The fascination with the occult and everything.
But I'm not sure how to get into it. I mean, where's the
female angle? That's what Frank Nussbaum wants from me.'

'Why don't you visit a palmist? They're everywhere.
Terrifically popular with women. Even my landlady sees one.'

'Of course!' Mary remembered that Lotte Klein regularly
read her horoscope in the *Bunte Wochenschau*. 'I know just
who to ask about that.'

They headed towards the bar. It was entirely circular, like
a giant zodiac, with the twelve signs imprinted under an illuminated glass top. In the centre a burly Bavarian, who had
exchanged his lederhosen for a dainty Moroccan fez, was
shaking some cocktails like they needed to be taught a lesson.

'Hey! Watch out.' Rupert protested as he stumbled over
the outstretched legs of a man sitting by the bar with a young
storm trooper perched on his knee.

Mary pulled him swiftly aside.

'Shh. That's Ernst Röhm.'

He was the size of a beer truck, with a little outcrop of hair marooned on the broad expanse of his pate, tiny eyes buried in flesh, and a broken nose that suggested a lifetime of fist-fights. He was an old colleague of Hitler's from the army and he had command of the storm troopers who were involved in most of the violence. As well as the boy on his knee he was surrounded by an attentive clique of young men in uniform, who hummed around him like brown-jacketed bees in a hive. He looked Rupert up and down, seemed to decide against a confrontation and turned away.

'Have one of these.' Mary handed him a packet of Trommers cigarettes, emblazoned with a little figure of a Brown Shirt, drumming a merry tune. 'Hey, isn't that your actress friend? Clara?'

Rupert turned. Emerging from the séance room was Clara Vine, alongside a tall, dark-haired German with a sardonic smile. One of his hands rested casually around Clara's waist, and far from shrinking at his touch she was snuggling into his side and smiling up at him, making some little joke that caused him to rock with laughter.

'My God,' breathed Rupert. 'She said she was getting friendly with the Promi's wife, but I didn't think that extended to necking with Nazis.'

Mary had registered before that she was a pretty girl, but that night there was no denying that Clara Vine looked beautiful. In stark contrast to her appearance in the newspaper, she was wearing an elegant, low-backed navy dress, the lamp spilling its soft, golden light over her shoulders and down the deep groove of her spine. She wore elbow-length white kid gloves and teardrop diamonds dangled from her ears. Her face was expertly made up, the eyes outlined in kohl and her lips painted a deep, burgundy red. The hair, pulled into a chignon, was sleek and glossy as a bird's wing. Beside her, Mary, in her old black dress, which had done doughty service at a hundred dinners and cocktail parties, felt distinctly drab. Her gaze flickered to Rupert, checking for signs of jealousy or dismay.

'Are you surprised?'

'A little. Her family are on warm terms with the English fascists. Her sister, Angela, is pretty strident, but for some reason I thought the younger sister was different. Seemed to have more sense about her.'

'You knew she was involved in that fashion enterprise. You saw in the paper.'

'I suppose. But I didn't have her down as one of those English girls who get their heads turned by the Führer.'

'Actually I thought she was getting on well with your friend Leo.'

'Nothing doing. Despite my attempts at matchmaking. And by the looks of it, he's well out of it. I don't think he'd go for a girl whose idea of fun is posing for National Socialist fashion week.' Rupert seized Mary's hand. 'Come on, let's quit before she sees us. The last thing I want is to stand around making small talk to Nazis when we could be having fun.'

As they made for the door, the booming voice of Hanussen could be heard issuing from the grand hall.

'Friends and fellow travellers in the occult realms. Tonight we have been privileged to glimpse into the future. We have been shown signs and portents of events that could shake the world. It is our sacred duty to treat these revelations with the respect they deserve. And I implore any journalists present tonight not to mention what they have just witnessed, for the sake of our nation and international peace.'

'A bit late now, I'd say,' said Rupert happily, tapping the notebook in his pocket.

★　　★　　★

There was a big mirror opposite, a speckled, silvered object whose gilt frame was etched with Masonic symbols, evil eyes and assorted hieroglyphs which were presumably meant to convey mystery and power, but in fact conveyed all the mystique of the furniture flea market at Charlottenburger Tor. Out of the corner of her eye, Clara surveyed herself. If Hanussen really had any clairvoyant powers, if he could see for a second what she was thinking, then Clara Vine with her Jewish grandmother would not be here sipping champagne in a dress that had been couriered over from the Ufa studios and a pair of diamond earrings given to her by Sturmhauptführer Klaus Müller. She would be standing in a police cell somewhere waiting to be interrogated or tortured or shot. That probably went for a lot of people in Berlin right now, but it didn't make the façade any easier to maintain.

As it was, though, Hanussen held no fears for her. His chances of taking in anybody but the most gullible were slight because although the Berliners might be suckers for astrology, their sense of humour kept their credulity in check. And besides, no evil eye could compete with the Gestapo themselves.

She was worried about Helga, however. She seemed to have disappeared, most likely abducted by the group of men who had been making eyes at her all evening. Yet again she had been drinking too much, Clara realized with dismay. First two glasses of champagne, then vodka paid for by one of the attentive Brown Shirts. She had already begun to sway. Thank God Bauer was not there tonight.

At that moment, at the far end of the hall, she spotted Helga arm in arm with two Nazi officers. She was leaning closely into them, one after the other, which Clara guessed was because she could not stand upright too well. Her dress was a pale pink gossamer silk which at first glance gave the impression that she was wearing nothing at all. The smile had slipped from her face and she was looking confused. The soldiers had the air of two large wild animals tussling over a gazelle. Either that or they were planning to share it.

'Leave me alone.' Helga pushed one man weakly, and he laughed, passing her over to his friend. 'All right then.'

'You too. Just leave me alone. My boyfriend is a very important man!'

Another laugh.

Instinctively Clara made to go over, but Müller tightened his grip on her arm.

'Leave her be.'

She smiled at him, and, despite her alarm for her friend, turned her back on Helga. She was not looking forward to the end of the evening, when she guessed Müller would invite her back to his apartment and she would have to disappoint him. Again. She planned on telling him it was a difficult time of the month, but there was only so long that excuse would work. And Müller might well be in no frame of mind to hear it. Already his brow shone with alcoholic sweat, and a frown of disgust darkened his face. During the séance, when the Egyptian woman had asked them all to link hands and fix their gaze on the symbols beneath the glass table top, Müller had kept his eyes on the participants, obviously noting their responses and weighing them up.

He wasn't going to like it when she called a cab. She hoped he was not the kind of man who became forceful when drunk. Sometimes, Clara wished she had the gift of second sight herself.

Chapter Thirty-seven

'Apparently, I'm going to marry my high school sweetheart.' Mary Harker closed the heavy street door behind her and laughed. 'Which would be tricky considering that I went to an all-girls school.'

'She told me I was going to have seven children,' said Lotte. 'In fact, she probably tells a lot of women that. It's what everyone wants to hear now.'

'The equivalent of winning on the horses?'

'Something like that.' Lotte smiled. Standing there on the pavement, unexpectedly released from the office, she seemed years younger. She took off her glasses and let the breeze ruffle her normally groomed hair. 'But it gave me a thrill all the same.'

'Well, she gave me the creeps.'

Frau Maria von Fischer, who advertised herself at the back of the *Bunte Wochenschau* as Madame Gypsy Rose, occupied a cramped office in Rosenthaler Strasse. It was a busy, mixed area close to the Scheunenviertel, where many of Eastern European Jews had settled and kosher shops and synagogues stood cheek by jowl with bars and brothels. Madame's room was lit by a dim red bulb and stank of sandalwood and Madame herself, who teamed an unwashed black dress with a Romany veil, had a creased, wily face, with clever little eyes that assessed immediately the state of her customer, marital, emotional and financial, and proceeded with her predictions accordingly.

Mary had guessed that Lotte would be keen to accompany her. She had an inexplicable addiction to all those horoscope magazines and could often be seen in her lunch-break eating a roll at her desk and flipping through the astrology journals, marvelling at their occult predictions, reading hungrily through the articles on magnetic healing or how to achieve marital bliss through hypnosis. They passed a small, traditional bakery, with oak panelling and fretted woodwork above the bar. Pretty gingham curtains were tied in the window, and the aroma of cinnamon and spiced apple cake rose tantalizingly from the kitchens. Mary let the scent flood through her with pleasure. She was ravenous. She pushed open the door.

'Let's go in here. I'll pay. Remember, it's for an article. Cake is compulsory!'

They sat down at a window table and ordered *Königsberger Klopse* and potato soup. Lotte tried to refuse, but Mary waved her hand.

'You're as thin as a stick! And the new German woman is supposed to be healthy, isn't she? They like their woman built like battleships, so the least you can do is oblige them.'

'I suppose.'

'And I need to thank you for putting me in contact with Gretl. She sends her love. She seemed happy when I saw her.'

'I know. She always makes the best of things, my little sister. I can't wait for her to come home. Fritz, my husband's, away, so it's quite lonely.'

Mary tried and failed to remember Fritz's job. He was a publisher's representative, she thought, but she wouldn't want to bet on it. He travelled a lot, she knew. Lotte was always sighing because he was out of the country on business.

'Where is he now?'

'Travelling in Europe again. He worries about me, I know. He's insisting I spend more time with his sister, Margarete.'

'And is she good company?'

'Not exactly. She's a staunch Party member.' She made a face. 'Last night she invited me to her sewing circle. They sew armbands and perform good deeds.'

'Good deeds?' asked Mary, through a mouthful of meatballs.

'Like taking in washing for SA men or cooking meals for Brown Shirts in need. Last night someone did a reading from *Mein Kampf*. I suppose it stopped them going on at me about when I was going to start a family.'

'Don't you want a child?'

Lotte blushed. 'Of course, I would love children. Wouldn't any woman?'

'So what's stopping you?'

'There's my job, for a start.'

'You'd have to give it up?'

'Almost certainly. They want you to. The government has just announced state loans for furniture and household necessities will be made to women who quit work.'

'That sounds like an expensive policy.'

'I know! And Fritz says the funny thing is, there are so many senior men who don't have many kids, their wives are going to look like members of the resistance.'

Mary was savouring the food. The soup was rich and creamy and the *Königsberger Klopse* were deliciously filling meatballs in a spicy gravy, served with nutty, brown bread. She let the tastes flood through her with satisfaction. She loved food, especially German food, and of all the German food she loved, desserts were her downfall. A swift glance at the menu suggested that today was going to be no different. She ordered apple cake with whipped cream and iced coffee for two.

'Tell me more about Margarete.'

'Oh, where do I start?' Lotte grimaced. 'Her latest excitement is the Strength Through Joy project. It's a brand new thing organized by the Labour Front. They have concerts and plays and day trips and they say they're going to have cruises on the Baltic too. It's amazing value. You can go on a walking holiday in the mountains for twenty eight marks a week. The mountains are glorious.'

'The company probably isn't.'

'I know. But she's booking a holiday for us all the same. Fritz and me, Margarete, Dieter and their children. Gretl's invited too. Margarete's planning our route and everything. Only before that, she's got her wedding to prepare for.'

'Her wedding?' Mary almost spat out her coffee. 'Isn't Margarete already married?'

'It's a group wedding. Lots of couples, twenty or so – some of them are already married – are going to the Lazarus church on Saturday to reaffirm their vows to show their dedication to the Party. Margarete and Dieter plan to take their children along and make a day of it. It'll be a huge event. Fritz is grumbling like mad about it already.'

'Well, that takes some beating. One wedding would be quite enough for me.'

'Perhaps you'd like to come along then? In fact . . .' Emboldened by the outing and the food, Lotte's habitual propriety was thrown to the winds, 'it might inspire you. They say you often meet someone at a wedding. I mean I'm not sure what kind of men you like?'

What kind of men did she like? If you'd asked Mary that ten years ago she would have answered without a beat, a man straight out of Jane Austen by way of Charlotte Bronte. A man who was capable of being intelligent, sensitive and elemental all at the same time. Matching all three was as hard as winning on a fruit machine, of course. She'd have settled for two out of three, but even those had been like hens' teeth in New Jersey, and nor had any appeared in the years since. And then, into the first press conference of the new Nazi Government had strolled Rupert Allingham, with a sceptical expression and volume of *Berlin Alexanderplatz* under his arm, and she was hooked.

'Is there someone special?' Lotte persisted.

'Maybe.' Mary finished her apple cake, licked a little whipped cream off her finger, then reached for her cigarettes. 'But it's early days.'

She had fallen for Rupert hard, but she still had not the faintest idea what he felt for her in return. On one level they got on so well. They had explored Berlin together and investigated the nightlife pretty thoroughly too, regularly tumbling out of clubs in the early hours. Mary adored hearing about Rupert's family and the Jacobean house with its deer park and its priest-hole. She pictured herself visiting London and walking with him past those dazzling white Nash crescents in Regent's Park or wandering through Soho streets discussing politics late into the night. Rupert, for his part, claimed to admire America, too. He even talked about settling there one day. But at other times she suspected there was something in his British background he would never break free of. Class, conformity, tradition – call it what you wanted. It was as though he was carved into his niche like a stone nobleman on a cathedral face. She feared that conformity might apply to women too. In her worst moments she imagined that somewhere back home Rupert's future wife already existed, tending roses or taking sketching classes, a slender, polished, ivory-skinned beauty, ensconced in one of those moneyed chunks of English countryside he so affected to despise.

As she lit up, a man came over and pointed aggressively at the sign above the bar. It was inscribed in the dense, curly letters of German Gothic script, and for good measure he read it aloud very slowly.

' "German women do not smoke".'

Mary inhaled deeply for his benefit.

'Then I'm thankful to be an American, sir.'

Chapter Thirty-eight

Gerhard Lamprecht descended from his platform on the crane camera like a god from heaven. Which he might as well have been, judging by the gaggle of technicians, script assistants, continuity staff and electricians who stood at his bidding in the wings, along with the girl whose whole job was to stand behind the camera with his cup of coffee, and replenish it every time it grew cold.

'I need to see Fräulein Vine. In private, please.'

The crowd behind the cameras parted like the Red Sea as he strode off the set, motioning to Clara to follow him. Olga Chekhova rolled her eyes and the other actors cast sympathetic glances as the director and actress proceeded in silence down the corridor to the elevator, and from there to an edit suite with blacked-out windows. Clara's stomach was a quivering knot of nerves. She felt certain Herr Lamprecht was about to deliver a stinging critique. Instead he closed the door behind them, turned to her and smiled.

'We've just had the rushes back of your first scenes. I thought you might like to see.'

He sat at the editing deck, rested his cigar on an empty film canister and started the reel of film. Images of Clara's face passed before them in a monochrome flicker. There was a short encounter between herself and Hans Albers against the background of the Venetian hotel, and then, slightly less convincingly, her hair blowing in a makeshift breeze as she rode a speedboat across the painted lagoon.

'It's just as I said. The camera loves you.'

Clara smiled awkwardly at the extravagance of the compliment. She felt deeply embarrassed. She wanted to say, *I understand why you are paying unusual attention to a junior actress with a miniscule speaking part. I realize you're acting out of concern for your own career.* But what good would it do to articulate such thoughts? It would only be disrespectful to Herr Lamprecht, whose kind nature and obvious skill she had grown to admire and, besides, she couldn't help feeling flattered that such an eminent director should devote any time to her, whatever his motives.

'It's only a tiny role!'

He nodded complicitly. 'Even the tiniest roles can be crucial, Clara. Never dismiss the importance of the cameo.'

Clara studied the rushes with interest. She had never seen herself on film before. There was something about watching the movement of her own limbs, the luminous sheen of her skin as the light slid across her face, that gave her quiet pleasure. Just as Herr Lamprecht said, the camera brought out certain qualities she did not even know she had. The skilful lighting sculpted and rounded her features so that she appeared more finished and self-possessed. She watched herself with none of the usual agonies of self-consciousness. The black-and-white girl in the rushes was both her and not her, and observing it was strangely liberating.

'Everyone starts with a small part. It's what you make of it that matters.' He was looking at her cryptically. 'Next time, I think we can find you something more promising.'

At the words 'next time' Clara felt a little pulse of pride.

'And by the way, you should look out for a little piece about yourself in *Filmwoche.*' He winked. 'A reporter called and asked me to tip some upcoming talent, and I may have slipped them your name.'

'Herr Lamprecht . . . I'm very grateful. I hope you don't think that—'

He silenced her with a wave of his hand.

'No need to be grateful. Just wait for the premiere.'

The premiere! She allowed herself to picture it. It would be, almost certainly, at the Ufa Palast am Zoo, which had its own Wurlitzer and could hold two thousand people. It was a favourite place for film premieres, and could regularly be seen decked with swastika banners as the top brass strutted in to sample the latest releases. The crowds would stand three deep as the stars walked down the red carpet, bathed in the metallic crackle of flashlights. The politicians loved it because it was their chance to be seen with the beautiful and the famous, and the actors loved it because what actor didn't love a red carpet? She would invite Leo, she thought impulsively, before sense intervened. She reminded herself that she could never be seen with Leo in a public gathering like that and besides, she was only in the film because Klaus Müller had arranged her part, and so it would be his arm she rested on at the film's opening night.

She was longing for Leo's next summons, even if she had nothing to tell him. The memory of that kiss in the cinema burnt in her mind. She returned to it again and again, feeling the imprint of his lips and the surprising passion in it which seemed to contradict the notion that it had been merely a gesture of desperate convenience. Either that, or he was a better actor than she was.

Days had gone past, however, without any fresh tickets appearing on the hall table. She spent the following week at the studio, and twice Klaus Müller arrived on set to see her, but fortunately he had been too busy to do anything more than give her a lift back to town, during which he complained bitterly of the workload that the establishment of the new ministry was placing on him and the foul temper of Goebbels, who was being distracted from important affairs of state by the hysterical moods of his wife.

Then, as Clara arrived home on the Friday evening, another call from Magda came.

Chapter Thirty-nine

The von Ribbentrops' villa in Lentzeallee, Dahlem might have been a Surrey stockbroker's home at the end of the Guildford line, if Surrey stockbrokers had a penchant for swastika flags on the gatepost. All around the neighbourhood Jews and shopkeepers were leaving, to be replaced by Nazi officials, who built high walls around their houses and parked pristine Mercedes in the drives. The Ribbentrops had a large, white building with wooden gables and balconied windows on the upper floors, and a flight of marble steps leading to a grandly porticoed front door. Outside a lawn as manicured as a Nazi haircut led to a swimming pool covered in water lilies. Crimson budding rhododendrons lined the beds where a gardener was digging in compost for the first flowers of spring.

A butler opened the door. He was around fifty with a white tie, a tailcoat and to Clara's surprise, a London accent.

'You are the first to arrive Fräulein. Frau von Ribbentrop will be with you soon.'

'You're British?'

'Indeed, Fräulein. As are all of Herr von Ribbentrop's staff.' The butler's face was a mask of decorum and his eyes focused flintily on the middle distance. He had that way of seeing without looking, which English people expected from their staff. It probably came in especially useful here.

He ushered her into a chilly drawing room. Although the furniture was austere and modern, the walls were hung lavishly with oils of the German countryside, French landscapes and, in pride of place, an exquisite Madonna and Child which, Clara recognized with a start, had been painted by Fra Angelico.

She drifted over to the bookcase, which to her surprise contained several books by British authors, and noted the customary photo gallery of Hitler looking misty-eyed. She was getting used to the idea that everyone liked to see pictures of their Führer at all times. There was a less than flattering photograph of Goering in field grey, resembling a sea lion at the zoo, and a tall man she recognized as Reinhard Heydrich, an angular figure with narrow eyes whose skin stretched skeletally over his face like a medieval martyr. Von Ribbentrop himself was wearing some kind of naval uniform, beaming out of the frame and rubbing his hands like the captain of a yacht nervously awaiting his latest client.

On a nearby table someone had left a copy of *Harper's Bazaar* open. It was turned to a page featuring a majestic Coco Chanel leaning against the fireplace in her Rue Cambon apartment. There was drawing of a bottle of Chanel No. 5 below the photo, accompanied by the caption: "Madame Gabrielle Chanel is above all an artist in living. Her dresses, her perfume, are created with a faultless instinct for drama. Her Perfume No. 5 is like the soft music that underlies the playing of a love scene."

Evidently Frau von Ribbentrop was not planning to forsake the soft music of Chanel couture anytime soon. Incredible, really, given the enterprise they were engaged in. Clara was just marvelling at this when she felt a draught of cold air behind her and turned to find the woman herself appraising her.

It was said that von Ribbentrop was terrified of his wife and it was easy to believe. Despite her pudgy face and the air of a dowdy librarian, she had a certain steely chic. A tight little string of pearls formed a genteel garrotte round her neck and a beige cardigan hung from her shoulders. That day she was favouring the Rhine maiden look, wearing her dark coiffure wound in earphones on each side of her head and the kind of smile that could freeze blood.

'I see you've found our English library. My husband is a great Anglophile. Our butler, as you might have noticed, doesn't speak a word of German and Joachim insists the children have an English nurse. We read a great many English books. Do borrow one, if you like.'

'Thank you. I'll take a John Buchan.' Clara selected *The Thirty-Nine Steps*.

'A spy novel.' Frau von Ribbentrop gave a narrow look. 'My husband likes that kind of thing. I find them rather unconvincing myself. Do you miss England, Fräulein Vine?'

'Not much.'

'My husband has a great affection for the place.' She paused for a beat then added, 'I wish I liked it better.'

'Oh?'

She sighed. 'It seems England doesn't like me.'

'I'm sure that's not true.'

'It's so dreadfully foggy, I find. So bad for the sinuses. I suffer terribly.' She sniffed, as if in illustration. 'Still, Joachim visits very often. Cornwall he loves very much. Do you know Cornwall?'

Cornwall, on whose chill south coast Clara had spent so many childhood holidays. The house they stayed in had been owned for centuries by her father's family. It was a large, slate-fronted building set in misty fields, where the sharp cries

of seagulls cut through the soft bleat of lambs and the implacable sea was framed by shards of dramatic granite.

'I know it very well.'

'The Führer is planning to send Joachim to England this
month actually. We have a friend, Ernest Tennant, who will
be arranging for us to meet the British Prime Minister.'

With a jolt Clara recognized the name of her father's
friend. Ernest Tennant was a red-faced banker who was
involved in the international friendship club. An eccentric
chap. She remembered him particularly because when she
was introduced one evening at Ponsonby Terrace he had
patted her approvingly on the cheek, which was totally inap-
propriate given that she was twenty at the time.

'He's a great friend of our family. Such a clever man.'

'And my husband says he has met your father too. Do send
him our regards.'

So they had checked her credentials. It would have been
naïve of her to assume otherwise. Perhaps it was von
Ribbentrop who had assured them that Clara would be
trustworthy.

The door opened soundlessly and the butler showed in
more guests. There was Frau Ley, smoking nervously, and a
couple of wives of attachés from the Foreign Office, both
portly and pearl-ridden and unlikely to need any encouragement to wear the folk look. Behind them were Magda, Frau
Helmuth Wohltat, the wife of the new cabinet councillor,
who turned out to be half-American, and the actress who
was to share the modelling with Clara. Lida Baarová, a shy
brunette with ringlets and high arched brows, was a new
discovery. The talent scouts from Ufa had come across her
acting in a series of low grade movies in Prague and brought
her back to Berlin to be turned into a star. Though she was
barely twenty, she was well on her way already, having

acquired a number of satin evening dresses and furs, and, courtesy of a strict diet, a pair of stunning Slav cheekbones.

Lunch was served on a vast dining table, polished to a high gleam, with enough flower arrangements to fill a funeral parlour. There were roses and lilies on the table and hothouse chrysanthemums in vases. The Ribbentrops, Clara had heard, held the best table in Berlin. The menu was in English, but the food was French. It was served with a fussy attention to detail on porcelain plates laced with gold. It couldn't be more obvious that Frau von Ribbentrop wanted to show off her chef. There was a green salad with prawn and caviar topping, then lamb chops wearing little crimped frills of paper, with a jellied terrine of vegetables followed by patisserie, cheese and coffee. It went without saying that hardly anyone ate a thing.

Magda and Frau von Ribbentrop set the tone, indulging in a type of competitive fasting, waving away plates that were barely touched, disturbing only the occasional vegetable from its decorative bed. The older women followed suit and only Emmy ate with abandon, clearing her plate with swift efficiency, as though if she didn't finish fast enough it might be taken away from her.

Through the thicket of lilies, Clara observed Magda. She had noticed Magda's make-up was an accurate barometer of her state of mind. The heavier it was, the unhappier she seemed. Today, it was as thick as paint, but still failed to cover the dark shadows under her eyes. Despite her refusal to touch the lunch, she cut a substantial figure, the flesh of her arms puckering against her sleeves and a bulge of pregnancy fat that she had failed to shake off. Next to the young actress, who was cradling her wine glass in slender hands, gazing through the flowery fronds with delight like a fawn in a forest, it seemed unfair.

Clara and Emmy were discussing Hermann Goering.

'When did you meet?'

'Only last year, can you believe it? It seems like a lifetime ago. I was acting in Weimar at the National Theatre. He saw me, and then he invited me to meet him the next day in a café, and we went for a walk, and everything went from there. It was what the French call a coup de foudre. When I got this job in Berlin, it made it so much easier, of course.'

'How fortunate.'

'Yes, wasn't it? Though I do so wish Hermann was an actor, not a politician. I don't know that I take well to the political life. On the night of the torchlight procession he gave me a gun! I was so shocked, I slipped it in my muff. I'd never handled a gun before, but as he told me, we have to be careful now.'

She sighed, and eased a button on her waistband. 'Still, I shouldn't complain. I've been so lucky. I often ask myself why Herr Hitler can't be as fortunate. Why can't he meet a sensitive normal woman? It would be such a help to him.'

From across the table, Magda widened her eyes. 'Frau Sonnemann, I think we have said enough.'

'Oh, I'm sorry,' said Emmy, wiping vinaigrette from her mouth. 'Hermann says I talk like a liberal newspaper that ought to be banned. And besides,' she mused, 'he does have Fräulein Braun, I suppose.'

'Who is Fräulein Braun?' enquired Lida Baarová. She had a slow sensual voice with a heavy Czech accent.

'I have no idea,' said Magda tartly.

'He keeps her in Berchtesgaden,' said Emmy more quietly to Clara. 'I tell you, I feel sorry for her. The house isn't bad, though a little poky, but there's no smoking anywhere. When you're craving a cigarette you have to go in the bathroom and it's absolutely crowded with all the senior men smoking out the window. Then everyone waves the towels around to get rid of the smoke. But you have to smoke because you'll do anything to keep awake. Everyone has to stay up until four in the morning, you see, because no one can go to bed before the Führer.'

'How tiring,' murmured Clara.

'And when they go out, he makes the poor girl travel with the secretaries so that she doesn't stand out. Their sedan is never allowed to travel in the same convoy as Hitler's. Even on walks she has to trudge behind. The only sign they have anything to do with each other is that they go up to the bedroom together at night.'

'Yet I have heard,' said Lida Baarová, leaning over, 'that the Führer says he cannot give himself to any woman because he belongs to Germany.'

'You mean they just talk? Well, goodness knows what they would talk about because Eva has absolutely no interest in politics! Herr Hitler told Hermann he thought the ideal woman was "tender, sweet and stupid" and I said to Hermann, "Eva's certainly that! She cares for nothing except clothes and watching all those trashy Ufa films." Oh I'm sorry, Fräulein Vine. I didn't intend any offence.' She placed a plump hand on Clara's arm.

'Of course not. None taken.'

Across the table, Magda's face was as dark as the sky before a thunderstorm.

'Ooh, I forgot to mention.' Emmy extracted a box, tied with ribbon. 'We were sent these as a gift. The Otto Boenicke company has started to make them. Delightful, aren't they?'

It was a cigar box, produced by the oldest cigar company in Berlin. The traditional design had been replaced with an image of Goering.

'I brought several. One for each of you.' Emmy handed them round, but Magda declined.

'Thank you, but no. Joseph doesn't enjoy cigars and nor do I.'

There followed a desultory half-hour discussing the progress of the Fashion Bureau. The Association of Aryan Clothing Manufacturers had produced a label that could be sewn into garments guaranteeing they had been manufactured by Aryan hands only. And plans were well in train for the first fashion show, which was to be held at the Grunewald race track. The date had already been earmarked in the diaries of all the top men who were, according to Magda, greatly looking forward to it.

After coffee and with almost indecent haste, Magda offered Clara a lift back to the centre of town in her green cabriolet, which Clara took as a signal that the meeting was over.

Once on the road, and heading towards town, Magda seemed to relax.

'I had to leave. I couldn't take a second more of listening to that Frau Sonnemann. I wonder what the Führer would think of such disrespectful remarks about his private life. What she said about Fräulein Braun . . . you must understand, my dear, Hitler has told me that he will never marry. The nation needs him too much.'

'Of course.'

'And I have begun to wonder about Frau von Ribbentrop too. I think it may be difficult converting her to our cause. She spends so much time abroad, collecting foreign fashions and perfumes. I wonder if she is fully committed to the whole idea of German culture. Did you notice the butler? And as for Frau Ley, poor thing. Have you seen how she drinks? I suppose she needs to.'

Magda seemed to have forgotten entirely the confessions of her own marital woes. Her face had softened as they headed back to the centre of town. She even smiled as the traffic was held up by a marching band, thumping out some brassy tune on its way towards the Tiergarten, and tapping her fingers in time on the steering wheel. Clara was emboldened to ask the question that had been at the back of her mind.

'I wonder, Frau Doktor, if I could ask your help.'

She gave a warm smile. 'But of course!'

'A favour really. For a friend of mine. A friend of a friend. She's a woman at the studios, and her friend is in a little trouble.'

Magda stopped her with a raised hand. 'Is it a Jew?'

'I think so . . . he's an artist.'

Magda sighed dismissively. 'Then I'm afraid, my dear, I can't help. It's always Jews.'

'It's just, he seems to have disappeared. She's trying to find out where he might have gone.'

'There's nothing I can do, Fräulein Vine,' Magda said briskly. 'Please don't ask me again.'

Her eyes had assumed the same impervious veil Clara had noticed before. The one that said *don't go any further*. It was infuriating, but also essential that Clara say nothing. Any kind of protest could only attract attention. Mildly, she said, 'I understand.'

But Magda continued. 'It's not as if I don't know. After all, my stepfather is Jewish.'

Clara attempted to contain her astonishment. 'Your stepfather?'

'Yes, my mother's name was Friedlander until my husband asked her to change it.'

'You mean Frau Behrend?' Clara thought of the timid woman she had met occasionally at the Goebbels' home, who always seemed to appear when Joseph was absent.

'She understands. It's rooted in the rationale of the regime. The Third Reich is opposed to Jews and if that is what the Führer wants, then that is what we have to obey.'

She spoke with the air of someone who has tussled with a seemingly illogical maths problem and come to accept the answer without remotely comprehending it.

'The thing is, my dear, it's hard to understand, but if we let them, the Jews and the Communists would take everything. It's their way. Look what the Bolsheviks did to the Russian royal family. I don't think I'll ever forget the newspaper picture, when all those children of the royal family were murdered. Murdered in cold blood. All those little faces lined up. What kind of person could do that? Those poor children. Images like that never leave your mind.'

Chapter Forty

All over Berlin impromptu prisons had appeared in basements, sheds, bunkers, even cinemas. There Ernst Röhm's storm troopers could provide *Schutzhaft*, "protective custody", for trade unionists, Social Democrats, Communists and whoever else they deemed an enemy. This custody protected them from everything except beatings, torture, and occasionally death. For the families of those abducted it could take days to discover where they had gone, provided they did not end up at Scharnhorststrasse hospital. And even when they had located their relatives, it was generally impossible to find a lawyer to represent them. But these SA prisons, Leo knew, were only for ordinary enemies. More important people went straight to the new Gestapo headquarters and lately there was another destination too. A different kind of prison in an old munitions factory at Dachau, a little village close to Munich. A concentration camp, it was called, for political subversives, especially Communists. Hundreds, maybe thousands had already been taken there, arrested without charge. The worry was that Bruno Weiss was one of them.

Having consulted his boss, that evening Leo caught a tram to Französische Strasse and entered a wine bar, where a good-looking dark suited man sat at the back smoking a cigar and perusing the *Berliner Morgenpost*. He had a brush of russet hair springing up from his brow, an immaculate handkerchief folded in his pocket and bright, intelligent eyes. He looked every inch the lawyer he was, so much so that anyone would assume the bulge in his jacket was a roll of court documents if they hadn't known it was a Mauser. He waved Leo over and lit a cigarette for him.

'A beer, my friend?'

Hubert Pollack now spent all his time setting up an advisory office for Jewish emigrants who wanted to leave for Palestine. To Leo and his boss, his co-operation was invaluable. He had already established a network of contacts amongst the police and was skilled in paying the right bribes to the right people. As far as locating and releasing prisoners went, there were few people more equipped than he. One beer later, Leo had established that Bruno Weiss was, in fact, still in Berlin.

'He's been taken to the SA barracks in Tempelhof on suspicion of Communist activity. From our point of view, the sooner you collect him the better. I wouldn't want him discussing our friend in Moabit.'

'I'm surprised he hasn't received a visit already.'

The friend was a small printer whose shop, right next to a church, sold religious texts and songbooks. Outside of working hours however, once the staff had left, the printer would go upstairs and produce pamphlets for Communist resistors. His expertise in the matters of ink and paper was also highly valued.

'Only a matter of time,' grimaced Pollack. He drained his beer and made to leave. 'Take this paper. I've finished with it. There's an excellent report on the threat of famine in Russia.'

It was a newspaper drop, one of the most trusted techniques. When Pollack had gone, Leo went to the lavatories at the back of the bar and found a release permit pinned to the inside page. He returned to the office, picked up his briefcase, and caught a tram to the south of the city.

The pleasant, red-brick building in Pape Strasse had once served as a barracks for Prussian soldiers, but it was a gang of smartly dressed storm troopers who now milled round the hall, observing the visitor with bored irritation. The officer in charge inspected the paperwork meticulously while Leo consulted his watch to conceal his nervousness. Pollack's work was known to be of the very best. Most of what he supplied was genuine, from his extensive network of contacts in the police, but what wasn't was forged with masterly skill, complete with the correct ink and rubber stamps. And the visa itself, of course, was perfectly genuine, stamped with the insignia of His Majesty's Government, and signed by Leo's boss, Foley, that morning.

The officer seemed to be taking an interminable time. Leo's mouth was dry and he was forced to check his watch again, with a show of irritation, before the man pursed his lips, returned the documents and gestured for Leo to follow a guard down the steps to the cellars.

It was dim below stairs, the ceiling punctuated with bare bulbs, the air freighted with urine and the unmistakable reek of fear. Despite himself, Leo was almost paralysed with horror as he peered down the long corridor, painted institutional green and lined with heavy steel doors with nine-inch barred inspection hatches. If this was what it felt like to visit, God knows how dreadful it would be to be frogmarched here with only the tender mercies of the SA to rely on. He forced himself to overcome his terror and go on.

From behind one of the doors low moans could be heard and from another a reedy, educated voice issued an indignant shout. 'I demand to see a laywer! I demand it!' For a moment

Leo stopped, almost overcome by the urge to turn round and hasten back to fresh air and the freedom of a Berlin evening. They passed an empty cell whose stained floor was the only witness to the horrors it had contained, and then the guard produced his keys, and opened a door onto a tiny space, just six feet wide, with no furniture except a wooden bench and a bed that let down from the wall. No window, but a single hanging bulb. Iron rings let into the brickwork. A stinking bucket stood in the corner and the wall was scratched with graffiti. On the bench a cadaverous man was hunched wearing a shabby suit but no tie. He sprung up as the door opened, his bony face white and sweating with fear, and looked from Leo to the guard in alarm.

'Weiss, your visa has arrived,' grunted the guard.

'My visa?'

Leo stepped forward, seized Bruno's hand and pumped it. 'My name is Mr Quinn. From the British Passport Control office. I have the visa you applied for to travel to England. Provided you sign your intention to leave the country, you will be free to go immediately.'

'You're . . .' Bruno's face was uncomprehending.

Leo was impassive, officious. A little bored. 'You made a visit to England, didn't you?'

'England?' After the hours of interrogation he had endured, Bruno was befuddled, and primed to deny any suggestion that was put to him.

Leo checked his watch. 'Really, Herr Weiss, if this is taking up your time.'

'No. No!' The voice was high and frantic. 'I remember now! England. I had an exhibition at the Whitechapel Gallery. In, er, '31, I think. That's it, 1931.'

Leo sighed and the guard shuffled his huge, polished boots.

'And while you were there you applied to British Passport Control for a visa to return?' He reached into his briefcase, every inch the bureaucrat whose overtime was going unappreciated. 'Well, I'm happy to tell you that that visa has now been approved.' He proffered the paper, with its indigo stamp and Foley's meticulous signature.

'Ah, yes. Thank you.' Bruno's mouth was trembling as he tried to smile, so it emerged as a contorted grimace of fear.

'So, if you'd like to accompany me, perhaps we can discuss the formalities.'

The SA officer motioned both of them out of the door and up the stairs.

'You have to sign for him.'

At the reception, another officer scrawled something in the record book, Leo added his signature, then Bruno was handed a bag containing his watch and glasses, and the two men walked out the door.

It wasn't until they had reached the street that Bruno seemed to stumble and clutched Leo's arm. He was trembling so violently that Leo decided it might be wise to steer him towards a bar.

'Have you eaten?'

'Eaten?' He looked at Leo as though he was mad.

'Let me buy you something. You can tell me what happened, Herr Weiss.'

They went into a small tavern beneath the S–Bahn and sat at a table as the trains thundered and clattered above them. Leo bought two plates of meatballs with mustard, pickled eggs and gherkins, salami, bread, cheese and two beers on the side. For a few minutes he refrained from questions, while the man fell ravenously on his meal. He had been handsome, from what Leo recalled, but now his eyes were pits sunk into the hollows of their sockets, gaunt shadows hollowed his

cheeks, and the entire side of his face was purpled with bruis-
ing. His hair was tangled and powdered with dust. He looked,
Leo couldn't help thinking, exactly like one of the figures in
his own work.

'When did they arrest you?'

Bruno put down his beer with a trembling hand. 'A week
ago. More, perhaps. It was before dawn, anyway. They
must have been hammering at my door for some time
before I answered it. I suppose I'm lucky they didn't break
it down entirely. There were about six of them, they came
in waving revolvers and I thought they were going to shoot
me. I said, "Can't you wait until I've put some clothes on?"
but when I went to my wardrobe, they flung all the stuff
out, saying, "Look at the finery this Jew can afford! All this
money he's been stealing from us!" Then they started asking
me about my Communist activity. I said I'm not a
Communist, just an artist, and one said, "What do you
make then? Bombs?" I said I had never made any bombs,
and he said they knew I was planning to bomb the Führer's
birthday parade. He was going to beat the truth out of me,
then another one said, "You think this is art? This repulsive
stuff?" There was something about this man . . .' Bruno
hesitated. 'He was different from the others. More aggressive. He really looked at the paintings before he ripped
them, and when he did he took his crop and slashed them
right across, the breasts and the legs, and you know, the
groin, as if they were real women, you know? As if he could
really hurt them.'

The food seemed to have revived him and he reached over
to grasp Leo's arm.

'Mr Quinn, I can't thank you enough.'

'Think nothing of it. I'm an admirer of your work, Herr
Weiss.'

'But you were running a risk yourself, weren't you? I never applied for a visa. You must know that.'

'Desperate times, et cetera.'

'But who told you I was there? Was it my parents?'

'A friend of yours got in touch. A woman called Helga.'

'Helga! Is she all right?'

'I think so.'

For the first time he smiled, and braced his shoulders.

'Is that visa real?'

'Of course. In fact, perhaps we should begin to think about your travel arrangements and so on. I take it there are people you could stay with briefly, when you arrive, just until you get settled?'

Bruno Weiss smiled and shook his head. 'Oh, my dear man, I'm not going,' he said lightly. 'I couldn't possibly.'

'With respect, I think you'd be foolish not to.'

Bruno shrugged. 'There's Helga to think of. As long as she's here, I'll be here too.'

'I don't know that I could guarantee a repeat performance.'

Across the plastic table top, however, a transformation had taken place. From the hunched and trembling figure of a few moments ago, Bruno now sat straight, eyes shining with defiance, the life flooding back into him as he talked.

'Mr Quinn, I love my country. Whatever my political sympathies, we Germans are not the same as Russians you know. We're civilized. Nor are we Italians. We will never turn Fascist. You'll see. The Nazis are having their moment now, but it's our turn next.'

Leo raised his eyebrows.

'You think it amazing that I can say that after what I've been through? Maybe. But these thugs, they're not everything. The great heart of this country is sleeping now. The people are slow to be provoked, but they'll rise. I promise you.'

Leo cast a swift, automatic glance at the drink-sodden loner he had noted, slumped over the bar. 'So you're not afraid?'

'No. It's not fear I feel now. It's shame. I'm ashamed that this murderous gang should be returning my country to the fourteenth century. But it won't last, dear Mr Quinn. It won't last.'

Leo's heart sank. Who was to say that Weiss was not right, and all those people who lined patiently up outside his office each day, eager for the unassuming indigo stamp that would mark them as exiles, ready to leave their homes and history for an uncertain impoverished future, were not wrong? Perhaps they were crazy to queue all day not just at the British Consulate, but the embassies of any godforsaken part of the world, just to obtain permission to escape the regime that hated them, but not enough to let them go. Yet how could it be that Bruno Weiss, of all people, whose desolate paintings testified to all the horror and despair of which human beings were capable, should feel any optimism about the fate of Germany now?

Bruno was devouring slices of bread and salami, as though he had just realized how hungry he was. He looked up and smiled, as if broaching a subject that Leo might find difficult to understand.

'One thing this dreadful experience has made me understand, Mr Quinn, is that I must be more outspoken from now on.'

'I would have thought you were quite outspoken enough already. Your paintings are pretty eloquent, Herr Weiss, let alone those pamphlets you help produce.'

Bruno laughed. 'I'm not talking about politics! I meant with women. You see, my feelings for Helga are very strong, yet I have always disliked that kind of discussion that women seem to want. Talk of love, and so on. But now I see that just as it would be cowardly of me to leave Helga in Germany while I seek safety elsewhere, so it is cowardly of me not to express my feelings for her.'

For some reason, the image of Clara's face in the shimmering darkness of the Neukölln cinema came into Leo's mind. Her mouth, with its teeth slightly crooked and the press of her lips as he kissed her. The astonishment in her eyes and the unexpected softness of her skin. He had acted on sheer operational instinct. He hoped she understood that.

Bruno wiped his mouth. 'There are times, Mr Quinn, when we need to be truthful about what we feel, don't you think?'

It was a curious thing to ask of a British Government passport official, Leo thought as he signalled for the bill. He decided to consider the question as strictly rhetorical.

Chapter Forty-one

'So what does Müller talk about?'

Two weeks had passed with no contact and then on Saturday another envelope was waiting for Clara on the hall table, containing a U-Bahn ticket for Krumme Lanke at the south-west end of the U1 line. There was also a ticket to a lunchtime concert at a lake-side restaurant.

The Grunewald's villa colonies grouped around the lakes were a favourite spot for Berliners who wanted to escape the city and get a breath of air. Although the area was being developed, with fresh roads being laid into the pine forest and pretty pale gabled houses being erected, there was still a rural feel, with jays and woodpeckers raucous in the trees around them and bluebells and prim-roses clumped on the banks. As she walked, Clara passed a group of boys running through the wood in shorts and gym shirts, and a band of Wandervogel scouts, marching along the footpath singing.

The café was right on the waterside, a number of wooden tables set inside fancy wrought-iron fencing surrounding a small dance floor, where couples and a few girls together were twirling in the sun. One of the girls, dancing with her soldier, was dressed in a blue dirndl with puffed sleeves. Magda would approve, Clara thought.

Leo had made a point of sitting as near as possible to the band so that it drowned out their voices and made Clara lean towards him to be heard. His face was thinner, she thought, and he looked more than usually sombre. She felt a lurch of desire so intense it surprised her. As he fiddled with the beer bottle, she badly wanted to take his hand in hers. She wanted him to lean across the table and kiss her again.

'Müller gossips. I think he's lonely. He's a widower, you know.'

'My heart bleeds. What does he gossip about?'

Clara knew what he was doing. She did the same now. She sieved her conversations with Müller like a prospector panning for gold, extracting those fragments that she thought might be useful to Leo.

'There was something. When he gave me a lift back from the studio the other day we passed an airfield. He began talking about rearming and how the Deutsche Luft Hansa is being readied for air warfare. But that's not supposed to happen, is it?'

'Under the terms of the Treaty of Versailles, Germany's not allowed an airforce. And they're supposed to restrict their flying activities to gliding. But if this regime stuck to what was supposed to happen, life would be very different.'

'Müller said underground airports and factories are being built. They're designing new planes and a school for pilots is being established near Gatow, twenty miles from here.'

'New planes?'

'Müller heard rumours that Goering was boasting of having five hundred operational aircraft by the end of next year. And civilian aircraft are being designed so that the baggage compartments can be deployed as bomb bays, if that should be needed.'

Leo made a swift note, then replaced his pad in his inside pocket.

'Sounds like he's still sweet on you.'

'Obviously.'

'Don't do anything to discourage that.'

His voice fell as a group of men in uniform passed, looking for a table, and then a waitress approached. Leo ordered herring in sour cream and onions along with a glass of beer. Although it was lunchtime Clara wasn't hungry. Being with Leo caused excitement to pulse through her, dulling her appetite.

'So tell me about the Führer's girlfriend? Do they talk about her much?'

'Eva Braun? She never mingles with the other women. I don't think it's because they refuse to invite her, I think it's because Hitler doesn't allow it.'

'Why not?'

'I suppose he knows what they would think.'

'And what do they think?'

'That she's not good enough for him. She's only twenty-one. She wears cheap jewellery, she loves fashion.'

'You might think she could help out in the Fashion Bureau then.'

'He never even lets her come to Berlin. She lives down in Munich with her sister in an apartment he bought for her. And she goes to stay with him at Obersalzberg. But really, she wouldn't fit in with the wives.'

Leo smiled wryly. 'I can imagine. And how are the Ribbentrops?'

'He is visiting England soon in a mission to cultivate pro-German feeling. He's to stay with a man called Ernest Tennant.'

'Ernest Tennant. A great enthusiast for Hitler.'

'My father knows him too. They're hoping he can fix up a meeting with the Prime Minister.'

'Mr MacDonald? Are they indeed?' He raised his eyebrows. 'And what about your father? Does Müller mention him?'

'Frequently. He hopes he'll be visiting me soon, which is a worry because I haven't even told my father where I'm staying. I'm going to have to write to him soon, Leo. That is all right, isn't it?'

'Keep it vague. But Müller trusts you because of your father, you know that?'

'I know.'

'Don't let him think otherwise.'

She focused on the couples on the dance floor without reply.

'Have you seen the first lady?'

'Yes. She's angry with Joseph.'

'Again. What's he done this time?'

'He's had her former husband arrested for tax irregularities. But it's really because Quandt has been restricting access to Harald, his son with Magda. Though I still think there's something else . . .'

Clara was now certain that some private matter was dominating Magda's thoughts. Since that day of the row, when Magda had seemed on the brink of confiding in her, Clara had puzzled over her comment. *"There's something you might help me with. A matter of some delicacy"*. Something was weighing on Magda's mind, she was sure of it.

'There must be a problem.' She traced a line down the condensed pearls of her beer glass. 'We weren't due to meet until the day of the fashion show at the Grunewald Race Track a couple of weeks away. But she left a message asking me to call at her house on Tuesday morning.'

Clara looked out across to the other side of the lake, where a border of pine trees ran along the sandy shoreline. The water was corrugated by a brisk breeze. A jetty protruded into the lake and a group of boys were taking turns to curl up into balls and hurl themselves into its silver depths. She watched how they hesitated for a second before plucking up the courage to jump, how the water fractured into a thousand sparkling shards and how exhilarated the boys looked as they emerged icy and dripping, their skin rosy from the freezing lake.

'Do you think she suspects something?' asked Leo.

'No. She trusts me. I'm good at concealing my feelings.'

'You must be. I can never tell what you're thinking.'

Clara allowed herself a quick smile.

'Have you always been that way?'

No one ever asked her that. But then no one had ever spoken to her the way Leo did, or shown an interest in her private feelings. Despite how recently she had met him, the peculiarity of their situation had forged a strange intimacy between them.

'Since my mother died.'

Her mother's funeral, at the village church of St Michael and All Angels, was the first time she had ever thought about the need to hide her emotions. It was absolutely essential, Angela had told her, not to cry. It was simply not done. '*If you feel the tears coming, dig your nails into the palm of your hand*'. And she had managed it. Even though the little country church had been full to bursting with friends and relations. Even at the graveside as the coffin bumped its way into the damp ground and Clara pictured her mother's tiny, wasted frame jolting against the inside of the box. Even as the family, like terrible conspirators, shared in the act of covering her with earth. So resolute was her self-control that for a few days afterwards she had continued dry-eyed, as if her mother had died merely to inconvenience her. "*My mother is dead*", she said to herself over and over in her head, as if practising the words of an unfamiliar part. It was days before she found herself lying as if paralysed on her bed as the great continent of grief inside her thawed and the dry heaving sobs turned into tears.

'I remember my brother, Kenneth, telling someone a few days later that he was over it.' She laughed, drily. 'I suppose in the short term children do get over it. In the long term, of course, never.'

Leo nodded. He was still regarding her with a peculiar fixity. She might almost have called it tenderness. She looked at the curve of his lips, which not so long ago had kissed her. She felt a desperate urge for him to take her on the dance floor, and hold her in the circle of his arms. It was a physical longing to be touched by him, to plunge beneath that cool exterior.

'Why don't we ever talk about you, Leo? I feel I know nothing about you.'

He shrugged and looked away. That was how it was supposed to be. Let others know as little about you as possible. He had spent so long trying to be unknowable that he barely knew himself.

'Not much to know.'

He wanted to talk to her. He longed to respond to that quick, inquisitive gaze, but he simply couldn't. It would complicate matters. Instead he took a long draught of beer and forced himself to the task in hand.

'Anyway. You say Müller is still sweet on you.'

Her face fell. She focused on the boys on the jetty. There was one, a flaxen-haired boy of around eight, who seemed more nervous than the rest. He was banging his arms against his sides for warmth, his chest concave beneath a ladder of ribs, gearing himself up for the plunge while his friends laughed. At last, unable to bear the jeers he took a run, folded up his knees and hurled himself into the implacable depths, surfacing with an expression of shocked delight.

'Müller's going to be making demands on you. He probably already has. You're going to have to make your mind up about that pretty soon.'

'Why?'

'You know why. For the same reason we're doing any of this. So that we can get valuable information. Like the tip about the pilot school. That kind of thing helps us enormously. You've no idea how helpful it is. How vital it might prove if relations between Britain and Germany take a turn for the worse. If the Germans really are rearming, we're going to need to keep up that flow of information, whatever it might take.'

'Whatever it might take?'

'To have someone close to the leadership, privy to all that uncensored chat. Seeing them socially, totally accepted by them. It's tremendously important, what you're doing. More important than you realize.'

'Perhaps I should get a medal for it.'

He ignored the sarcasm. 'It's appreciated.'

'Is it?'

Quietly he said, 'Look, Clara, this isn't cricket. Nor is it the kind of game you play in some English drawing room on a wet Sunday afternoon. We can't always play by the rules. There are more important things at stake than ourselves.'

'There's a big difference between ignoring the rules and sleeping with a Nazi captain.'

He cast his eyes around quickly. 'It's your call,' he said quietly. 'I thought I made that clear. It's always going to be your call.'

For a second she didn't say anything. Then in a low voice she said, 'What would you think of me, Leo, if I did?'

He was saved from a reply when a bird landed on the table right in front of them. It was a sparrow with a bright, enquiring eye, hopping with a delicate frisk of feathers to peck at a crumb. He thought how endearing it was that such a tiny, fragile thing should be unafraid of the larger creatures around it. The laughing soldier in SA uniform and his girlfriend stopped to look at it.

'It's beautiful,' cooed the girl, and her boyfriend leant over and kissed her. 'So are you.'

The couple smiled at their slight indiscretion, and Leo grinned back at them.

Clara waited until the young couple had returned to the dance floor. The image she had a few moments ago of dancing with Leo had evaporated, supplanted in her mind by the idea of Klaus Müller, and the trip she had arranged with him the following day, to examine the country house he had discovered, just outside Potsdam. She rubbed her arms as a chill breeze blew in from the lake.

Bitterly she said, 'That's the thing about this place. It's like a picture book. Everything looks sweet and clean but inside it's rotten to the core.'

Leo reached across to her and lightly brushed the back of her hand, then pulled away.

'Clara, if you're finding this too hard . . .'

She shrugged, her face set, chin jutting defiantly. Physically she was still right next to him, but he sensed she had receded from him.

She was remembering something Paul Croker said to her when she was tackling a tricky role.

"Whatever you do, Clara, if you really want to do it convincingly, you need to find your motivation".

"My motivation?"

"The trigger that makes your character act the way she does. The emotion that guides her. The reason that carries her through. If you have your character's motivation, you have everything you need".

She had that, at least. Her motivation. It remained to be seen if it would be enough to carry her through.

Chapter Forty-two

Klaus Müller's find was in Caputh, a village on the fringes of a pine forest, a few miles outside Berlin. To get there they took the autobahn in the direction of Babelsberg and travelled past Potsdam into the countryside. Clara wore sunglasses and a red cotton scarf tied round her neck in a way she had copied from Olga Chekhova. It was a fine day and the blue sky was lightly feathered with clouds as Müller's BMW convertible, freshly waxed and polished, sped along the empty road. He had the hood down and the wind rushed against her face with an intoxicating edge of grass and damp earth. Looking into the dark coniferous forests as they passed, she almost expected to see girls with braids and baskets weaving their way through the trees, the way they did in Germany's deep ancestral imagination, and would do again, if Hitler had anything to do with it. But it being Sunday, the sides of the autobahn were dotted with picnickers, sitting on rugs watching the cars go by.

The road moved out from the forest to run between wide meadows, waving with great lances of wildflowers, and fields blunt with the stubble of early crops. Clara looked at everything they passed with interest. She fed greedily on the beauty of the landscape, as if by focusing on the journey she could forestall the arrival.

'When Elsa was alive we always planned to find a place out here,' Müller shouted to her, above the rushing air. 'But it's taken me a while to get round to it. Luckily, there's plenty of property available right now.'

Caputh was set in a beautiful position between two lakes, in which, he explained, he planned to do some sailing and fishing, should work ever let up enough to give him the chance. But the village's most notable feature, he told her, was that it contained a house that had been built for Albert Einstein, a two-storey, timber-framed construction looking out over Lake Templin, which had been a fiftieth birthday present from the city of Berlin to its eminent resident. Unfortunately, the eminent resident had recently decided to reside anywhere but Germany and just two weeks ago had turned up at the German Consulate in Antwerp to renounce his German citizenship.

'So a great use of taxpayers' money that was.' Müller waved a contemptuous hand in the direction of the house. 'I hear the local police had to raid the place the other evening. They were tipped off that they might find weapons left there by Communist agitators.'

'You'd never have thought of Professor Einstein as the sort to hide machine guns under the bed,' said Clara mildly.

He cast her a quick glance to assess the level of her flippancy so she shot him a bright smile, glad that her eyes were hidden by the glasses.

'That's exactly the point. He may have looked like a crazy professor – no doubt he was – but he was also a lying Jewish Communist and there's no depths to which those people won't stoop. We're better off without him.'

Müller was wearing a leather jacket and open-necked shirt with braces. He looked different in his weekend clothes, fleshier, and less intimidating. He retained his air of jocular cynicism, but he looked more like the businessman he had once been than a Nazi officer. Clara wondered if in normal times she might have been attracted to him, but she doubted it. There was a flatness in his brown gaze, a lack of depth and questioning, that reminded her of a Rottweiler dog that Kenneth had once looked after. She shifted in the seat, her flesh sticking to the warm leather. Part of her was impatient to arrive, the other part hoping the journey would never end.

He drew up at the end of a track, where a small wooden house with sloping gables stood, surrounded on three sides by forest. It was quiet here. The air was mossy and tinged with woodsmoke. A tiny garden was falling into genteel disrepair and weeds were beginning to thread through the gravelled drive. The only sound was the birds squabbling in nearby branches. Müller hauled a picnic basket from the back seat, fished out the house keys and flung open the door.

'So what do you think? It's charming, isn't it? Not big, but I don't need much space. It's just me, after all, for now.'

Clara looked around her. The door opened straight into a small sitting room where a couple of armchairs were arranged before a wood-burning stove and a pair of antlers fixed incongruously above it. Apart from the sparse furnishings, the house had the pitiful look of the recently abandoned. On the walls she noticed pale rectangles where the pictures of the last occupants had hung. She imagined they might have been family photographs and how the people in them had turned into a blank shadow of themselves, inverted negatives, remaining only as ghostly reminders of absence.

'How did you find it?'

'The people who owned it had to leave in a hurry so the house had become available quite suddenly. Fortunately I keep my ear to the ground.' He shrugged happily. 'I tend to know what's going on.'

At the back of the house was a tiny kitchen, no more than a work surface in solid pine, a cooker and a sink. Clara peered through the back door to the forest outside.

'It's rather remote, isn't it?'

'Not really. There's houses on both sides. It just seems so. And that's what I like about it. I love a little rural tranquillity. More than ever right now.'

She had felt sick in the car, a rising nausea that all her improvization couldn't dampen. It was plain from the moment she stepped into the car what the purpose of this outing would be. Images of what was to come flashed through her mind. This was what she had been dreading and it had arrived. She half worried that she would be incapable of it, but she wasn't entirely inexperienced. It would be hard to have come through several seasons in rep and remain a virgin, and her time with Dennis had taught her that the physical act required only passive acquiescence. Yet she knew also that a show of enthusiasm would be required if Müller was to continue trusting her and feeding her information in the future. The future! The very thought was too difficult to contemplate just then. All she could do was focus on the here and now. She must make everything shrink to the essence of herself, standing there in the silent house. She must let all distractions and thoughts fall away and enter fully into the act. She had decided to do this and as there was no getting out of it, there was no point waiting either.

Müller seemed to have the same idea. He took her in his arms.

'Do you know why I brought you here?'

'To see the house?'

He gave a short, impatient laugh. 'I hope you're not going to behave like a little tease again.'

He ran a hand down her body and an unexpected shudder of fear ran through her. He was so much larger and stronger than her and whatever he said, the place seemed so remote. She flinched and took a step backwards.

'Don't avoid me. You're a grown woman. You wouldn't have come if you didn't want to.' His lips were wet against her ear. 'You're no little innocent, my dear. Don't imagine I'm taken in by that lovely, pure face.

He reached for the belt of her dress, and with deft fingers eased the buttons and pulled it off. Suddenly a wave of panic rose within her and she fought against the impulse to flee. Feeling her struggle he grasped her more firmly.

'Come now, my little actress. Stop your play acting.'

He tipped up her face and kissed her greedily. His tongue was large and thick and his moustache scratched her. It took everything in her not to push him away. Leo's remark burned in her mind. "Don't do anything to discourage him."

He cupped her breasts roughly and she sensed the excitement and lust coursing through him. He let his hands roam down, over her bottom, plucking at her suspender belt.

She looked away and said, 'Is that a Riesling in your basket?'

Reluctantly he detached himself and took out a bottle and two glasses.

'I was going to chill it for later, but why wait?'

They chinked glasses and she drank it down. It was intense and fruity. He poured her another, then half unwound the scarf from her neck, using it to draw her towards him.

'You might think I spend my life with beautiful women, but you'd be wrong.' His face was flushed and drops of sweat had formed on his temples. 'I was attracted to you from the moment I saw you.'

The drink was a good idea. It meant his mouth now tasted of wine, not cigars, and Clara, whose tolerance for alcohol was low, knew that her head would very soon be swimming.

'Come here.'

He took off his shirt and Clara, unprompted, removed her bra. Muscle barred his chest like the ridges of a barrel and he was surprisingly hairy. She ran her hand down it. At her touch, he quickened and turned away, fumbling with a contraceptive, then drew her down to the carpet and laid her beneath him.

She had wondered if she might, despite herself, become aroused. Just as a mechanical reaction to his caresses, as had happened momentarily in the opera house. But as it was, she remained entirely cold. His earlier comments about Einstein had helped.

He placed one meaty thigh between her legs and pushed them apart. Clara imagined watching herself, studying her own performance the way she had done with Herr Lamprecht in the editing suite, detaching herself from any connection with the girl there on the floor of the house in the German countryside, the sound of birds loud in the trees outside. It was important that she throw herself into this. Convincingly, she shut her eyes.

It was quick, and he apologized, a little shamefacedly.

'You've made me wait too long, *Schatzi*.'

He lay on the rug beside her and stroked her naked body, while she stared away from him, up into the timber ceiling.

'What a girl you are. You're full of surprises, aren't you?'

'I certainly am.'

For once, the sardonic edge in his voice had given way to a note of unguarded gentleness. She thought of Leo. She had done her bit all right. She had done "whatever it takes". Soon she would have to figure out what she did next.

'Do you remember those roses I sent you?'

'Of course.'

He dawdled a finger on her bare skin. 'When you pluck a rose, you know it's beautiful but you also know you might get hurt. That's what I'm wondering right now.'

There was nothing to say to this. She tried not to look him in the eye.

'When I told you the other day about not liking to be unmarried, well, it's not just because of my needs as a man. It's not good for a senior man to be without a woman. The party doesn't like it. It gives the wrong impression.'

'I'm sure there are plenty of women who would like to be with you.'

'Of course there are! I wasn't saying that.' He frowned at her lack of understanding. 'I'm the aide to the Minister of Propaganda. I could have any actress I wanted. But I don't want just any actress. I want a woman of refinement.'

She smiled.

'You think I'm being sentimental, don't you? You're right!' He gave a bark of laughter. 'It's the German vice! I'll stop at once.' He sprang up, suddenly boyish, and pulled his trousers on.

'Stay here. I'll get some food together.'

She went into the bathroom to wash and he went out to the car to carry in a box of possessions he had brought from the Berlin apartment. Cups and plates, knives and forks. A stack of books, soap and shaving things. The bread, ham and apples he had brought for their lunch. A Luger pistol, wrapped in a cloth. He seemed utterly happy here. Relaxed from the straightjacket of his professional duties he had also shed the carapace of vicious cynicism he habitually wore. Whistling a tune, he carefully began setting out photographs on the mantelpiece. First the face of Elsa, the dead wife, and then the inevitable image of the Führer. Clara turned away.

Chapter Forty-three

'Fräulein Vine. A pleasure as always.'

Goebbels' gaze was intent as he stepped out of the way to allow her into the house. The stare from his large brown eyes had a peculiar quality, and his expression was unmistakable. He distrusted her, sure, that much was plain, but that didn't mean she didn't also intrigue him. He stood pulling on pale, calfskin gloves to go with his silk striped trousers and patent leather shoes. A newspaper was rolled under his arm. Fortunately he was on his way to the Ministry. A uniformed chauffeur stood outside holding the door of his Mercedes, but he hesitated.

'So what is it today, Fräulein?'

'The show we are preparing for the Winterhilfsverk, Herr Doktor,' Clara replied smoothly. It was an invention, but it was easier to volunteer something than to reveal she had no idea why Magda had sent so suddenly for her. Helping out the poor with food and fuel was everyone's favourite charity, despite what people said about the funds being funnelled directly back to the Nazi Party.

'Of course. A good cause. You must give me a private view of these fashions you are modelling for my wife. It would be of great interest to me. I am, after all, in charge of all aspects of German culture.'

'I know, Herr Doktor.'

He cast a quick, instinctive glance up at the house. 'Perhaps you would like to call at the ministry one day soon. Do you know it?'

'Of course, Herr Doktor. Everyone knows it.'

The Propaganda Ministry was an imposing building in front of the Reich Chancellery.

'It would be interesting to have a longer talk with you.'

She quailed. She knew what long talks with Goebbels meant, and talking was not a big part of it.

'I'll look forward to it, Herr Doktor.'

'Well, then. I shall send for you. Good day!'

He got in his car, slammed the door and was driven away, swastika pennant fluttering in the breeze.

The maid showed Clara up to the yellow dressing room where Madga sat with her back to the door, her eyes huge and dark in her pale face. She was dressed smartly, in a rose satin shift and matching jacket, but she was plainly in no state to go anywhere. The ashtray was full of stubs and she was sucking at another cigarette, her cheeks hollowing with each breath.

'Thank you for coming, Fräulein. You don't mind?'

It was unusual for Magda to register that other people might have work or social lives or any kind of priority that couldn't be dropped at a moment's notice.

'Of course not.'

She gestured towards a tray containing blue and white Meissen coffee cups and a silver coffee pot.

'Help yourself. I had to talk to someone and I didn't know who else to call.'

If this seemed like an extraordinary confession of weakness, she didn't elaborate. She wasn't looking at Clara. She was leaning towards the table, knotting a handkerchief distractedly, as if speaking to herself. From the opened window came the scents of spring grass and the distant rumble of traffic. Clara poured herself a cup of coffee and added cream.

'You might have noticed in the past few weeks, that I have had something on my mind.'

So she had been right: the instinct Clara had from the moment she met Magda that some emotional struggle was tearing her apart. The melancholy face, the rows, the tears. What Müller described as her 'hysteria'.

'I know it's been a difficult time for you.'

'Yes, it has. Would you mind if I told you something? A story?'

'Of course not. I'd like it.'

'It's about someone I met. Someone from the past.' Magda gave a huge sigh and dabbed her eyes where the mascara had run.

'When I was fourteen, I think I told you my family was forced to move from Brussels to Berlin. The war and so on. I went to the Kollmorgen Lyceum and I became best friends with a girl called Lisa Arlosoroff. Her family had come from the Ukraine but her father was dead, so Lisa's mother had to cope alone. She had a sister, Dora, and a brother called Victor. Perhaps because I was an only child, I loved their family. They were so lively and welcoming. I spent a lot of time with them at their apartment, which was quite humble, you know, but always full of people, quite unlike my own home. Anyway, Victor became a good friend too. He was a very clever young man. A Zionist actually. It was his ambition to establish a Jewish homeland in Palestine and for a while I was quite convinced by his arguments . . .' She shot a quick glance at Clara. 'Well, you don't need to know all that. All you need to know is that we had a youthful attachment and at one point I agreed to marry him.'

Clara put down her coffee. Had Magda really just told her that she had agreed to marry a Jew? The wife of Adolf Hitler's right hand man, the First Lady of the Reich, had once been engaged to a Jewish man? But now was not the time to express amazement. Clara leant forward to take a cigarette from the silver box and the only sign of her astonishment was a slight widening of the eyes.

Magda sniffed. 'As it happened I decided I was not a part of his world and we separated. But some years later, when I was married to Gunter Quandt, I met him again. It was back in '29. I was unhappily married.'

She tapped a cylinder of cigarette ash in the cut-glass ashtray. 'I was so bored. My husband left at seven in the morning and didn't come back until late at night. I had a big house with fourteen staff, and only little Harald at home. I played the piano, I helped with the child's homework, I went shopping. I drank coffee on the Ku'damm and I went to dinner with bankers. And that was it. Christ! It was like being buried alive.'

She lifted a cup of coffee to her lips but the delicate porcelain shuddered in her hand.

'It was like living in a doll's house. I had luxury everywhere, but no life. I had begged Gunther for a divorce. I even had him watched because I hoped I might find he had been unfaithful himself. Then Victor came back and, you can probably guess, I started an affair.' She cast a glance at Clara. 'You don't look surprised?'

'Should I?'

'There had been another man in between. He was a law student. Very attentive. He sent flowers, he took me on a trip to the Hotel Dreesen at Godesberg. But he was a boy and I was playing with him really. It was Victor I cared for. You can't imagine how I felt when we met again. But he was a serious man. Tremendously passionate, you know, but intelligent too. He was committed to building a homeland in Palestine.'

Clara nodded, careful not to interrupt her flow.

'Anyhow, the result was that my husband threw me out. He left me standing in the street with a suitcase in my hand and just enough money to take a taxi to my mother's house.'

'This was four years ago?'

'That's right. Before I met Joseph. And then, in the exhilaration of love, I told Joseph all about it, fool that I was. He was crazy with jealousy. He raved for days.'

It was all too easy to imagine how Magda, with her strange, humourless candour would have had Goebbels stamping his crippled foot with rage.

'But, Frau Goebbels, does all this really matter now? You're married and you have the baby and—'

Magda gave a savage laugh and pulled a fresh lace handkerchief from her sleeve. 'And I'm so happy, yes? You've noticed that, have you?'

'Men are often jealous of their wives' past lives. It's normal.'

'But this is not my *past* life. That's the point.'

From the garden outside came the sounds of the child playing with her nanny. The child was toddling across the lawn, pushing a wagon full of dolls, but the wagon hit a stone and overturned, throwing the dolls in a froth of lace dresses out onto the grass. The little girl began to wail and at the sound Magda rose and stood at the window impassively. Then she turned away, drew the shutters and began pacing restlessly round the room.

'A few days ago I received a call. We were giving a dinner and I happened to be passing the telephone in the hall so I picked it up. You can't imagine how fortunate that was. It was Victor. I recognized his voice at once.'

'And what did he want?'

'How would I know?' she spat. 'I put the phone straight down again. I was actually shaking. How could he not be aware that our telephone line is listened to by others? What if Joseph had answered, or any of the staff? Rudolf Hess and his wife were in the next room.'

'So did he call again?'

'I received a letter.'

'He sent you a letter!'

'Not here. To my mother's house. He evidently has enough sense not to post it here. And it was hand delivered, so obviously someone has told him about the censors. He is back in Berlin and swears his love for me.'

Involuntarily, Clara put her hand to her mouth. The shock must have registered on her face because Magda reached over to her arm. It was the first time Magda had ever touched her, other than to shake hands. She gripped so tightly Clara could feel the fingers digging into her flesh.

'You must promise me solemnly that you will tell no one. If Joseph finds out he will kill him. I wouldn't be surprised if he killed me too.'

'Surely not.'

Magda dragged another cigarette from the box, snatched up a table lighter and lit it with shaky fingers. She inhaled, the tendons standing out on her neck like wires, then she resumed pacing the room.

'Nothing is sure.'

'But your husband . . .'

'Would not hesitate to end the life of someone who stood in his way.' There was a contemptuous edge in her voice, as though Clara was being deliberately obtuse. 'With some people . . .' She shrugged. 'Well, killing is not a difficult thing for them.'

A clatter in the distance caused them both to startle.

'It's all right. My husband's at his office. It can't possibly be him.'

She leaned towards Clara, and spoke in a low, urgent tone. 'There is something I need you to do. I want you to take Victor a letter.'

'But . . .'

'I ask you this from the bottom of my heart. You have to do it. The fact is, there is simply no one else I can ask. There's no one here I trust.'

'And what will you tell him?'

'That is between me and Victor. It's better for you not to know. Will you do it? For me?'

As Clara stared at her, the words stalled on her lips. She was being asked to act as a courier between the wife of the Propaganda Minister and her Jewish lover. It was hard to imagine a crazier risk to take. What punishment might be devised in the dark recesses of Goebbel's bitter heart for a crime like that?

Magda observed her hesitation impassively.

'There's nothing for you to gain from this. Unless you choose to betray me. But you have always struck me as a sympathetic person.'

Clara didn't reply.

'Will you at least think about it?'

Clara nodded. Magda rose and the breach in her glacial surface was healed, like the surface of an icy lake, as though it had never been.

'Good. If you decide to help me you must come back next Wednesday evening at seven and I will have a letter for you to collect. You can take it to him the next day. I will tell you where to meet him. And I want you to promise me. No one must know.'

Clara was not needed at work that afternoon, so she got off the bus at the end of the Tiergarten and walked for a while as the conversation with Magda churned in her mind. People and traffic passed by without her seeing them. Eventually she stopped in a coffee shop and sat in a trance as the bright chatter of Berlin housewives rose and fell around her. Sunlight strained through the windows catching in the glitter of cutlery and glancing off the little tin tables. Clara envied these women their gossip and confidences. She longed to unburden herself of the events of the last few days, but there was no one in the world she could talk to. How could she utter a word about Magda's request? Who could she tell about her day with Klaus Müller? She felt desolately alone. For the first time since she had arrived in Berlin, Clara missed her own family. She missed Kenneth saying 'Chin up!' in his jovial English way, and Angela, with her familiar impatient frown. Her mother, lost so long ago, now felt more distant than ever. For a moment Clara even contemplated contacting her cousin Hans Neumann in Hamburg, before dismissing it from her mind.

The only person she could confide in was Leo, and she had no idea when he would contact her again. Even when he did, how could she possibly tell him about her day with Müller, the details of which were now engrained in her mind? The dense bulk of his torso as he rose above her and his shuddering groan of release. The sentimental memories of childhood he told her over lunch, the jokes and stories he shared as he drove her home, planning their next encounter.

Shaking herself out of her trance, Clara paid the bill and looked out at the street. Directly opposite was an optician's shop that had been desecrated with anti-semitic slogans, the usual combination of threats and warnings about the danger of buying from Jews. It was not the graffiti, however, but the contents of the shop, that caught her eye. Behind the paint-spattered glass were rows of spectacles, men's and women's, wire and horn-rimmed, tortoiseshell and pink plastic, bottle-thick and bifocal, packed on shelves that filled the entire window. There must have been hundreds of spectacles in there, jammed indiscriminately together, ranked from floor to ceiling, all staring emptily ahead. Something about the dinginess of the display meant the spectacles on sale didn't even look new. They looked as though they had been abandoned by their owners, who no longer had any use for them.

Chapter Forty-four

'Doesn't he just look like a waiter carrying a tray?' said Rupert. 'Every time a Nazi gives me that salute, it makes me want to order a Martini.'

Mary snorted with laughter. It was true that many Party officials, in trying to emulate as much as possible the way the Leader flipped his arm upwards to his shoulder, made the gesture look ridiculous, as if it wasn't ridiculous enough already. No matter how demoralizing they were, the morning press conferences at the Propaganda Ministry always contained a merciful element of humour.

Having given his salute, Goebbels sat at the red-cloth-covered conference table, and Putzi Hanfstaengl, Dr Boehmer, chief of the Foreign Press department, and a bevy of officials and bureaucrats, variously attired in brown shirts, army uniform or suits, deposited themselves around him.

'They always remind me of an identification line-up,' she murmured.

'Only difference is, they're all guilty.'

Goebbels proceeded to announce a long and boring report on improvements to domestic and social policy, rounding it off with a reprimand for the press for focusing on invented stories about Jewish atrocities, when they should be writing about radical innovations such as the new law for the encouragement of marriage, which would offer couples a thousand-mark gift as a wedding present from the state. Eventually, he drew to a close and the journalists dispersed in relief to write their reports.

'Thinking about it, I really could do with that Martini,' said Rupert, as they headed out. 'How about a quick drink at the Adlon?'

It had become their routine. The Adlon bar was a favoured watering hole for foreign journalists and reliably full of people they knew, downing a whisky or several before heading off to the office to file. Mary thought that some of her happiest times here in Berlin were ensconced in the Adlon's capacious leather armchairs, staging a mock quarrel with Rupert or sharing the latest political news with the other correspondents.

As they made their way down the steps of the Ministry she saw a face she recognized amongst the Ministerial staff.

'Isn't that the guy we saw the other night? The one with Clara Vine?'

'Doktor Müller, you mean?'

'What is she thinking of?'

'He's pretty handsome, isn't he? Quite a beefcake.' Rupert assessed him with interest. 'I'm not a woman and I wouldn't like to presume what goes through your heads but . . .'

Mary aimed a mock blow at him with her notebook. 'Please, Rupert. Give us some credit.'

It was a short walk down the Wilhelmstrasse and round the corner to the Adlon. The bar itself, across the lobby, up a flight of marble steps and through a pair of leather doors, was a place of discreet luxury, thickly carpeted and smelling of expensive tobacco. They ordered their Martinis and armed with a bowl of nuts, wandered over to Sigrid Schultz, who was deep in a red leather chair, leafing through the international newspapers that were provided.

'Hello, stranger,' said Rupert, handing her a press release. 'You missed this morning's press conference.'

'But I didn't miss it that much. How was it?'

'Oh, another chance for Goebbels to rail at "fake Jewish atrocity stories". He was really needled by the reaction to his boycott of Jewish shops.'

'Says it was propaganda spread by international Jewry,' added Mary.

'He's getting into his stride now. He wants complete control of the press, and once he's got the domestic press under his thumb, it'll be our turn. The Foreign Office is already complaining we're unfairly prejudiced against Germany. If it goes any further, they'll start to expel people.'

'He's started already actually,' said Sigrid languidly. 'Didn't you hear about Angus MacLeish? He was summoned to the Propaganda Ministry and they told him he had to leave because Hitler had read his book and couldn't stand it.'

'What did he say?'

'He said he'd read Hitler's book and couldn't stand it either.'

They laughed, but it was laughter tinged with apprehension.

'You'll be all right though, won't you Sigrid?' asked Mary.

Sigrid Schulz was so petite and pretty that a lot of the German officers fell over themselves to please her. Goering was rumoured to be especially smitten.

'Oh sure,' Sigrid said with a laconic wave. 'I can take care of myself. But listen. Have you seen this?'

She held up a copy of the *Berliner Morgenpost* and adjusted the glasses which hung on a gold chain round her neck. 'A body has been found in a field. It is identified as that of Erik Jan Hanussen.'

Mary felt the hairs rise on her neck. Rupert whistled through his teeth.

'A farmer discovered the remains near Staakower woods north of Berlin. Two bullets in the head and nothing on the body but thirty marks.'

'But we saw him only the other night!' gasped Mary.

'He was arrested at his home in Bendlerstrasse and taken to the SA barracks at Pape Strasse in his own red Bugatti,' read Sigrid. 'It says here he wrote a last letter in invisible ink.'

'But why would they kill him? He was Hitler's favourite!'

'He was a Jew, apparently,' said Rupert, taking the paper. 'This report says he was born in a gaol cell in Vienna to a father who was the caretaker of a synagogue. The rumours have been going round for months. Eventually someone mailed a copy of his Jewish marriage contract to the Führer's office.'

He drained his Martini, ate the olive it came with, and picked up his jacket.

'Thank God I haven't filed my piece on the House of the Occult yet. This is going to make a fantastic feature. High society, sex and violence, a cameo appearance from Herr Hitler himself. And plenty of pictures to go with it. Just the thing the *Daily Chronicle* reader wants to read over his toast and marmalade in Tunbridge Wells. If I hurry I can do two thousand words for the morning edition.'

Mary took the paper from Rupert and looked at the picture of Hanussen. It was a stock publicity shot, the hypnotist intense and swarthy with his veiled, far-seeing eyes, as though he was able to perceive something hidden from ordinary folk. He looked, she realized, like a character from *Dr Caligari*, one of those old Expressionist movies that Ufa didn't make any more, full of mysticism and magic and other dark forces. But his look reminded her of something else too. She recalled the front page of Lotte Klein's *Bunte Wochenschau,* which that week featured an image of Hitler, eyes straining mystically into the distance, as though he perceived a future that no one else could see.

'So much for fortune-telling. That man was reckless,' said Sigrid coolly, lighting her pipe. 'He bragged about his sessions with the Führer. All that stuff about being able to foresee the success of the Reich. Too bad he didn't foresee he was about to be shot in a field by a bunch of brown-shirted thugs.'

Chapter Forty-five

Clara didn't see him at first. She remembered what he had said about looking confident and natural; as though you belonged in a place, so that staff or authorities wouldn't bother you. And he did. Leo was standing in the courtyard of Charlottenburg Palace, Frederick I of Prussia's baroque fantasy with its egg-yolk façade and copper cupola. He was sketching a towering bronze of the emperor on horseback, as if pencil drawings of corpulent equestrians were his speciality. He was wearing a shabby old tweed jacket and brushing his hair out of his eyes as he squinted up in the sunlight. Anyone looking at him would assume he was an art student, entirely devoted to his aesthetic efforts. Indeed, he seemed so absorbed, Clara even wondered if he would notice her approach, but as she drifted towards him he dropped his pencil and she stepped forward to pick it up.

'Thank you.' Leo acknowledged her with a cool nod and turned towards the palace. She wandered in alongside him and presented her ticket. She wondered if he had been thinking about her day with Müller and how it had turned out.

The ticket had been waiting for her when she got back to Frau Lehmann's from the studio the previous night.

Schloss Charlottenburg. Admit one. And underneath, scrawled in ink, *4 p.m.*

There had also been a message from Helga, but as Clara never used Frau Lehmann's telephone any more, she decided it would have to wait until she was out the following day. She had tried to call her from a telephone cabin on the way here but there was no reply from Helga's number so she hurried on. Since her friend Bruno had been freed, Helga's happiness was entirely restored. Indeed, her celebrations had tipped into risky exuberance. Two days ago she had appeared on set stinking of alcohol and much the worse for wear. The next day she had failed to turn up entirely. Clara, however, was too preoccupied to worry about Helga's self-destructive tendencies. She had barely been sleeping. Her outing with Müller, and Magda's request, drove everything else from her mind.

'So how are Beauty and the Beast?' Leo asked now.

'In quite a state at the moment.'

'Squabbling?'

'Not really. They're hardly speaking to each other. She can't bear the sight of him.'

'A lot of people feel like that.'

They entered a room in the east wing lined with glass cabinets featuring decorative objects that had belonged to Queen Louise. Clara was getting used to the way Leo would glance about him, rarely making eye contact, the way he always found the guidebook terrifically absorbing. "The construction of Schloss Charlottenburg, designed as a summer residence for Sophie Charlotte, wife of the Elector Friedrich III, began in 1695."

For a Thursday afternoon, the Schloss was fairly busy with tourists, craning to see the trinkets and china shepherdesses in their glass cabinets. A swift head-count told Clara there were five other people in the room, so she knew she needed to tell Leo in a way that would not cause him to react overtly.

'The thing is, there are so many contradictions about her.'

'What do you mean?'

'She mystifies me.'

'Oh yes?'

'She started out a Catholic, you know. She went to convent school. Now she's actually a Buddhist, at least that's what she says. She believes strongly in reincarnation.'

'Doesn't stop her being a Nazi.'

'That's true. But people can't always be judged by their labels.'

'What's that supposed to mean?' Leo asked.

'Perhaps, sometimes, wearing a swastika tells you no more about a person than wearing Ferragamo shoes. I suspect she wanted a political philosophy to believe in. It could as well have been Communism. The National Socialists came along at the right time.'

'Are you making apologies for her?'

'No. I'm not defending her. Of course not. It's just . . .'

Why were these women so willing to adopt the poisonous politics that their husbands espoused? Why did women always try to smooth things over? Why didn't they question more? Stand up for themselves?

'Just what?' he said impatiently.

Clara cast a glance at Leo. She had felt a thrill of excitement when she saw the ticket on the hall table the previous day. A rush of pure relief. At last she would be able to see him. At last there was someone to confide in. Yet, now it had come to it, Leo seemed even more terse than usual. His face was closed and guarded, his hands rammed in his pockets. He stood at a slight distance from her. Was he impatient because he imagined she sympathized with Magda Goebbels? Or was it something a little more personal? Could it be distaste about her weekend jaunt with Müller? That having asked her to do 'whatever it takes' Leo was now appalled she might have done it?

'Nothing. Anyway. Something's happened.'

'Another squabble is it?'

'Not exactly.'

'What, then?'

He was so curt and businesslike, as though she had dragged him from his valuable work specifically to waste his time with women's gossip. As though domestic tittle-tattle was all Clara was good for.

'Forget it.'

She stalked away, heart thudding with annoyance, into a dazzling room of sun and gold, all panelled with mirrors that reflected back the gleaming parquet floor. It was the Porcelain Room. Each gilded wall was lined by blue and white Chinese porcelain running from floor to ceiling, drawing the eye upwards to a swirl of ethereal clouds. There were vases, with a delicate tracery of indigo, and plates and figurines whose translucent willow patterns seemed to symbolize the very fragility of antiquity. An entire culture, centuries and centuries of it, was hanging precariously there in front of them. In a flash Clara was reminded of Erich on the china stall at Luna Park, hurling his little rubber balls for the pleasure of hearing the crockery smash. Jumping with satisfaction as plates and cups dropped in shards to the ground.

Leo came up behind her and murmured, 'If you were trying to draw attention to yourself just then, you succeeded.'

She braced her shoulders and didn't reply. He stood rigidly beside her, staring grimly at the chinoiserie, the guidebook clenched in his hand.

'Let's start again, shall we? You said something's happened.'

'It has.'

'Is it to do with Müller? You haven't said anything about him.'

'What would you like me to say?'

'You saw him, didn't you? How did it go?'

For a moment she didn't speak. She couldn't find the words to tell him. Her exhaustion weighed on her. She looked at the golden walls of china and wondered how something could be simultaneously so precious and so precarious.

'Clara, I asked you . . . what happened with Müller?'

Something flipped in her. She looked around quickly – the German glance – saw there was no one else in the room, and hissed, 'You really want me to be sleeping with him, don't you, Leo? That's actually what you'd like. And then every little detail of it to be delivered to you afterwards in triplicate. For consideration by Head Office. Time, date, marks out of ten. Perhaps that's what I should do. I should prepare a report. How Sturmhauptführer Müller performs in bed.'

He recoiled slightly and she saw herself caught in the green amber of his eyes. Her anger melted into an ache. She wanted to be there, trapped in that small space, enclosed within him. She wanted to tell him that every minute of that Sunday with Müller she had thought of him. For a second he seemed stunned. Then he brought his face closer to hers and spoke in a low voice.

'Sleep with him? Do you think I even want you to *see* that man? Don't you think it's tearing me apart that a woman like you is dallying with a senior Nazi and having to employ every feminine wile she has in order to extract information from him? Is that what you think I want? That every time I meet you I have to encourage you to lead him on a little further. To forego everything you have, your integrity, your innocence and God knows what else, to coax a little more out of him? Can you honestly imagine that's what I want?'

It was as if his words had opened a floodgate. Something in his expression released and his eyes shone with a kind of passionate anger. His face was transformed, and it was as though she had never seen him properly before. She reached for his hand and he grasped it.

He pulled her towards him and said in her ear, 'Listen carefully. There's a place we keep. Just a couple of rooms. In Xantener Strasse, a block south of the Ku'damm. One down from the Hotel Rheingold. Third floor next door to a bakery shop, in the name of Zink. We can talk there. Go now. Wait an hour and take a cab to the top of the street. Ring twice.'

The bakery had shut for the evening by the time she reached the house in Xantener Strasse and it appeared no one was in on any of the other floors. From the plaques and bells beside the front door she divined that most of the apartments were let to corporate concerns, rather than private residents. She found a small ivory bell for Zink and Sons and rang it twice. Eventually she heard his footsteps. It was dark in the hall and she could see his shape behind the frosted glass, but he waited until she had come in and shut the door behind her before switching on the light. In his shirtsleeves and braces, he led the way wordlessly up the creaking wooden stairs.

The door opened into a narrow room, with a bathroom and a bedroom leading off. Inside he stuffed the keyhole with chewing gum, and unplugged the light from its socket. Then he turned to her. She leant into him and felt the length of his body. His mouth reached for hers and it was surprisingly hard and forceful as he kissed her.

Clasping her to him, he pulled her jacket off and felt for the buttons on her blouse, but his fingers were trembling and she needed to help. She stepped out of her skirt and stood on the cold floorboards in her heels, stockings, plain cotton underwear and white cotton bra embroidered with pale blue forget-me-nots. She was shivering uncontrollably as his hands ran over her.

'Come here.'

He pulled her towards the bedroom.

The bed was uncomfortable and narrow, presumably what His Majesty's Government considered appropriate to a travelling salesman. Some box-ticker must have decreed it should be three feet wide and not an inch more, and that the mattress should be the precise texture of blancmange with walnuts in it.

Leo took her face in his hands and kissed her again, all over, on her eyes and cheek and neck. Then he leant down and kissed her nipples and she arched her back beneath him, abandoning all inhibition. She ran her hands over his body, tentatively at first, then with increasing confidence. He was so much bigger than her. He was lean and well defined, with only a smattering of hair on his chest. His shoulders were surprisingly muscled, and when she reached round them she felt the deep groove of his spine and caught the faint, masculine tang of sweat as he rose above her. His movements were practised and careful and she was glad he was not a novice. His assured taking of pleasure absolved her of responsibility for a moment, and allowed her to lose herself in the sensation. She hadn't realized until then what a strain her self-consciousness could be or how thrilling it was to be freed of it. Leo made love with a particular intensity, as if he wanted to claim her as his own and eliminate all memory of Müller. She recognized that, though he need not have worried. Just his touch had erased the print of Müller on her at a stroke.

Afterwards he lay on one side of her and propped himself up on one elbow. He was unshaven and a haze of golden stubble covered his chin. She saw herself captured in his eyes, the way she had wanted.

She said, 'Are you going to stay in Berlin?'

'As long as they need me. If I had children, I wouldn't want them to be here right now, but as it is, I can do as I please.'

'What about your family?'

'I'm half-Irish. Hence the name. Both parents still living.'

'Do you see much of them?'

His father missed him, he knew, and he felt a deep weight of guilt there. His mother's love was silent, in the English way, and Leo took after her in that aspect, but his father, with Irish blood in his veins, never shied from expressing his feelings. Just a few weeks ago he had begun a letter to him, "My dear child," and then corrected himself. "I know you are a man now, but you will always be my child and I wanted to remind myself of it by using the words."

'I see them whenever I'm back, of course. But I don't feel I belong there any more.'

'I know that feeling.'

After her mother died, Clara's childhood home in Surrey seemed to sag into gradual decline. The grass grew high on the tennis court. Dust collected on the Bösendorfer. The tall-ceilinged rooms grew shabby and the chintz on the armchairs faded. Eventually, when Kenneth went off to university, father announced that they would 'shut up shop' and move to Ponsonby Terrace, which was a handy distance from Parliament. Secretly though, Clara had dreaded leaving the old house. She had leant against the wall as though she could physically embrace it, and wet the wallpaper with her tears.

'I hated leaving our home when we moved to London. The new place was never the same.'

'Why did you come to Berlin?'

'It's a long story,' she reflected. 'No, it's not. It's a short story. There was a man who wanted to marry me. He's called

Dennis Beaumont. My father thinks the world of him. When I discovered that Dennis thought acting was incompatible with marriage, everything else became clear in a second. In a single second. It was like the scales falling from my eyes and seeing things properly for the first time. I was shocked at the misjudgement I'd made. To think it could have spoilt my whole life. So I was running away really. From Dennis, and the terrible marriage I might have had.'

'It's easy to fall into a terrible marriage.'

'Do you mean . . .?' Suddenly uncertain, she looked up at him. 'Are you married?'

'No.' He brushed her hair with his hand. 'I was thinking of someone else.' He reached out and freed a cigarette from its packet. 'Ovid, in fact.'

'Ovid!' she burst out laughing, then seeing his surprise said, 'It just sounded so funny. Why Ovid?'

'I'm translating *Metamorphoses* at the moment. I try to do a little each evening. I find it relaxing. Anyway, Ovid had an ill-advised affair, and it cost him his life.'

She was still laughing. 'Sorry. I don't know anything about Ovid. I hardly know who he is.'

'He was a Roman poet writing at the time of Christ. He wrote a series of poems about the Greek myths. They're all about human motivations and human delusions. People changing shape and adopting disguises.'

'So what about the terrible affair then?'

'It changed the whole course of his life. He was all set for a brilliant political career, he was going to be a senator, but he got involved in a scandalous love affair. The Emperor Augustus exiled him to Constanța on the Black Sea. He hated it. The ghastly climate, the bleak terrain, the lack of any civilized company. He described the landscape as a grey sea, patched with wormwood, where there was no birdsong, no vines, and wine was broken off and sold in frozen chunks. He lasted ten years there before he died.'

Clara liked the rhythm of his voice. It was like being told a story. Thinking of Ovid in exile, isolated among the barbarians, transported her far from Berlin, with its frenetic streets and clanging trams. Perhaps it was the same for Leo. Maybe that was why he spent his evenings immersing himself in poems about transfiguration and disguise.

'The local people were under constant siege from rivals who sent poisoned arrows across the roofs. There was a pitiless local wind which ripped the skin. You can't help but feel for Ovid, a civilized man, fallen among savages.'

Clara shifted a little in his arms, pressed herself back into the unfamiliar contours of his body and looked around the room. It was utterly impersonal. There was only the bed with a chair by the side and a chest of drawers. A picture of a German alpine landscape, a worn Persian rug over the floorboards. Outside, against the tessellated rooftops, lines of pigeons shuffled and puffed their chests like army generals. Clara felt a powerful urge to stay there for as long as possible, shut off from the world of politicians and films, without need of dissembling, without fear, making love with Leo, having him tell her stories. She marvelled at the beauty of his body, the way the muscles moved beneath the skin of his back like the ripple of piano keys. The ridges of his chest, the strong line of his jaw and the dark tufts beneath his arms.

After a while he climbed out of bed, tied a towel round his waist and went into the kitchen. He returned carrying two white china cups and a bag containing two rolls.

'I got these from the bakery before it shut.'

They sat up against the pillows, sipping hot tea, and Clara pulled the sheet around her.

'Does anyone live here?'

'No. People stay here occasionally. We could use it.'

She wondered if they could stay the night. She had no clean clothes, of course, or toothbrush, or anything belonging to the mundane, everyday world. All she had was this burning excitement that came from being with him, and having her feelings reciprocated and despite having just made love, a tingling feeling of anticipation at the pulsing, male nakedness beside her. She was about to ask him what they should do when he put down his cup, drew her back into his arms and kissed her again.

Later, when the sheets were tangled and the sky was violet and the room lit only by the wash of the streetlight outside, Clara grew suddenly serious.

'On the subject of ill-advised love affairs, that's what I was going to tell you. Magda is having one too.'

'An affair?' The information caused Leo to sit up with a start.

'That's what I was trying to tell you at the Schloss. She wants me to deliver a letter to the man who used to be her lover.'

'Are you serious? Who is he?'

'No one I'd heard of before.'

'Do you know his name?'

'Victor Arlosoroff.'

Arlosoroff. He knew that name. It was the name Heinz had written on the piece of paper in that same apartment just a few weeks ago. "A big fish is about to swim into your net." When Leo had briefed Archie Dyson and the others on the meeting, the name of Arlosoroff had caused a palpable ripple of excitement. Even Dyson, who prided himself on his Etonian sang-froid, had uttered an excited curse before explaining the reason.

Victor Arlosoroff, also known as Chaim Arlosoroff, was already well known to the Foreign Office. A powerful man with a magnetic personality, he was an ardent Zionist, associated with the dominant Jewish political party in Palestine. Though he had held many confidential meetings with British officials, he was also known to bear a special grudge against Britain on account of its Palestine policy. The British, he complained, always sided with the Arabs. There had long been a suspicion, said Dyson, that Arlosoroff might have "something up his sleeve" and recent events seemed to have borne that out. Just a few weeks ago a letter had been intercepted from Arlosoroff to Chaim Weizmann, the former president of the Zionist World Congress, suggesting an armed uprising against British authorities in Palestine. Everyone at Head Office was on the alert for his next move.

As Dyson explained, Arlosoroff was heading up a plan to encourage the Germans to fund Jewish emigration to Palestine. If, as Heinz now claimed, Arlosoroff was also in league with the Reds, it was entirely possible that some of the money funnelled out of Germany might also be going to the Communists. This was something that needed to be conveyed to the highest authorities.

None of this Leo mentioned to Clara.

'What do you know about this man?'

'He and Magda were engaged, but they broke up because he wanted her to leave with him and settle in Palestine. Now he's back in Berlin, he's got in touch again and she wants to respond.'

'Good God.'

'She's asked me to deliver a message to him. She's frightened to meet him herself and she doesn't trust anyone else.'

'I'm not surprised. She must assume anyone else would be bribed by agents of her husband to give up their information. Or, at the very least, be followed.'

'Would I be followed?'

'It's a possibility, though I don't think they have any doubts about you.'

'But I might be?'

'If you are, I've told you what to do. You're observant. You know how to check for surveillance and how to escape it. You know to keep your wits about you. Did you say you'd do it?'

'I haven't told her yet. I just don't know.' Clara bit her thumb and gazed out at the fading sky. 'Perhaps it's too risky.'

'It's your choice.'

'You mean you think I should do it? You think I should see Arlosoroff?'

He traced a finger down the side of her cheek. 'You know I can't tell you that.'

'She wants me to collect the letter next Wednesday and take it the following day.'

'How clever of her.'

'Why?'

'Next Thursday is the 20th. April 20th is Hitler's birthday. The whole of Berlin will be swarming with devoted follow-ers. You won't be able to move for screaming citizens waving flags. It's the ideal distraction. She's obviously given it some thought.'

'Probably because she's frightened.'

'She's right to be.'

He hesitated a moment, then got out of bed and reached over to where his jacket hung. She saw the dull glint of metal and, to her alarm, realized he had drawn a pistol. He placed it on the sheet between them.

'It's a Beretta. A semi-automatic. It's very simple. Here's the safety lever on the back of the slide. Pull the slide back to chamber a round and only put your finger on the trigger when you're ready to fire, then squeeze it, don't pull it, it gives a steadier shot. I'll give you a holster so you can carry it inside your coat.'

'No, Leo!' She recoiled in shock. 'I don't want to shoot anyone. Not for any reason.'

'Are you sure?'

'Of course.' She pushed the gun from her. 'Put it away.'

'All right.' He replaced the Beretta, then reached out a hand and pressed it against her cheek. 'If you do it then, Clara, you're going to need to be careful. Very careful. Remember everything I've told you. And come here afterwards, so I know you're safe.'

It was late when she reached home and she felt glad that Frau Lehmann had furnished her with a key. She tiptoed up the stairs, desperate not to disturb the little dog, whose bark could wake sleepers as reliably as a Gestapo arrest squad. But the following morning, as she was sipping the bitter, over-brewed coffee that was always served at breakfast, Frau Lehmann approached her tight-lipped.

'That friend of yours telephoned again, Fräulein Vine. Repeatedly. I think she had recently had a drink.'

'Did she leave a name?'

'She said you would know who it was. She wanted you to get in touch.'

Helga. She must be dying for a talk. But Clara was expected at the studio by nine o'clock. She'd make it up to her at the weekend.

Chapter Forty-six

'Enjoy golf, do you, Quinn?' asked Hitchcock.

'Loathe it, actually,' he replied.

It was Saturday and the pair of them were driving out in Hitchcock's cabriolet to Wannsee, the leafy area outside Berlin where the ambassador and his wife rented a villa next to the lake. This was their holiday sanctuary, the place they could relax, entertain, play tennis and sail their small motor boat with its Union Jack flag fluttering at the stern. Sir Horace's favourite recreation, however, was golf. He was a good golfer, having spent much of his life in the diplomatic service on the links, yet for safety's sake any embassy staff who received an invitation to a game were quietly instructed to lose.

'You know he hates being beaten,' grumbled Hitchcock, narrowly overtaking a family of cyclists at speed.

'That's not going to be a problem.'

'For you, maybe.' Hitchcock considered himself a superior sportsman. He had been tennis champion or something at Charterhouse and then a boxing blue and was almost congenitally incapable of losing at any game.

'Look on it as a challenge,' said Leo mildly.

Hitchcock frowned. He was wearing regulation golfing attire of plus fours, argyle stockings, open-necked shirt and windcheater. His personal set of clubs in a stitched cream leather holdall sat in the back seat of the car. Leo, by contrast, had on his Saturday flannels, a sleeveless sweater and his worn tweed jacket. Hitchcock had lent him a pair of shoes, white and purple monstrosities with tassels. They were two sizes too big, like clown's shoes, but there didn't seem to be much choice.

'It is a fairly decent course. Excellent greens. I've played there a couple of times. Won, actually.'

'He's probably heard. Perhaps that's why he's asked us.'

'I assume that's supposed to be a joke, Quinn. You know the only reason he's asked us is because of your girlfriend.'

Leo knew it was best not to react. Hitchcock was always jumping to conclusions where the opposite sex was concerned. He had that boorishness mixed with a dash of desperation that was common among ex-public school boys. The first night they had met, Hitchcock had insisted on drinking himself silly, then tried to persuade Leo to visit a brothel.

'Indeed,' he said quietly.

It had been forty-eight hours since his night with Clara and he had barely slept. His nerves tingled with a mixture of exhilaration and anxiety. He was half dazed with pleasure, half stymied by fear at what might be yet to come. Clara's information about Arlosoroff was obviously important, but the nagging worry that she would undertake Magda's mission and place herself in even greater danger made him desperate to protect her. He cursed himself for not being more forthright and telling her not to involve herself. But what guarantee did he have anyway that she would follow his instructions?

He had, of course, relayed the information about Magda's affair the very next day. They were interested, but when he revealed that the man in question was Victor Arlosoroff, the room had suddenly reverberated with excitement. That the man they had just been warned of, the very Zionist agent whom the British were intent on tracking, should be having an affair with the Propaganda Minister's wife, well, it beggared belief. But so did many things that were happening in Berlin just then.

A few hours later had come Sir Horace's invitation to an unwelcome game of golf.

The Wannsee Golf Club was everything Leo distrusted, a vista of silky grass, rich weekenders and sunlit greens. Sir Horace waited until he had teed up at the first hole, a simple par three, sent the ball arcing high over the fairway and landing straight on the edge of the green, before turning to the matter in hand.

'I'm glad we had that little conversation the other week, Quinn,' he remarked as they strolled ahead of Hitchcock along the shaven turf. 'You followed up very well. Your news about Arlosoroff is a gift.'

'Thank you, sir.'

'We know what he's doing here, of course. He's aiming to negotiate with the Nazis over Jewish emigration to Palestine.'

'Something we're broadly in favour of, I take it.'

'Sure. Though the Nazis, as you know, are making it fiendishly difficult. They don't want the Jews to take their money with them, but they don't like the alternative, which is a boycott of German goods round the world. So Arlosoroff's plan is to hammer out a deal in which they would set up a special bank account, get the German Jews to deposit all their money there, and then use that money to purchase German goods, for export to Palestine. Germans happy, Jews happy, is the idea.'

'Do you think it could work?'

'Not a chance. It's a pact with the devil. At best optimistic, at the worst naïve. Once the National Socialists realize the Jews will surrender the threat of a boycott, they'll play fast and loose. A lot of Arlosoroff's colleagues are already condemning him for even trying to fraternise with them. However . . .' he paused, 'that issue is not what's concerning us right now. As far as we're concerned, just now it's very much in British interests that Arlosoroff should be discredited.'

'Discredited?'

'Perhaps side-lined is a better way of putting it.'

'Because of the Communist ties?'

'Because we can't trust Arlosoroff as far as we can throw him. As you know, we recently intercepted a letter he sent, outlining plans for an armed uprising against the British mandate in Palestine. That was not entirely unexpected, there are rumblings like that going on all the time. But this looked like a serious threat and it could be extremely troublesome. Add on your friend from the Red Fighters' Front and his warnings about Arlosoroff's possible Communist links and it would be terrifically useful right now if the fellow was off the scene. Or even just compromised. And thanks to you, Quinn, it seems the perfect excuse has presented itself. Fancy a gasper?'

Sir Horace halted in the dappled shade of a pine tree and extracted a silver box from his pocket. Leo took a cigarette, snapped open his lighter, then stood back to inhale.

'So how exactly would we go about . . . compromising him?'

'We shall have to give that some thought. But it's my feeling that it would help if your source were to let Goebbels know who his wife is fooling around with.'

Leo stared at him aghast. 'Let Goebbels know! With respect, sir, that course of action seems to me extraordinarily wrong-headed. And terrifically dangerous.'

Sir Horace sighed and Leo divined in the milky vagueness of his eyes a shrewd cunning entirely at odds with his avuncular air.

'Not at all. Quite the reverse in fact. It's for her own safety.'

'I'm not sure I follow your thinking.'

'If Goebbels believes she has knowingly led him to Arlosoroff, he will trust her. It will cement her position. She will be useful to him.' Observing Leo's horrified gaze, he added, 'It's only an idea.'

'It's too dangerous.'

Sir Horace stroked his moustache thoughtfully. 'Isn't that for the girl to decide? It might be she felt, as a decent, morally worthy person, that a husband would want to know his wife was betraying him. Yet she would not want to cause problems in her own friendship with the wife. So she could let him know discreetly. A note perhaps, something like that. Goes on all the time, I would have thought. Marital politics are always damned awkward.'

'I'm sorry sir. I just can't agree. Apart from anything else, it would probably cause the Goebbels to separate, and what use is Clara's friendship then? Just being the daughter of a Nazi sympathizer would never be enough to secure her the kind of access she has now.'

'That's possible, of course.'

'And why would Goebbels believe that Clara would betray her friend's confidence? What possible motivation could she have?'

Sir Horace ground his cigarette out on the perfect green.

'What motivation does anyone have to do what the Nazis want? Fear. Pure and simple. Goebbels knows that.'

'Well, I'm sorry,' said Leo, stabbing a tee into the grass. 'I can't ask her to take that risk. With respect, sir, I really must insist that she is protected from anything like that.'

'Fair enough,' said Sir Horace mildly, watching Leo flail his shot wildly out into the rough. 'Just running an idea up the flagpole.'

The ambassador stepped onto the green and performed an exaggerated waggle of his hips before sending his own ball soaring up the fairway. Leo watched him distrustfully. The proposal he had sounded out was suicidally dangerous. The leap from double-crossing Goebbels' wife to performing what amounted to a triple-cross, was a lot to ask even of an experienced agent. It would require nerves of steel and a sober realization of the consequences. To ask it of Clara was entirely unacceptable. The memory of her sitting in bed beside him, and the horror on her face when he produced the pistol, caused a surge of protective feeling to rise that he must on no account betray. At the same time he felt a stab of tenderness, and a desperate urge to find the opportunity to be with her again.

'I know her father, of course,' said Sir Horace as Hitchcock joined them, brandishing a four iron. 'Ronald Vine. I was at school with him.'

'What's he like?' said Hitchcock.

'Miserable beggar. A junior minister in the mid-twenties. He was badly affected by the loss of his wife, obviously, and consequently very devoted to the cause of Anglo-German friendship. You know the type. These people who go off on beer-drinking weekends and frightful hiking trips in Saxony. Only in Vine's case, as we rapidly discovered, it went a bit further. There have been serious, high-level contacts with the regime here. We've had an eye on him because of who he is. He's a name, and the Nazis want names. They're after the highest society, the best people. Bank directors, members of the House of Lords, influential writers, industrialists. But from the sound of it, the daughter's cut from a different cloth. She's obviously got guts.'

'She has,' Leo agreed.

'Curious that the daughter would go a different path from the father. What's she like, Quinn? She's sounds an unusual girl.'

Leo considered. In one way, of course, Clara was like hundreds of other girls from her background, who lived in the Home Counties and attended bridge parties and played tennis and worked at small jobs which they gave up the moment they married. But there was something different about her too. To march out on her family and fiancé like that without a backward glance. To step into a different country with no idea of what to expect.

'I think she is quite unusual.'

'A cracker to look at, by all accounts,' added Hitchcock.

'Well, I hope you're being nice to her. Access like that can't be taken for granted. We're lucky to have found her. And having a woman is a stroke of genius.'

'In what way, sir?' said Hitchcock.

'Oh, the National Socialists are tremendously arrogant, you know. They think an awful lot of themselves. They would never expect a woman to get the better of them. It would be practically impossible for them to imagine that a girl in silk stockings and Elizabeth Arden face cream would be able to outwit them.' He paused a moment to reflect on his own image. 'A spy in silk stockings. What about that then?'

'That's exactly why we shouldn't expose her to any unnecessary risk,' said Leo tersely. 'As you say, access like that is invaluable.'

'It was just a thought,' Sir Horace conceded. 'Though I'm amazed at what you tell me about Frau Goebbels. Quite frankly, I've found myself next to her at a couple of dinners and she seems one of the most godawful frigid women you've ever met. You break the ice only to discover a terrific lot of cold water underneath.'

The golf game went exactly as Leo had anticipated. His own performance was disastrous and Hitchcock could not restrain himself from offering tips. Hitchcock himself had enormous difficulty in managing to lose and at first he couldn't help himself. Sir Horace watched his impressive swings with dismay until Hitchcock got the message and then overdid it, first by hacking out clods of turf, then deliberately mishandling a dogleg and landing in a water hazard, and then getting stuck badly in the rough. He took his frustration out in a heated argument with a caddy. Sir Horace and Leo managed to shake him off as they returned to the club house.

They had reached the terrace when Sir Horace stopped and looked at him levelly.

'You know I'm leaving next month?'

'I do, sir. You'll be much missed.'

'Thank you. Though I'm not sure how much I'll miss Berlin. Anyway, I've mentioned you to my successor, Phipps. He's a good chap. Brother-in-law of Bobby Vansittart. He takes a robust view so keep in touch with him.'

By this, Leo understood that the next ambassador, Sir Eric Phipps, was under no illusions about Nazi aims or methods. And Sir Robert Vansittart, the Permanent Under-secretary at the Foreign Office who was deeply suspicious of Germany, was known for having cultivated his own secret network of contacts in Berlin government circles.

'And thank you for a jolly good game. Especially as you don't get a round in too often.' His gaze travelled down to Leo's feet. 'I must say those are most extraordinary shoes. Did you hire them?'

'I borrowed them from Hitchcock.'

Sir Horace cast a glance back at Hitchcock, who was hurrying pink-faced to catch them up.

'Our friend looks in need of a drink. Now, what do you say to a quick gin and tonic here and then back to the house? As far as I know my lady wife is expecting us for lunch.'

Chapter Forty-seven

The light was falling by the time Clara arrived at the end of Helga's road, past the water tower. Its gates were just closing and a police car was passing through. She wondered if what Helga had said about it being taken over as a prison was true. Vans bundled with prisoners could be glimpsed at all hours of the day and night she said, and though Helga was prone to exaggeration, there was something about the sight of the sentry standing to attention inside, and next to him a panting dog on a leash, that made Clara fear Helga had got something right for a change.

She felt a little guilty that it had taken her so long to come. She had called by on Saturday, but there was no answer from the bell, so she spent the afternoon walking in the Tiergarten instead and returned to find that Helga had telephoned Frau Lehmann several times again. On Monday she had not shown up at the studios and all of Tuesday had passed without any sign of her. Clara knew perfectly well that Helga only wanted to talk to her about Bruno. She just hoped she had managed to stop herself talking to Bauer about him too.

Her first inkling of alarm came when she saw the huddle of people outside Helga's apartment. Berlin had become a city of huddles, whether it was buying black market goods or sharing dramatic news, and a cluster of citizens signified trouble. Either trouble or tragedy. From their backs and craned necks alone Clara felt this particular huddle meant something terrible.

And then she saw the shoes. And as soon as she saw them, she knew the truth. With a throb of fear, Magda's words came into her mind.

"Killing is not a difficult thing for them."

The old men in the street assumed Helga had killed herself, but this was no suicide. This was what Nazis like Walter Bauer did to people who crossed them. A gun in the night, a battered body that surfaced at a local hospital, or a mangled heap on the pavement. Perhaps they would bother to stage a story. The suicidal actress, the girl of unsteady mental state. There must be plenty of them in Berlin these days.

Once she had sprinted up to the apartment, Clara was even more convinced. Nothing she found contradicted her belief of what had happened. Helga's coffee still warm in the cup, her fur-collared coat laid out on the bed, and the postcard. Most of all the postcard.

She thought again of the red shoes. Those shoes, which Helga had begged for a 'special occasion'. Why would she wear them if she was intending to die? Killing yourself was not a special occasion. Helga had not wanted to die. She had tried desperately to get in contact. She must have been in constant fear of Bauer. Perhaps he had even threatened her with what he might do, yet in her time of greatest need, Clara hadn't been there.

Having seen all she needed to, she walked quickly out of the block and back towards the city centre. At Alexanderplatz she caught a tram up west and made for Frau Lehmann's, where she went straight to her room, turned the picture of the Führer to the wall, pulled the curtains and got in bed. She clutched herself beneath the mounds of musty green eiderdown, shivering uncontrollably. She thought of Angela and Kenneth and her father back in England going about their lives, waking up each day and having breakfast, taking a bus to the office beneath the unfurling plane trees of Millbank, attending parties, and perhaps even talking about Clara, who had skipped off to Babelsberg and had sent postcards saying she was having a glorious time. She had never felt so alone or frightened in her life. She had come to Berlin to feel closer to her mother, and had found instead danger and death. Magda had warned her what happened to those who crossed the regime, but no warning could prepare her for the shock of that crumpled body or Helga's piteous face. And if she had been killed for the crime of telling jokes, how would they view Clara's far greater betrayal?

Poor sweet Helga. With her vanity and her kind nature and her messy love life. What had she ever done to deserve this? And who would tell little Erich that his film-star mother was gone? Lying on her bed, Clara made the only resolution she could – to carry on. She would do anything in her power to impede these people, no matter how small the act, or how seemingly insignificant. She would carry her secret as close as her own shadow. She would find a way to contact Helga's mother, and assure her Helga had not suffered before she died. She would see Erich, and try to give him some comfort. She would make sure he knew how much his mother had adored him. And as for Helga, she would do everything she could to avenge her.

Chapter Forty-eight

The following morning passed in a blur. Clara was needed on set to shoot a scene with Hans Albers, and she was glad of it. She rose at seven, stared blankly at her empty face in the mirror and rubbed a dab of rouge into her pallid cheeks. She ate Frau Lehmann's chill porridge without noticing for once how its starchy globules stuck to the roof of her mouth and she drank her burnt coffee, trying hard to avoid eye contact with Professor Hahn. The studio's Mercedes saloon collected her at eight, and it took a full morning to shoot a single scene in which she had a conversation with Albers in the hotel. She had tried to learn the script on the way, a task that would normally be effortless, but the words on the page danced in front of her eyes. On set Herr Lamprecht seemed uncharacteristically tetchy, which put everyone on edge and meant an unusual number of takes. At one point, when the film in the camera was being changed, Albers leant over to her and explained why.

'I shall have to take my leave of you soon. I've just told Gerhard I'm going after this film. We're heading for Starnberger See.'

'But, Hans, why?'

He spread his hands. 'It's Hansi, you see. We've no choice.'

Clara understood. Albers' girlfriend, Hansi Berg, was half-Jewish and had already been forced to leave the studio. Didn't the Nazis care that they were driving away their best talent? Or did they think they could manufacture brand-new actors, like guns and ships and aircraft?

Clara told no one what had happened to Helga. She was desperate to talk to Leo, but she could not contact him. She wanted to tell Albert, and at one point she looked up from the hall and instinctively sought out the window of his office, but there was no Albert staring back down at her and she was glad of it. It was important that she didn't break down.

It was late afternoon by the time she had returned to town, changed into her blue polka-dot dress, eaten a quick sandwich, then caught a tram to the Goebbels' home. Her initial hesitation over the wisdom of delivering Magda's letter had vanished now. She had no idea what Magda wanted to tell this man and if the penalty for laughing at the authorities was death, then assisting the Minister's wife in adultery was surely equally grave. Yet she was more certain than ever that keeping Magda's confidence would be vital if she wanted to continue helping Leo.

Unusually, Magda answered the door herself. The turbulence of her last visit had gone, to be replaced by an iron composure.

'Thank you for coming. I knew I could rely on you. I've sent the maid to take the baby for a walk.'

She ushered Clara quickly up the stairs and into her dressing room.

'I have it ready for you. Here.'

Magda felt under the blotter on the desk and withdrew a letter. The expensive cream notepaper was covered in curious stubby letters, like nothing she had seen before.

'Is it in code?'

Magda gave a strange guttural laugh. 'That's Hebrew. You didn't expect that, did you? My stepfather taught me. Victor always liked that about me.'

She folded the letter, then folded it again with precision, as though it was an elaborate piece of origami, whose perfect shape must echo the perfection of its sentiments. She stared at it a moment, then bundled it into a plain envelope. There was something else in there, something metallic, Clara saw.

'Hide it, please. No . . . not in your bag.' Her eyes scanned Clara thoughtfully. 'In your brassiere please. Keep it there.'

Clara unbuttoned her dress, folded the letter awkwardly and placed it inside her bra, where it wedged uncomfortably next to her skin.

'When do you want me to take it?'

'Tomorrow night. Tomorrow is the Führer's birthday. Everyone will be busy. You are to meet him at Brucknerstrasse 46, Steglitz. At seven o'clock. Repeat it.'

'Brucknerstrasse 46, Steglitz. At seven o'clock.'

Her face was so pale it seemed almost translucent. A narrow blue vein throbbed down the side of her temple, like the tracery on a piece of fine porcelain.

'And when you knock on the door, just say you're a friend of Lisa.'

'A friend of Lisa.'

'He'll understand.'

Clara decided to walk back to Frau Lehmann's. She had adopted the practice of changing her routes around the city, trying to avoid patterns in the way that Leo had advised. Skirting the Kroll Opera House she proceeded along the northern side of the Tiergarten, barely noticing how far she was walking in the darkening streets.

As she went, she mulled the astonishing matter over in her mind. Magda was in love with a Jewish man. Magda, whose marriage and ambitions and entire life were founded on a violent antipathy to Jews, was in love with Victor Arlosoroff.

Perhaps it shouldn't come as such a surprise. After all, Magda's stepfather, Richard Friedlander, was Jewish. The Friedlander household observed all the major laws and festivals of his faith. How was it then that Magda should now ally herself with someone like Goebbels? How did that angry and emotional woman come under the spell of such a violent and tyrannical man?

Magda did not, Clara was sure, share Goebbels' relish for physical violence. Although Leo had said she had actively campaigned to have SA members freed when they were convicted of murder, it was hard to imagine her enjoying the scuffles in the streets, the smashed heads and brutal humiliation of the Jews. Yet she had been merely uninterested in the plight of Bruno Weiss. Could it be that Magda was merely yearning for drama in her life? If so, she certainly had it now. Magda Goebbels had all the drama she could ever want.

Clara was walking quickly. Her palms prickled with sweat and her dress was sticking to her back. One sharp edge of the envelope was digging into the flesh of her breast. She shook her shoulders to try to move it but she didn't dare touch it. Not there in plain view. She would adjust it in the shelter of a shop front.

As she slowed to duck into the porch of a delicatessen, she heard the grunt of brakes and a saloon car pulled up alongside her. She barely had time to look around in the gloom before, with the engine still running, the driver sprang out. He was wearing a dark suit and tie, and he gestured as he opened the back door.

'Get in please.'

A jolt of fear ran through her.

'What do you mean?'

'Fräulein Vine, you are to come with me.'

So he knew her name.

'What's this about?'

The driver didn't reply. He gestured again to the seat. Clara contemplated running but saw immediately that there would be no point, so she climbed inside. The car pulled out into the traffic. Her entire body was shaking.

'Where am I being taken?'

The driver murmured something about "orders". He was driving far too fast. They headed north, across a sullen canal, oily water glinting beneath a bridge, and she couldn't help thinking of Rosa Luxemburg, shot and dumped in the depths of the Landwehr Canal and only dragged up four months later. They cut through badly-lit back streets, and she saw a prostitute in a doorway, arms wrapped round her chest to keep warm. They must be in the Moabit area, Clara calculated. Tall blocks loomed above and the belching stack of a factory sent clouds of soot into the air. She stared out in panic and tried to orient herself, or at least memorize the street names, but she had lost all sense of direction and guessed that the driver was taking a deliberately circuitous route, looping back on himself, to disorientate or torment her. It was too dark to see. She eyed the rolls of flesh on the neck in front of her.

'On whose orders exactly?'

He must have heard her, but he said nothing. The iron railings of another bridge passed and Clara glimpsed a barge sliding beneath and rubbish floating on the inky water. The sign of an S-Bahn entrance flashed by, too fast for her to read. Through a street of cobbles they passed a man sweeping the pavement and a shopkeeper putting up the steel grille on his window. Then another stretch of canal and the halo of street-lights wavering in the mist. Clara had a mad impulse to wrest open the door and jump out, but dismissed it instantly. She would need to rely on her wits.

'Am I being arrested?'

She caught a flicker of his eyes in the mirror, then nothing. She fell silent, feeling the powerful thrum of the well-oiled Mercedes beneath her, attempting to quell the dread that was rising within her. There was an acrid taste in her mouth, a sharp wash of adrenalin. What lay at the end of this journey? A cell, or something worse? And who would she contact for help, even assuming she was given the chance?

After perhaps twenty minutes the car slowed and drew up at the entrance of a building of pale stone, with arched Palladian windows. The driver held the door for her and then led the way up a flight of white steps. They entered a vast marble hall, crossed it, and Clara followed him up more stairs and down a long, ill-lit corridor, past rooms where, even at this hour, the clattering of typewriters could be heard. The driver kept a couple of steps ahead. Though he had uttered barely a word, he was enjoying this, just as he had enjoyed their unnecessary diversion around the backstreets. They reached some red-carpeted marble steps and came to a door. He put out his hand and took her handbag.

'I'll look after that.'

Then he knocked and gestured her inside.

The Reich Minister for Public Enlightenment and Propaganda was sitting behind an enormous desk, wearing a dark suit and a natty pink and green striped tie in a wide Windsor knot. He sprang up with a smile.

'Fräulein Vine, what a pleasure. Do come in. What do you think of my new headquarters?'

'It's very smart.'

'Do you think so? I think it's hideously old-fashioned. I detest all this damask and brocade and silk. So drab. I'm having it entirely redecorated by Herr Speer. Ocean liner style, he says. I want walnut veneers and smooth curves everywhere. And I want frescoes running along the tops of the walls. But it's very slow going. A few days ago I got so frustrated I tore off a load of old plaster and wood lining and tossed it down the stairs. How can people work without light and air?' He threw up his hands. 'We're also planning a thea-tre hall with state-of-the-art equipment for all the latest movies. You'd be interested in that. There have been some hitches with the electrical components apparently, but Speer possesses great technological wizardry. I'm a big believer in technology, aren't you? I rather think technology can solve any problem, no matter how complex. Please sit down.'

He walked over to a cocktail tray, poured her a whisky and soda and came over to her with two glasses. He smelt strongly of pomade. She noticed the immaculate fingernails and thought again of the nail file in his study.

He leant back against his desk and said casually, 'I under-stand there was a suicide of one of the Ufa actresses. A friend of yours. My condolences.'

Clara looked up at him, and felt her mask almost slip. How could he have heard so soon about Helga's death? And, what was more, how could he know that she knew? He must have had her followed, that much was obvious.

'You knew Helga, I think, Herr Doktor.'

'Yes. As I said, I'm sorry.'

'And do you think she committed suicide?'

'I will await the police report, as we all must.' He lit a cigarette and crossed his legs. 'Though from what I heard she was a fantasist. Possibly that pointed towards some form of mental disorder.'

Clara sat rigidly. She knew it was better not to reply. He must know what she thought, yet it was essential she said nothing. Danger flickered from his skinny form like an elec-tric spark from a wire. She wondered what he wanted of her.

'I understand she jumped out of the window just as some storm troopers were coming to interview her about vicious gossip she had spread concerning the Führer. She was a girl-friend of Walter Bauer, I heard. Some men can be very zealous in their loyalty to our leader.'

'I see.'

'She was also known to fraternize with Jews and Communist criminals.'

'I didn't know that.'

'On the other hand,' he spread one hand, inspected the moons of his fingernails and blew lightly on them, 'amongst all these theories, there will be people who say let her death be a warning. Perhaps that's what happens to young women who don't do as they should.'

His eyes held hers, steadily, as he waited for recognition to dawn on her. And when it did, Clara's shock deepened to horror.

Helga hadn't been killed because of her loose mouth and off-colour jokes. She hadn't been murdered because she made fun of Hitler's sex life or Goering's weight or Goebbels' crippled foot. It wasn't even because she fraternized with a Jewish artist of Communist sympathies. If Clara read Goebbels' implication correctly, the order for her death was a specific message to Clara herself. "Let her death be a warning." But a warning about what?

While his message was sinking in, Goebbels stopped for a meticulous moment to pick a strand of tobacco from his teeth.

'Commiserations aside, that's not why I wanted to see you, Fräulein. I wanted to see you because I think you can help me.'

It was dark in the room. The chief source of light was the green shaded lamp on the desk. Goebbels' shadow fell huge against the wall behind him. It was hard to make out his mood from the intonation of his voice.

'I can help you, Herr Doktor?'

'That's what I said. It's about my wife.'

'Frau Goebbels . . .'

'Indeed.'

He indicated a painting of Magda on the adjacent wall. It was a full-length official portrait, painted in the lush, idealized style that was popular with the Nazi leadership, and the spotlight above the frame caused Magda's face to loom out like a ghost. Her complexion was milky and there were no shadows beneath her eyes. She was holding a spray of flowers and gazing radiantly towards some distant Nirvana. For some reason Clara heard a poem running through her head.

"That's my last Duchess painted on the wall,
Looking as if she were alive."

'Magda likes you, I know,' said Goebbels. 'She's told me. She trusts you. But you need to understand she's frail. She's not herself sometimes.'

'She takes on a lot of work,' said Clara carefully.

'Yes, yes. As must we all.'

'What with the baby and all her social duties, and then the Fashion Bureau.'

'I'm not sure how long I'll allow her to carry on with that.'

'But Herr Doktor, I thought it was the Führer's own wish?'

'Let's just say I'm not sure it's proper for the First Lady of the Reich to be gallivanting around with film actresses and people of low morals.'

Was this meant to include her? Everything he said seemed

double–edged. He flashed her his famous broad smile. It was impossible to tell.

'You need to understand that my wife has had a difficult life. She had an unhappy marriage in the past and she became prey to people who took advantage of her. Sometimes she feels obligations to people which she doesn't really need to fulfil, but she is easily pressured and has a very high sense of duty. The thing about her is . . . she's all too quick to see the good in people. She's often blinded to their faults. Now that can be an admirable quality – as a husband I have benefited from her generous nature myself – but I don't feel the same about other people. In fact, if I discovered that someone was deceiving her, I don't know what I'd do.'

'Deceiving her?'

'Yes. And I have reason to think that may be happening. Do you understand what I am referring to?'

His voice now carried an undertone of menace. He scanned her face intently. Into Clara's mind the face of her sister came, that afternoon a long time ago. Angela's warning.

"Don't talk about being an actress. You won't ever be an actress. I can tell everything you're thinking. Every single thing you think is written all over your face. You couldn't act to save your life."

Clara's face barely flickered. Though her heart was pulsating so hard that it was making her chest shake, she kept her eyes steadily on his.

'I can't imagine what you mean, Herr Doktor.'

'What I mean is, I have suspicions that someone is taking advantage of my wife for disreputable ends. If I discovered that was happening . . . well, let's just say, I would not tolerate it.'

Averting her gaze, Clara glanced out of the window. Some lights were burning in the Chancellery, where a few dedicated secretaries worked on late into the night, processing the burgeoning bureaucracy of the new Reich. Down the hall the distant peck of a typewriter could faintly be heard. But most people had packed up for the day. In the cavernous room she felt acutely alone. How much did Goebbels know? Did he know about Arlosoroff's deception, or about Clara herself? He was having her followed, that much was obvious by the fact that the car had been able to waylay her, so did he know she was deceiving his wife? Yet if he did, surely she would not be sitting here in his office calmly sipping a whisky and soda? Surely she would be lying crumpled on a street like Helga, or bleeding by the side of the road after a car accident, or sinking slowly beneath the foul waters of a Berlin canal.

He got up and came over, pulling up a chair to sit next to her.

'You're not very talkative tonight, Fräulein.'

He reached towards her. She was still wearing her coat, but at his touch Magda's letter in her bra pressed against her skin, its sharp edges digging into her flesh. His hand moved to cup her breast and she recoiled, as if electrified. He withdrew his hand and laughed.

'I think you dislike me.'

'I—'

'Don't say anything. The fact that you dislike me makes me like you more. I'm funny that way. Perhaps I trust you more. So many of these actresses just want to sleep with an important man for advancement. I'm sure no one could accuse you of that, could they?'

She tried to take a sip of her drink, but her hand was trembling so hard she put it down again. Was that a reference to Müller? Or to himself?

'You see,' he continued, 'I know a little more about you than you think.'

She didn't answer. If he had had her followed he must know something, but how much did he know? For one dreadful moment, she wondered if he knew about Xantener Strasse. That in the dark of that one, blissful night a Gestapo shadow had lurked. Yet if Goebbels knew that, surely the smile on his face would be a far more sadistic sneer.

He sat back in his chair, as if her dismissal of his advances was a purely temporary hitch, and removed a long strand of hair from his suit sleeve. It was a woman's hair, but not blonde like Magda's. Clara wondered if it was another X in his diary.

'Enough of that. We can talk more on that subject later. Let's get down to business. My wife is in need of a good friend. Someone who has her best interests at heart, as I do. Someone who understands that she is fragile and sometimes needs protecting from herself. She's taken to you, I can see that. So you are well placed to keep an eye out. For my sake, and her own.'

'I suppose that's true.'

'So here's what I had in mind. I'm assuming I can count on you to help me in future?'

'I will help you in any way I can, Herr Doktor,' she replied smoothly.

'I hoped you would say that. So let's stay in touch.'

He got up abruptly and returned to his desk, pulling a pile of paperwork towards him.

'Oh, I almost forgot. I have some sad news for you. I'm afraid Herr Müller is to be temporarily transferred. I've decided the Propaganda Ministry needs a film of the Victory Rally at Nuremberg in August, so I'm sending him down there to make the arrangements. I'm thinking of Fräulein Riefenstahl as a director. I think she could make a skilled job of it, don't you?'

'I'm sure.'

'Perhaps you'd like to come to the Rally?'

'If I'm free.'

'Of course. Your handbag will be with the receptionist. It's a security issue. Tiresome, I know.'

He bent his head over the paperwork and she realized she was dismissed. She thanked God that she had the letter in her bra, not in her bag where it would surely have been found by some inquisitive SA official. She had one hand on the door handle when he called after her.

'Oh, and forgive me, but I notice a little blood on that dress. Down there on the hem. I hope you don't mind me pointing it out. It's a fad of mine. I have a bit of an obsession with cleanliness.'

It was Helga's blood. And he knew.

Chapter Forty-Nine

"If you buy a packet of Kurmark cirgarettes in Berlin right now, you will find inside an embossed colour card of a film star to collect. There's Marlene Dietrich and Brigitte Helm, Lil Dagover and Renate Müller, and every one of those beautiful women has a cigarette perched delicately between her fingers. But if you're an ordinary woman in Germany today, you light up at your peril. And if you're standing next to an SA man beware, because you might just have the cigarette slapped from your hand. All cafés and restaurants in Berlin have been requested to place signs telling women not to smoke. Ordinary citizens have been advised that if they see a woman smoking in public, they should remind her of her duty as a German woman to preserve her health and fertility. Some shops won't even sell you a cigarette. What's a girl to do?"

Rupert chuckled and handed the newspaper back to Mary.

'I can see why they like it. It makes a change from talking about the League of Nations.'

They were in a restaurant on the Gendarmenmarkt, looking out at the dome of the New Church across the busy square. The room was a sea of tables draped with crisp white linen, busy with the chink of glasses and the hum of upmarket conversation. All this Mary saw mistily, because her heavy spectacles were tucked away in her handbag and her naked eyes were primed with kohl and mascara. She was as blind as a mole as she blinked helplessly at the menu. It was *Spargelzeit*, asparagus season, and everywhere they went, whether it was a high-end restaurant like this or a lowly bar, the plump white stalks were on offer. The average German was said to eat asparagus once a day and the restaurants were full of it, in soup, rice dishes, *mit Butter*, *mit Schinken*, *mit Holländischer Sauce*. You couldn't escape it if you wanted to. For Rupert and Mary it had become a running joke. Each time they were served it, they remarked how weird it was that an entire country could so unilaterally love the same vegetable. Asparagus was about as ubiqitous as National Socialism. The difference was, as Rupert said, they both liked asparagus.

Rupert noticed that his compliment had caused only a fleeting smile to pass across Mary's face. He poured her a little more Gewürztraminer.

'So now you're going to tell me what's wrong.'

She looked up gratefully. Because Rupert generally kept up such a banter, it was sometimes difficult to be serious with him. He had a light-hearted English habit of turning everything into a joke. She had no real idea even now whether he saw her as a girl, or a colleague, or simply one of the guys. Their dates had generally ended with a chaste peck on the cheek, no matter how hard she tried to signal that she would like something more. This time she had vowed to make her feelings clear. After the day she'd had, she had been looking forward to it intensely.

'Oh, I had a bad encounter this morning. At the Ministry.'

'I saw Dr Dietrich collar you. What happened?'

Her heart buckled to see a touch of concern in his face.

'They hated the last article I wrote. That interview with Rosenberg about the sterilization of women who are deemed unfit to reproduce. It's Rosenberg's pet subject. He says if the

Nordic races are to survive there will be no place for weak-
lings. It's no different from farming, he says, and the Reich
needs to establish breeding programmes to produce the
strongest specimens.'

'Breeding programmes? You're not telling me this is this
Party policy?'

'I'm not sure. Rosenberg's an eccentric. But Dietrich was
mad at me. He said I had no right to spread erroneous conjec-
ture. He told me they've appointed a translator who in future
will go through all my pieces and next time I write something they take exception to, my visa will be cancelled. He
also said under the new Ordinance for the Defence against
Malicious Attacks on the Government of National Renewal,
or whatever it's called, there's a two-year prison sentence for
anything critical of the regime.'

'Come on, Mary. This is 1933 and year one of the
Thousand-Year Reich. No one's going to get off to a bad
start by putting an American journalist in prison. Not when
they're desperate to cosy up to the United States.'

'I guess not. But if I wrote anything else they objected to,
I could get thrown out.'

'Other people have been thrown out. They come back
again.'

'But I'd hate to be thrown out! This is where the action
is!'

'If you do get thrown out for what you write, make sure
it's a great piece. You want to go out with a bang.'

Mary smiled despite herself. Why was Rupert incapable of
taking anything seriously? Perhaps now was the moment to
broach the subject. Her heart began to beat the way it had as
a teenager when her horse, Dora, came up to a jump. Her
stomach clenched with nerves as she hunted for the right
words. She felt angry with herself. She was supposed to be a

journalist, wasn't she? Getting people to confide the truth
was her speciality.

'You sound like you don't care if I stay or go.'

'Surely not.'

'Well, do you?'

'Do I what?' he smiled, draining his glass and pouring
another.

'Do you care, Rupert?' she said, reaching her hand across
the table to him. 'If I went, would you miss me?'

'Of course I'd miss you.' He gave her hand a little pat.
'You know, Mary, you are the only person, and moreover
the only woman I know who . . .' His brow knitted and he
looked at her steadily, as if trying to summon the right words.

The tension overcame her. 'Who what?'

'Who likes asparagus as much as I do!' He burst out laugh-
ing. 'If you went who else would I spend *Spargelzeit* with?'
He wiped his lips. 'And to be honest, you're the only woman
I've ever met who can really make me laugh.'

'I'm glad.' It wasn't a protestation of love, but perhaps that
had been too much to hope for. 'Because I sure as hell don't
want to go.'

'So try keeping on their good side then. Make an effort not
to annoy them for a while. You're specialising in women,
after all. That should be fairly uncontroversial.'

For a second she paused, as she replaced her glass and
looked at him in amazement. *Uncontroversial?* Had he really
not heard anything she'd said?

'Do you mean that?'

'Sure. I bet there are a million stories around. I saw something
the other day in the *Tageblatt*. A young woman who wants to be
the first female Lufthansa pilot. Germany's own Amelia Earhart.
Aged twenty-three. Lives with her proud parents on a potato
farm just outside Berlin. You could interview her.'

Mary had to wait a moment, while the waiters arrived with platters of *Wiener Schnitzel* and whipped off the silver covers with a flourish. She felt the emotion rising within her as a flush crept up her face. Then in a low voice she said, 'You know, Rupert, when Frank Nussbaum first asked me to write colour pieces about women's lives in the new Reich I thought, Jesus, all this politics going on and I'm having to do pieces about weddings and babies! I told him that. I complained like hell.'

'I can imagine.'

'But you know what I found out?' She was twisting the tablecloth in her hands in an effort to keep her voice steady. 'I found out it's so much more than that.'

'Is it?' he said, slicing hungrily into the crisp golden veal.

'Yes, Rupert, it is! Frank's right. Reporting on women is about the most important thing you can do right now. The way a country treats its women is an exact measure of its moral health. Even though women are Hitler's strongest supporters, he intends to change their lives radically.'

'In what way?'

'To start with, for the first time since 1919 there are no female deputies in the Reichstag. They'll probably take the vote away too if they can.'

'I think that's just propaganda.'

'You can't deny it's the Nazis aim to remove women from public life?'

'That's just their rhetoric. It's crowd pleasing.'

'Rupert! Don't you see?'

She was blinking back tears, but it was her own fault. Her fault for expecting Brits to be different. It was all part of her fantasy that went with a childhood burying herself in *Wuthering Heights* and *Jane Eyre* and going to every Shakespeare play that was available in the state of New Jersey in the 1920s.

She had a crazy, romantic idea that British men would be somehow more sensitive and refined than the boys she had been brought up with. Sure, they liked to turn everything into a great big joke, but underneath it all they believed that women were their equals and needed to be treated as such. What a fool she had been to think that.

She pushed away her plate in annoyance and leant over to him urgently, elbows on the table. 'It's straight from their mouths, Rupert. Hitler says German women don't need to be emancipated. He's determined to turn them back into a nation of hausfraus.'

'Don't women like staying at home?' He emptied the Gewurtztraminer into his glass. 'I mean, let's talk more personally. What if it were you, Mary? If some man came along and said he wanted to marry you and for you to keep home, are you really saying you wouldn't consider it?'

For a moment her chest tightened, and she marvelled at the way Rupert's easy charm could slide like a knife between the ribs. How those dancing, humorous eyes could almost make her say, '*All you have to do is ask me, Rupert, and I'll raise babies and bake cookies with the best of them.*'

'After all,' he added casually, looking around for the wine waiter, 'that's what women really want, isn't it?'

A wave of frustration rose over her. 'And what would you know about what women really want, Rupert?' she snapped. 'Do you actually have any interest in women at all?'

The glance he gave her, sharp and unadorned, explained everything. It was as though she had touched something raw and deep within him. It was like opening the wrong page in a book and discovering the ending before you were ready for it. She realized, though she wouldn't feel capable of accepting it for a while, that not only did Rupert have no understanding of women, but he had no real interest in them either.

Sure, he would have girlfriends, and might marry even, in good time. But men were the focus of his interest and always would be. She thought of how his eyes lit up when he saw Leo. Of how happy he was, joking and laughing with the male correspondents. How his highest praise for a female journalist was that she was 'a good chap'. Rupert was no Heathcliff, and no Mr Darcy either. In that instant Mary understood something about him that he probably didn't understand himself and perhaps would never confront.

She took a long swig of wine and looked at him resolutely.

'In answer to your question, I could never be a housewife. I love my job too much.'

'That's exactly what I thought.' Rupert smiled with visible relief as the waiter uncorked a fresh bottle. 'I knew that from the moment I met you.'

Mary took out her glasses from her handbag and the world swam back into focus. She could carry on breaking her heart over Rupert as long as she liked, but it would never do her any good. She might as well concentrate on breaking stories instead.

Chapter Fifty

The sky could not be bluer. It was as though the weather itself had received orders from some newly formed Ministry of Meteorological Events. It was unnaturally sunny for April. A clever journalist with an eye on promotion had even come up with a name for it: Führerweather. The newspapers were full of congratulations for Hitler having reached the grand age of forty-four. Lapels everywhere were spattered with swastikas. The Brandenburger Tor was wrapped up like a Christmas present in scarlet ribbons, and school children from out of town who had been woken before dawn for the occasion, larked and yawned in the streets.

Clara had to turn out for the parade. It would have looked strange if she didn't. The whole city was streaked with billowing red flags, and in the shops the Führer's photograph was displayed, wreathed in ribbons or studded with crimson carnations. The *Graf Zeppelin*, a long, hydrogen-filled airship, sailed like a great silver salmon above the trees, the sun glinting off its sides. All this, she thought, the banners and the formations and the flags, were no more substantial than the struts and props you saw at the Ufa studios. They were merely flimsy, colourful surfaces, concealing hard, gritty rubble underneath.

As she made her way towards Mitte the noise was extraordinary. Church bells were ringing and horses clattering. A

new linden tree had been planted to mark the occasion and
stalls had been set up where people could donate towards
Hitler's birthday. And all this without the star himself. Hitler
was in Bavaria, opening the first of the prestigious Napola
academies, the schools Erich wanted to attend, if his intellect
proved enough to make up for his asthmatic chest.

A stream of schoolchildren passed her, their faces alight
with excitement as they were guided to a specially reserved
place at the front of the crowd. Clara thought of the Pied
Piper of Hamelin, all those laughing children dancing to the
irresistible tune of the piper, and following him to their
uncertain fate.

She took up a place behind a barrier on the Siegesallee
where the crowd was five deep. Beside her, boys twined like
ivy around a bronze Prussian on horseback, so only his helm-
eted head peered above the crowd, gazing out at the parade.
Just about everyone was there; goose-stepping soldiers and
the Hitler Youth with spades slung over their shoulders, and
finally, way behind them, the motorcade of Nazi officials.

From the east it came, like a flutter of breeze in the trees.
A low sound at first, but when the crowd saw the first cars in
the distance, a roar went up like a great murmuring wind and
the *Heil Hitlers* began. The faces of soldiers lining the street
turned like the leaves of a book as the motorcade passed. A
little boy in front of Clara, dressed in army uniform, put his
fingers in his ears to stop the noise, but his father gently
moved them away.

That morning, Frau Lehmann had insisted they listen to
what Doktor Goebbels had to say about the Führer's
birthday.

'Normally the great men that we admire from a distance
lose their magic when one knows them well. With Hitler the
opposite is true. The longer one knows him, the more one

admires him, and the more one is ready to give oneself fully
to his cause.'

Fräulein Viktor's knitting had fallen to her lap as she
listened with rapt attention. Clara had not dared to meet the
eyes of Professor Hahn.

Once the parade had passed and the crowds began to
disperse she went and sat in a café reading the *Morgenpost*. A
telegram of congratulations for the Führer had been sent
from Rome, assuring him of "unflinching co-operation"
from the Vatican. More than four thousand cities had awarded
Hitler honorary citizenship. Clara tried to concentrate on the
news but her eyes kept sliding off the page. Helga's death had
left her not just scared, but stunned. And the only person
who had spoken of it was Goebbels himself.

Goebbels. The meeting with him the previous evening
had filled her with a fresh terror. What did he mean by his
request to "keep an eye" on his wife? How could she possibly
fulfil that? Could she really manage to act like a double agent
in the Goebbels' marriage, all the while reporting to Leo?
Such a prospect would surely test her acting skills to the
utmost. Besides, she didn't need reminding, this was the man
who had had her friend killed. And who would not hesitate
to kill again. Until Helga's death the idea that she might be
risking her life had never seemed real to her. Now she wished
she had accepted the pistol Leo had offered her.

She became aware of a man watching her. He sat two
tables to her left, between her and the door, and was ostensibly reading a newspaper but in fact stealing frequent glances
in her direction. He was in his fifties, a creased, anonymous-
looking character with steel-grey hair cropped close to the
skull, and a hat beside him on the seat. Worn shoes, but
neatly pressed trousers. Shabby, yet clean. Either he was a
slow reader or he was especially fascinated by the page of

foreign news in front of him. He was no longer taking sips from his cup, plainly suggesting that he had finished his coffee long ago.

Clara was immediately alert. She wondered if there was a back way out of the place but apart from a single doorway to a half-glimpsed kitchen, it was clear that the café considered itself too small to provide toilet facilities for its customers. She had instinctively chosen the table furthest from the front window, right at the back of the café, but that meant if she wanted to leave she would have to walk right past him, giving him the advantage of observing the direction she took and following at his own pace. For twenty minutes she sat it out, till her own coffee was just a grainy, brown puddle at the bottom of the cup, willing him to leave, but noticing that his glances had become more frequent and less disguised. She was about to get up when he stood himself and approached her, proffering a packet of cigarettes.

'I saw you were alone.'

His voice was hesitant and eager, his eyes had all the pathos of the lonely pick-up. Instantly she perceived that his interest in her was not as a shadow but as a solitary man, hoping to have found a fellow loner.

'I wondered, would you care for another coffee, or a drink perhaps?'

'Oh, I'm sorry. I have to leave.'

Folding some notes beneath the saucer, she stepped quickly out into the street, almost laughing with relief, and remembered Leo's remark: '*A girl like you must get used to being looked at.*'

It was true. The sensation of men's eyes on her, attracted by her face first, then running over her breasts or her legs, was perfectly normal to her. It was the same for most women. No matter how professional or polished the man, a woman could tell in a split second when he was assessing her looks. Yet how far off that kind of innocent observation seemed now.

She moved cafés and sat until five o'clock, overdosing on caffeine and toying with a *Mokke* cake she couldn't eat, until she decided it was time.

Magda had been right. It was a good day to choose. It couldn't be better. Though it was early evening, the streets were still thronged and busy, with crowds jostling the streets and strolling through the parks, enjoying their day out. The sun had gone and an edge of chill had entered the air, mingling with the scent of wurst and beer and a trail of cordite from the celebratory fireworks.

Clara stood opposite the Friedrichstrasse station, waited until the conductor of the 177 tram had rung the bell then jumped into the back carriage. A stop later she entered the U-Bahn, catching a train to Leipziger Strasse, from which she emerged straight into the front door of Wertheim's. The department store, hung with plate glass and mirrors, was ideal for her purposes. Each time she passed a mirror she studied the reflection of the faces among the shoppers for any she recognized. It was nearly closing time but the shop was still packed with customers taking advantage of the day out to see the country's biggest department store. She took the escalator up to the second floor, stepped off and came down the opposite side immediately, allowing her to glance at the people passing her on the way up. There was no sign of a shadow. There was a moment when she noticed that a trout-faced middle-aged woman who she had seen on the ground floor buying perfume appeared alongside her at the gloves on the first floor. She got into a dispute with the assistant, which was exactly what Clara would have done if she had been the shadow, drawing attention to herself and behaving atypically because she had been spotted. For safety's sake, Clara slipped into a door marked 'Staff Only'. Pausing to remove her cherry beret and bright cotton scarf, she walked along a corridor and down a flight of concrete steps, emerging in the china and glass department. Leaving the store she crossed Potsdamer Platz to Stresemannstrasse and entered the Haus Vaterland.

The Kempinski Haus Vaterland was five towering storeys of entertainment beneath a brilliantly lit dome, the idea behind it being spelt out in large neon letters on the frontage: "The World in One House". Clara remembered Helga talking about it. It was a kind of world tour under one roof with twelve international restaurants catering for up to six thousand diners at any one time. Clara had thought it sounded pretty dreadful then, but it suited her purpose now. And it was gratifyingly busy. Passing the Spanish bodega, the Turkish bar and the Viennese café she made for the first-floor Rhine Terrace, a cavernous hall set with tables where murals depicted a Rhine landscape complete with castles and the Lorelei rock. From the sound alone, she knew she was in luck. The particular draw of the Rhine Terrace was that once an hour the lighting was dimmed and a thunderstorm was simulated. Lightning flashed, thunder rumbled and artificial rain spattered down on the landscape, misting the nearest diners to their evident delight. As Clara entered, the weather show had just begun. She stopped a moment and looked about her. All eyes were on the far end of the hall. No one was looking at her. Weaving her way through the tables, she slipped into the ladies' lavatory, locked herself in a cubicle and removed the blonde wig from the studio which she had brought in her satchel. Fixing it, she smiled at herself in the mirror, seeing a lighter, gayer self emerge, then took out a navy soft-brimmed felt hat and a gabardine which she had

carried rolled up, covered herself up and became immediately less conspicuous. When she came out she checked the
faces of those around her, and saw nothing but entranced
diners, watching the display and enjoying the sensation of
having the whole world at their feet.

She turned right and walked down the street to the
Anhalter Bahnhof, took the U-Bahn one stop, then got off
quickly and changed carriages, choosing a seat next to a fat
woman, leaning in to her slightly, inhaling the greasy air of
cooking that arose from her. Clara felt intensely in control of
herself, keeping her expression deadpan, every movement
deliberately relaxed. She crossed her legs and an old man
seated opposite caught her eye then looked away. Both of
them noticed the small swastika flag lying crumpled on the
floor of the carriage, but neither of them picked it up. She
travelled a further two stops, watching the lights reflected in
the window veer towards them and slide away, before alight-
ing at Steglitz.

Steglitz-Rathaus station was almost deserted apart from a
youngish man smoking in the yellow-tiled waiting room. It
was as though everyone in the locality had gone into the
centre to watch the festivities and decided to make an
evening of it. Turning out of the station, she passed into a
tree-lined street. With the thrum of traffic heading towards
the city centre behind her, the quiet was deep and domestic.
She heard a mother calling children in to bed, and from
another house a sweet female voice issued from a wireless
singing. She came to a road lined with shops. One was
boarded up, the streetlamp glinting on a tidy rubble of
broken glass, and next to it were the lighted, steamy windows
of a restaurant, the Bar Axel. A celebration of some kind was
underway. The light spilt around the animated figures like
players on a set, yet it was she, in the dusk, who felt the

intense concentration, the heightened alertness of an actor
on a stage.

A Persian cat stalked by on a wall, its feathery tail aloft.
The occasional car passed, but from what she could tell no
vehicle followed her. She checked each parked car for occupants, but saw none. Look for any unusual activity, Leo had
told her. She watched for anyone behaving aimlessly, or
pretending interest in shop windows, who might look away
if she caught their eye. But there was no one. She was just
thinking that she was being absurdly cautious, and priding
herself on the thoroughness of her route, when she caught
the flicker of a figure a few yards behind.

Leo had told her what to do. 'Stop a while. See if he stops
too. Cross the road.'

So she stopped and made to look into a shop front, and
when she glanced behind she saw nothing.

She was being hypersensitive, she told herself. She had
followed every step of Leo's lesson and had no reason at all to
suppose that she was being tailed. She carried on as the shops
gave way to apartment buildings and the pavement darkened
in the intervals between the street lamps. Two blocks on a
ticking sound approached from behind and she looked into
the side of a gleaming car to see a boy wheeling a bicycle
coming past her. Though her nerves were jangling she forced
herself to keep in steady step and felt glad for the anonymous
gaberdine and the soft-brimmed hat, which shaded half her
face.

She carried on for half a block, but moments later she
heard a faint, metallic clatter. She had trodden on a drain
cover a few moments before and her heel had made that very
sound. This time, in the reflection of a window she saw him,
a man in a trench coat, pale hat, and newspaper rolled up in
one pocket. A pale tie and dark suit trousers. There was no

doubt about it. She was being followed. A kick of nerves assaulted her but she forced herself on. Though she managed to keep herself from trembling, fear ran through her like electricity snaking along a wire.

A bus trundled past and as it did, Clara took the opportunity to step into a narrow, unlit passageway, smelling of urine and litter. A few steps along was a doorway and she wedged herself in, her heart jolting with fear, until she saw the man following her pass on the other side of the street. He proceeded with a firm tread, looking neither left nor right, as though he was a private citizen, entirely lost in thought. But he would soon realize that he had lost her and retrace his steps.

Clara saw that the passageway was in fact an alley, a narrow space between the brick walls of the houses, barely wide enough for a single person to pass. The stench of garbage was overpowering. Squeezing along, she emerged at the other end into a residential street, cursing herself for being so complacent before. For assuming that, because the man in the café had been a well-intentioned stranger, it meant no one else was on her tail.

According to the map she had memorized, she was getting near to Brucknerstrasse. She readjusted her directions and turned down a street full of prosperous-looking villas set back from the road. At a crossroads, she turned left into a street of undistinguished blocks with scrubby front gardens. The perfect place to sink into anonymity. She counted the numbers and checking the road quickly right and left, crossed to a tall, red-brick mansion house, went up the steps and knocked five times. When the door opened, she said, 'I am an old friend of Lisa's,' and he let her in.

Victor Arlosoroff was a tall, densely-packed man with tight curly hair the texture of wire wool, round horn-rimmed glasses, and a belligerent air. He had a hard, knuckly brow, bulbous nose, and a protruding lower jaw. His forehead was heavily scored with lines and his face was bunched as a fist. Not even his mother could call him good-looking. As she followed him through a shadowy hall into a cluttered front room where thick curtains were drawn, Clara was amazed yet again at why Magda should be attracted to men who were so physically unprepossessing. He was smoking a pipe with short, savage puffs, and looked at Clara searchingly. His eyes, through the thick glasses, were tiny.

He waved her to a chair, and sat down. There was a piano, with a Beethoven score open, and dusty glass cabinets stacked with books. Many of them, she noticed, had titles in Hebrew, just like Magda's letter. A quick scan of the photographs on the shelves suggested that this house did not belong to Arlosoroff and the clatter of dishes in the distance confirmed that other people were in residence.

She handed him the envelope and he read the letter through, then leant back and surveyed her.

'So you are a friend of Magda's.'

'Yes. My name is Clara Vine.'

He chuckled. 'She doesn't like me sending letters to her mother's house. It's come to something when old friends can't communicate, eh?'

'She is quite frightened.'

'I'm sorry.' He removed his glasses and rubbed his eyes. 'Do you know, I wasn't even aware until a few weeks ago that she'd married that club-footed loudmouth. How could she be taken in by him? And the gall of him, holding the wedding at the country estate of her first husband! I suppose she told you there was a time she was going to emigrate to Palestine with me?'

'She did.'

He tipped up the envelope she had given him and Clara
caught the flash of something gold. A necklace.

'Do you know what this is?'

'A Star of David?'

'I gave it to her as a present. She loved this necklace. She
wore it all the time. She has sent it as proof that this letter
could have come from nobody but her. A Nazi minister's
wife using the Star of David to vouch for her identity. You
have to admit that's original!'

'So what went wrong?'

For the first time the anger seeped out of his face and his
stubby features drooped. He tapped his pipe, which was issuing gouts of smoke like a badly laid fire, got up and hunted
round the musty, brown room for a book of matches, then
sat down again.

'I wish I knew. Our friendship goes back a long time. She
was a friend of my sister Lisa. Her own family seemed pretty
remote, so she was always around our place, for dinner or
playing music. Then, in 1920 I left for Palestine for the first
time and whenever I came back to see my family, it meant I
saw Magda too. And she'd grown so lovely, I don't mind
telling you. A beautiful woman and so . . . so feminine. We
grew very close, and I shared all my dreams and plans with
her. My ambitions for a Jewish homeland in Palestine. Proper
co-operation between Jews and Arabs. We discussed everything. Anyhow, it stayed like that, on and off, until three
years ago. At that time she had split up from her first husband
and had another lover, a young man called Ernst who was
crazy about her. He fired a revolver at her when she refused
to go with him and it only just missed. She simply laughed at
him. She's got guts, you see. She's very strong-minded.'

'I've noticed.'

'Can I offer you something? A drink?'

He waved a bottle at her and she nodded, accepting the glass of rough brandy he proffered and taking a tiny, fiery sip.

'This time, when I came back, a good friend, Robert Weltsch, the editor of *Jüdische Rundschau*, met me at the station and he had some news for me. "Remember that pretty woman you used to see?" he said. "Well she's married to the Minister of Propaganda now." Magda was married to Joseph Goebbels! I almost passed out. Magda Friedlander! My beautiful girlfriend. The woman who once discussed coming to Palestine with me to establish a proper homeland for the Jews!'

He stood up and crossed the room to correct a chink in the curtains.

'But then it crossed my mind that this could also be a blessing in disguise. It fitted with my plan.' He fixed Clara with a shrewd look, as if still uncertain of her motivation. 'You see, it's my view that the Jews in Germany should be helped to come to Palestine. We already have Jewish organizations here training people in the practical skills they need for our homeland. They're learning everything under the sun! Cooking and baking, sewing and tailoring courses, typing, shorthand, bookkeeping, photography, and language classes. Agriculture, nursing, all these things. And the National Socialists say they want as many Jews as possible to emigrate, so why should they not help fund the transit of people who want to leave? Perhaps, I thought, Magda could help me with that.'

Was he brave, Clara thought, or foolhardy? It was dreadful to imagine him making this proposition to some sadist of a Sturmhauptführer, his features contorting with incredulous contempt. Even Klaus Müller would laugh in his face, before having him arrested for audacity. The Nazis may have convoluted morals, but the idea of them using the coffers of the Reich to assist their declared enemies was simply unimaginable.

'I assume it didn't work?'

'No. In fact it has been made clear to me that not only do the Nazis have no interest in helping us out, but I may myself be in serious danger.'

'Herr Arlosoroff. Victor. I think everything you're doing, training Jews to start a new life, helping people to leave Germany, is invaluable. It was brave of you to come back. But if the Nazis won't co-operate, and they've already threatened you, I would advise you to leave straight away.'

He smiled, acknowledging her concern with a tilt of his head. 'That's what I'm telling everyone I know. There's no way a Jew can stay in Germany much longer. The Germans won't rest until they have locked every one of us up. I'm well aware that Berlin is not safe for me.' He took his pipe out and gazed searchingly at her. 'Yet there is something I need to do before I leave. A proposal I have for my dear Magda. I am wondering, my friend, how far I can trust you.'

'You know Magda sent me.'

'Plainly. But, forgive me, you are not the type of woman Magda normally calls a friend. Far too pretty, for one. She must be terrified her husband will make a play for you, if he hasn't already. Indeed, I'd be surprised if she has many friends. She never used to. You're younger than her, too. I'm having difficulty seeing where you fit in her life. For all I know, you could be one of her husband's spies. What's in it for you? Why are you taking this risk?'

She thought of telling him about Grandmother Hannah. How since she had arrived in Berlin her own life had become far more closely intertwined with events than she could ever have imagined. But she had determined that her Jewishness would be a secret to be carried close. Just like her mother, though for different reasons.

'I'm doing this because they murdered Helga Schmidt.'

It was the first time the words had come out of her mouth, though she had played the scene over and over in her head. The moment Helga fell, the dreadful moment of realization, as she plummeted towards the paving, that her life was finished, broken off mid-sentence. And how scared she must have been. Because Helga was not brave. She was foolish, friendly, and life-affirming. But not brave. Her death was so unnecessary, so callous and wasteful. Merely thinking of it brought the tears back to Clara's eyes. Angrily she blinked them away.

'Helga was an actress, like me. She made the mistake of joking about Hitler and they pushed her out of a fifth-floor window. You might read about her in the next few days and it will probably say she committed suicide because she was depressed, or a fantasist, but that wasn't the case. Her only crime was laughing at them. I would do anything I could to avenge her.'

He put an awkward hand out to her. 'I'm sorry for your loss. There's an old Jewish saying, "All things grow with time, except grief." I hope it will prove so with you.'

He shuffled closer in his chair. 'But what you say convinces me. The sooner Magda gets away from those thugs, the better. I hope you will agree to take a message back to her.'

'A letter?'

'No. She has specifically asked me not to give you a letter. It's more of a risk. You will just have to memorize what I tell you. This is my plan. I need to leave Berlin. There's no way I can stay much longer here before I find myself involved in the same kind of accident as your unfortunate friend. After tonight I am going to move each day from house to house so I cannot be traced. But what I most want is for Magda to come away with me. To make a fresh start. Will you tell her, that if she comes to the Anhalter Bahnhof at six o'clock next Friday evening I will be waiting for her? Just inside, beneath the clock. She can bring her child too, if she likes. I will have tickets for Vienna and we will travel from there to Switzerland. All she needs to do is turn up.'

'And if she doesn't want to?'

He shook his head, as if refusing to admit the possibility. 'I'm sure she will. Once she has thought about it.'

'It would be difficult for her.'

'Not as difficult as her life will be if she stays. This is her chance to escape.'

'You seem very confident.'

'Why should I not be? Magda writes to say she still loves me. She has always been a woman of strong passions. She will follow her heart.'

He stood up and led the way to the darkened hall, but as they reached the glass-fronted door he hesitated. He seemed unwilling, Clara felt, to let her go. As if with her he lost his last link to Magda.

'I envy you seeing her, Clara. Take my blessing with you. Do you think she'll come?'

'I couldn't say.'

Outside a car backfired, startling them both, then Arlosoroff moved closer to her so that she could smell his breath, slightly rank, and see the open pores in his skin.

'She couldn't ever be happy with that man, could she?'

'I doubt it.'

He put a hand on her shoulder. The sudden intimacy unnerved her, but he was holding out the Star of David.

'Take it back to her. If she comes with me, she'll need it.'

Clara pocketed the necklace, walked out into the cool, evening air and checked her watch. It had been only thirty minutes, but while she was with Arlosoroff she had lost all sense of time. It felt like hours had passed.

She went down the steps, her mind racing. She had done what Magda had asked of her. She had passed the letter on. And she was glad of it. But Arlosoroff's proposition astounded her. Would Magda really go with him? She was desperately unhappy with Goebbels, that was certain, but could she really give up the luxury, the clothes, the society evenings, the newspaper features, to scrape a new life in the relentless heat of the Palestinian desert? From everything she knew, Clara doubted it. And then, a second consideration came to her. If Magda did elope with Arlosoroff, what would that mean for Clara? What access would she have? How could she continue what she had started?

She made a decision and crossed the street.

It was properly dark now, and the trees made bars of shadow across the road. She took a different, more convoluted route back up the street towards the station, but she was convinced that she had lost the tail before she even arrived on Brucknerstrasse. Leo would be pleased with her. She knew for certain she had been followed that evening, and, though the confirmation terrified her, she felt giddily excited at having given Goebbels' man the slip.

She walked quickly, too absorbed by the events of the evening to notice the figure in the trench coat who crossed the street from under the elm trees opposite and followed at a languid pace behind.

Chapter Fifty-one

The garden of the Press Club in the Tiergarten reminded Mary of sunlit afternoons at her grandparents' home in New Jersey. Grandpa was rich – he had his own business manufacturing luxury boats – and they owned a colonial-style mansion near Salem with eighteen acres and a swimming pool. If she closed her eyes she could almost imagine herself back there, a jug of iced tea beside her, and the regular thwack of journalists' racquets on the Club's grass tennis court reminded her of the insanely competitive sporting contests that took place regularly between her brother, father and grandfather. No one in the Harker family liked to lose.

Berlin in 1933, however, was nothing like New Jersey. For one thing, as far as Mary was concerned, summers in New Jersey were a somnolent, unexciting space of time strung between the school semesters of spring and autumn, whereas this city was gripped by a kind of frenetic tension that rippled through the air like an electric current. For another thing, in Grandpa's garden you saw a relaxing vista of horses snorting in a distant paddock, but when you opened your eyes here you could see right across to the windows of the Reichswehr Ministry which cast their chilly glance on Bendlerstrasse. That wasn't the kind of place to make anyone feel relaxed. It was behind the vast façade of the Bendlerblock last month that Hitler had apparently told senior generals he planned to exterminate Marxism and conquer more living space in the east.

Sitting on the terrace in a patch of warm sunshine, Mary drained another cup of coffee and read the letter again.

It had arrived that morning. In typical style, her mother had devoted several pages to news about her bridge partners and the grandchild (walking already!) and the charity evening she had been organising at the country club, before she got to the point.

"Daddy had a turn last week, when he was walking round the garden, and Doctor Hillman said it was a stroke. A rather bad one I guess. He can't talk too well and is very weak down one side. He's confined to bed and we both of us think it would be a good time for you to come back."

This piece of news she put on page five. Why had her mother not sent a telegram in 72 point capitals: YOUR FATHER IS MORTALLY ILL? She had a gift for what Frank Nussbaum would call 'burying the lead'.

Her dear father. The first man who had faith in her. The man who when she was just twelve had silenced a roomful of belittling female relatives with the firm declaration, "Of course Mary can be a journalist. A girl like Mary can be anything she wants." The man she loved more than anyone else. Thinking of his powerful, craggy form, with its ramrod back and steely sinews, crumpled in a heap on the garden path caused her a vicarious physical pain.

After her announcement her mother had, with typical insouciance, added an afterthought.

"I'm sure there's plenty of journalism to be done in America, after all. You are our only daughter, Mary, and

right now, for however long it may be, I think your place
is with us."

Her mother's request – 'demand' was more like it – couldn't
have come at a worse time. The feature about the labour
camp had gone down well. So well, in fact, that it had been
picked up by the wire services and syndicated round America.
There had been plenty of correspondence about it, many
readers suggesting the United States adopt a similar system for
the good of the young. Frank Nussbaum had called her piece
about the threat to sterilize unfit women "a powerful condem-
nation" of the regime. The story of Lotte's sister-in-law
Margarete and her mass wedding, which had run the following week, earned Mary a telegram of praise from the editor-
in-chief himself. Even down the telephone line, she could
hear Frank breaking into one of his rare grins. There was an
appetite for this kind of feature, he said. They had decided
from now on she should have her own regular column. It
would start next week and be called '*Mary Harker's Berlin Life*'.
They would run a picture by-line of her on top. A picture
by-line! Mary had needed to clear her throat to mask her gasp
of delight. The truth was, Frank went on, Germany was a
complex picture right now. In some ways perhaps America
had something to learn from it – like the way it had motivated
its workforce, for example, and channelled the energies of its
young people. But there were horror stories too, and Mary
should get on with a piece about how the state was planning
to fire all married women on the grounds that they took work
away from their husbands. How women teachers would be
banned from giving private lessons and how the number of
women going to university was being reduced. If she took it
carefully and managed not to get thrown out, Frank thought
this new column could make her name.

Absently Mary stretched out her hand and took another of the *Lebkuchen* the Press Club did so well. And another. Those delicious little gingerbread biscuits with cinnamon and spices weren't good for the waistline, but who cared about that after her disappointment with Rupert the other night? Rupert, who was now grimly relegated to a long list of men labelled Just Good Friends. She sighed. She had been completely honest when she told him she could never be a hausfrau. What she had come to realize was that as someone who loved chatting to people, gossiping and asking all sorts of nosy questions about their lives, journalism was simply ideal for her. It wasn't so much a job as a continuation of her natural persona.

Staying in Germany. Perhaps becoming a great correspondent. Her own column. It was everything she had ever hoped for. Or going home to America and putting everything on hold. What kind of daughter did it make her if she wasn't prepared to make a sacrifice for her dying father? Should she please her mother, or Frank Nussbaum? And which of those choices would please herself? Her head ached with the effort of trying to resolve the conflicting forces tearing her in two.

A shadow fell across her face and she looked up to see a waiter standing in front of her.

'Excuse me, Fräulein. There's someone waiting for you at reception. A lady. She says it's urgent.'

'Did she give a name?'

'A Fräulein Vine.'

Clara Vine. Rupert's little English Nazi-lover. What on earth could she want? Mary hauled herself up and pulled on a cardigan. She supposed she would have to see her. But she seriously hoped it wasn't a social call.

Chapter Fifty-two

When Leo went out into the silver morning and saw work-men spraying the sticky residue of the lime leaves from Unter den Linden he thought of the old song he had heard: "So long as the old trees bloom on Unter den Linden nothing can defeat us, Berlin will stay Berlin."

But now they were cutting down the limes to make way for more marches. Not just limes, but maples and planes too. Hitler wanted his troops to be able to walk twelve abreast.

Leo thought again of Ovid in exile watching the barbarians and wondered if he too was catching a glimpse of what humanity could become.

He came to a church and quite on impulse stepped inside, walked down the dim aisle and sat on a wooden pew, a few feet away from the altar. There was no one inside but the hunched form of a cleaning woman on her knees, polishing the brass fittings of the lectern. A shaft of light, pure Protestant light, unfiltered by the rich complexity of Catholic stained glass, pierced the gloom. Leo bent his head in a hypocritical semblance of prayer.

It was the first time he had been in this church, but he had often passed and felt a visceral urge to come inside and pray. Indeed, he almost ached for prayer. What must it be like to unburden yourself like that? To release the straps and buckles that bound your secrecy to you? But he couldn't do it. Caution and duplicity were engraved too deeply within him.

The SIS had been right to recruit him. They had seen in him what he had never seen in himself: a combination of immense plausibility masking a profound scepticism which made him perfect for handling the betrayals and blackmail of others. The advantage was that he was never likely to suffer blind fidelity to an ideology. The disadvantage was, between these shifting layers of distrust, it was hard to work out just where his real self lay.

Sitting there, in the church, the image of Clara came to him. Two nights ago she had come back exhausted to Xantener Strasse and fallen into his arms. She didn't say where she had been or what she had done. She flung her coat over the arm of the chair, drank the coffee he had prepared for her, and ate a cheese sandwich. Then, just as hungrily, she had made love to him.

The next morning when he woke she was still fast asleep beside him. He could tell by the trembling of her eyelids, light as a moth's wing, that she was dreaming. Happy dreams, he hoped, of England perhaps and all that she had left there. Watching her eyelids with their faint trellis of veins, the long, dark lashes, and her face, smoothed in sleep, he felt flattered that she should relax with such abandon in his presence. To surrender yourself to sleep was a form of trust, a faith that he would still be there when she woke up, and that she could drop her guard.

He remembered her standing barefoot at the mirror and pushing a grip into her hair, and seeing him watching her. Her breasts, milk white where they met the scalloped sunburn of her neckline. The heart-shaped face with angular cheekbones suggesting something faintly exotic beneath the English veneer. The watchful, intelligent eyes. As she stood washing

at the basin, entirely naked and unembarrassed, she turned to
him and smiled and he thought that was the kind of face he
wanted to see every day smiling at him. That was what he
wanted. Ordinary life.

Even now he could still feel the touch of her against his
skin, and the memory of that sensual pleasure surrounded
him like an invisible embrace. Her body in bed, her curving
back and taut loins, had awakened a hunger in him, for the
exhilaration of sex coupled with being in love, which he had
never experienced before. In the past few weeks he had
understood for the first time what poets had always written
about. He had changed since he met her. She connected him
with everything that was good in his life, and talking to her
about poetry, about Ovid, had even brought him back to an
idea he once had of committing himself entirely to the world
of scholarship and literature, losing himself in some place of
learning where he could be Dr Leo Quinn, with leather
elbow patches and an oak-panelled study, buried safely in the
misty past.

He tried not to think about her with Müller. Of her body,
with its sleek, downy flesh, beneath that brute of a man,
perhaps responding to him, the way she had done with him.
Her reddened lips, the colour of crushed strawberries, slightly
parted. The veined neck arched, the whole body tense and
then relaxing as the flush rose into her face and neck. He
hadn't asked her about it, and she hadn't told him. She was a
skilled actress, he reminded himself.

As he sat in bed beside her, thinking of everything that lay
beneath the vault of her chest, the heart and its secret internal
workings, he was reminded of something that had been said
to him in that week of training at the country house. One of
the chaps there, the effete young man who talked about
tradecraft, had told him that an agent needed to think like a

schizophrenic might. To imagine his body as something different and separate from the mind, like a piece of wood or metal rather than flesh with nerves and sensations. Entirely disassociated from the self. That kind of detachment was necessary in this line of work.

Leo had managed that, he thought, but could Clara? Could she ever become what he had become? He knew it was old-fashioned, but he had a deep instinct that women should be protected, rather than put in the way of danger. His mind rebelled at Rumbold's little epithet, "a spy in silk stockings".

And yet, she had proved a fast learner so far. He was proud of what he had taught her.

He had hoped that Clara had not yet attracted surveillance. They had been so careful every time they had met, and he had never seen any sign of a tail. But on Thursday night it was abundantly clear that Goebbels was having her followed. The tail was a feckless type in standard issue Gestapo clothing with a dark, peasant face, a sweaty suit and rubber raincoat. He had pursued her from Mitte all the way to Steglitz and almost as far as the rendezvous with Arlosoroff himself before Clara became aware of him. Once she did, she had done exactly what Leo had told her. She had waited and watched and taken avoiding strategy and managed to dispose of him. Leo had felt a burning feeling of pride as he observed her.

Perhaps that had been his mistake: to ever imagine that he could protect her.

Somehow, shortly before she reached Brucknerstrasse, the shadow had picked up her trail again. As Leo approached the house from a group of elm trees across the road, he could see the shape of Clara behind the frosted glass in the door, by the looks of it preparing to leave. The image of Arlosoroff was by her side. Suddenly, a glimmer of movement caught his eye.

A few feet away from him, shrouded in darkness and merged with the shadow of a tree, the man was standing. His outline was barely visible, and his tread was silent on the mossy earth, but in the damp air Leo caught the smell of him, a rank combination of beer and cheap aftershave. And even from behind it was possible to see hanging from his palm the unmistakable shape of a handgun. In the glint of moonlight Leo recognized it as a small Walther PPK, the *Polizeipistol Kriminal*, standard issue to all Nazi undercover agents.

The shock of seeing the pistol, prepared and ready to use, astonished him. Was Goebbels really planning to shoot the messenger? What was the point of that? Unless, in Goebbels' twisted mind, the death of Magda's little go-between was intended as a stark message to cease her assignations with other men.

For a moment, it was as though the four of them – Clara, Arlosoroff, Leo and the agent – were suspended outside time. Behind the glass door the figure of Clara and Arlosoroff remained talking. Arlosoroff had extended his arm to Clara's shoulder. Leo heard the slide of greased metal as the man cocked his trigger.

Was it the crack of a twig or some minute muscular twitch in Leo's body? Whatever it was, like a rabbit scenting movement, the man sensed him and turned blindly, pointing the gun straight in Leo's direction. Without hesitating, Leo felt for the Beretta that hung in a leather sheath just below his left armpit and for the first time in his life, in a single smooth movement, managed to fire directly at the figure in his sights.

It was almost startling to see how swiftly the man crumpled and fell. He would never have guessed how easy it was to kill someone. How quickly life evaporated from the body, lifting off into the air like dew, even while his blood darkened the dirt. The man lay on the ground, arm splayed in surrender to his approaching death. Coming closer Leo saw that the shot had punctured his chest directly in the area of the heart. He was an ugly fellow, with a lantern jaw and a brow you could break your fist on. He gave a last cough, bringing a bubble of blood to his mouth, before turning his head aside, as if in a gesture of resignation. *A clean kill*, were the words Leo heard running through his head.

He looked around him. If any local resident had heard the shot, they had probably pulled their curtains a bit closer and turned up the wireless. Turning a deaf ear to nocturnal crime was the best policy in Berlin right now. Shaking himself out of his shock, Leo caught the man by the armpits and hauled him up. He was a bruiser of an agent but the rush of adrenaline coursing through Leo's veins made the effort almost negligible. He found a spot a few yards away where tree trimmers had left a pile of branches. That was unusual in an area like this. Tidiness was not just a civic but a moral virtue in Berlin. The danger was that someone would be back to clean it up all too soon. He had no choice, though. He covered the corpse as best he could, then followed Clara back to the city.

Sitting there, in the pew, Leo buried his face in his hands and thought he detected the faintest trace of that perfume she wore. Evening in Paris. He had noted the bottle in her bag the first time they met, and his habit of scanning and memorizing peripheral detail meant he had consigned the name to memory instantly, without thinking about it. Clara had managed her double-dealing so far, but with Goebbels on her trail how much longer could she go on? He bitterly regretted encouraging her to become involved. How could he want her to become more like himself, gathering intelligence and engaging in deception? It was a rotten, corrupted way to live, lying to your friends, lying to people you loved.

Yet, for him, what alternative could there be? Could you simply walk out of this and start again, as though it was a role you assumed and then shrugged off, like some ham actor in a forgettable B feature? He and Clara had talked about exile, but working for SIS was a permanent exile from everything that most people considered normal – a quiet life, a house and family and dreams that were not filled with horror and fear.

A priest was approaching, with an enquiring look on his face. Leo got up quickly and walked back down the aisle. He left the church and took a big breath. At least the air was clean.

Chapter Fifty-three

Dressed in sky-blue silk by the Jewish designer Max Becker, with a matching cloche hat and sable stole, Frau Bella Fromm had arrived. Frau Bella, as everyone called her, was the social editor of the *Vossische Zeitung* and the acknowledged queen of high-society gossip. She attended every diplomatic cocktail party and foreign embassy dinner going and her accounts were read each morning on all the best breakfast tables in Berlin. The fact that she was Jewish gave her reports an especially barbed edge, which in turn encouraged the denizens of high society to overlook her racial flaws, at least for the moment. Something about her quick eye and sharp, intelligent face reminded Clara of a beautiful bird of prey. One with an especially merciless method of dispatch. Her prey that day at the Grunewald horse track was Magda Goebbels, who was playing hostess at the Bureau's first fashion show.

Meticulously planted with rose beds between the stands and the paddock, the horse track in west Berlin was a popular society destination and Magda's enterprise had brought them out in droves. Not only the Nazi top brass with their wives, but owners of fashion boutiques, representatives from the influential Horn fashion house and the big department stores, all coasting round the club house, viewing the exhibition of German clothes, complete with wholly German accessories of amber buttons, satin, flowers, feathers and lace. As if to make up for any restraint in the fashion, the female guests were decked out in glittering jewels, sapphire cuffs, ruby bracelets, teardrop pearls and enough diamonds to fill a mine.

The idea was that all members of the Fashion Bureau should wear the Bureau's own designs. Magda presided in a cowl-necked velvet dress in black, whose voluminous swathes lent her the air of a mournful nun. Clara had performed her catwalk in an olive-green pin-striped flannel suit, cut to mid-calf, and beneath it a silk blouse with a fussy bow. It was teamed with a soft green hat, to which a spray of silk roses was attached and another artificial rose served as a corsage. These token gestures of femininity did nothing to alleviate the drabness of the outfit. Clara couldn't think what it reminded her of, until it suddenly came to her. She looked exactly like a ticket collector on a London bus. A clippie! She might just as well have been clumping her way up and down the stairs of a big red bus with a leather satchel on one shoulder. Though she performed with as much elegance as she could muster, it was clear that the ripples of applause for her outfit were about as genuine as the flowers in her hat.

Now everyone had settled, with flutes of bubbling Sekt in hand, to hear Hans Horst, the Bureau's acting director, make a speech about the future of German fashion. He was a pompous man with a deep love of his own voice, which boomed out of the Tannoy.

'A beginning has been made. We know that the path will be difficult and full of thorns, but our belief in the new Germany and our conscious knowledge that we are fellow fighters in the work of Adolf Hitler will make our goal attainable.'

This was about as much as Clara could bear. She moved unobtrusively to one side and headed out of the club house.

But no sooner had she left than she found herself cornered by Bella Fromm. She came close, her beaky face eyeing Clara with a penetrating gaze.

'Fräulein Vine. I wonder if I could have a quiet word.' She communicated in a low, professional whisper, finely calibrated to deter eavesdroppers. 'I suppose you saw this.'

From her bag protruded a copy of the *Herald Tribune*, folded to expose the article it had picked up from yesterday's *New York Evening Post*, headed: "German actress in suspicious death plunge. Mary Harker traces the strange fate of one actress and her relations with the Nazi élite."

'You knew Helga Schmidt, didn't you?'

For a second, the sight of Helga's face, beaming out of the newspaper in black-and-white, transfixed Clara. She longed to seize the article and examine it more closely, but with a supreme effort of self-control she composed her features. She had to admire Frau Bella's perspicacity.

'She was a friend of mine.'

'And do you think she committed suicide?'

'I couldn't say.'

'This writer obviously doesn't. She thinks her suicide was staged. She says she had become an embarrassment to the élite. She made jokes. She laughed about Hitler's sex life. Until someone decided she should be pushed out of her window by a gang of storm troopers.'

'As I said, Frau Bella, I really couldn't say.'

'Well, Goebbels is furious. He's told the paper the journalist's visa will be retracted immediately. Apparently she's packing her bags right now. She has a ticket booked on the night train to Holland.' She eyed Clara sceptically. 'I just wonder where she got all that inside information. She seemed to know everything about the woman. Right down to the jokes she told.'

Clara recalled her meeting with Mary Harker two days ago at the Press Club. As soon as she had established why Clara was there, Mary had hailed a cab, and taken them back to her office, high above Unter den Linden. She ushered out her secretary, closed the blinds, and turned on the wireless. It felt intensely intimate in that room together, with a single desk lamp casting a pool of light on the table. Once there was no chance of being overheard, Mary had sat down, notebook in hand, as Clara told the story of Helga from beginning to end. Mary listened intently, and the only sign of her growing horror was the slight quiver in her fingers as she wrote it down.

'Do you think you can use it?'

'Put it this way. If I'm going to get thrown out for a story, I want to go out with a bang.'

So right now, Mary was packing up her apartment in Nollendorfplatz and preparing to leave Berlin. Clara felt an unexpected sense of dismay. That single hour in the newspaper office had sparked a closeness between the two women. She regretted that they had not been friends before. They parted with a brief hug, but both knew, if Mary had stayed, they would have become true allies.

'Suicide seems unlikely, doesn't it?' persisted Bella Fromm. 'I mean, Helga Schmidt had a son to look after. And a part in a new film.'

'Frau Bella, please forgive me, but I wouldn't know.'

At that moment Emmy Sonnemann bustled up, a small dog clamped under one arm like a furry clutch bag.

'So this is our most popular design.' She plucked at Clara's sleeve with undisguised dismay. 'Well, I suppose it is our patriotic duty.'

Emmy herself was encased in the teal hunting outfit, which was straining slightly at the seams. A burst of pheasant feathers sprouted from her hat.

'May I say how charming you look Frau Sonneman?' said Bella Fromm sinuously.

'I suppose you may.'

'And did you hear this morning's new law?' Bella Fromm smiled. 'The Propaganda Ministry has just issued an edict. From now on, all German actresses must wear only German fashion.'

'I will decide what this German actress wears, thank you,' said Emmy grandly, taking Clara's elbow and steering her towards a buffet groaning with salmon, cold meats and potato salads. There were exotic fruit, oysters, lobsters and crabs. The buffet was making up for the domestic theme of the fashion show with an extravagant international spread of English pies, French pastries and Italian desserts.

'Come and eat. You need something. You look pale as a sheet. Is something keeping you awake?' She nudged. 'Not Herr Doktor Müller, I hope!'

As Emmy dumped the dog down and dug into an iced platter of caviar, Clara looked over at Frau Ley, surrounded by a bevy of men. She had selected a black velvet sheath with a low neck and a jet necklace at her slender throat.

'I don't remember that dress in the collection.'

'Something tells me it's not her dress they're interested in,' said Emmy, archly. 'Didn't you hear? That husband of hers commissioned a life-sized portrait of her in the nude and has hung it in the hall of their home? Can you imagine the shame? Apparently the men are queuing up to visit.'

She stooped to pop a plate of caviar under the table for the dog. Its small pink tongue began slurping hungrily.

'But then, I suppose, it's all irrelevant. Magda won't be around for much longer.'

Clara stared at her.

'Oh, hadn't she told you? Joseph has decided it's wrong for his wife to be involved in the enterprise. Doesn't think it's fitting for her to be mingling with actresses, I think is what he said.'

'But the Führer—'

'Agrees with him apparently.'

They both looked over at Goebbels, who was deep in conversation with Hela Strehl, a simpering blonde fashion journalist from *Elegante Welt*. Just the sight of him caused a shudder of fear to run through Clara. There stood the man who had ordered Helga's death as a warning to her, and whose shadows kept a constant watch on her. A barbarous man, clever and callous, who would use her if he could, but would never trust her. Right then she had the better of him, but she knew she could not let down her guard for a second.

As if he could read her thoughts he broke off, came over, took her hand in his and kissed it. For a killer, he had beautiful hands.

'Frau Sonneman. Fräulein Vine. I must say, you model with conviction. You both look like truly authentic representatives of German womanhood.'

As usual his words were hard to read, suggesting a barbed double meaning. He dealt in ambiguities, sugared threats, a smiling sweetness concealing the savagery.

'That's very kind,' said Clara.

'No, Fräulein, it is we who are in debt to you. Which reminds me. It's a little thing really. I wanted to thank you.' His eyes fixed on her. 'Personally.'

'Herr Minister, you really don't need to.'

'Oh, but I think I do.'

Clara was keenly aware that a small crowd had followed in his wake and were avidly listening in. Frau von Ribbentrop was hovering, her ample bust imprisoned in a faux riding jacket. Emmy was looking on with frank disdain. Magda gazed impassively from across the room. Bella Fromm already had her notebook out. Around them the chatter had died down as attention was fixed on the minister and the actress. This exchange was evidently going to be all round Berlin by the afternoon. It would no doubt make something juicy for the braver of the gossip columnists, those that still remained and dared to speculate on the complicated private life of the Propaganda chief. All eyes were trained on Clara's face, eager to detect some scintilla of secret intrigue, a lover's knowing look or flash of sexual chemistry. Probably Goebbels meant it that way. As she returned his look deadpan, Clara realized this encounter was as stage-managed as any march or rally he had a hand in. But why?

'I wanted to give you a modest token to thank you for everything you've done and will continue to do. Please, take it.' Astonished, Clara stared at him as he reached into his pocket and passed her a square box of navy leather, embossed in gold with the name of a Berlin jeweller.

'Go on. Open it.'

She remembered to smile lightly, but when she opened it and saw the brooch, nestling in satin, her face lost its composure. Her astonishment was unfeigned.

'I hope you like it.'

It was expensive, she could tell that at once. Made of silver and studded with diamonds, it must have cost Goebbels hundreds of marks, unless the jeweller, like so many tradesmen who supplied the regime, had insisted on providing a patriotic discount. Or had been informed, when he submitted a bill, that providing his services to the Nazi leadership was an honour in itself. Clara looked down at it with amazement as the brooch sat heavily in her palm. A glittering swastika.

'Here,' he lent towards her, 'let me pin it on.'

Chapter Fifty-four

The only good thing about the frenetic level of activity at the Passport Control Office was that it made it impossible to think about anything else. That morning the usual queue system of anxious professionals had been disrupted early on by a hysterical woman who was desperate to obtain a visa for her husband, a Jewish doctor. He had refused to come himself, insisting that his patients needed him and he would never leave Germany, so his wife, who had relatives in Hampshire, was there on his behalf. But as the receptionists explained, nothing could be done unless they saw her husband in person. The woman, who had flaming red hair and a figure as sturdy as her personality, had plonked herself in the front office and refused to budge. The queue had begun to fray at this unexpected obstacle, edging around her like a river bursting its banks, until it broke down completely and became a single pressing mass of people bearing documents and wielding briefcases and announcing their case to no one in particular.

The front office staff were becoming increasingly impatient with the obstructive woman who had spoilt their immaculate queue, but it wasn't until someone suggested a policeman be summoned that Leo took the woman gently aside, fetched her a cup of tea and sat her down at his desk. After an hour working through her case, along with coaxing and tears and the forfeit of his clean handkerchief, he decided to volunteer to talk to her husband himself. It would mean going out to Treptow the next evening, and foregoing his supper, but the offer had the effect of calming the wife, who grudgingly agreed to leave. All of which meant that when Hitchcock telephoned, asking Leo to drop by in his lunch hour, he did not respond with undimmed enthusiasm. He grabbed a lukewarm cup of coffee and an egg sandwich and made his way across the Tiergarten.

The elevator at the British Embassy was a splendid fin de siècle affair, with an interior of panelled walnut and a set of elaborately twisted wrought-iron double doors. As Leo reached the third floor the ancient lift keeper rose from his seat and drew back the creaking gate with a nod, his watery eyes following Leo's progress down the corridor to the room where Hitchcock was waiting for him behind a typewriter, smirking slightly.

'I was wondering, Quinn,' he looked up briefly, 'if you might know anything about a Helmut Kappel, aged thirty-six, believed to work for the political police? Found under a heap of leaves in, where was it now . . .' he leaned forward and consulted a note, 'Brucknerstrasse, Steglitz.'

'Should I?'

'Someone shot him through the heart. On the evening of Hilter's birthday.'

'Perhaps someone was celebrating.'

'Pretty violent kind of celebration, wouldn't you say?'

'I'd say it's a pretty violent kind of city.'

Hitchcock gave him a suspicious glance, then flicked a cigarette out of the box on the table and tossed it across to Leo.

'I hope none of our people are engaging in freelance operations. That kind of business can cause us problems, you know.'

Leo kept his eyes trained on the photograph on the desk. She was a lovely-looking thing, with her shining eyes and glossy black hair, squinting up at the camera. Hitchcock was obviously very attached to his Labrador. Following Leo's gaze, Hitchcock turned the picture away from him, reclined in his chair and planted one foot on the desk.

'Anyway. About your love affair.' For a second he paused deliberately, then said, 'Mrs Goebbels, I mean.' He hesitated, revelling momentarily in the possession of information that Leo had been denied.

'I just thought you ought to know that Head Office decided on balance that it was better if Goebbels did have wind of it.'

'I'm sorry?'

'The Minister received an anonymous note telling him about Arlosoroff. Very nicely done by all accounts. Fountain pen. Flowery script. Posted in Wilmersdorf and signed "A Friend and Patriot".'

Leo sat back in the chair as if Hitchcock had just delivered one of those brutal punches to the solar plexus that had apparently won him a Cambridge boxing blue. As the acid rose in his gullet, everything became suddenly clear. So that was why the man had been hovering in Brucknerstrasse with a pistol! He was there to kill Arlosoroff. All that time Leo had been fearing for Clara, and it was Arlosoroff who was the target. Goebbels, in full knowledge of his wife's deception, had sent a Gestapo agent to shoot her lover. He must have guessed, or worked out somehow, that Clara would be used as a go-between, so he calculated that he would have her followed until she led him to the quarry. Once she did, there were orders to eliminate him.

Leo cursed himself silently. Why had he not realized the explanation that was staring him in the face? The answer was just as obvious. Love had blinkered him. Clara and her safety had commanded his full attention. He had been so intent on ensuring that she came to no harm, that he'd failed to assess the situation with the judgement required. Clara's protection, he had foolishly imagined, was in his gift. As if he could ever protect her, once forces like these had been unleashed.

'What a bloody reckless, irresponsible idea.' Looking at Hitchcock's complacent face made him doubly furious, but he kept his voice hushed and steady. 'I thought we'd discussed all this with Sir Horace. We have a duty to protect our source, instead of which we exposed her quite unnecessarily to terrible danger. She could very easily have been shot.'

Hitchcock spread his hands. 'It was Dyson's idea.'

'Damn Dyson.'

'Just delivering the message,' Hitchcock said mildly, taking refuge in his paperwork. 'Take it up with him if you have an objection.'

'Objection?'

The way Leo was looking was beginning to intimidate Hitchcock. He hoped he would leave soon.

'Surely you realize my objection means nothing now? Don't you see what you've done? As a result of this meddling, Goebbels will continue to follow Clara until she leads him to Arlosoroff. He's not going to let her out of his sight. She'll have the Gestapo on her heels for weeks. They'll haunt her like a ghost. Goebbels won't stop until he's hunted down Arlosoroff and disposed of him. And then most likely he'll turn on Clara. The only decent thing we can do now is let her know the full picture as soon as possible.'

Leo strode out of the room without a word. He could have strangled Dyson for his double-dealing, until he reminded himself that being two-faced was part of the job description.

Chapter Fifty-five

'I'm trying to work out your secret,' said Karin Hardt as she passed Clara in the shadows of the studio's great hall. They were shooting the farewell scene where Alicia, the character they played, took leave of her lover beside the Grand Canal. It was to be filmed in German first, then English and both actresses were wearing identical, tight, burgundy satin evening dresses, with three strands of pearls around their throats.

'What secret?' asked Clara, standing aside in the wings to let Karin pass.

'Why you're so popular. It's either your natural acting ability or something else you're not telling us.'

'Who says I'm popular?'

Karin ducked past the camera, straightened her costume and stepped out into the limelight.

'Go to your dressing room and you'll find out,' she called.

Clara made her way down the corridor as fast as her constricting dress would allow, taking off the wig and freeing her curls with her fingers as she went. As soon as she pushed open the door, she saw what Karin meant.

The dressing room was filled with roses. Roses stuffed in a vase among the pots of make-up and cold cream on the dressing table, roses massed by the lighted mirror, roses thrust in a jar on the wash basin, and another on the table top. Roses relaxing their furled petals into glorious bloom. Dozens of vermilion roses, sharply scented, eloquently expensive, their colour blazing against the silvery dazzle of the dressing table lights.

'Lovely, aren't they?' said Klaus Müller from behind her, shutting the door and looking around with satisfaction. 'Roses are my weakness.'

Unusually for a working day, he was in full uniform, black tie, buttoned shirt and the leather of his brown belt and knee boots gleaming.

'You're my weakness too, of course.' He bent towards her and gave her a kiss so rough it hurt her mouth. 'A serious weakness.'

To hide her astonishment she ran a hand over her mouth, where he had smudged the lipstick.

'They're beautiful, Klaus! You must have emptied a flower shop!'

He tipped one crimson bloom towards him critically, as if inspecting it for defects.

'Almost. I waited till you went on set and had the florist come in with them.'

She turned away. 'You should have told me you were coming.'

'And spoil the surprise? But, wait . . .' He stopped for a moment and took a step back, affecting a look of puzzlement. He spread his hands. 'Perhaps you made a mistake? Perhaps you thought these flowers were from your other boyfriend?'

There was a deathly pause. With her back towards him for a moment, fright turned Clara's mind blank. From the menacing tone of his voice it was clear he wasn't joking. What did he mean by her "other boyfriend"? Was it possible that Klaus Müller could have discovered Leo when they had

both been so careful? Had the Gestapo observed them
together – photographed them or noted down the details of
their meetings? How much did Müller know?

With an enormous effort, she shook her head lightly,
turned to him and laughed. 'Klaus. I don't—'

A stinging slap landed on her cheek.

'Forget it! You're not on a film set now.' His face had
darkened with rage and his voice was thick with disgust.
'Don't try and string me along with that innocent act. It
makes me sick.' He grasped her shoulders and dug his fingers
painfully into her flesh. 'In fact it makes me want to take your
clothes off right here and give you a beating. I've half a mind
to. It's less than treacherous girls like you deserve. I mean, my
dear, your boyfriend in Steglitz.'

Gazing up at Müller's furious face, feeling the grip of his
fingers, a single thought clamoured in the tumult of Clara's
mind. Talking about Steglitz meant Müller didn't know
about Leo. He knew nothing of Leo. Müller knew about her
visit to Brucknerstrasse, but Leo was safe. Which meant,
perhaps, she was safe too, if she could just keep her wits. She
managed an appropriately indignant frown and shook herself
out of his grasp.

'Stop this, Klaus! What are you doing? I don't know what
you're talking about.'

'I'm talking about a man found face down in the bushes in
Steglitz. Murdered. What have you got to say about that?'

'A dead man?' Astonished, she shook her head. 'What the
hell would a dead man have to do with me? I promise you, I
know nothing about it.'

'As it happens, I don't believe you. And the Doktor doesn't
believe it either. He ordered me in early this morning because
a Gestapo agent was shot dead on the evening of the Führer's
birthday and Goebbels thinks you may have been involved.

He must have some reason to suspect you. He said I was to get an answer out of you, even if I had to beat it out of you. Otherwise he was going to haul you into Prinz Albrecht Strasse to find out what the hell's going on. I don't think I've ever seen him so angry. He had some idea you were sympathetic to his problems with his wife. That you were going to be some help to him. Instead of which—'.

'Klaus, you have to believe me! I don't know anything about any police agent!'

He pulled over a chair, lit a cigarette and crossed his legs. 'You're going to need to try harder than that.'

She was calculating frantically in her head. She knew Goebbels had had her followed to Steglitz but she had lost the tail, hadn't she? So how had the man ended up dead? In the claustrophobic confines of the dressing room, Müller was able to scrutinise her every move. To buy herself time she turned away to the mirror and reapplied her lipstick where he had smudged it.

'I'll be honest with you.' She capped the lipstick and pursed her lips at him in the mirror. 'I did go to Steglitz that evening. It was a social visit. I can't tell you what I was doing there, but the person I went to see was certainly not a boyfriend.' She faced him, hands on hips. 'And if you really think I'm the kind of girl who goes around shooting people in my spare time, then you certainly don't know much about me.'

'It seems I don't know much about your social life.'

'I was doing a girlfriend a favour. The person I went to see was her ex-boyfriend. She wants to keep it that way. And it's no good talking about beating anything out of me. That doesn't scare me. You can tell the Herr Doktor that's all I'm going to say.'

It was a gamble, Clara knew, this show of defiance. But it was one she had to take. Though Müller's face was a mask of icy fury, and her face stung where he had hit her, something about his extravagance with the roses suggested that his loyalties were divided. She was determined to stay silent, not for Magda's sake, but to protect Victor Arlosoroff himself. The brief time she had spent with him, hearing his plans for a Jewish homeland and his ideas to help Jews escape Germany, had inspired a deep respect in Clara. He was a brave and resourceful man, even if he was a foolish one too. The Magda Friedlander he knew was a changed woman now. She had grown cold and severe, and her passion for politics had hardened into fanaticism. If Arlosoroff thought the Reich's First Lady would throw up the dinners and cocktail parties and the status she had now for an impoverished and dangerous existence with him, he was deluded. Yet all too soon he would be standing at the Anhalter Bahnhof with a pair of tickets, hoping to start a new life with Magda. And she would not be there to meet him.

Müller ground out his cigarette and chucked the stub in the basin. 'These girlfriends of yours seem to lead complicated lives. Let's hope this one doesn't end up throwing herself out of the window.'

At this remark Clara felt her composure shatter. How dare Müller talk of Helga so casually and with such contempt?

'Helga didn't throw herself out of the window, as you know. She was murdered. Ask yourself why no one's investigating that!'

Müller rose and came close to her, forcing her to step backwards.

'Stop acting like a child, Clara. You don't seem to understand the trouble you could be in. Goebbels was all for having you arrested right away. He was muttering that you were untrustworthy, that you had betrayed him. He wanted to know what I had to say about it.'

'So what did you say?' Clara glared at him but braced herself against the back of a chair to stop herself shaking.

Müller gave her a searching look. 'I told the Doktor there was no way you could have been in Steglitz that night and you had nothing to do with his dead policeman. Because all that evening you were celebrating the Führer's birthday with me. In bed.'

He sank back against the table, pulled out a handkerchief and wiped his face. Running a hand through his immaculate hair, he looked around at the rose-strewn dressing room and sighed.

'I suppose you know I'm being redeployed to Nuremberg.'

'I heard.'

'I leave tomorrow. It's an honour, really. Quite a professional challenge to oversee the filming of the Party rally with Fräulein Riefenstahl. I should be happy. But to tell the truth, I'm not pleased to be leaving Berlin. A while ago I wouldn't have minded, but now that I've just found the new house, and you . . .'

He drew her towards him so that their faces were level and ran a hand down the length of her satin dress, letting it rest on her bottom.

'The right thing to do would be to hand you over to Goebbels' policemen and let them do what they like with you. You're probably not telling the truth, and I don't like women who mess me about. Apart from anything else, it reflects badly on me. But then nor do I want those careless policemen spoiling this body, or this charming, deceitful face.' He tilted her chin as if to inspect her more closely. 'I found you, after all.'

Inches away from him, Clara held his gaze.

'Don't think you're escaping me, Clara. Or that because I'm going away that I won't be able to keep an eye on you.

I will be keeping the closest of eyes on you. As will the Herr Doktor, I fear. So think of it this way. You need me now.'

He kissed her, pushed her away, and strode off down the corridor.

Chapter Fifty-six

Leo went straight to Xantener Strasse, let himself in and proceeded through the unlit hallway and up the stone steps. He noted that one of the pigeonholes that held the post for each resident of the block had been emptied. Evidently, the owner of the flat downstairs, the proprietor of the Munich ceramics factory, was in town. With a resident in the flat below they would need to be careful.

Closing the door behind him, he took a look around the flat as if seeing it for the first time. This place was meant to be anonymous. Everything about it from its matted carpet to its chipped bathroom and tired furniture covered with dingy chintz had been chosen for precisely that effect. The kitchen, clumsily partitioned from the living room, with its single-ring cooker and nicotine-stained walls. The dreary view of rooftops and a brick wall advertizing Lufthansa, featuring an aeroplane escaping through grimy clouds to sunnier climes. The wallpaper, with its pattern of flowers imprisoned between bars of stripes, which no one with an ounce of taste could ever have chosen. It was a transitional place, where people met and passed like ghosts, and yet now this space of nothingness was filled with her. For him, the flat was resonant with images of Clara. She stood at the basin and leant against the pillows of the bed. The sheets bore her imprint. Her face laughed at him in the mirror.

He threw himself down in the armchair, lit a cigarette and waited. It would be the last time they could use Xantener Strasse. If Clara was being followed it was compromised now. But for one afternoon, for just a few hours, Leo wanted to indulge himself. To pretend that they were ordinary lovers, meeting for the reasons that ordinary lovers do.

Precisely at three the bell rang and he went downstairs. Opening the door, he put his finger to his lips, and brought her inside. It was raining outside and minute beads of fine rain powdered her coat. The damp air had caused her hair to curl and framed a few crystalline drops in the tendrils around her face. Her skin, bearing the remnants of studio make-up, had an absurdly healthy glow. Once in the apartment Leo caught her in his arms for a deep, lingering kiss.

She pushed him to arm's length and scrutinized him.

'This is a bit reckless, isn't it? I thought we were supposed to be following procedure?'

His hands were running through her hair, stroking down over her hips and thighs. He began to slip her clothes off, first the coat, then the blue dress he liked with the polka dots.

'I'd only just got back from the studio. Frau Lehmann thought it rather odd that I should be needed urgently for a poetry reading at three o'clock in the afternoon.'

'She's right.' He was kissing her neck. 'The poetry reading is postponed.'

'So why did you need to see me?'

'Do you need to ask?'

He flicked apart the clip of her bra and tugged her slip so that it rode up to her waist. She felt his fingers, probing and caressing, and the excitement of being with him beginning to overpower her. She pressed herself closer and inhaled the warm musk of his skin as he dipped his face to her neck, then her breasts, then lifted her up, with her legs around his waist and carried her through to the bed.

After they had made love, he lay and studied her with the close, meticulous attention that was part of everything he did. His lust for her extended to every physical detail. He wanted to capture and swallow everything about her, from the delicate shoulder blades, to the flicker of the pulse in her throat, right down to the violet network of veins on the arch of her foot. Every curve and hollow of her body. He would have liked to study her close-up, as you would in a film, without making her self-conscious or embarrassed. Seeing her naked made it easier for him to imagine that they were somewhere else entirely, somewhere uncomplicated and dull, where people laughed and argued and loved without subterfuge. But as he looked at her he noticed a faint purple line of bruises along the top of each arm.

'What happened here?'

She rubbed her arms instinctively. 'Müller came to the studio this morning. He said Goebbels was furious with me. He seemed to think I had something to do with a man being killed the night I delivered Magda's message. He warned me Goebbels might have me arrested.'

'A man was killed?'

'A police agent, apparently. I have no idea what why Goebbels should think I'm involved in it. But I'm worried, Leo. He knew I was in Steglitz, so I think he must know about Magda's lover.'

Leo's throat constricted. He felt the words stall in his mouth, as if reluctant to emerge and change everything.

'He does. That's why I got in contact. I needed to warn you.'

'But how could he possibly have found out?'

'Head Office let him know.'

'Head Office? You mean you told him!'

'Not me. People I work for.' Leo was about to launch into some kind of defence of their strategy, but why bother? One look at her face, cheeks scarlet with shock and betrayal, and he felt the same.

'But why, Leo?'

'They thought it would be safer for you if Goebbels believed you were helping him. That you had felt some kind of moral conflict about Magda's affair. They did it without telling me, Clara. You know I wouldn't have agreed to it.'

She moved away from him and stared straight ahead. 'Exactly what happened?'

'Goebbels received an anonymous note about Magda and Arlosoroff. I only discovered this morning. I needed to tell you straight away.'

She looked at him, comprehension suddenly dawning. 'So that's why.'

'Why what?'

'Goebbels had asked me to keep an eye on Magda. He must have had his suspicions. Then a few days ago at the Fashion Show he thanked me personally. For everything I'd done.'

She sprang out of bed, shattering the spell of her nakedness, covering herself again, clipping on her stockings and pulling on her blouse.

'I need to warn Arlosoroff.'

'How can you? Do you even know where he is?'

She picked up the watch she had left beside the bed.

'He'll be at the Anhalter Bahnhof in one hour.'

'How on earth do you know that?'

'I just do.' She pulled on her coat and buckled her shoes, the transformation complete.

Leo sprang up and caught her arms urgently. 'Clara, you can't go. If they're following you, they'll pick up your trail and you'll lead them straight to him. It's exactly the wrong thing to do. It places you both at risk.'

She was buttoning her coat. 'I have to warn him. I owe it to him.'

He wanted to restrain her, but she was pulling herself from his arms.

'Listen to me. You don't owe Arlosoroff anything.'

'But I do, you see, Leo. It's my fault. He sent a message to Magda and I didn't pass it on. He's expecting to meet her at the station. If she doesn't turn up he'll stay on in Berlin, trying to get her to leave. He's a stubborn man. An honourable man. He'll seek her out and try to persuade her. He'll get in touch, only this time, Goebbels will be waiting. It's me who has put him in danger and I need to tell him he must leave straight away. Tonight.'

'If you go, I can't protect you. Müller is right. It would be, very, very bad for you if you were arrested.'

He saw himself as if from above, naked and white-faced with rumpled hair, pleading with her, trying to make her understand.

'They could lock you up. They could torture you. You know about torture, don't you? I couldn't help you. I wouldn't be able to do a thing about it.'

A thought ran through her head. It was the question she had asked herself on her first day in Berlin. *What is the worst that could happen?*

'I know what I'm doing, Leo.'

'And I couldn't bear anything to happen to you, because . . .' He caught her face in his hands. 'I have known from the day I first saw you and every second since that you are the most remarkable woman I've met. I'm thirty-three years old and I've never felt like this about anyone.'

He saw her falter, and her eyes fill, but she didn't reply.

'What was the first rule I told you, Clara? Keep yourself safe. Otherwise you endanger other people too.'

'And the second rule was, sometimes you have to abandon the rules.'

She reached up and kissed him. Her face was intent and removed in that completely focused way he had seen before. Though he watched, agonized, as she walked out the door, he still marvelled at her resolution. Whatever had made him think she was unsuited to this life?

Dusk was falling as Clara approached the Anhalter Bahnhof. The crowd flowed in one direction on the pavements. Commuters with briefcases and determined expressions were making their way from the office and back to the suburbs, no doubt thinking about the supper that waited for them, and the children to be played with and the pleasures of the week-end ahead.

A few streets away she got off the bus, merged into the crowd and walked briskly, head down and lost in thought. She was a shop girl, anxious to get home after a day spent on aching feet.

She might not have noticed them at all if it hadn't been for the woman's shoes. Her suit was a dull brown, just the kind of thing any office worker might wear, but the shoes were a contrast, a rich claret colour, accessorized with white daisies stitched into the leather and a midsize heel. Lovely shoes, they were, suggesting a frivolity quite at odds with the utilitarian suit. Helga would have liked those, Clara thought, keeping her eyes to the ground. The shoes clipped along in front of her in the crowd, but paused as their owner stopped to look in a shop. Then, to Clara's surprise, a few minutes later, the shoes appeared ahead of her again. How did that happen? Looking up, her senses tensed and she realized she had company.

From what she could make out there were two of them, one in front and one behind. The woman was young, perhaps her own age, with a headscarf and glasses. The man wore a black fedora above ginger hair. He carried a briefcase and had a languid stride, just fast enough to suggest purpose, but slow enough to change tack if necessary. He had a scar on his face, which drew down the side of one eye, like a perpetual wink. They kept a couple of yards' distance, dodging the people in their way, weaving in and out of the crowds in a determined manner. From what she could tell they seemed to be moving in a co-ordinated fashion, one falling back as the other overtook. Leo had told her about this strategy. A box, it was called. For all she knew there was a trio, with another in a car cruising by.

In the hope of losing them Clara took an abrupt right off Stresemannstrasse, and found herself heading away from the station down Prinz Albrecht Strasse, past the new Gestapo headquarters, where political prisoners lined the cells and the names of thousands more Communists, trade unionists, Jews, freemasons, religious leaders and other enemies of the state were imprisoned in a vast, automated filing system. She wondered if there was a file on her, with instructions perhaps on surveillance, and details of her habits and associates. Instinctively she crossed the road. No one walked past that place now without a shudder. She took another right at the end of the road and then right again down Anhalter Strasse, which brought her in a circle. She didn't dare glance at her watch. What better way could there be of signalling that a meeting was planned?

At the end of the street the tall portal of the Anhalter Bahnhof loomed into view, with its twin figures above the entrance, Night and Day, one with its eyes closed and the other staring out into the distance. Her diversion had been pointless. By now the woman was at two o'clock and the man behind her at seven o'clock, and despite the crowds they were keeping increasingly close, boxing her in and restricting her movement as if trapping her in a net. Clara's heart was pumping and fear was slicing through her, settling in the marrow of her bones. Did they want her, or Arlosoroff? She needed to lose them quickly, but how?

The station was no more than a hundred meters away on the other side of Stresemannstrasse when she passed a stately building that she recognized with a jolt of surprise as the Hotel Excelsior. The very same hotel that had featured in *Grand Hotel*. The place Greta Garbo made famous when she said she wanted to be alone. Well, Clara knew exactly what Garbo meant. She wanted to be alone too, so she ducked through the revolving doors and looked around.

She really didn't have the first idea what she could do there, other than achieve a moment's respite from her followers on the street. There was an air of hushed luxury in the lobby. Receptionists in gold-braided jackets manned a vast desk and bellhops in navy uniforms with brass buttons pushed expensive cases around. She knew within seconds the tails would be making their way through the revolving doors.

As she glanced across the expanse of chequered black and white tiles, a sign caught her eye, "*Verkaufsladen Im Tunnel*", and beneath it the mahogany doors of an elevator. The famous tunnel! She remembered now. Because the Excelsior was designed for business travellers, a tunnel had been built to run directly beneath the street through to the station opposite. It was all part of the five-star experience. It meant guests could go straight from their hotel to their train without having to negotiate the chaotic traffic above them. Clara almost sighed with relief. Walking across to reception, she asked in English for Herr Winkelman in room 368.

'I'm sorry Fräulein. There is no one of that name in that room.'

'But he told me! Room 368! Fourth floor.'

'You must be mistaken, I'm afraid. For a start that room is not on the fourth floor.'

Leaning closer towards the receptionist, in a confidential tone she said, 'But he's waiting for me. Fourth floor, he said. I remember exactly. And it's very important that I see him.'

The man licked a finger and began running through the register.

'We have a Herr Henkell in room 368.'

'It's Herr Winkelman,' she pouted. 'And he very specifically told me the fourth floor.'

'I'm sorry.' The man gestured at a bank of telephones in little wooden cabins across the lobby. 'I can't help you. Perhaps if you would like to make a call?'

'Oh, don't bother.'

She turned away, a picture of sulky indignation, then as if on impulse, made a sharp left and walked swiftly up the red-carpeted staircase. When she reached the first floor, she walked along the corridor, waited two minutes, then took the lift back down to the lobby. She hoped Herr Henkell in room 368 wasn't taking a shower, because he could expect a couple of uninvited visitors ringing his bell before too long.

Crossing the lobby she entered the tunnel lift and descended to a gleaming underground stretch of marble, lined with shops selling jewellery and cosmetics. A last deluxe retail opportunity for the hotel's guests before they re-entered the grimy streets of Berlin. There were high class fashion boutiques with stiff-limbed mannequins frozen in their furs and displays of finely stitched leather gloves. The plate windows gave her every opportunity to see there was no one behind her. A hundred metres later she clipped up a flight of steps and emerged in the vast glass cathedral of the Anhalter Bahnhof itself.

At five minutes to six on a Friday evening the station was a single heaving mass of people flowing towards the platforms and funnelling themselves into the six trains that left every three minutes. The great trains heaved and exhaled, their clanking adding to the cacophony of sound that rose high into the ribs of the sooty glass ceiling. The forecourt was thronged with shoe shine boys, newspaper vendors, flower sellers, men unloading carts and porters hauling luggage. And right there beneath the clock, blinking and looking around him with a distinctly nervous air, was Arlosoroff, accompanied by a stained suitcase and a coat folded over his arm.

Scanning the crowd Clara realized how difficult it would be to spot her followers if they had managed to catch up with her. The forecourt was a seething press of travellers, milling around the booking halls, cramming the waiting rooms and gazing up at the destination board, which registered services, not just to Leipzig, Frankfurt and Munich but as far away as Prague, Naples and Athens. The train to Vienna, she noted, was leaving from Platform 6. It was the Express, no stops all the way to Austria.

Her eyes swept the concourse. There was a man sitting on a bench a little way off who was ostensibly reading a magazine but kept glancing at her. An old fellow with a gold watch chain and a bow-tie had her directly in his line of sight. A plump girl in a crimson jacket standing in line at one ticket desk seemed to be staring right at her. But no sign of the pair from the street. The air was filled with the clash of iron on steel and the bitter hiss of gas.

At that moment her gaze snagged on something familiar. The ginger hair of the briefcase man. He had sat himself up on one of the tall mahogany seats used by the shoe-shine boys, high enough to afford him an excellent view of the passing masses. The wispy ginger locks were visible because the fedora sat on his knee. It looked to her as though he had taken his hat off to conceal something beneath it, and it wasn't the evening newspaper.

When Arlosoroff saw Clara approach his knuckly face registered first relief, then dismay.

'She's not coming,' said Clara quietly.

'You're lying to me.'

'I wouldn't lie.'

He made to pick up his suitcase. 'Then I'm going to see her. You don't write a letter like that and then abandon someone.'

'Listen to me, Victor. Her husband has discovered. His men are following you. You have to leave as soon as possible.'

His face was incredulous, wounded. 'He's told you to say this, hasn't he? You're one of his spies.'

'I'm not. But they are here all right. Ten yards away from us there's a man having his shoes shined. Don't look. He's holding a pistol under his hat. The faster you can get on this train, the less chance he has of using it.'

'What is this nonsensical melodrama?'

'I'm trying to explain. Goebbels knows all about you and Magda and he's aiming to kill you.'

Arlosoroff's eyes peered myopically through the furling steam. Clara snatched a glance at the briefcase man and saw him tense for a second before a family of children passed in front of him, obscuring his view.

Arlosoroff was scratching his densely curled head, as though tackling some obscure Talmudic question.

'Now what I have to ask myself is, why should I believe what you have to say? Magda loves me. She wouldn't change her mind without a word.'

Clara remained still, willing him to pick up his suitcase and focus on the train standing at Platform 6 which was issuing the kind of grunts and sighs that generally preceded departure.

He continued, 'It may be that she needs some time to decide. Leaving home is a serious business, after all. She'll need to make plans.'

'She doesn't want to come, Victor.'

'What did she say?'

'She wants to stay with her husband. She urges you to leave immediately.'

'And yet, I have only your word for this. What I am wondering,' he continued ponderously, 'is why I should trust you?'

Clara reached into her pocket and passed something into his fleshy palm. The golden Star of David.

'There.'

He stared at it for a moment and closed his hand over it. Clara looked round with a start as she was jostled by a passing commuter. Behind the barrier that led to Platform 6 a whistle sounded. But Arlosoroff's drooping sadness moored him to the spot.

'Does she realize what it means for her if she stays?'

Clara took his hands in hers. 'Victor, she's not coming and it's not safe for you. Think of all those people you've been helping. They need you more than Magda does. Getting people out of Germany and setting them up with new lives, teaching them new skills, helping them to survive in a different country, that's what matters. Who knows how bad it will get here? Magda can choose what she does, but the Jews can't. You have to go, right now. Please get on the train.'

Doors were slamming as, with creaks and wheezes, the train began pulling out. Behind them the man on the shoe-shine chair was jumping down. With an alacrity that surprised her, Arlosoroff gave a curt nod, plucked up his case and strode towards the barrier waving his ticket. Once through he sprinted for the final compartment and slammed the door. Clara turned away at once, so she didn't see the fedora man reach the barrier and conduct a furious dispute with the railway official, as the Express train headed off through the Berlin suburbs into the darkening night.

She was out of the station and about to hail a cab when she became aware of him. It was the man she had spotted in the station, on the bench by the booking hall, reading the magazine. He was pacing after her now, his hat bobbing above the crowd.

'Wait a moment please!'

There was no time to wait for the cab. She would have to evade him on foot. She turned from the taxi queue, quickening her step.

'Please. Wait!'

Hurrying against the flow of commuters, she turned her collar up and walked briskly towards the U-Bahn, her slight figure weaving easily through the thicket of overcoats and mackintoshes flooding towards her. But as she made to duck into the subway a passing woman detained her with a friendly hand on her arm.

'Fräulein, I think there's someone who wants to talk to you.'

'I've never seen him before in my life.'

She shook the woman's hand off and clattered down the steps to the underground. Her plan was to insert herself at the far end of the platform, deep amid the thick of the crowd, take the first train that came for a couple of stops and then switch routes. But the man pursuing her was faster than she was. His steps thudded heavily after her until, panting, he drew level.

'Am I right in thinking that you are Clara Vine?'

He had an upper-class English accent. How clever of them to choose someone so unthreatening. A genial English gentleman. She squared her shoulders and turned to face him. He wore a tartan scarf round his neck, and a heavy overcoat that looked a little too large for him. He blinked at her through wire-rimmed spectacles.

'Yes.'

'I thought so. You know, I was back there in the station looking at your picture in *Filmwoche*. Upcoming talent, it said. I recognized you at once.'

He held out his hand. He had an extravagant manner and a slight lisp.

'I'm sorry. I should have introduced myself. My name's Max Townsend. Friend of Rupert Allingham. I've only just arrived, actually. Got rather caught up in London.'

'You're Max Townsend?'

'Weren't we going to meet up about this film I'm planning? Would you like to come for a drink? I see you've got off to an awfully good start.'

Chapter Fifty-seven

Berlin, June 1933

It had rained again that morning. Lightning cracked the charcoal sky and brought rain drumming on the ground, drenching the air and bringing the scent of the Grunewald deep into the city's heart. It spattered on the statues, ran down the awnings of the shops and soaked the geraniums in the municipal beds. At midday, as sunlight warmed the chalky air, Clara walked slowly along the side of the canal.

The day before, news had come that the bullet-ridden body of Victor Arlosoroff had been found on a beach in Tel Aviv. The death was attributed to a feud between factions of the Zionist movement. At least that was what the *Jüdische Rundschau* said. She had found the newspaper in her dressing room, tucked into a basket of fruit and inked with a stamp that said "Property of the Office of the Reich Minister of Public Enlightenment and Propaganda". When she read the report the familiar fist of fear balled up in her stomach once again, and the tears welled in her eyes. But by the time she was called on set, her expression was as sunny and carefree as any heroine of a Nazi spy caper should be.

She wondered how the news would affect Magda, but guessed that whatever she privately thought, her demeanour would not betray a dent. The moment Clara told her that Arlosoroff had no reply to her letter, her expression had hardened and she turned away, dismissing Clara from her presence with a terse wave. In the weeks that followed, it was as though Magda had decided she was now inescapably bound to her fate. Life with Joseph and the baby. Perhaps even a little sister for the child, but preferably a brother, as her husband so publicly hoped, because a man always wanted sons. There even began to be a detectable show of affection between the two of them. Joseph was *"Engelchen"* again. They had just returned from a holiday in Heiligendamn on the Baltic. Very soon they were off to Rome.

Soon after Arlosoroff left a man called Archie Dyson had telephoned Clara, asking to meet up. He had an instant familiarity. He reminded her of Angela's friends, right down to the tan, which suggested a year-round presence on the tennis court, the smooth Etonian self-assurance and the name-checking of mutual acquaintances. They had met at a bar up west, a place full of hothouse flowers and pale leather furniture, and Dyson ordered her a gin and tonic without asking before outlining his request. He thanked her for everything she had done so far and was interested to know if Clara intended to stay in Berlin? If so, whether she might continue to help them? He avoided specifics but Clara detected the deadly seriousness beneath the veneer of charm. She told Dyson she would think about it.

Leo's proposition, however, was rather different.

They had spent the previous night at the new apartment, in a yellow-painted nineteenth century block in the east of the city in Friedrichshain, rented indirectly by His Majesty's Government. It had a hallway of speckled marble, heavy brass lamps and a grandly sweeping staircase. It was bigger than the place in Xantener Strasse, boasting two rooms and a separate kitchen, but the bed was just as narrow.

It was the first night they had spent together for weeks, and it had been a joyful reunion, folded in each other's arms. Yet in the morning Leo seemed preoccupied, dawdling over his coffee and glancing up at her from time to time with a frown. Eventually he told Clara that he had something to say and she need not answer right away. The apartment was safe, of course, but he still turned on the radio, filling the room with a burst of Viennese dance music, before he spoke. She should have guessed right then, but Leo was always exceptionally hard to read, even when he standing before her in his shirt and braces, regarding her with that unwavering, deep green gaze.

He asked her to marry him. But if she did, they couldn't live here. She should leave Germany and return to London. In time, when the flood of refugees had abated, he would take another job, and escape the fevered violence that pervaded daily life in Berlin. Meanwhile, he would go over to London and rent a flat for them. She could get in contact with the people at the Gaumont-British, where other German exiles had headed, because with one film already under her belt and Gerhard Lamprecht's recommendation it wouldn't be hard to resume her career, and then as soon as he possibly could he would join her.

Marriage. England. Peace. Or Berlin, where Max Townsend had finally announced that work was due to start on *Black Roses*. Where the studio executives had been admiring of her cameo in *Ein gewisser Herr Gran*. Fresh scripts had been sent to her and Gerhard Lamprecht was talking seriously about a role he had for her in his next film. And where death was all around.

As she was about to speak Leo placed a finger on her lips.

'Don't answer straight away.'

He held her tightly, so she felt his breath on her cheek, and the slow drumbeat of his heart. They stood frozen as the music whirled around them, like dancers moving to their own, silent tune.

She said, 'I haven't told you about Erich, have I?'

'Who's Erich?'

Clara pulled the postcard from her pocket, the one she had taken from Helga's room. The face of Marlene Dietrich had acquired an uncharacteristic number of wrinkles from being carried around so long.

' "Dear Mutti",' she read, ' "I have an interview for the Napola school! It will be on Saturday 24 June in Berlin. Can you meet me off the train from Havelberg, 2 p.m.?" Erich is Helga's son. He's ten years old. I found this postcard in Helga's apartment, the day she died. He lives with his grand-mother. I want to tell him how much his mother loved him, Leo, and that she wanted him to study hard and do well. That's where I'm going this morning. To meet Erich from the train and take him to the interview.'

By one o'clock she realized she still had plenty of time before Erich's train arrived. At Magdeburger Platz there was a small park with scuffed grass and benches set beneath the linden trees so she sat for a moment and shut her eyes. The air was like a soft blue veil, pierced by the sharp cries of thrushes in the branches around. Sitting there, with the sun's warmth on her face and its tangled scarlet on her eyelids, the breeze satu-rated with the scent of grass, the clip–clip sound of a garden-er's shears and a child's laugh against the city's rumble, it was possible to remember the peace that came before this tumult, and would come after it.

A gentle brush against her arm caused her to open her eyes. She hadn't heard him coming, but she guessed she would never be able to match his soundless tread or invisible approach. Leo must have followed her all the way from

Friedrichshain without her noticing. He sat beside her and his hand closed briefly over hers.

'One day you must teach me how you do that,' she said.

'I'm beginning to doubt I could teach you anything.'

'You'll have to promise you won't make a habit of this.'

'I won't. Just this once. I'd like to see Erich, that's all.'

He squeezed her hand, crossed the park, slipped behind the railings and was gone.

As she got nearer the station Clara passed more building work and was obliged to skirt round the edge of the scaffolding. There was so much construction going on now. Another huge block was being erected in the Government quarter, alongside Goebbels' planned new ministry and the proposed new Reich Chancellery in Voss Strasse. There probably hadn't been this much scaffolding here since Gothic times. It was said that Hitler was planning to turn Berlin into the *Welthauptstadt*, the capital of the world, and that his new young architect Speer was planning enormous arches that would make the Brandeburg Tor look like a children's plaything. Monstrous edifices that would rise above the baroque skyline with its delicate verdigris, dwarfing the human scale and making the inhabitants feel even more insignificant than they already did. Already these blank-faced towers were carving a deep, indelible groove in the surface of the earth. Something about their solidity, their dense metal and steel, made human flesh more fragile, and the crowds that surrounded them more transitory, like passing clouds reflected in a flat bronze facade. Clara wondered how long Hitler's monuments would be erected in this city. Would it be decades? Or even centuries? Would Hitler be like Ozymandias? 'Look on my works, ye Mighty, and despair!' She wondered what would have to happen to cause these monuments to fall.

Author's Note

Magda Goebbels, the wife of Hitler's Propaganda Minister, is most notorious for killing her six children in Hitler's bunker at the end of the war. But her life was a dramatic one before then and much of this novel is based on genuine events. In 1933, shortly after coming to power, Hitler decreed the establishment of a *Deutsches Modeamt*, a Reich Fashion Bureau, with the aim of creating "independent and tasteful German fashion products". He appointed Magda Goebbels as honorary president, and although her association with it was ended some months later by her husband, the Bureau continued.

Magda Goebbels did have a youthful liaison with Victor Chaim Arlosoroff. Arlosoroff, a prominent Zionist, who was involved in the establishment of the State of Israel, returned to Berlin in April 1933 with the aim of encouraging the regime to contribute to Jewish emigration to Palestine, to no avail. He got in touch with Magda again, and though the substance of their conversation is unknown and I have fictionalized their subsequent exchanges, she did tell him she feared for her own life. Historical sources suggest that British Intelligence was alerted to his plan for an armed uprising in Palestine, although nothing came of it. He was gunned down on a beach in Tel Aviv in June of 1933. Joseph Goebbels was suspected of involvement in his murder, although that remains unproven.

Magda Goebbels, Joseph Goebbels and their six children died on 1 May 1945 as Berlin was overrun by the Red Army. The day after Hitler and Eva Braun killed themselves, Magda drugged the children and broke cyanide capsules into their mouths. She wrote to her older son, Harald Quant, who was in a prisoner of war camp in north Africa, that the children were "too good for the life that would follow." She and Joseph then committed suicide.

Magda's stepfather, Richard Friedlander, died in Buchenwald concentration camp. There is no record of her intervening to save him.

Emmy Sonneman married Hermann Goering in 1935. She survived the war and wrote a biography, *My Life With Goering*, which provided this author with much incidental detail.

The heroic achievement of Frank Foley in rescuing thousands of Jews from Berlin under the auspices of British Passport Control won him the accolade of Righteous Among the Nations from Yad Vashem, the Israeli Holocaust Memorial Centre. His story is superbly told by Michael Smith in *Foley, the Spy Who Saved 10,000 Jews*.

Ein gewisser Herr Gran was produced by Ufa in 1933, directed by Gerhard Lamprecht. *Schwarze Rosen* starring Lilian Harvey, came out in 1935.

This era of German history is richly documented. Amongst books which I have used for research, *Nazi Chic?: Fashioning Women in the Third Reich (Dress, Body, Culture)* by Irene Guenther, was invaluable, exploring how the Third Reich attempted to construct German women's identity through fashion. Anja Klabunde's comprehensive biography of Magda Goebbels was also excellent, as were Anna Maria Sigmund's

Women of the Third Reich and Guido Kopp's *Hitler's Women*. Hans Otto Meissner's *Magda Goebbels, First Lady of the Third Reich* contains an interesting first-hand account from a man who knew his subject for many years and Bella Fromm's *Blood and Banquets, A Berlin Social Diary, 1930-1938* is an astonishing eyewitness testimony of the doings of the Nazi élite in the increasingly brutal lead-up to war.

Thank you so much to Caradoc King for his unstinting encouragement and to his colleagues at A.P. Watt. I am in awe of Suzanne Baboneau for her inspiring editing and wonderful enthusiasm, and grateful to all at Simon & Schuster. And, as ever, thanks and love to Philip.